THE Ebony

OUT OF THE FOG

BOOK TWO OF THE EBONY SERIES

———

HEATHER FISHER

THE *Ebony*

OUT OF THE FOG

BOOK TWO OF THE EBONY SERIES

SWEETWATER BOOKS
An imprint of Cedar Fort, Inc.
Springville, Utah

This is a work of fiction. The characters, names, incidents, places, and dialogue are products of the author's imagination and are not to be construed as real. The opinions and views expressed herein belong solely to the author and do not necessarily represent the opinions or views of Cedar Fort, Inc. Permission for the use of sources, graphics, and photos is also solely the responsibility of the author.

ISBN 13: 978-1-4621-4226-2

Published by Sweetwater Books, an imprint of Cedar Fort, Inc.
2373 W. 700 S., Springville, UT 84663
Distributed by Cedar Fort, Inc., www.cedarfort.com

Library of Congress Control Number: 2021950597

Cover design by Shawnda T. Craig
Cover design © 2022 Cedar Fort, Inc.
Edited and typeset by Valene Wood

Printed in the United States of America

10 9 8 7 6 5 4 3 2 1

Printed on acid-free paper

I would like to dedicate this book to my sister, Jenn. Jenn you were my rock throughout this whole journey. I will always cherish our late-night chats as we laughed and discussed my entries. Brainstorming ideas with you have brought my story to life. Thank you for believing in me and always being there for me.

Prologue

Jane stared out the library window of the governor's plantation, a forgotten novel laid open across her lap. For two lengthy weeks she'd mused over the kiss she shared with the one and only Captain James McCannon. She closed her eyes and smiled. Details from the night before he shipped off to patrol the island were still fresh in her mind. The vibrant glow of the southern lights. The chill in the air but feeling warm in his arms. And his lips! Her fingers brushed her lips as she could still feel the sweet, tingling sensation he left when he kissed her.

She leaned against the plush chair in the library. Releasing a contented sigh, she closed the book. Sophie would be in for a surprise when she received Jane's letter. Her best friend from Bombay had never seen Jane Sawyer smitten. *Let alone with a naval captain.* She smiled at the irony. As the surgeon's niece, Jane was quite acquainted with the militiamen from her time spent at the hospital. But the extent of her relationship with any of them was never more than a greeting. Not from her own doing, but because of her uncle's protectiveness. Being the finest surgeon in all of England, he always made certain the gentlemen and the officers stayed clear of her. Essentially, they did. Being that he was their surgeon.

Since being in Jamestown, Saint Helena, she noticed her uncle more at ease and less protective. Especially when it came to James.

Having allowed him to call on her on a few occasions, it seemed he had accepted him, rank and all.

But what of England? How could she set sail in a few weeks when their relationship was heading into uncharted territory? Not that she didn't mind the course they were heading. More than anything she was enthralled with the idea. Her racing heart could validate that. But she found it difficult because for the first time in her life, she couldn't think clearly. Her thoughts were all muddled with James. The idea of carrying on to England with her uncle, let alone pursuing midwifery, had been drowned out many times with nothing but reminiscing memories and feelings towards the captain. *Good gracious! How was one to plan for England with such an unexpected distraction?*

"Jane!"

She jumped and caught her book before it tumbled to the floor.

Elaine hurried into the room with a scowl on her face. Throwing herself across the sofa, she covered her face with her hands. Little whimpers escaped from behind her palms.

Jane blinked and hesitantly scooted over to the edge of her cushion. Reaching out to her friend, she asks. "Elaine? Are you alright?"

"No." She threw her hands in the air and sat up. "I said my goodbyes with Richard."

"Oh?" Uncertain of what she meant by her "goodbyes," she asked, "As in farewell because of his patrol?" *Not of their relationship,* Jane hoped.

Captain Richard and Elaine had been courting since the picnic auction. Instead of carrying out his assignment in Bombay, he opted to extend his stay on the island. Not because of his affection towards Elaine, but due to the increasing attacks on the merchant ships. Reinforcements were still weeks away, and with how merciless the French were proving to be, it was only a matter of time before they attempted to overrun the island.

"Of course because of his patrol." Elaine glowered at Jane, appearing flushed with her golden hair disheveled.

Jane's eyes widened. She leaned away in her chair, being certain not to press any further. Nothing about Elaine read torn and heartbroken. Quite the contrary, judging by the flared nostrils and fire in her eyes, she was disgruntled. *Perhaps they got into a disagreement?*

She watched Elaine take to her feet and pace circles in front of her. For a lady with such a petite frame, nothing about Elaine's emotions were small. When she became excited, she would burst at the seams, when she was sad, she would burst at the seams, and when she'd get angry, well, she would burst at the seams.

Stopping to point an accusing finger at Jane, she muttered, "Your captain is despicable."

Jane's mouth fell. Despite the flattering words of "your captain," she quickly brushed aside the excitement the notion brought to focus on her friend's accusation.

"How do you mean?" *Perhaps, Elaine was being over dramatic about a little mishap. It wouldn't have been the first. Besides, James had been absent for the past few weeks.* "He's been absent for—"

"Oh no," her friend's voice shook with frustration. "This all happened before he left." Breathless, Elaine rested her hand on her chest. "I can't believe he did such a thing. Actually," she paused and looked at Jane. "I can! He'd do anything to push me aside. Not that I'm interested in him anymore."

Jane ignored the last two statements. "I'm not sure I follow."

"Poetry!" Elaine waved her hands in the air.

"Poetry?" Jane rested her chin on her palm. *What harm could poetry do?*

"Yes! That scoundrel told me how much Captain Richard loves poetry."

"I don't follow. Why is that upsetting?"

Elaine released an exasperated laugh. "Poetry?! Why, it's the dullest nonsense I've ever had to read! Believe me, if you saw what I saw today, you would withdraw that comment."

Jane bit her cheeks as a smile formed. She remembered how James and Captain Richard played jokes on each other. "So, you became a pawn in their game?"

"More like the trusting horse in their game!" Elaine plopped back onto the sofa. Thin, blonde strands escaped from her loose bun and framed her face.

"Do you mean the knight?" Jane teased, understanding her friend was referring to the game of chess.

Waving off the comment with her hand, Elaine exclaimed, "Yes! Or an innocent bishop. Today I grabbed *two* books of poetry that I thought he'd enjoy. And then took him to the gardens to read. Halfway through my poem about lovers parting, I looked at him and saw—" She began to giggle then drew back the laughter to hold her angry facade. "I saw Richard, raking his fingers through his hair. He had such an anguished expression."

"Anguished?" Jane lowered her hand from her chin and caught hold of her friend's cold stare.

"I continued to read all the while thinking how sweet it was that he was becoming emotional from the poem. I even fooled myself into thinking that perhaps he was relating this lovestruck couple to us— seeing that he may be leaving for Bombay after the reinforcements arrive."

"Of course," Jane assured her. She bit her lip to keep from smiling. She had an idea on where the story was going.

"But much to my dismay, I couldn't have been further from the truth." She blew an exasperated sigh and continued. "For, towards the end, he stood and uttered this torturous groan that made me jump, causing me to tear my page. And then, I began to fear he was going to kick at Mother's rose bush with all his heavy stomping." Elaine hid her giggle behind a throw pillow. Lifting her chin over the pillow's edge, she said with a high-pitched tone, "Why, he entangled his hair around his fingers and appeared to be refraining from yelling out. After a minute of his horrid display, he uttered the most dreadful thing,"

Jane leaned closer to her. "What was that?"

"He told me how he despises poetry!" Elaine threw her face into the pillow to hide her torn expression of humor and frustration.

Jane held in a giggle. "He didn't."

"He did!" Elaine let out another groan and threw herself back against the sofa. "For weeks I've been thinking how I was sacrificing my own state of mind, just to read Richard those endless, mind-numbing words."

Biting her cheeks to keep from laughing, Jane began to oppose her friend's notion, "Poetry can be quite beautiful."

"No, Jane." Elaine raised a disapproving brow at her. "No, it's not. Not what I was reading. Your captain fooled me into reading Richard poems about religion, nature, and politics. All because—surprise, surprise—that's what he had informed me Richard favored."

"He didn't!" She covered her mouth with astonishment and laughed.

"Yes! It was right after the picnic at Heartshaped Falls. Your captain told me Richard had an eye for me. In order to capture his heart, I was then directed to read those poems. Oh, and to show him the gardens." Elaine's face paled. "Dear me," she straightened and ran her hand over her cheek. "Did Richard have an eye for me at all? Do you suppose your captain said that because at first Richard didn't find me interesting?" She began to re-pin a few loosened curls.

"Based on the way he stares whenever you walk in the room, Elaine, I'm certain he finds you interesting." Her friend shot her a humored smile. "And if he didn't fancy you then, he's definitely smitten with you now."

Appearing satisfied with Jane's response, Elaine leaned back against the sofa. She began to twirl a curl around her finger. "That he is," she mumbled, with a far-off gleam in her eyes.

Relieved their relationship was still intact, Jane asked, "Elaine, may I ask why you read him a poem of forbidden lovers if James said he preferred the other topics?"

She rolled her eyes at her. "I couldn't take another day— nay! Another *word* of some boring political outcry! Nor how a frail flower blossomed in the bitter, cold of winter." Elaine thrusted her fist into the air. "Besides, whatever kind of flower would blossom in that condition?"

"I suspect it's a metaphor for enduring . . ." Jane stopped herself from continuing as Elaine stared at her with annoyance. "Well, at least that's all settled. No more poems for the both of you," she finished, and wiped her remaining tears of laughter. Thank goodness Elaine's theatrical entrance was nothing more than frustration with having been tricked into a joke between the two captains.

"Mm," Elaine responded with hesitation. She scooted herself towards the edge of her cushion. "As your dearest friend, may I offer you a fair warning?"

"Oh?"

"Richard won't forget those treacherous hours that we had to endure with poetry. I'm certain he's going to return the favor to Captain James. To be safe, you'll want to avoid getting caught in their crossfire."

"I'll be extra cautious." Jane replied with a smile.

Elaine lifted a brow. "With how those two play, I wouldn't be so sure it makes a difference."

Jane nodded. "We'll have to keep an eye out for each other."

"Yes! Thank goodness that's over with."

Chapter One

James's pounding heart echoed in his ears as he awoke in his dark cabin. He lifted his dampened shirt off his chest and started shaking it out. The cool air whisked over his clammy skin, raising little bumps across his body. He shivered and sat up. Releasing a shaky breath, he threw open the drapes that fell next to his bedside. Light seeped into the dim cabin as a thick gray cloud enveloped his window.

He grunted, flinging his covers off. It would be impossible for them to spot any ship. Particularly an enemy's vessel. Shaking out his uniform from off his chair, he dressed and pulled on his boots. Patting his left pocket, he smiled to himself as Jane's chess piece laid secure in the wool material. Ready to carry on with his duties, he left his quarters to head on deck.

It had been two weeks since he'd last seen her. His stomach leapt every time she came into his mind. And it was no surprise that it happened frequently during the still hours at sea. The first thing he wanted to do was ask her uncle if he could court her.

Judging by the doctor's acceptance of him in the past, he would probably accept his courtship of his niece. But then what? That's where the future becomes a blur. Would the doctor really accept his offer, when he and Jane were to set sail in a few weeks' time? And what of Jane's plans while she was in England. From what he knew of her, she wasn't one to sit in parlor rooms all day, twirling her finger in her hair. What would she do during the day while her uncle was away teaching at the university? James slowed his steps while he passed the galley way. He had yet to discover any passions she may want to pursue, other than her hint of wanting to be a surgeon. Knowing that wasn't plausible, due to her being a woman, he paused to consider Thomas's cousin, Jenny. Before he set sail, she made an off-handed comment about how Jane should consider midwifery. It was Jenny who encouraged Jane to assist him with the goat's delivery. It was quite brilliant of her. Considering Jane's excitement with helping him deliver the baby goats, and her eagerness to learn, she would be remarkable.

The curl of her soft lips, smiling like she was capturing the moment of the baby goats, seeped into his mind. He rubbed at the back of his neck as he remembered how he fought against the strong desire to pull her into his arms that day. Had it not been for Thomas's interruption, he would have easily surrendered his battle.

James cleared his throat as a smile began to form on his face. A sailor strutted in his direction in the darkened hallway.

"Captain," the young man straightened his posture and saluted. The shadows under his eyes darkened when he passed a lantern in the hall.

"Timothy," James replied. The man's red hair gave an orange tint in the lamplight. "Finished with the night watch?"

"Yes, sir." He attempted to hide his yawn, pausing to address James.

"Anything to report?" James asked, though he intended to receive the answer from his first in command, Lieutenant Fletch.

"No, sir. There's been nothing but fog. Thicker than my mum's porridge."

James couldn't help but smile. Knowing how Mrs. Haymore, Timothy's mother, was concerned about him wasting away at sea, he pictured her feeding him everything she had to thicken him up before he left for patrol. "Well, carry on Timothy. Your mother wouldn't approve of you missing out on your shuteye." James patted the lad's shoulder and smiled.

The corner of the young man's mouth raised. "I wouldn't put it past her, captain."

James chuckled and continued forward. Approaching the door to the outer decks, he drew a deep breath. The time came when his thoughts of Jane were tucked away, and his duty to search for the mercenaries commenced.

There had been reports of two more attacks within the week. The pressure to find the ghost ships was taking a toll on him and his men.

He stepped onto the freshly mopped deck. The salty air from the ocean spray misted the ship where his somber crew administered their tasks. The ship creaked as it swayed over the waves. The sound added to the uncanny stillness of the atmosphere. Holding onto the rail, he ascended the stairs to the quarterdeck.

Thomas manned the wheel of the Ebony through the murkiness. The sails above rippled in the breeze.

"Good morning, lieutenant," James's voice carried deep into the mist. He couldn't help but notice his friend's uncomfortable stance. Thomas's eyes, though weary, were alert, his jaw clenched and his shoulders rigid. He wasn't his usual chipper self, whistling or humming to a tune of his own. Just quiet. Unusually quiet.

"Captain," Thomas replied in an apprehensive tone. His thick brows furrowed with unease.

"Any reports for me?" James inquired, sensing the severity in his mood. Thomas's knuckles whitened as he shifted his grip on the handles of the helm.

"We've been in this fog for hours. Something doesn't feel right." He peeled his eyes from the thick haze and looked at James. "The further we go the more unsettling it's become."

James glanced around the deck and stepped forward to take over the helm. The hair on the back of his neck began to stand. Whenever Thomas had an inkling, he was usually right. The last time he had one of his impressions, they had been swimming in the ocean. They had been cooling off from the sun's heat when he ordered everyone out of the water. As the last man climbed the ladder, two sharks appeared.

"Alert the men. Ready the crew and loose the cannons," James ordered.

"Aye, aye, captain," Thomas's pinched expression relaxed with relief.

"Lieutenant?" James said in a hushed tone. "Order the men to be as quiet as possible. If those ghost ships are out there, I'd rather have the element of surprise, rather than an announcement."

"Yes, sir."

James observed the orders carried out as his men darted to their assignments. All sixty-four of their eighteen-pounder cannons rumbled below deck. Rolling into their portholes. Their ship was one of the largest in Her Majesty's Navy. It carried the second highest number of cannons of any ship in the world. James felt a sense of honor being assigned to such a magnificent vessel. And at the moment, he'd never felt more relieved.

Weapons in hand, the crew scurried across the deck, hovering into positions. Thomas approached James and offered a salute.

"The crew is ready and are waiting for further orders, captain." His brown eyes were bright and eager.

"Thank you, lieutenant." James broadened his stance. He squinted towards the sky with hopes to see any sign of the fog lifting. Nothing. Nothing but a white, heavy mist. Disappointed, James shifted in his boots. He held the wheel steady, continuing to navigate them north, towards the latest attack. Thirty-two thousand meters east of Saint Helena's cliffs. *Far too close to home,* he scowled, tightening his grip.

Their ship creaked and moaned, filling the silence as it splashed through the choppy water. A bead of sweat rolled from under his hat towards his temple. He wiped it off.

They had been scanning the dense fog for over an hour. Some of his crew grew restless as they fidgeted at their posts. James threw his head side to side, attempting to loosen the stiffness in his neck. Since awaking that morning, his body had been tense.

"Look," Thomas whispered, pointing to a patch of blue sky.

James's thoughts lightened with hope to be free from the white, encompassing snare. Beautiful blue sky trickled through the mist as the fog dispersed. Prying his fingers from his handle, he adjusted his cravat. The disturbing feeling since he had awoken that morning continued to manifest.

"Lieutenant Daniels, man the wheel," he ordered. Grabbing his spyglass, he stalked to where Thomas stood.

"Do you still feel it?" James asked.

Thomas lowered his hand from his squared chin. "I can't seem to shake it. You?"

"I thought it was from a dream, but I'm beginning to have my doubts."

They were emerging from the last bit of fog. Even with the welcoming sight of the bright day, something was amiss. James dashed to the front of the quarterdeck. Raising the spyglass, he scanned the glistening water. Eager to search for the cause of the unsettling feeling. Sweat began to prickle his back. He held his breath, sensing he was getting closer. There! His pulse raced in alarm.

"Thomas," he called to his friend in a hoarse whisper. Thomas rushed to his side. "Look, a little on the starboard side." James didn't have to give Thomas the spyglass for him to see.

"Two of them," he exclaimed. James tightened his grip on the spyglass. "One of them has sixty-five, sixty-six...seventy-four cannons! That ship alone could annihilate us with one blast!"

James swallowed the lump that made its way into his throat. He took a side glimpse at his anxious friend.

It would be a fool's errand to pursue the two frigates by themselves. James rubbed at his stiff neck. They were less than thirty-two kilometers from shore. If they're brazen enough to be this close to the island, what's stopping them from attacking Jamestown next? How many more innocent lives would they lose?

"Get the men ready. We still may have the element of surprise."

With wide eyes, his childhood friend regarded James's uniform for a moment. James stiffened as he read what was in his eyes. Had he not been his captain, Thomas would have been blunt and spoken his mind. He knew how foolish they were for not waiting for reinforcements. Unfortunately, so did James. Yet as sailors for Her Majesty's Navy they had a specific duty to protect their crown and country. Turning around now would make their months of searching for these ruthless barbarians all for naught. It could take weeks to find them again. Within that time, who knew how many innocent lives would be destroyed by their hands. James wasn't willing to risk that. He wanted nothing more than to inflict every round of ammunition and cannonball they had before these mercenaries could cause any more harm. He gazed across his crew, feeling humbled to be serving among them. They had given years of their service under his command. He knew where their hearts stood. They were ready. James clenched his jaw and gave a curt nod.

"Aye, aye, captain." Thomas saluted with respect. Before he left James's side, he gave a quick squeeze on his shoulder to show his support and hurried to the other officers on the deck below.

Twisting the spyglass, James peered through it. Both French battleships sat anchored side by side with their stern facing them. He released a ragged breath as luck appeared to be on their side. There was a large enough gap between the two vessels that their ship could squeeze through, providing at least another forty meters on either side of their ship from the enemies. With their guns in position, they'd fire thirty-two shots from each side. It would cause a great amount of damage to both the French ships. A perfect setup. Perhaps they did stand a chance. Unless they went through with the French expecting them. Then it would be a suicide mission. James wiped his forehead again. He prayed they'd go unnoticed.

"Captain, the crew are ready." Thomas reported. James gave a nod.

"Lieutenant Daniels." He took confident strides to the Lieutenant at the wheel. "I want you to steer her right between those ships."

"Captain?" Lieutenant Daniels's eyes widened with confused panic. James peered through the spyglass. He wanted to double check that the enemies gun ports stayed closed. *Excellent,* he thought to himself. *Even their decks are quiet from the morning hours.*

"It's too late to turn back now. This is the only shot we have to survive. Their gun ports are closed. Most of the crew are below deck. If we hesitate and shoot at only one ship, we have little chance of surviving their guns." He turned to Thomas who listened with determination.

"I'll go give the order," he responded.

James adjusted his constraining cravat. Beads of sweat rolled down his back. Lieutenant Daniels steered them towards their passageway. James gripped the spyglass tight to control his trembling hands.

"Come on, come on, a few more meters," James muttered to himself, peering through the glass. Thomas returned to James's side, panting as he had run back up the deck. He gave James a curt nod, letting him know the men were ready.

A bell clanged rapidly in the distance. The alarm blared from one of the French battleships. James's head snapped forward as shouts from the other ships erupted. Blast, they'd been spotted! It was too late to maneuver elsewhere. There wasn't enough room as they drew closer to their point of entry.

"Steady!" James bellowed down to his men. Their muskets and pistols were in close range, but not close enough to make a difference. His sailors on deck obeyed with anticipation as they crouched behind the ship's sides, their muskets loaded and ready to fire. The Ebony's sails fluttered as a gust of wind blew from the south, increasing their speed. The French began to raise their anchors hastily. This might work. It had to!

Hunched behind one of the masts, James glanced over at his life-long friend. His stomach took a turn for the worse. Thomas's face was fierce and uneasy with anticipation for the battle at hand. His cheeks tightened. He was serious. Too serious for his own good. No, he can't focus when he's like that. *This isn't good. I need him focused.* Panic rose in his chest.

"Thomas," James whispered, staring at the ships. With their enemies' gun ports now open, he could see the Frenchmen frantically, readying their cannons. They were about to enter the death trap. "I have a confession," he took a breath. "I was the one who told Miss Keaton you liked her when we were younger."

Breaking from his frightful state, Thomas looked at him dumbfounded. James knew that year in grade school had taken a toll on Thomas. The other children had been ruthless in their teasing. Taunting whenever Miss Elaine Keaton was around. It had been a constant thorn in his side.

James pulled out his pistol and cocked it back in its ready position.

"Steady!" he ordered. Their ship started to ease its way through the narrow gap of the two frantic ships. Shouts rang out from the French quarterdecks. Members of their crew scrambled aloft to release the gaskets.

"Why did you do that? That was the most miserable year of my life!" Thomas hissed.

"You stole my lunch." James shrugged his shoulders. "She asked me if you did and at the time, I obliged and said yes..."

"I never stole your lunch!" Thomas argued. Of all things to get Thomas fired up, James knew that this topic would ignite him.

Cries bellowed through the air. The Ebony's stern entered the alley between their enemies' ships. James wiped away the sweat on his face. The French scattered across their decks in a disorganized fashion. *Right where I want them.* Loud cracking of musket fire erupted on either side of their ship. He ducked as splinters of shattered wood exploded off the rail next to him.

With the sails unfurled and rippling in the wind, the French ships had a stronger chance to keep pace with the Ebony. Their escape from being between them would be narrow, if yet impossible. James tightened his trembling fingers around his pistol.

"Fire the muskets!" he roared, shooting off his pistol towards the helmsman on the ship to his right. Entering between the two ships, they had just a few more meters before they were aligned in the heart of the French hulls. His gun's smoke filled his nostrils as he loaded the pistol with more gunpowder.

Deafening sounds of shots rang from all around them. Lead balls whizzed by, striking the timber of their ship. Pieces of wood shredded, exploding into the air.

"Thomas!" James shouted over the snapping and cracking of muskets. "I lied!" He cocked his gun and fired towards the French's quarterdeck. The sharp loud crack from his gun echoed through his ears. He ducked once more from shattering lumber. He'd never spoken to Miss Keaton about Thomas. Quite the contrary; he'd gotten himself in a few tussles with the other lads for standing up for his friend. He had even faced quite a few thrashings from their headmaster that year.

Crouched down, Thomas smirked at him as understanding crossed his face. He chuckled and fired another shot.

James watched in alarm as their enemies rolled their guns through the gunports. He rushed through the sulfur-filled air towards their bell. With both ships taking sail, they were a few meters from where he wanted, but with the heavy fire they were receiving, they were going to have to make do. He rang the shiny brass bell two times, signaling their cannons.

"*Fire the guns!*" he thundered.

His chest pounded with the vibrations from explosions they inflicted on their enemy. He gripped a post, holding himself steady as their ship jerked with each eruption from cannons below. BOOM!

BOOM! BOOM! Timber cracked sharply and popped from the French vessels. Glass shattered through the air. A powerful blast erupted on his left, rattling their ship. James covered his head with his arm as debris poured down on them.

Black smoke curled through the air, watering his eyes. Peering through the haze, he noticed an orange flickering light in the thick black air from the ship on his left. Fire! His pulse raced with triumph. If the fire spread, the French would be down forty-eight cannons!

"Keep her steady, Daniels!" James yelled out to the lieutenant as their stern passed the bows of the other ships. James squinted through the thick vapor to be certain he heard him. Crouched behind the wheel and covered in debris, Daniels carried out the order. Single shots were fired from the French, striking their ship and piercing the water as they lost visibility of the ships in the smoke. Relieved that their ship was no longer sandwiched between the French vessels, James wiped at his stinging, watery eyes.

Rubbing his ears, he attempted to stop the high-pitched ringing caused by the blasts. Coughs, screams, and crying groans echoed all around him. Feeling heavy at heart, he knew the battle had only just begun.

James drew in a deep breath of the fresh salty air tinged with gunpowder. He couldn't make out the damage they caused to the French with them still submerged in smoke. Any hesitation on their next attack could result in defeat.

"Lieutenant Fletch," James called. Thomas hurried to James's side. Blood trickled down his temple from a small gash. He looked to him with urgency.

"Have the men clear the deck, we're going back around."

"Aye, aye!"

James wrung his hands together, drawing in deep breaths to keep his nerves under control. If he were to make an assumption, their battle took mere minutes compared to the eternity that it felt. Fortunately, the damage to their ship was a fraction of what he pictured being the worst outcome.

"Captain!" Lieutenant Daniels yelled from behind the wheel. "The French vessel is gaining on us!"

Looking over his shoulder, James watched one of the two French frigates emerge from a thick cloud of smoke. She was the largest of the two with minimal damage. Much less than James would have liked. Luckily, she appeared to be the only ship that stormed after them.

"Reload the ammunition!" he thundered down to the crew on deck.

"Lieutenant Daniels, circle her around," James ordered.

Daniels nodded and threw the wheel to a hard left. James held onto a rail as the ship tilted to the right and crashed over a wave. Water sprayed the deck as his men clasped onto ropes and railings while the ship continued to tilt to its side.

The enemy vessel turned sharp to the left in an attempt to cut them off.

"Straighten her out, Lieutenant!" James hollered. The Ebony was sailing almost parallel with the French ship. The race was fierce as the ships rushed to be the first to aim their cannons at each other.

Deep, reverberating explosions rumbled through the air. Smoke seeped from their enemy's cannon ports. Now was their only chance.

"Fire The Cannons! Fire! Fire! *Fire*!" James roared. He clasped the rail and braced himself as cannonballs soared towards them.

Their ship rocked as loud booms detonated from the Ebony's cannon ports. The rumble vibrated deep in his chest. With mere moments to spare, loud, intense whistles began to strike them. Timber snapped all around the deck. Splinters and spikes of wood exploded into the air as sharp daggers. Men ducked, covering their heads, some screaming out in agony. A sharp, stabbing pain shot through James's upper arm. He gritted his teeth and looked to see a piece of wood sticking out of his frock. Baring his teeth, he grabbed and pulled out the wood dagger.

"Gah!" He clenched his teeth harder.

"Watch out!" someone cried. Large pieces of lumber snapped from the quarterdeck. The Ebony's rigs twisted and groaned as they came crashing down onto another. Men yelled, diving from falling ropes and chunks of masts. James glanced at the other ship.

"Ugh!" he raged. The Ebony cannons had caused limited damage to their hull.

The French frigate sped closer to James's ship.

Clasping his bloodied arm, James hurried and rang their bell twice.

"Fire at will!" he commanded.

Explosions of musket fire rang out from both ships. Lead rounds whizzed past them, devouring the surface they struck. Sulfur tinged his nose as he shot at the Frenchmen. Bumps raised on his skin when he heard a round whistle past his ear.

Reverberated booms erupted from the French vessel, firing more cannonballs at the Ebony. A loud, thunderous crack of snapping wood sounded from their ship. His men cried out to each other and lunged out of the way of a large piece of timber and sails.

"We're taking on water!" one of his officers reported.

"Keep firing!" James ordered. They weren't going to stop. Not yet. A smoky haze filled the air. More cannons boomed from the Ebony. Through the smoke, James saw the enemy's masts and a few cannon ports damaged beyond repair. They were close, but not close enough! The Ebony began to lean towards the port side as the water weighed them down. She could handle a few more blasts before they'd be forced to abandon ship. Which he prayed would never happen.

If captured, judging by the ruthless attacks from the past few months, the French would never accept a lawful surrender. But these murderers showed no honor among the merchants. They would most likely murder James and his crew as well, instead of taking them hostage. He fired another shot. They would just have to fight to the end.

"Give it all you've got!" he bellowed. His men crouched behind any shattered object offering them protection. Once reloaded, they fired their muskets. Through the smoke, James glanced over his shoulder to see Thomas raise from behind a barrel, firing a shot. Relieved to see him unharmed, James hurried to blast a round.

His finger hovered over the trigger, waiting for his order, but James couldn't move. The muscles in his body tensed, locking him in place. Peering through the smoke he saw three Frenchman carrying a small cannon to the quarterdeck. His mouth fell. A swivel gun! James aimed and fired but panicked as his gun's flintlock caused him to misfire. The bullet struck the railing of their enemy ship. His stomach dropped. The men began positioning the cannon towards Thomas and a few of James's crew. "Thomas!" James screamed. "*Thomas!*"

The shrill cries of wounded men and explosions of muskets blasting, drowned out his cries. James's hand shook as he attempted to reload his pistol.

"Come on, come on," he muttered as his gunpowder spilled.

"*Thomas!*" he cried out again. Drops of sweat rolled down his back. Through the gray smoke, his friend crunched down as a bullet struck the barrel in front of him.

"Ahh! Forget it!" James sprinted towards his friend. From the corner of his eye, he saw a Frenchman drop a cannon ball down the barrel. "Thomas!" James bellowed covering the side of his face from splintering pieces of wood. Thomas glanced at him. His eyes grew wide as he watched him run through the commotion. "Take cover!" James pointed at the small cannon and threw his arm down as he motioned to his friend and their comrades to run.

A high-pitched whistle pierced the air followed by an awful thump as it struck its target. A hot ache spread through James's side. He clutched at the spot and fell forward with a groan. Excruciating pain burned from his side through his torso. All the resonating cries of wounded men and explosions became a haunted silence. The ship swayed and he heard gentle thumps of their cannons firing again. He thought it peculiar how everything sounded so distant. His eyes grew heavy. Blinking many times, he failed to clear his blurry vision. He coughed and he attempted to roll his heavy body to his side. He reached his shaking hand into his frock pocket. *Where is it? Where is it?!*

Relief rushed through him as the tips of his fingers brushed over the smooth surface. Clasping the wood carving, he pulled out his chess piece. Shooting, scorching heat in his stomach forced him to choke out in anguish. Warm liquid trickled through his fingers as he continued to clutch his side. He ran his thumb over the cool small surface of Jane's token. Through the silent commotion, he watched images of men scrambling across the deck.

"James! James! You foolish man!" Jane's sweet velvety voice muffled through his ears.

James peered through his heavy lids. Thomas came into his blurred vision.

"Stay with me!" she rushed, but it was Thomas's mouth that moved. How could that be? The pain sharpened. He groaned in agony. It felt as if he were being stabbed by a hundred scorching knives. He clenched his chess piece in his hand, bringing her to his chest. Opening his watery eyes, he saw a radiating sight—Jane stared down at him with her big blue-green eyes. Her dark curls draped over her shoulder and light illuminated around her. James took in a sharp breath, causing more fits of coughing.

"Jane," his voice was hoarse and faint. She smiled before her angelic face began fading into darkness. *No!* He sought to call her. *"Don't go,"* he choked out. But there was nothing he could do, she was gone. A dark abyss filled his consciousness. His hand dropped from his chest to the deck, his queen rolled from his feeble grasp.

Chapter Two

Swirling her fork around the peas that now surrounded her pota-
toes and ham, Jane stared at evening meal. She wasn't hungry. An
unsettling feeling had consumed her all day. She had a restless sleep
the evening prior. Startled awake from a horrific nightmare, tears were
streaming down her face. It was James. He was sinking into the deep,
blue ocean, reaching up to her. She tried to dive in to grab him, but no
matter how hard she kicked and pumped her arms she couldn't reach
him. She was helpless, crying out for him. The emotions were so real
that she hadn't been able to rid the dreadful feeling all day.

"Jane, my dear, are you alright?" her uncle asked. He sat across
from her, observing her through his spectacles.

"You do look rather pale," Governor Terry pointed out, placing
down his fork.

"I'm fine," she whispered, giving them a small smile. That was all
she could muster.

Sniffing came from the other side of the table. Elaine wiped her
tears with her napkin then proceeded to fidget with her water glass.

"Elaine darling, please control yourself." Lady Keaton gave her
daughter a loving but stern expression.

"I'm new to this area, Terry, but I'm afraid our young ladies are
lost in love," her uncle stated with a small smile.

His friend, the governor, chuckled.

"There's nothing to fret about. Captain McCannon will be back in a week. And Elaine, why, Captain Norton only left yesterday. Cheer up you two. They'll be back in no time."

Jane's uncle and Governor Keaton nodded with confidence at each other. Lady Keaton rolled her eyes. Of course, they thought those were fine words of wisdom, but it did little to comfort Jane and Elaine. Elaine let out a loud sob, causing the men to cringe from their victory smiles.

A loud knock resounded down the hall, interrupting Elaine's cries.

"Are you expecting anyone, Terry?" Lady Keaton asked.

"No, my dear, not tonight. Duncan?"

"I'm not."

The butler opened the dining room door, admitting a militiaman.

"Governor Keaton, sir!" The soldier was perspiring as he took off his hat and bowed to the ladies. "You're needed at the hospital. There's been an attack on two of our ships."

"Merchant ships?" the governor asked, rising from his chair. Jane froze as she watched the militia man's head shake. Everything in the room became stilled.

"No, sir, they were two of Her Majesty's naval ships. The Sphinx and the Ebony."

A fork dropped against a dinner plate, echoing through the silence. Jane swallowed down a cry and looked to Elaine with horror.

"Both ships made it back to the harbor but there's been many casualties with many wounded, sir."

Jane continued to stare at Elaine who turned ghostly white with wide eyes looking back at her.

"Retrieve the carriage!" the governor ordered the butler, while hurrying out the room.

"You'll need my help, Terry." Uncle Duncan stood, leaving to retrieve his bag.

Pushing aside her fear, Jane staggered to her feet. "I'm coming too!"

"So am I!" she heard Elaine exclaim as Jane departed.

"Jane, I can't promise they'll let you through. And what of your reputation?" her uncle asked over his shoulder.

"I don't care about my reputation! If it means I can save someone's life, then I'll risk it. Please, Uncle," she blinked back her tears. "What if he's there? He'll need me!" Her voice dwindled. "I need to see that he's alive and well."

His eyes softened as he pulled her into his arms for a loving embrace.

"Go get your bag and hurry down."

"Thank you!"

"But Jane, if they don't allow you in, we'll need supplies. The hospital isn't stocked like they should be."

"Yes, Uncle," gathering her skirts, Jane sprinted up to her room. The medical bag her uncle gave her when she was younger laid under her bed.

Within minutes, Governor Terry, Uncle Duncan, Elaine, and Jane were riding in the carriage. Their driver, Samuel, had the horses at a full gallop racing their way down to the harbor. Uncle Duncan and Governor Terry sat next to each other. Together they discussed how to handle the wounded and the townspeople.

Jane scooted forward on the bench. She couldn't catch what they were saying. Not with the rickety carriage and the horses' hooves pounding against the dirt road. She clasped the ends of her shawl, twisting them around her fingers so tightly she could feel her pulse. Her anxiety was getting the best of her and she wanted to burst from the carriage and run to the harbor herself. Even if the horses were galloping, she felt she could be faster.

Next to her, Elaine sniffled. Jane knew the dread she was feeling. She too had worried over many of her friends during the war against the Mysore. Elaine had grown up knowing most of the sailors on The Ebony. She was either friends with them or their families. Jane gripped Elaine's hand. Elaine glanced at her with tears glistening at the brim of her eyes.

"It will be okay," Jane whispered, "they'll be alright." At least that's what she'd been repeating in her mind most of the ride. Elaine sniffled again and nodded. Since she's known Elaine, she's never been one to be quiet. But for the first time in their friendship, she remained silent during the duration of their ride. The two stared out their carriage window into the dark night.

The carriage began to slow as it made its way through the town into a crowded street. It was like the festival a few weeks back, as the whole town was awake. Except instead of cheers and laughter, there were mournful cries and shouts. The lamps along the street flickered against the moonless sky. Men in tattered, smoked-stained uniforms with faces blackened with ash hugged their crying loved ones. Bodies of soldiers covered in sheets were laid in a row along the dock. People were hurrying along with lanterns in search of answers. Her chest tightened as women screamed in anguish amongst the crowd on the dock. Children, wide-eyed, clung to their mother's skirts with hope of their father's return. A tear rolled down Jane's cheek while she stared.

"Jane," her uncle said, bringing her attention back to him. She never noticed the carriage had stopped. Her uncle was already on the street extending his hand towards her through the open carriage door. Grasping it for support, she stepped down into the frantic mass of people. The scene was like many scenes she had witnessed after an attack in Bombay. Chaotic. An overwhelming swarm of people yelled at the guards who barricaded the entrance to the hospital. Some guards attempted to calm a few of the women. Jane listened to them assure the women that they'll have their chance to enter after the sailors were all tended to. The rest of the guards stared blankly ahead, with clenched jaws and a stiff posture, ready to intervene if needed.

She peered through the distraught people towards the ships in the harbor. She spotted what looked to be their vessels. One of the ships had lost its rigs. Broken masts were completely shattered, laying on top of one another and the decks. The lamp lights on the piers outlined splintered stumps where masts used to stand upright. The ship was listing to one side, clearly taking on water. She clutched her medical bag in her hand. How it stayed afloat was beyond her. The other ship remained in fairer condition. All the masts but one was intact. From the darkness she couldn't tell what other damages they had suffered. She forced herself to inhale deeper even though each breath was harder to muster. Her uncle kept tension on her arm, pulling her with him.

"You'll find him, my dear," he assured. "Now let's go save some of these families' loved ones." He pointed towards the large crowd that formed around the two-story building of the hospital. Soldiers acted as barriers, standing shoulder to shoulder, keeping the people back. The four of them went through and rushed up the stairs to the guarded doors.

The soldiers allowed Governor Terry and her uncle through but stopped Elaine and Jane.

"I'm sorry, but no citizens allowed past this point," one of the soldiers stated. He immediately brought up his arm, blocking Jane and Elaine from entering the doorway. Not moving from his firm stance, he peered over the dark circles from under his eyes to give them a cold, hard stare. Jane's uncle paused in the doorway. She peeked over the soldier's shoulder and motioned her uncle to proceed without her.

"I'll gather what you'll need!" she called out to him. He nodded before disappearing behind the heavy door.

"But my father's the governor," Elaine stated, clearly annoyed.

"The rules go beyond your father," the soldier snapped. "These are orders by the king himself. No citizens beyond this point until we have everything in order."

Elaine glanced at Jane with a helpless expression.

"There are other ways we can help. Come." Jane grabbed Elaine's arm and rushed towards Samuel, who was waiting at the carriage.

"What are we going to do?" Elaine asked, confused.

"I'll tell you in a moment. Samuel!" Jane called up to their carriage driver.

"Miss Sawyer? Are you two all right?" He stood from his bench with a puzzled expression.

"We need you to go back to the plantation. Have the maids collect extra linens, lanterns, candles, and baskets and bring them back here." She turned to Elaine. "We're going to make strips of gauze."

"Right away, Miss Sawyer." Samuel flicked the reins and parted the crowd with the four stallions. "Hyah!"

"Jane! Elaine!" Jenny hollered while squeezing through the crowd.

"Have you seen them?!" she breathed as she threw her arms around them.

"No," Jane managed to choke out. The three of them embraced each other. Jane shuddered in her friends' arms. Her chest tightened, shortening her breaths.

"Have you searched—" Jenny couldn't finish her sentence. Tears rolled down her cheeks as she pointed down to the dock where the were bodies laid, waiting for their proper sea burial.

"No. And we won't," Jane answered. "They're not there. They can't—" her voice cracked as she swallowed down another sob that fought its way to the surface. She knew if they were to find any of them down there, they wouldn't be able to be of any more help. Jenny nodded in understanding. Elaine placed her hand on Jenny's arm and softly spoke, "Come, help us. We're going to make strips of gauze for the wounded."

"What do we need?" Jenny asked.

Jane wiped at an escaped tear. Clearing the lump that made its way to her throat she spoke, "Samuel's on his way to the plantation to get linen. We'll need to set up stations. One for the gauze and one for laundry. They're going to need hot water for the linens and instruments. Though I haven't figured out where we're going to get the water buckets." Jane was about to suggest going to the tavern for a laundry tub when a woman approached her.

"Excuse me, miss?" The woman looked to Jane with fear and worry. A piece of graying hair escaped from her loose bun and draped across her temple. Two wide-eyed little girls clung to her hips.

"Yes?" Jane did the best she could to sound pleasant given the circumstance.

"I beg your pardon, miss. I couldn't help but overhear you saying you want to pull together stations to help the men. My boy, Timothy, was on the Ebony, and I'd like to offer my service, if you wouldn't mind?" The woman's eyes pleaded with desperation.

"That would be wonderful. What is your name?"

"Francine Haymore. Please, call me Francine."

"Francine. I'm Miss Sawyer, this is Miss Oakley and Miss Keaton." They all gave a quick curtsy.

"What are you in need of, miss?" Francine asked.

"So many things. Tables, tubs, buckets, lanterns, linens, bars of soap, water. We're going to need a washing station and a linen station." Jane was trying to remember what they had during some of the attacks in Bombay.

"Miss Sawyer, would you mind if I recruit a few other ladies?" Francine asked.

"By all means! We could use all the help we can get." Jane smiled. A glimmer of hope shined through the turmoil. The woman nodded, then turned and yelled, "Betty! Sarah! Camille! Come over here!"

Three women from different sections of the crowd weaved their way to Francine.

"Ladies, meet Miss Sawyer, Miss Keaton, and Miss Oakley." The women gave a curtsy. They appeared wary about why their friend had called them over to make introductions.

"Miss Sawyer here is pulling together stations to help our men. Come, there are supplies we need to gather. We'll be back soon, Miss Sawyer." The women's faces brightened as they listened earnestly to Francine and hurried into town.

"Jane?" Jenny asked. "Where are we setting up?"

Jane scanned around them. Across the street was Mrs. Kimble's son's supply store and the blacksmith. To her right, the chapel doors of the whitewashed building stood ajar for people to enter for prayer. Of course!

"The churchyard," Jane declared. It was next to the hospital, only a few yards away.

Within the hour, people from town were tearing up sheets and folding them to place in baskets. Four large tubs of water boiled, with washing boards and sticks set ready for use. Jenny had an idea to collect food donations to give to the men. The table she set up was quickly filled with baskets full of all types of bread and fruit. Jane rushed up the stairs of the hospital to the same guard who forbade her to enter.

"Excuse me, sir. My uncle is Doctor Duncan Brown. He's asked me to get supplies for him. Can I go through to speak with him?"

"Sorry, miss," he huffed. "I can't allow you through until I'm given further instructions." The soldier kept his stance stern, though his shoulders began to relax.

"Sir, I understand, but this is to help the men and the surgeons there."

"Until I'm given further orders, you are to remain outside," he snapped.

"Miss Sawyer!"

Jane turned at the sound of a gentleman's voice calling to her. Her heart leapt into her throat as she tried to distinguish to whom it belonged to.

"Lieutenant Woods! You're alive!" Jane ran down the two stairs to give him a quick embrace, sighing in relief that he made it through. "What of Captain McCannon? Lieutenant Fletch? Captain Norton? Have you seen them?"

His smile faded. Long black sideburns framed his solemn expression. He took her hands in his.

"I wasn't on the ship. I was given the assignment to stay at the fort. We haven't heard any news about their whereabouts, as they're still trying to take account of the wounded."

Jane's stomach dropped. She nodded, taking in his pristine uniform.

"Are you trying to get into the hospital?" he asked.

She released a heavy sigh. "Yes, we have extra bandages and supplies for my uncle."

He squeezed her hand then headed up the stairs to the guard.

"This here is Miss Jane Sawyer," he said with authority. "Doctor Brown's niece. She needs to enter."

"Do you know how chaotic it is in there? They're dealing with their own battle. The last thing they need to be dealing with is a woman fainting in their workspace. I have my orders." The soldier scowled.

"Johnathan," Lieutenant Woods said with firmness. He took off his glove and held up his finely scarred hand. "I can assure you, she will not faint."

"That was her?" Astonished, Jonathan took a second look at Jane then back at Lieutenant Woods's hand.

"Send her back now," Lieutenant Woods ordered.

"Of course!" The man stepped aside.

"Miss Sawyer," Lieutenant Woods grabbed her hand before she stepped towards the doors. "It's a bloodbath in there, stay strong." She squeezed his hand.

"Thank you, Lieutenant."

He nodded then headed back down towards the barricade.

She pulled open the heavy doors and walked through with a wave of recognition. The overcrowded hall flooded with both conscious and unconscious men. Each wrapped in blood-stained bandages that covered their injuries. Some of the conscious men stared in front of them with a haunted gleam in their eye. Others cried or wailed in pain as they waited for treatment. Clasping her skirt, she scooted around them to the open room. Searching their faces in the dim light for James and their friends along the way. Her nose twitched with the familiar smell of burning flesh from cauterizing.

Once in the candlelit room, Jane trembled, taking in the disturbing scene before her. Rows and rows of cots filled the room with battered men. Dark puddles smeared across sections of the floor where the surgeons worked. Surgeons and nurses frantically yelled out demands to militiamen assigned to help. The scene brought haunted memories from battles in her past. Drawing in quick fervent breaths, she straightened her shoulders. *Take courage, Jane!* she ordered herself, clasping her shaking hands together. Spotting her uncle across the room, she rushed to his side.

"Jane!" He wiped the back of his hand across his forehead. His pinched brows relaxed as he glanced at her. In one swift motion, he clamped a blood vessel on a soldier's leg. "Hold him steady, Alfred," he ordered to the young militiaman who was clutching the wounded man's legs. "Louis," he said in a firm tone, to the injured man. "Whatever you do, don't move. Otherwise, I could cause you more harm." The man nodded through clenched teeth. Jane grabbed a washcloth from the table next to her uncle and dampened it in the water basin. She began to wipe away the beads of sweat from the wounded soldier's forehead. With the signal from her uncle, Alfred pushed down with all his might above the soldier's injured calf. Straight away, her uncle grabbed a hot poker stick from a large burning lantern. Jane cringed, hating what was about to come next. Her stomach tightened in anticipation. Strategically he placed the glowing orange stick against the wound and cauterized the bleeding. Louis twisted the sheet he laid on and cried out in pain. Biting her lip, she continued to blot the man's anguished face with the cool damp cloth.

"Shh, it will be alright." she soothed. "That should be the worst of it." The man's cry calmed to a whimper, as her uncle began to stitch the wound.

"There's not enough staff to help," he muttered to her. She went to his side, picked up the scissors and began to cut the thread he pulled taut for her, above the knot. Together, they moved as a fast team while he stitched. "I'm glad they let you through," he exclaimed. He stitched, tied the knot, and she cut.

"Uncle, I know there are many people who are eager to help. Please, let me get them. They can help slow the bleeding and give the wounded water until others can attend to them." Again, he stitched and knotted the thread. Jane made her precise cut with a steady hand.

"If they allow them in, by all means! Most of the men will bleed out if we don't hurry." She cut the last stitch.

"I'll see what I can do." Placing the scissors back on the tray, she gave him a kiss on his smooth cheek. He smiled encouragingly and began to wrap Louis's leg.

"I'll have Alfred here spread the word to the staff that some towns-folk will aid us in saving these men's lives." Her uncle eyed Alfred. The militiaman nodded at him, then left to speak with members of the staff. Feeling nothing but admiration for her uncle, she hurried outside to inform Lieutenant Woods of the conditions in the hospital.

❦

"Listen up!" Lieutenant Woods roared through the banter of the crowd. "We need healthy volunteers that don't faint at the sight of blood. The men need more bandaging and water. Please step forward if you can help."

Jane counted twelve men and women volunteers.

"I'm certain you have heard of England's finest surgeon, Doctor Duncan Brown. This is his niece, Miss Jane Sawyer." Lieutenant Woods introduced her. "She'll be giving you your instructions."

"Come with me," she ordered, walking to the churchyard. Gathering the linens, lanterns, food, and water buckets, they headed towards the hospital.

"Now, if you see any bandages that are bleeding through, what-ever you do, don't take them off. Leave the bandages on and apply

29

more bandages on top. If you notice they're still soaking through, inform a surgeon right away. Use your best judgment. If you have any questions or concerns, please don't hesitate to ask any of the militiamen or nurses. You're going to start from the front entry hall and work your way inside."

The volunteers stared at her with mixed expressions ranging from uncertainty to determination. She clasped her hands together as they shook. Feeling she did all she could to instruct them, she led them past the guards into the hospital.

After entering the hall, her volunteers were eager to get to work. Questions began bombarding her and she answered them the best she could. Each of the volunteers worked the best to their knowledge. Some hunched down to talk with the men on the ground, others gave them water and checked their wounds. A few of the uninjured militiamen joined the volunteers, working by their sides and giving guidance if needed. Seeing no need to be there at the moment, Jane left the group to grab more bandages.

"Jane! Jane! Come quick!" Elaine pressed, pulling her hand away from a linen basket. Elaine began dragging her towards the harbor.

"Elaine, what is it?" she panicked.

"There's no time to explain. Just come!"

Jane's stomach sank as they drew nearer to the dead, laid there for families to give their final goodbye before being laid to rest. Twisting her hand out of Elaine's grasp, she cried, "No! I can't." Tears began pouring over the rim of her tired eyes. So much loss. She couldn't bear to see James's face among them. Her heart ached as she pictured his one dimpled smile beaming down at her, his blue eyes twinkling in the light, taunting her. She needed him to be alive and whole and well. How she yearned to be in his arms knowing that he was safe.

"Jane. It's alright. I overheard a sailor talking and—Richard? Richard!" Elaine screamed out his name, releasing Jane's hand. Elaine ran towards the pier between the two distressed ships. Jane's spirits lifted when she saw two figures. One ran towards Elaine and swung her in his arms. The other man patted Captain Norton on his shoulder and continued walking forward in a rush. He was shorter than Captain Norton and wore an officer's uniform. Passing a lantern, the light exposed his weary face. His square jaw was clenched tight and his thick brows were pinched together with concern.

"Thomas," Jane choked out. She ran and wrapped her arms around his thick neck and sobbed in his broad shoulders. All the tension and worry the past few hours began to dwindle. If Thomas was here, then so was James.

"Lieutenant Thomas! I'm so glad to see you."

"Why Miss Jane! Aren't you a sight for sore eyes?"

Chuckling, she drew back and wiped her tears on her shawl.

"Where is he?" She looked up, searching his face for answers. Thomas's strained smile fell. His chocolate brown eyes were apprehensive and worried. "Please," her voice became frail. "Where is he?" she pleaded, clasping the sleeves of his uniform. Elaine and Captain Norton approached Thomas's side. Captain Norton held the same concerning expression, his black brows drawn tight together.

"Miss Jane," Thomas said carefully. "He's on the Sphinx. He's been wounded—" Elaine gasped through Thomas's now muffled words. "—I'm on my way to find a doctor who can examine—" Jane tried to control her emotions while processing what he said, but she desperately needed to see for herself.

"Excuse me," she broke away from the group, running towards the Sphinx.

She boarded, keeping her hands off the splintered rails that were once smooth. Sulfur tainted the air. Round holes scattered around the dark deck. Grabbing an extra lantern from a hook, she rushed towards a guard blocking the entrance of the ship.

"I need through," she ordered. The man didn't budge. Fire burned inside her. Her hands clenched into fists. She would fight him if needed.

"It's okay, Theo," Thomas came up from behind her. His light sandy hair tousled from his run. "She can pass." The soldier nodded and moved to the side, allowing her passage. Jane raced down the stairs, stumbling on the last step. The lantern's light swung, casting shadows across the dark walls of the hall. Thomas went to help steady her but she brushed his hands away. Hurrying down the dark hallway, she came to an abrupt stop at a door.

"Is this it?" she asked. Her chest heaved while she tried to catch her breath. Thomas slowed from his quick walk to stand by her side.

"Yes," he muttered. "We didn't want to move him into the hospital where his men were." He lowered his eyes to the ground. "Not with their cries." For the first time, Jane noticed Thomas's powder-smudged face. Two sutured abrasions hid under his disheveled hair above his left brow. Dark circles framed under his heavy eyes. Without his usual cheerful, boyish smile, he appeared much older than before. She swallowed and placed her hand on his arm. "You did well."

She stared at the dark door. She had seen wounded men in all states of injuries but for the most part, she had never known them, not like she did James.

"It will be alright, Miss Jane." His face hid in the shadows of the dim lamplight, making it impossible for her to tell if his expression said otherwise. He twisted the handle and opened the door. "He'll want to see you."

Chapter Three

A candle burned on a small table. It was the only light source in the room. A form that breathed heavily under a blanket hid partially in the darkness. In an attempt to not disturb him, she eased her way through the doorway. A board creaked under her foot, breaking the silence in the room. James's face turned towards her lantern, illuminating his ghastly pale, glistening skin. His pale-blue eyes shimmered from the flame's glow as he squinted. Lowering the lantern, she swallowed a cry of relief and ran to his side.

"James!" Jane exclaimed, burying her head in his chest.

"Jane?" he muttered in an unfamiliar, faint, dry voice. "Are you really here?"

"Yes," she whispered, choking back a sob. "I've never been so scared in my life." She lifted her face to look into his tired eyes. With his fingertips, he stroked the tears off her cheeks.

"I'm sorry, I'm getting your shirt all wet." She sniffed, wiping where her tears had fallen on his shirt. He let out a chortle and began to cough. He winced in pain, gritting his teeth. Alarmed, Jane looked down at his shirt. It was damp and certainly from more than just her tears. She felt across his rather warm chest. Lifting her lamp above her head, she noted his shirt adhered to his body. Quickly, she pressed the back of her hand to his forehead. It was clammy and hot. Her head spun as she scoured his body to find the injury.

"You're burning up." She tried to control her emotion, but her voice kept quivering. "Tell me, where were you wounded?"

James let out a cough and tried to lift his arm to point to where the injury was but failed. His arm fell back to his side. Thomas, who had been standing outside the door, hurried next to her.

"The worst of it is on his side," he whispered. "A lead ball and some shrapnel struck him as he ran to warn us of the enemy's cannon. We managed to shoot them before they shot us, but for James . . ." Thomas's voice cracked. He cleared his throat and continued, "Our ship's doctor, Doctor Bentley, removed all he could."

Jane stared at Thomas, mortified. "If he didn't remove all the shrapnel," she muttered to Thomas, "then it would explain his fever. He's developed an infection. Thomas," she lowered her voice further to keep James from hearing. "He could die."

Thomas's eyes widened. "I'm going to show her your wound, James. She may be able to help with the pain."

"Okay," James groaned.

Thomas pulled off the covers. He began to tremble. Jane held the lantern higher while Thomas lifted his shirt, exposing the saturated bandage wrapped around his muscular torso.

"James," she said, releasing her breath. "I'm going to press on your stomach. It will be extremely tender, but I only want you to inform me if you feel a sharp, stabbing pain."

He nodded, clenching his jaw. She pressed her free hand to the right of his wound, where the blood saturated his bandage the most. A subtle grunt escaped James's lips. Relieved he didn't react too strongly, she slid her hand to a different location on his side and pressed.

"There!" he moaned, curling up in agony.

She drew her shaking hand back. Her mind raced while she assessed his condition. It was critical that all the shrapnel be removed, especially being so close to his organs. Looking up, she saw Thomas's expression match her dread.

"Can you remove it?"

"No," she whispered. "I need you to fetch my uncle, with great haste! Tell him that James has a piece of shrapnel in his side and that he's burning with a fever. He'll know what to do."

"I'm on it," he replied, before rushing out of the room.

"Jane," James mumbled. He groaned when he turned towards her. Taking his hand, she noted how it grew heavier in hers.

"Shh, James. Try not to move." She urged, running her fingers through his damp, dark hair. From the corner of her eye, she spotted a washcloth and a water pitcher. She dipped the cloth in the cool water. Wringing it out, she dabbed his forehead. His pained expression began to relax and he closed his eyes.

"Jane," he whispered again, his breathing more labored. "Stay with me."

She picked up his cut-up hand and kissed it. "I promise."

He cupped his hand on her cheek. She held his arm with both her hands offering him extra support while it grew heavier.

"You're so beautiful," he murmured. She smiled at the absurdity. She was a mess with her curls falling out of their pins and puffy red eyes.

He coughed, wincing again in pain. "If you only knew," he whispered, under his breath. "From the first day I saw you." he paused, closing his eyes for a moment, then opened them again. "I . . . I've never experienced that feeling before." He brushed her cheek with the back of his hand to wipe a tear.

"James McCannon," she breathed. "Don't start talking like we're never going to see each other again." Another tear dropped from her cheek. "You have yet to take me riding around the island."

"I look forward to that ride." He gave a half smile, exposing her favorite dimple.

Temptation took over and she leaned over to kiss it. His hand rested on her arm, causing her to stop. Inches apart from each other, she looked at him. The beating in her chest intensified as he glanced down at her lips with longing. His fingers weaved through her hair stopping at the nape of her neck. He brought her face towards him until his lips pressed tenderly against hers. It was sweet and everything she dreamt of while he was away. Drawing away, his hand traced her cheek. "I've thought of nothing other than seeing you again."

"And I you."

His eyes glistened in the lamplight as he held her gaze. Feeling desperate to keep him comfortable, she pulled his blanket higher over his shoulders when he began to shiver. It was a failed attempt to warm him as his teeth started to chatter. Blotting his face with the cloth, she watched his lids grow heavier. She'd seen his condition play out in the hospital and it was never promising. Hiding her tears, she turned to wipe her eyes. *Please, let him make it,* she earnestly prayed. It's felt like a lifetime since she's felt this scared of losing someone close to her.

Hurried steps and heavy panting echoed down the hall. A soft thud sounded as though something dropped.

"Theo!" A fierce whisper erupted outside the door. "It's just a rat! Hurry and gather those up."

Jane exchanged a curious expression with James and smiled at his faint smirk. The door swung open and Thomas stormed through, with his wide shoulders brushing the doorframe. His hands were full with a bucket of steaming water and—Jane took a double look—her medical bag. How did he find that? She couldn't remember the last place she'd put it. He blew out an exasperated breath and set the bag next to the lantern on the table. Swiftly, Thomas turned to Theo in the doorway and snatched the basket of linens and a bottle of liquor from him.

"When Doctor Brown arrives, I need you to show him down immediately," he ordered.

"Yes, sir," the guard replied before disappearing into the darkened hall.

"Alright, Miss Jane." Thomas rushed to her side and set the basket down. He ran the back of his hand across his damp forehead. "Your uncle gave me strict instructions to bring you all of these supplies. It took Jenny a while to find your bag but she did it. Shall we get started?" Her eyes widened at Thomas. He appeared quite determined as he shrugged out of his smoked-stained jacket.

"We?" She stood, holding tight to James's weakened grip. Panic pricked up her spine. If he was thinking she would perform the surgery, then he was mistaken! Thomas nodded and began rolling up his sleeves.

"I'm afraid your uncle is in the middle of a surgery and said, given the situation, you best get started as soon as possible." Jane frowned at him when he peered from his sleeves at her. "He also said you would do a far better job than half the doctors on the island." Thomas bit the cork of the bottle and popped it off. Spitting it across the room he poured the alcohol on his hands. "And to be frank, after watching you suture Lieutenant Woods's hand, I couldn't agree more. Now," he placed the bottle on the table and clapped his hands, "What would you have me do?"

Jane sucked in a breath. She didn't have much time to process any of it. But what she did understand was James's condition was worsening. Nodding with understanding, she looked to James. His ashen face glistened in the lamplight. He coughed an exhausted-sounding cough and lightly squeezed her hand. His heavy-lidded eyes met hers. With his dimple faint on his cheek, he nodded.

"I have full confidence in you," he said with encouragement.

She kissed his hand. If only she felt the same way. She knew her uncle wouldn't have asked her to carry on without him if the situation wasn't so dire.

"And not to worry, Miss Jane. Your proficient embroidery skills will stay between us." Thomas winked with a smile as he referred to what she had told them after suturing the lieutenant's hand.

James went to laugh but winced in pain. She offered him a small smile. It wasn't her reputation that she was concerned about. She knew both gentlemen would be discreet about her performing a surgery. It was the surgery itself that she feared.

"Very well," she said with more confidence than she felt. She didn't dare show the men in the room any of her uncertainties. She'd seen the procedure performed many times by her uncle, but doing it herself; that was something she used to dream of, but not like this, not on the man she deeply cared for. Clearing her throat, she tucked a fallen piece of hair behind her ear. "Thomas, I need you to cut the bandages off of him."

He gave a curt nod and pulled scissors from the linen basket.

"James, I need you to drink this." She raised the bottle Thomas had brought towards his mouth.

James shook his head. "I don't need it."

"But it will help with the pain."

"Not for me," he answered with a short breath.

"I suppose you could say it's not his cup of tea," Thomas muttered when he saw her scrunch her brows in confusion.

"Very well. Bite down on this." Jane rolled a rag and brought it to James's chapped lips. He clamped down, exhaling through his nose.

Opening her medical bag, she peered at the sterile instruments wrapped in fabric. Sucking in a breath, she proceeded and poured the alcohol on her hands. With eyes closed, she shook the residue of the liquid off her fingers. If her uncle said she would do better than some of the doctors in the hospital, he either felt she needed encouragement, or he wasn't impressed with their procedures. Either way, it didn't help her nerves.

She unwrapped her instruments and approached James's side. The bruises blended into the shadow around the sutures.

"Lieutenant Thomas, I need you to hold the lantern above me, please."

Light illuminated the injury as Thomas reached out and rested the lantern on a hook hanging from a beam above her. A six-inch gash with brown and yellow pus oozed between the sutures on James's side. The skin surrounding the suture was bright red with purple and blue bruises expanding in different directions like a drop of paint splashed on a wet surface. It was grim, yet something she'd seen before. They were fortunate there wasn't any rotting flesh . . . not yet. Biting her lip, Jane snipped each of the sutures. Her hand shook after each cut. Keeping her breaths steady, she inhaled the foul stench of infection. Yellow and brown liquid seeped out of the open cut. She turned towards the basket to grab a cloth but found Thomas ahead of her with his hand pressing a clean piece of fabric against the bleed. James gritted his teeth into the rag and groaned.

Thomas raised a concerning brow at her. Her heart sank, knowing that was the least painful part. James's stomach rapidly raised and dropped under Thomas's hand. She reached for her pickups and bottle of alcohol.

"James, I'm going to clean the wound and then proceed with removing the shrapnel." With her forearm, she wiped a curl off her forehead. "I need you to stay as still as possible." James puffed a heavy breath through his nose and nodded.

"Lieutenant, be ready to hold him down," she instructed. "When you see an area that's bleeding profusely, I'll need you to apply pressure and keep it there until I can cauterize." She glanced at the thin iron rod sticking out of the lantern.

Thomas repositioned himself and leaned his body over James's. "Thank goodness you don't smell as bad as I thought you would," he spoke with a hoarse tone. James scoffed through the rag. Thomas smiled, but it didn't reach his eyes. He looked to Jane, letting her know he was ready.

Sucking in a breath, she dabbed the alcohol into his gash. Every muscle in James's body flexed, pushing his veins to the surface. An anguished howl rumbled through the quarters, jarring through Jane's body and piercing her heart. The lantern's light shook as Thomas pushed his weight against James's shoulders. Tears stung her eyes and she squeezed them shut.

"It's alright, it's alright," she stammered aloud. She wasn't sure if she was trying to calm the trembling within her body or James's anguished cry.

"Miss Jane, it will be fine," Thomas assured, his tone sounding more of an order rather than one being comforting. He raised a thick, sandy-colored brow, encouraging her to proceed.

"Yes," she whispered, blinking away her tears. Knowing time being the essence for James's life, she straightened her shoulders and jumped into action. She maneuvered through the motions of the procedure she's watched countless times. Careful to not dig too deep, she searched for the debris.

"Thomas," Jane's voice shook as James cried out another muffled groan. Grateful that Thomas blocked her from seeing the pain in James's face, she focused on keeping her hands steady. "Tell me, what happened?"

Thomas spoke in a low hushed tone, while keeping himself positioned over James. "We were in a fog when we came upon two French frigates, anchored about thirty kilometers from the island. James had this absurd, yet brilliant, idea to lead us through the two ships while we had the element of surprise."

Jane felt herself getting woozy as she noticed James's cries had disappeared. All his flexed muscles relaxed and, judging by his steady breaths, he had passed out. Thomas continued to talk. "We fired at them while we passed, eliminating one of their frigates."

Another groan escaped from James when she tugged a piece of shrapnel free.

"But that wasn't enough." Thomas proceeded. "Our sixty-four cannons didn't have a chance against their seventy-four-cannon ship. But that didn't sway James."

"Seventy-four cannons?" she exclaimed with surprise. With a solemn expression, Thomas held out a metal tray for her to drop the sharp sliver of wood onto. "There's only a handful of ships in the world that carry that kind of gunpower."

"My word," she breathed. Taking advantage of James's given state, she went deeper into the wound.

"If James hadn't directed us through the two ships like he had, we wouldn't have had a chance against their ships."

"How did Captain Norton get involved?" A vexing strand of hair fell across her eyes and she brushed it away with the back of her hand.

"Captain Richard," she heard Thomas swallow before he continued, "happened to be patrolling the area when he and his crew heard the cannon fire. It was impeccable timing when he intervened. For if the French blasted us once more, we would have been done for."

"Captain Norton was the one that sunk the large French vessel?" She briefly peered at the small, jagged sliver she removed. A tiny piece of cloth was attached to it. If they were lucky, then that would be the only piece of fabric lodged into the wound. Being thorough with her exam, she searched for any other pieces of fabric.

"They did." Thomas's voice sounded pinched. Peeking at him from the corner of her eye, she watched his face pale as he stared at James. He cleared his throat. "As you can tell from the ship, they ended up having a battle of their own. Fortunately, we caused a lot of damage, so their fight didn't last long. Those Frenchies had what was coming to them."

After hearing about all the innocent lives the French had taken, she was grateful they couldn't do any more harm.

"I'm very grateful it wasn't worse," she whispered, focusing on a particular area. Maneuvering her pickups, she felt along a section that had the most bruising on the surface. She had removed a great deal of tiny pieces of shrapnel and fabric and prayed she had found them all. Right when she suspected the wound was clean, the tip of the metal pickups scraped across a hard surface. James cried out and started to snap forward from his unconscious state. Thomas roughly pushed him down before the object could cause further harm.

"Easy there, James," he responded, his voice shaking from either adrenaline or force.

Heavy pants came from Thomas's other side as James breathed unevenly through his nose. He grunted with painful cries through the saturated rag. Jane froze, unable to move while she watched in horror as James's stomach rose and fell swiftly with his panting. She had tapped something that was deep—too deep.

"Miss Jane . . . Jane!"

She blinked realizing Thomas was calling to her from over his shoulder. Sweat ran down his temples. His sculpted arms quivered while he strained to hold James against the bed.

"What do you need?"

"A miracle." Blotting the wound, her voice hitched. "The shrapnel is deep." She blinked again, looking back at the gaping hole that filled with blood. Drawing in a breath, she blotted the area and held pressure to stop the bleeding. James's muscles in his stomach began to relax.

"He's passed out again." Thomas's words floated through the stillness of the dark room.

Drawing in a shaken breath, Jane removed the saturated cloth. A prickle of panic shot up her back. The area flooded immediately with blood again. The pressure she used wasn't enough to stop the bleeding. His sudden movements must have caused the shrapnel to nick a small artery.

"He won't be for long. I have to cauterize," she rushed. With the back of her arm, she wiped at a drop of sweat that itched her forehead. "Try to keep him extremely still." Her voice quivered. "There's shrapnel lodged deep towards an organ. Any sharp movement and it—" She swallowed, meeting Thomas's eyes. "—it could be fatal."

Thomas nodded. His arms flexed as he pushed on James's shoulders. Maintaining pressure on the bleed, she grabbed the metal stick from the lantern. Angling the red-orange tip towards the saturated cloth, she held her breath. Exhaling, she pressed it against the severed artery. Smoke, tainted with burning flesh, tinged her nose. Jane bit her lip as all James's muscles tightened in unison across his body. Once again, his anguished cries broke through his unconscious state.

"I'm so sorry, James." Her voice shook along with her shaking hand as she removed the torture device. She fervently blinked, unable to evaluate James through her moisture-filled eyes. "Thomas, how is he?"

"Better. He's not fighting me and the muscles in his neck relaxed again. I reckon he's out."

With a sniff, she wiped her eyes on her arm. "Very good." Satisfied the bleeding had stopped, she placed the poker stick back in the lantern's flame above her. Fumes of burning flesh lingered in the air. Clasping the forceps, she locked her breath in her lungs and held her wrist steady while she attempted to tug at the shrapnel. The metal pickups slid across the hard surface pinching themselves at the tips. She exhaled and tried again, only to have the same disheartening result. The shrapnel was securely lodged.

Hurried footsteps sounded outside the room. Jane looked hopeful at Thomas. There was one gentleman who she wanted more than anything to belong to those steps.

"Jane," her uncle gasped, while opening the door. Beads of sweat rolled down his temples. His cheeks were flushed and his spectacles had slid further down the bridge of his nose.

"Thank goodness, you're here!" she exclaimed.

"I tried to get here as fast as I could. How is he?" Uncle Duncan darted to her side. He placed his medical bag on the floor and pushed his spectacles higher on his nose.

Her words tumbled out while her chin started to quiver. "He's unconscious at the moment. I was able to retrieve all the shrapnel except there's a piece that will need to be carefully removed. He's lost a fair amount of blood. I'm afraid to proceed any further in fear I'll either cause him to bleed out or accidentally nick an organ while removing the shrapnel." She paused to take a breath. "This is beyond anything I've ever done."

Her uncle eyed her while she brushed hair off her face with the back of her shaking hand. He gave her a small smile and patted her shoulder.

"You've done well, my dear. I shall take it from here."

Without hesitation Jane withdrew herself from her post and moved towards James's head. Washing the sticky residue from her trembling hands, she grabbed a cloth and began dabbing the perspiring drops off James's face.

The rag between his lips slipped to his chin. "Jane," he whispered, fighting to open his eyes. "Stay with me," he muttered.

"I promise."

With an incomprehensible mumble, his head turned to the side.

"Uncle," Jane glanced around Thomas's broad frame. "The shrapnel is on the left of the opening. About eight centimeters deep." With her free hand she pointed in front of Thomas to the side of James's wound. He didn't look her way but gave her a nod of acknowledgment. Grabbing a pair of long forceps, and with a steady hand, he maneuvered them into James's wound. James's pale face crimsoned as it pinched in pain.

"I am going to have to cut it out," her uncle warned, after his examination. Jane caught his eye and nodded with understanding.

"James," she whispered, bringing the rag to his lips. "It's critical that you hold very still."

Keeping his eyes tight, he weakly clamped on the cloth. Thomas leaned over James's shoulders, readying himself, should he move. Her uncle worked inside the opening of his wound, pulling out bloody pieces of the large shard. Under Thomas's fierce grip, James shook with muffled howls of pain. Through flared nostrils, he breathed heavily into the rag.

"Got it," her uncle exclaimed. A whimper escaped James's lips. Drops of sweat rolled down his temples meeting the tears on his cheeks.

"You're doing well," she soothed.

"That looks to be the last of it." Her uncle dropped the large sliver of wood on the metal tray with a low clang. Jane rolled her stiff shoulders back and repositioned herself. Little pieces of sharp, jagged wood littered the tray. How on earth did their ship's doctor miss all that?! As if Thomas read her mind, he answered her, "There were so many casualties, our doctor did the best he could with what little time he had."

To keep from objecting to the matter, she focused on blotting the drops of sweat from James's face.

"He did fine, given the circumstances." Her uncle reassured, applying a salve around James's wound. James grunted, releasing the rag from his mouth.

"Were there any prisoners?" her uncle inquired.

"No." Thomas stared at his feet and shook his head. "The Frenchmen didn't believe in being taken alive."

Jane's eyes widened. "You mean, they . . ." She couldn't finish what she was about to ask. It was too disturbing to think.

He gave her a grave nod. "The brutes were all dead from their own doing."

The room fell silent as her uncle began to suture the wound closed. On cue, Jane picked up a pair of scissors to assist him. James's cries had stopped yet she couldn't help but notice how heavy his breathing came. Her uncle held up his thread, waiting for her to cut it free. Switching places with Thomas, her hands shook as she reached out and cut the taut thread. She swallowed, feeling a loss for words. For the first time since she had started learning how to suture, she had cut the thread too high above the knot. Hurrying, she trimmed the excess thread while her uncle proceeded with his next knot. She watched the faltering rise and fall of James's breaths. *Were they faltering breaths or was her mind playing tricks on her in the dim light?*

"There you have it my friend, the worst is over," Thomas whispered to James. "I'm certain that was no worse than the time you broke your leg falling out of a tree when we were younger."

A subtle grunt came from James. He laid with his eyes closed, no longer fighting to open them.

"Ahem."

Jane jumped and tore her eyes from him. Her uncle held the next thread up for her to cut.

"My apologies." Holding her shaking wrist in an attempt to hold herself steady, she squeezed the scissors close. Blast! She cut the knot! She glanced up at her uncle, with astonishment. Never had she cut the knot. Only a slight raise of her uncle's brow gave away his surprise. He carried on and re-stitched the knot, as though nothing had happened.

"Jane, dear," he said softly, "Why don't you gather the bandages from my bag?"

"Yes, Uncle." Reluctant to comply, she released the scissors. It was for the best.

"Captain McCannon?" her uncle called.

Her head snapped up as she recognized the change of tone in her uncle's voice. The same tone that was used whenever his patients weren't responding,

"James?" She hurried around Thomas. James's chest sank down, barely raising to fill his lungs. She stroked his hair. "James?" her voice rose with alarm. He didn't respond. His chest raised for a brief second and fell. She stared, waiting for it to rise again.

"James," Thomas shook his shoulder. Nothing. James's chest held in its sunken position with no sign of movement. Thomas shook it again, but this time with more urgency, and trembling hands. "Come on, James!" he blurted with a sob.

No, no, no! Panic scattered from her head to her toes, draining the blood in her limbs. "Please!" She begged, desperate to see his chest rise again. Tears poured down her cheeks. Stroking his hair, she whispered, "Please, James. Stay with me."

Chapter Four

"Miss Jane? Are you awake?"

Thomas's quiet voice pulled her from her sleep. Her eyes opened wide and she sat up with abruptness. Fervently she blinked trying to adjust to the darkness in the room of the governor's manor. The muscles in her body cried out in protest from the wooden chair she had sat on for what felt like hours since their arrival from the harbor. She looked at James's dark figure on the bed. Smoke and melted wax lingered in the air. The haunted memories from losing her parents when she was a child resurfaced from their dark, forgotten abyss. Tightening her arms over her chest, she braced herself. She was surprised to have those feelings resurface throughout the night. She'd known him for just a few weeks, yet she couldn't fathom how he made her feel so vulnerable.

"Yes," she claimed, almost forgetting what Thomas had asked. Blindly, she patted the table beside her in search of matchsticks. Her fingers grazed the box that held the slender pieces of wood. Striking the match, she lit the wick and held the candle towards James. In front of her, he lay unconscious on the feathered mattress. Tiny cuts marked the side of his shadowed cheek. The battle still etched a devastating story on his skin, yet he appeared peaceful with a little color in his cheeks. She released her held breath.

Her uncle had reassured her multiple times that she didn't cause James's heart to stop. A faint voice in the corner of her mind informed her that he was right but that didn't stop the doubt from spreading.

On rare occasion she had heard other doctors mention a pattern they've seen with labored breaths. That when the patient experiences those breaths for some time, their heart stops soon after. Witnessing what happened with James, with his breathing, and then his heart stopping, she could attest to the pattern. Thank goodness her uncle was there. Much to her surprise he began pounding on James's chest. It was as though the action caused his heart to wake up. But that seems implausible.

Guilt ate at her, knowing that she was the one who had caused his labored breaths. She practically tortured him during the surgery. Squeezing her eyes, she failed to push the horrid thought aside. Why she ever wanted to pursue being a surgeon was beyond her. Emotionally, she could never make it. Not after the screams she forced from him. She squeezed her eyes tighter, focusing on drowning out his cries. The thought left her with a terrible feeling of regret in the pit of her stomach.

"I'm afraid I must be going," Thomas whispered. In the corner of the room, she heard a soft snore coming from Millie. Poor girl refused to have one of the maids take her place. "I need to return to the fort, to report and check on our men."

She held the candle towards the sound of his voice. Standing by her side, the small halo of light glistened in his weary eyes and the dark hues under them told her of the hours of sleep he still required. Still wearing his tattered uniform, his light brown hair was in disarray, with residue of black powder smudged around his hairline. Being the first lieutenant on the Ebony, Thomas was now in command. She knew he had pushed off his responsibilities to be by James's side for as long as he deemed possible. "I understand. I'll be certain to inform you of the details of James's condition."

He gave her a short nod. A dark shadow had formed around his square jaw. Any signs of his jolly demeanor were hidden with the downward corners of his mouth. A shiver ran up Jane's spine. It was hard to see him so solemn.

"Thank you. I look forward to it." He offered her a stiff bow.

"Thomas?" she asked, before he departed. "Will you be alright?"

"As long as he keeps improving, I'll be more than alright."

She smiled at his hope-filled response. The candlestick's flame flickered a shadow across James's unshaven cheek, making him appear lifeless. Her eyes trailed down to his chapped lips that parted with a breath. His chest raised with a slow, steady inhale. It was a miraculous sight that she was relieved to see.

"Yes. I'm certain his condition will only do just that," she replied.

"That's all one can pray for."

"Yes." And she had. She had kept a prayer in her heart ever since James had departed for the patrol. "Will you make certain my uncle takes a moment to get some rest? I'm certain he'll lose track of time with all the surgeries at the hospital and I want to be sure he doesn't over exert himself."

Had her uncle not bid her to return with James to the plantation, she would have insisted on helping him. But she was grateful to be where she was, especially while James still laid unconscious.

"I'll inform him of your order." The corner of his mouth raised with hesitation. "Jane, I hope you know that none of this was your fault."

Tears that had been pooling on the surface poured down her cheeks. She wiped them away with her hand. "How do you mean?"

"I watched the whole procedure. There was nothing you did that caused this nor was there anything you could have done to prevent it. I feel you should know."

A sob broke free from her lips. She covered her mouth. The guilt that stuck like tar to her thoughts lightened from his words. He laid the knitted blanket that she gave him earlier over her shoulders. She tugged at the ends, hugging it over her body for comfort.

"I can't tell you how much that means to hear that from you," she managed to say through her tears.

"He's fortunate you did what you did. Never doubt that, Jane."

She wiped her tired eyes on the blanket.

"I won't." Hearing his padded steps draw closer towards the door she whispered through the darkness, "Goodnight, Lieutenant Thomas."

"Goodnight."

A low moan echoed in James's ears. Dull pain spread through his side. The moan grew louder as the pain intensified. He gasped, waking up with a torturous throb coursing through his side. A rosy hue of light seeped through his lashes as he attempted to open his eyes.

"Good morning, Captain. You've been asleep for two days, a lot longer than I expected," Doctor Brown's cheerful voice brought confusion.

Unable to hide the pain any longer, James grasped the blanket his hands laid on and pressed his head against his pillow. His breaths grew shorter. He closed his eyes, focusing on keeping the nausea down as the pain magnified.

"Captain, I need you to drink this," the doctor's urgency in his tone carried through James's gasps. With his eyes squeezed tight, he felt a cup press to his lips. Obediently he separated his clenched teeth and swallowed the foul liquid, desperate for whatever it was the doctor offered that would help with the agony.

"Now that should relieve some of the pain."

James winced when he coughed as the last of the drops slid down his throat. "What was that?" he croaked.

Blinking open his tear-filled eyes, he watched the doctor chuckle.

"That was a medicinal concoction I created with a few herbs from India. Given how your fever broke, I added a few additional herbs to calm the inflammation."

"I've never tasted something so horrid." James gladly accepted the glass of water Doctor Brown handed him. The water sloshed over the cup's lip from the tremors in his hands. Rinsing the sour taste out of his mouth, he lowered the glass and looked down at his soaked-filled shirt. Across the room he noted a floral sofa and a plush chair to the opposite corner, both had blankets folded neatly on top of them.

"Very good." Doctor Brown smiled. "Let's get your bandages changed, shall we?"

When he went to nod, James felt his body become light. The excruciating pain that he had, faded into a dull ache. "What exactly did you give me?" he asked, feeling as though everything around him was beginning to float.

"Just a few tonics. Raise your arms for me. We need to get your shirt off while you're still conscious."

"Still conscious?" he slurred. The door to his room squeaked open.

"Ah, perfect timing. Jane, can you assist me? I need you to grab me the bandages while I remove his shirt."

"I can do . . ." James started but couldn't finish. A feeling like someone poured sand in his arms, legs, and body overcame him making every part feel weighed down. The doctor began tugging at his garment and James's vision became white from the shirt slipping over his head. Then, from the corner of his eye he saw her with tear-filled eyes and a bright radiant smile. The woman who was everything that mattered to him. *His life. His soul. His sails. His dreams. His compass. His love. His—what's happening?* Jane tucked a piece of hair behind her ear. James sighed. Isn't her skin so soft and creamy? Like a tall pitcher of milk, that he could drink. Her lips looked like strawberries but tasted like peppermint. *Wait. What did the doctor give me?* James swallowed and concentrated even more to keep her in his line of sight. Jane's cheeks flushed when her eyes gazed down to his wound. Or was she looking at him? Did he not have his shirt on anymore? Where did it go? She quickly glanced to her side, her cheeks as pink as the peculiar wallpaper. *Where was he?* James went to smile at her, but it felt lopsided, and his eyes fell hard against his lids.

Jane blinked away the moisture in her eyes. It was easier to breathe knowing James had awoken. Her uncle carefully laid him against his pillows, making it even more impossible not to gawk at James with his shirt now tossed on his bed. Earnest to avoid the indecency of his lack of clothing, she gathered the used bandages.

"It's looking better," her uncle murmured.

Tempted to see for herself, she peeked over her uncle's shoulder to evaluate his wound. The scar stretched across James's side with normal amount of seeping. No sign of infection. The bruises, vibrant in color, covered part of the curvature of James's finely toned abdomen. Her eyes trailed up towards a bruise on his chest from where her uncle had pounded. Her mind took a turn as her eyes traced his chest to across his broad shoulders, down his well-defined arms. *Goodness. Every muscle is smooth like a sculpture of a roman warrior.* Heat scorched up her neck to her cheeks. Tearing her eyes away, she released a hitched breath. With muddled thoughts she began tearing strips of fabric for fresh bandages.

"Jane, I'm going to hold him up, can you wrap the bandage around his torso?"

She stared at her uncle like he had asked her to dip her toes in crocodile-infested waters. Of course, he was expecting her assistance. She was usually there to aid him whenever he did procedures in their home in Bombay. But this wasn't any ordinary patient. It was James . . . a half-dressed James with a body. . . her eyes gave into the temptation to peek at his arms. Biting her lip, she tore her eyes away. With a body that needed covering—immediately! She looked from the empty room towards the open doorway. Perhaps, she had time to fetch the valet, the butler, or even Governor Keaton to assist her uncle? The blaze in her cheeks intensified. Standing next to James, her uncle pulled him from the pillows.

"Jane?" he grunted over his shoulder. "Let's make this quick, he's not as light as I hoped he would be."

Swallowing down her hesitation, she tore her eyes away from the doorway and grabbed the strips of fabric. "This is just another soldier in Bombay," she muttered to herself. Folding a strip of fabric, she added a paste her uncle made and pressed it against *the soldier's* sutured wound. Unraveling the roll of fabric across his torso, her hand grazed the firm muscles of his stomach. Every fiber of her body shrieked from the touch. *Just another soldier!* she assured herself, glancing up to find her face inches from his parted lips. She swallowed, forgetting what it was she was doing.

"Jane?" her uncle wheezed, pressing his body against James's shoulder. "Please hurry, he's slipping."

Grateful her uncle didn't witness her gawking, she slipped her arm between him and James and began to unravel the roll further. She paused. Holding her breath, she stretched her arm as far as she could without having to get her body closer to his. She waved her free hand around him, hoping to grab the fabric, but she wasn't close enough.

"Were you able to get it around?" her uncle breathed. "Jane, I need you to hurry."

She bit her trembling lip, ashamed she wasn't performing how she usually did. Doing everything she could do to focus, she drew in a breath, closed her eyes, and took a daring step closer to the unconscious patient. Keeping her feet planted, and her body from touching his, she leaned forward, reaching her arms further around his torso. Goosebumps formed along her neck as James's stubble tickled her skin. She exhaled slowly, concentrating on stretching her fingers towards each other. She raised to her toes to close the gap.

"I'm going to—" her uncle began, but with James's steady breaths in her ear she struggled to understand what he was saying. Her fingers clasped the roll.

In a brief moment, she felt a solid mass of weight press against her arm pulling her down. Losing her balance, she fell on top of James with her arm trapped under his back. The touch of his firm chest against her hand sent a flare up her arm, igniting her entire body. Mortified to be in such a position, she scurried to get to her feet, but her arm didn't budge under the boulder that trapped her. With the frantic attempt to escape, momentum flung her back onto James's chest. A whimper escaped her lips.

"Forgive me, Jane! I thought you heard me say I needed to lower him. Are you able to slide your arm out?"

James's firm chest rose and fell steadily under her hand, opposite from her frantic breaths. Before she could reply, she watched in horror as James slowly peeked through his lashes, exposing his glazed blue eyes. She gasped. Terror plucked at her sprinting heart. A heavy arm fell against her back, locking her against him. Closing his eyes, he continued to sleep.

"Uncle?" She panicked, looking over her shoulder at him. "I'm trapped." She kept her voice low so not to wake James, but she couldn't control the horror from her tone. What would James think if he actually was coherent when he found her on top of him like she was? *And my uncle! Why must he witness this?* Peeking back at Uncle Duncan, she watched him tuck his lips under to hide a smile and quickly grabbed James's shoulder.

"He's a bit heavier than most of the soldiers I've worked on," he said with a grunt, his glasses lifting up on one side by James's shoulder.

Freeing her arm, she managed to slide herself from James's ensnaring arm. Her uncle laid him back down as though nothing humiliating took place. "Is your arm okay?"

"Yes," she nearly squeaked. Smoothing out the front of her dress, she tried to rid any sign of what just occurred.

"Were you able to get the roll out from under him?" He dabbed at his forehead, his spectacles now balancing at the tip of his nose.

Trying to rid the thoughts of her body against his flesh, she rubbed her arm. "Uh, yes, I managed to get it out from under him. It should be on his other side." Feeling breathless, she looked up at the ceiling, avoiding any more contact with James and the situation.

"Jane," Elaine whispered from the doorway.

Grateful for the excuse to depart from the uncomfortable scene she endured, she hurried to where Elaine stood, appearing all fresh.

"Did he wake up?" Elaine whispered. Her blonde curls were loosely pulled back into a low bun, her blue eyes were bright and well rested.

Jane nodded freely and was about to respond when Elaine gasped and covered her mouth.

"Great heavens, please tell me he didn't wake up to you looking like that?"

Her eyes trailed from Jane's hair to the hem of her skirt. Jane's mouth fell. She'd never considered how she appeared. Having changed into a new dress after the harbor, she hadn't had time to change since. Insisting on being there for James should he wake, she had never left his side. That was not until her uncle asked for her assistance in gathering a few tonics from his room a few moments ago. Her curls were probably flat and frizzy, no doubt she had circles under her eyes. What a fright she must have given him! No wonder he smiled. He'd probably never seen such a mess. She gathered the fabric of her skirt in her hands, wishing the past few moments all disappeared.

"My goodness, your cheeks are more flushed than Mother's roses. Come, we must take care of you before he wakes next." Elaine clasped her arm. "We must leave him in awe by the time he opens his eyes. Doctor Brown?" Elaine glanced around Jane. "When will the patient awake again?"

Uncle Duncan finished tying off the bandage. Jane was grateful his body blocked any view of James's torso, giving him that privacy.

"Depends on the patient. We'll see how long the medicine lasts on him." Uncle Duncan dabbed at his forehead. "I'm going to assume it will take but a few hours. Jane I'm going to ask one of the servants to watch him until you've returned. As soon as I've cleaned up here, I'll be returning to the fort."

"Very well," she replied.

All the coiled muscles that formed during the past two days began to make their presence known in her shoulders. Elaine glanced at her and offered a soft, sympathetic smile. "Come, I had Millie warm a bath for you."

Jane rubbed the small knot on her neck. James had woken up. And with her uncle at his side, she knew he was in good hands. "That sounds divine."

Elaine wrapped her arm through hers and led the way. Walking in the hall of the west wing, the walls were a lighter shade of blush compared to James's bedchamber. This section of the house was where Elaine's mother had free range of the interior decorating. Gold-trimmed paintings of lovers lined the hall. Large vases filled with wild-flowers sat on two long tables. She began to wonder if James minded being in the more feminine wing. Or if he would even notice, though, after passing a painting of an intimate couple, how could one not.

"You know, you certainly set expectations high for me," Elaine stated humorously, while interrupting Jane's thoughts. "Richard told me how he expects me to stay by his side if he were to ever be wounded."

"Oh?" She peered over at her friend. "And what did you say?"

"Of course," Elaine hesitated a moment. Her fingers twisted among each other, and she held a pinched expression. "But I didn't tell him that I wouldn't stay through the night." She released a breath as though the confession had weighed heavy on her. "I treasure my dear Richard very much, but I also treasure my sleep. I fear I will dis-appoint him. I'm facing such a dilemma."

Tears glistened in Elaine's blue eyes. Mindful of her friend's feel-ings, even if they sounded a bit absurd, Jane wrapped her arm around her and pulled her into her side.

"You'd be surprised what you'd be willing to sacrifice when the one you care about is lying wounded before you."

"I suppose. But just as long as I'm not having to clean him up." Her petite nose scrunched up with disdain. "I'm not used to seeing wounds like you are. There were many times I had to avoid a few of the men at the harbor when I saw their bloody bandages. I came close to fainting on multiple occasions that night."

The idea of Elaine keeping her distance from Captain Norton made Jane laugh, for they were never apart. "Oh Elaine, you'll have to continue to pray that he stays unscathed."

"I certainly intend to," she assured and rested her head against Jane's shoulder before releasing a dramatic sigh.

Jane indulged herself in the warm bath water. With the lack of sleep, she felt herself drifting off into a sweet slumber. She didn't know how long she had slept before Millie had awoken her to help her dress, but judging by the water's cool temperature, it had been a while. With her curls pinned on her head, and wearing her soft blue dress, she headed through the corridor to see if James was awake.

Straightening her skirt, she knocked on the door. Padded footsteps came from the other side of the wooden barrier. With a squeak of the doorknob, the door opened to reveal her uncle. His bag in hand, he walked through the doorway like he was on an errand.

"Jane," he greeted. "Impeccable timing."

"Uncle," she said with surprise as she expected someone other than him. "I thought you had already left for the hospital."

"Not yet," his eyes twinkled as he looked at her. "Our patient has exceeded my expectations."

"How do you mean?"

"Take a look for yourself." He pushed the door wider, inviting her in. "I must be going. Keep an eye on him. I don't want him to make any sudden movements or else his sutures may break."

Doing everything to keep herself from sprinting into the room, she bounced on her toes to give her uncle a peck on his cheek. "Thank you. I'll make certain he's taken care of."

"Splendid." With a pressed smile, he departed down the hall.

"James!" she exclaimed, bounding into the room. He turned his head in her direction and smiled. Clasping his hand, she felt comforted when he ran his thumb across her fingers. "We were so worried," her voice broke.

His blue eyes were repentant while they bore into hers. "I'm sorry to have put you through that."

She scoffed with a sob. "You shouldn't apologize." She blinked back her tears. "You did everything right."

"Mm," he muttered as though he doubted her words. His gaze turned towards the ceiling with a distant look. She recognized the daunting expression. Any man who endured a catastrophic battle faced much turmoil and grief. Sadly, from what she's heard from her uncle, the effects lasted a few of the men an extended amount of time. Meeting his eyes again, she felt herself slip into their depths as his focus turned towards her. Clasping her hand with his, she watched as his pain disappeared behind his softened gaze. It was as if a tide rushed over the sand, covering what was once exposed.

"Ahem," Millie stood in the doorway. Her blonde braid hung over her shoulder. She had been Jane's shadow and companion, every time she entered James's bedchamber. "I beg your pardon, Miss Jane. Would you like me to inform Lieutenant Fletch that the captain's awake?"

Jane looked back to James. He offered a small smile of confirmation. "Yes, please."

She dipped into a curtsy and grinned at Jane. Probably the biggest grin she had seen from her in weeks.

"And Millie?" Jane called before she hurried away. "Please be certain that word is sent to Miss Jenny, and Captain Norton as well."

"Of course, Miss."

James squeezed her hand and brought it against his blanket-covered chest. "I hope there's a delay in her message," he remarked, his voice sounding less hoarse.

"If everyone is at the harbor, I'm certain there will be."

"Mm," he agreed. He stared up at the ceiling as though confused. "What day is it?" he asked, his voice barely above a whisper.

"Wednesday." Patting his arm, she stood to pour him a glass of water. "I'm going to have to fetch someone to assist you to prop against these pillows."

His eyes shone bright like she told him a humorous joke. "I believe I can manage." He winked at her and tucked his good arm under him.

"But James, you're not in the best condition—"

It was too late. James was already attempting to sit up. She hurried and slipped her arm behind his back. His body fiercely shook.

"Not too much," she warned, worried he'd injure his stomach further. "Keep your back straight." Swiftly, she slid another pillow behind his shoulders. She watched with dread at how his pale cheeks flushed to crimson. His lips were pressed together as though he held in a cry. He puffed out a heavy breath through gritted teeth while he relaxed against the pillows.

She grabbed a cloth from the table and quickly wiped at his dampened forehead. Feelings of regret soured in her stomach. With the extent of his wounds, she shouldn't have mentioned anything about him sitting up.

"Do you mind if I lift your blanket?" she asked, worried he may be bleeding through his bandage more so than usual. James lifted a questionable brow. Any thought of his wound became a mere speck in the horizon. Warmth spread through Jane's cheeks.

"And your bandage." She gave him a stern look to hide her embarrassment. "I need to examine your wound, to make certain you didn't tear any sutures."

He chuckled but thought better of the laughter as he winced in pain. "By all means, Jane. I couldn't resist giving you a hard time."

"Of course, you couldn't," she mumbled. After their little encounter earlier, her uncle left the man's shirt off so they could access his bandages easier. Now that he was awake, well, she should fetch him a shirt—and soon.

Flustered, she uncovered his torso. Keeping her gaze locked on his bandages, she lifted them to peek at his sutures. Thankfully, they were secure, and his wound appeared to have seeped a small amount from his efforts.

"Your bandages will need to be changed within an hour," she declared, releasing his wrappings as though they would scorch her skin. With trembling hands, she tucked his blanket under his shoulders. Keeping her eyes from wandering, she made certain to cover every well-pronounced muscle of his body.

"I appreciate you checking," he said, still breathing heavily from his effort.

She kept her gaze away from his and retrieved his glass. She aided many of the patients in Bombay with their recoveries, but at the moment she felt out of sorts. Glancing at the glass, she tried to determine her next step.

"Would you care for some help with the water or do you feel well enough to do it on your own?" She studied him. Determined to catch any flinch of hesitation in his face.

He didn't move, except for the corners of his mouth. "Considering how you've shackled me up to my chin in this blanket, I'm afraid I may never get my arm out." She bit back a smile. He continued to look at her with a humorous gaze. "Would you mind?"

Pressing her lips, a laugh of embarrassment caught in her throat. She had been carried away, and for a very good reason. He was indecent and distracting—she flicked her eyes to the ceiling so he wouldn't fluster her thoughts any further.

"I didn't want you to catch a chill," she retorted at his shackled remark and leaned down to bring the glass to his lips.

"Mm hmm," he mumbled into the cup, "That was considerate."

A knock sounded at the door. Not wanting to be caught being so close to James, she straightened as Captain Norton entered.

"I was just on my way to visit with Elaine when a little maid told me that the heroic Captain James McCannon was awake, so I've come to see for myself," he announced, striding further into the room. The captain appeared pristine in his attire. His raven, short-cropped hair was combed forward and up like he had been facing the wind. His thin mustache was freshly trimmed. Only tiny scratches on his cheek gave away that he had been in the battle.

"If you've come to short sheet my bed, you're a little late," James noted as he nodded towards his blankets. He held a gleam in his eyes that told Jane there was a story behind his remark.

Captain Norton smirked. "I believe I could still do the honors, considering how your blankets are all but covering your face."

James smiled and glanced at Jane for a brief moment. She bit her lip and abruptly looked away, mortified that Captain Norton even noticed. Not that it wasn't blatantly obvious. She had made James appear like he was sewn into a bundling bag! One would have thought her uncle came to make certain James was being chaste with her in his unconscious state.

"Have you the chills on this warm morning?" She detected a hint of concern in the captain's voice.

"I may have given Jane the impression that I needed more covering." He gave her a knowing smile which made the temperature in the room rise.

Straightening her shoulders, Jane peered at him from the corner of her eye. "Your grinding of teeth certainly indicated you had a chill."

A grin spread across James's face. She ignored how she felt like a sheer piece of fabric for him to see through her facade. "Well, I best be going to see that you get a shirt, *and some broth*," she added, more flustered. If James had any suspicion that he made her uncomfortable being half clothed, she certainly solidified it.

Handing the water glass to Captain Norton, he accepted it, looking a bit confused as to what to do with the cup. "The captain will be needing your assistance with taking sips. Be certain he drinks all of this within the next half hour," she instructed.

Captain Norton looked at her and his eyes began to twinkle with mischief. "I'll be sure to do just that."

James winced as he untucked his well-toned arm from under the blankets. "I'm confident that I'm capable of drinking on my own." He held a slightly shaky hand out for the glass.

"Sorry, chap, Miss Sawyer has entrusted me with the honors, and I intend to do so myself, now tilt your head back."

Jane retreated for the door, all the while suppressing a smile. Had she not been too flustered at the moment, she would have thought better than to give the glass to the captain.

"I would have to decline, respectfully," James's tone held one of command. "Miss Jane, please inform Captain Richard otherwise." He peered at her from around the man's tall figure.

"I do believe you're capable, Captain, but considering how you couldn't get your arm untucked earlier has me questioning your strength."

The corner of James's mouth lifted and his voice lowered. "If I may be so bold, Miss Jane. I'm certain any gentleman in my circumstance would have happily refrained from moving their arm as well."

She stared wide-eyed at James who then gave her an unforgiving dimpled smile.

"Captain Norton?" She turned to the pristine captain who was looking at James with a smug grin. "Be certain it's empty within the half hour. I have some broth I need to get for our patient."

"Not a drop will be wasted," he replied with enthusiasm that hinted he had other intentions.

From the corner of her eye, she saw James lay his head against the pillow and heard him muffle a groan.

She pressed her lips together and escaped the scene that was about to unravel.

Closing her novel, Jane left her room towards the kitchen. She couldn't concentrate on any of the pages knowing he was close by. Hoping to distract herself, she wanted to see how the cook was fairing with the broth.

"Miss Sawyer?"

She paused on one of the steps and glanced up. Captain Norton stood at the top of the staircase. His crisp, blue waistcoat was now spotted with patches of dark hues. Water dripped off his white drooping cravat onto the floor like a flower that had been flattened by a rainstorm.

"May I have a moment of your time?" he asked in a composed manner. Jane's eyes widened as he calmly descended the steps, appearing unphased by his saturated coat.

She pressed her lips together to hold back a smile. "Not a drop wasted?"

"Only a few drops, but the rest was certainly put to good use." His thin mustache curved with his smirk.

"As long as it didn't go near his bandages."

She raised a brow of warning. Captain Norton chuckled and tugged on his sleeves.

"There's nothing to fret about. Much to my dismay, his reflexes were never wounded. James also managed to drink all that you had required of him." His smile grew. "And perhaps, a little more."

"I had asked that you'd help him drink, Captain, not force him to drink." She wasn't certain what had played out between the two, but if James wasn't careful, he could reopen his wound.

The corner of Captain Norton's thin lips dropped into a more serious manner. "Yes, forgive me. I promise to encourage him to behave himself the next time we're together."

She began to smile. "You two are intolerable."

Captain Norton laughed and nodded in agreement.

"Uh, Miss Sawyer, I have a concern I would like to address with you," his voice dipped into a low hush.

"What is it?" Seeing the worry in his eyes, Jane grabbed the mahogany banister and ascended towards him. He leaned his body forward, leaving a small gap between them. Whatever he had to say, he wanted to say without being overheard.

"Miss Sawyer." He attempted to fluff his cravat but miserably failed to bring the limp cloth to life. With defeat, he shrugged his shoulders and disregarded it as he clasped his hands behind his back. "I know you mean a great deal to James." His brows drew together to form a deep crease. "And this duration of healing will be treacherous for him. He gets extremely restless staying in one place for a significant amount of time. Might I suggest something to help pass this phase?"

"What is that, Captain?" Jane quietly released the breath that she held, grateful it wasn't anything about James's condition worsening.

"James enjoys poetry."

"Poetry?" She pressed her lips to keep from indicating her knowledge of how she knew Captain Norton's despair of the subject.

"That's correct, I've come to discover that he loves poetry. Why, when we were in Bombay together, he used to carry a book of poems around with him. He'd pull it out whenever he had a moment to spare. Though, he's too modest to ever admit that." Captain Norton tugged on the cuffs of his sleeves with an indifferent expression. Satisfied with how they laid, he tucked a hand behind his back and carried on. "Might I suggest, given his weakened condition, that you read to him? William Wordsworth is especially a favorite of his." Jane was extremely impressed with how convincing Captain Norton was of James's secret passion. Particularly of the romantic poet. Had she not known what James had done to Captain Norton and Elaine after their picnic to the falls, she might have believed him.

"Thank you, captain. I'll be sure to keep that in mind."

"Please do." He beamed and tugged on his lapels with satisfaction. "Oh, and if you ever need to borrow any books, by all means, ask Elaine. She has a plethora, I'm sure she'd love to loan to you."

A squeak of laughter escaped her lips. Forcing herself to look at his black, polished boots she nodded, and attempted to collect herself.

Through clenched teeth and a smile, she managed, "Will do. Thank you, Captain."

He offered her a bow, and walked down the stairs with a buoyant bounce, only to pause on the last step, "Miss Sawyer? One more thing." Jane bit her cheeks and raised him a questionable brow. "Promise me you'll keep this conversation between us? He gets extremely uncomfortable if anyone knows of his secret. Let him be the one to tell you—in time."

"Of course," her voice pitched higher than usual. The muscles in her cheeks shook while she strained to keep them relaxed. "I'll be certain not to mention it." Swallowing her laughter, she curtsied him a farewell. He grinned, a victorious grin, and departed the manor.

Once in the hallway, she released her giggle. Never did she expect the captain to ask that of her. Especially not while James sustained his injuries. She would have thought there was a truce between them. Wiping her laughter-filled eyes, she sighed. She had no intention of reading James any of the poems.

Raising her hand to his bedchamber door, she knocked. After seeing Captain Norton's manner of dress, she could only imagine how he fared.

"Come in," he called.

Turning the knob, she pushed her way through the doorway but abruptly halted. A gasp escaped her lips and she covered her mouth to quiet it. James sat in the same position as she had left him. Sections of his blanket soaked to his body. His wet hair was slicked back, off his face. She bit her lip as she watched a drop of water roll down his forehead and into his eye. He glanced at her while squinting one eye shut as more drops descended down his face. Keeping his composure indifferent, he said, "Jane, would you be so kind as to have a valet retrieve me another set of sheets?"

She entered the room and picked up the pitcher from off the floor. "Yes, and perhaps more water?" she teased, sensing he wasn't upset from the matter.

"Mm," he nodded, staring into his glass. "That would be nice considering my cup is now empty."

"Yes, I see that you were thirsty." At least Captain Norton kept to his word by keeping his sutures dry. Otherwise, they would have faced an encounter by not only her but by her uncle as well.

His eyes gleamed with laughter. "Very," the corner of his mouth lifted. She took a step closer to his side and wiped away the drop from his jaw.

"Well, now that you're cleaned," she smiled innocently as he gave her a scowl. "Would you like me to see that you were given a shave?"

"As much as I appreciate the service being offered, but if that was my bath, I must admit I fear for my shave."

She laughed and squeezed his hand. "Not to worry, Captain Norton is otherwise engaged."

"Like changing into drier clothes?"

"Perhaps," she smiled. "But all jesting aside, I'll see that the governor's valet assists you with a clean shirt and a fresh shave."

James's blue eyes brightened. "I never did thank you for all that you've done for me."

"Including leaving you at the mercy of Captain Norton?" She smiled and sat next to him, on the all too familiar chair.

"I suppose we can forgo that part." He lifted his cut-up, weathered hand to her cheek. She leaned into his touch, welcoming the comfort it brought her. "Thank you, Jane." His tone held the deepest respect and regard. Her heartbeat became loud in her ears as his thumb caressed her cheek. He stared into her eyes like he yearned for her to understand what he was about to say. "I wouldn't be here without you."

She bit her lip as shameful tears pooled in the rim of her eyes. His words didn't assure her. They reminded her of the pain she had inflicted on him, and the hollowing ache that a loss of a loved one brought. Thomas's reassuring words as well as her uncle's replayed in her mind. She drew in a shaking breath. She did nothing wrong. And he was still here. Squeezing his hand, she met his gaze.

"Really, you should be thanking my uncle," she managed to whisper. She broke from his grasp and kept her eyes low to hide the agony that night brought. "I'll see that you're tended to." With a strained smile, she left the room.

Chapter Five

"Reading or painting?" James watched Jane concentrate on her cards. Satisfied with his hand, he laid his cards on the empty food tray that laid next to him. The morning sun poured into his room, making her blue-green eyes even more striking. His heart skipped a beat when she began to smile at her cards.

"Reading," she replied to his question, which he had already forgotten about. The corner of her mouth raised and she played the winning hand to the game twenty-one.

Knitting needles clicked at the other end of the room. Millie was humming to herself as she created . . . something yellow. Scorching heat stabbed his side with every twist and turn he made. He puffed out a breath, hoping to hide any sign of pain on his face. The last thing he wanted was for Jane to insist he get his rest.

"Parlor rooms or waterfalls?" London came to his mind. *Would she consider staying?*

"Waterfalls." She laughed at the odd comparison. "Ship decks or ballrooms?"

"Ballrooms with you, ship decks if I were on my own."

She pressed her lips like she was attempting to hide a smile.

He continued, "Sunshine or endless cloudy days?" *She couldn't possibly go to England.*

"Sunshine." She dealt him two cards. "Cloudy days are tolerable, but not when they're endless." Raising her dark brow, she continued, "Sunset or sunrise?"

"Both. Smog or ocean views?"

She laughed at the absurdity. "Ocean views, of course. I'm not sure I know of anyone who enjoys smog. Picnics or rowboats?" She flashed him a teasing smile. James tapped the tray, and she dealt him another card.

"Rowboat."

"Why's that?" She gave him a curious look that made him even more desperate to know more of her passions in life. Holding his side, he carefully repositioned himself against his pillows.

"I had great company." Realizing she could easily misinterpret his company to being with Miss Harrlow, he quickly added. "There was a reason why I was out on the pond after the picnic auction."

"Was it so you could rescue Lieutenant Wood and I?" she smiled.

He chuckled. "Actually yes, I knew the lieutenant wouldn't have been able to hold those oars."

"You did?" her lips parted with surprise. It took every ounce of strength he had to swallow the lure they had on him. His eyes trailed up her petite nose to her eyes.

"The day prior, he struggled grasping one of the lines to tie off. Having seen you two go out on the water, I thought I'd make certain there weren't any problems." He rubbed his neck. "I just never expected him to lose *both* oars." He held his side and chuckled.

The arch of her brow raised in confusion. "How do you mean?"

An opportunity presented itself and James couldn't hold back. "Well, if it was just us on the pond, had I thought of it, I would have done the same thing. And the location the lieutenant picked was perfect, given it was away from prying eyes." Her mouth fell further. He offered a wink, unashamed of his taunting. Snapping her mouth closed, she straightened in her chair as though she knew he would never do that.

"Not unless I made you dive in to retrieve those oars."

"At your request I would have gladly done it. Though, that wouldn't have been the first time I dived in the water for you,"

As though on cue, her eyes flicked up to his. The fire in her stare could warm a man's heart and soul. Fighting a laugh, he continued to hold his smile.

"I had no control over that. Well, any of those. They were pure accidents."

"Of course, except I do have my doubts the lieutenant's was an accident," he teased. "That being said, if you're ever near the water, I'll make certain to be on the lookout."

Her lips twitched and she rolled her eyes at him. "That is very considerate of you, Captain McCannon."

Staring deep into her eyes, everything within the past few days disappeared. His heart pounding echoed in his ears as he desperately wanted to take her away to the pond. The scraping of Millie's knitting needles brought him back to the moment. Releasing a staggered breath, he ran his hand through his hair.

"I believe it's my turn to ask you the question."

She smiled. "By all means."

He rubbed the back of his neck. "What are your passions in life?"

She grew quiet and stared at her cards with a torn expression. "I'm not so sure I know anymore." Her voice was soft like that of a saddened child who became lost. She stared down at her hand, her lashes fanning above her cheeks.

This didn't sound like the woman he encountered skipping through the field at the governor's plantation the day after she sutured the lieutenant's hand. She had even asked him what his thoughts were of a woman performing a surgery. Was that not her passion? Something with medicine?

"Would you like to talk about it?" James treaded carefully as not to come on too strong but the desire to know was eating at him.

Releasing a heavy sigh, she looked up at him. "I'm not so certain I can."

He searched her eyes, hoping they'd give him a clue of what held her back. "Perhaps if I asked a few questions?"

The corner of her mouth twitched. "Now I'm more curious as to what you will ask." Tilting her head to the side, she gazed to the corner of the room as though it held the answer. "Very well, help me understand what it is I'm passionate about."

He couldn't help but smile at her enthusiasm. "Do you enjoy embroidery?"

Her smile began to fade. "Sometimes."

James laid his head back against his pillow. It was his surgery! Wanting to make it right, he clasped her hand and stared into her eyes, hoping she'd understand how he felt.

"Jane, if you fear I will think less of you for knowing how to surgically remove shrapnel, I don't. Quite the opposite. I've never met such a remarkable woman as you." He began to smile when the corner of her mouth lifted. "And I've never met a woman who's been able to embroider perfectly straight lines—on people."

She pressed her lips together as though to keep from laughing. "James," she looked down at their hands. "Thank you. I appreciate the compliments."

He watched her hesitation, "But that's not what's holding you back."

She stared into his eyes with vulnerability. "No. It's not."

His mind raced to remember all that occurred during the surgery. Over Thomas's shoulders he remembered a glimpse of the calmness in her face. She appeared confident, like she'd performed the procedure many times, yet there was more behind her facade. At one point when he was conscious, he had watched her hands tremble after she dropped a piece of something bloody on a tray. Her eyes were full of remorse. And then came her tears. His heart fell into his stomach. "You must have been terrified," he whispered with dawning.

Her eyes began to fill. "I was."

"I'm so sorry to have put you through that."

"No. Don't apologize." Her chin quivered and she breathed in deeply as though to calm it. Staring at their hands, she continued, "I used to dream of performing a surgery. I never was able to until . . ."

"Me," he finished.

She sighed and pulled her hand away from his and folded it in her lap. Keeping her eyes on the cards, she spoke with a low and soft voice. "I used to assist my uncle when he performed minor surgeries from our home. And whenever I visited the hospital, at times I'd see the relief in soldiers' eyes after he saved their lives or even their limbs. Those experiences inspired me to do the same for others." She peeked up at him as though she were assessing his reaction. Being consumed by her words, he closed his mouth and offered her a slight nod. He wasn't certain how he looked and thankfully it wasn't too startling for her as she continued, "You see, there's an art to what he does, and I developed the passion to do the same. I just never realized how much it would affect me. The risk of losing you was too high." Her voice hitched. "I never wanted to hurt you like I did."

James shook his head. He pushed aside the pain that throbbed on his side as he focused on the torn expression she held. He recalled a few moments during his surgery where it was unbearable but most of that was not done by her hands themselves, but by the solution she used to clean his wound and by the scorching poker.

"Hurt me?" He couldn't help but chuckle at that. "Let me assure you, Jane, I was worked on by our ship's doctor before you graced me with your mercy. I may put a word in to the queen herself for you to be his replacement. You were by far the gentlest person who's ever worked on me." She wiped her eye before a tear escaped. "And may I add the most beautiful."

His sincere compliment brought a small smile to her face. "Well, I certainly don't think she would approve of my lack of propriety with what I did. I may be shunned by all of England."

"Not all." He offered her a wink. She laughed and tucked her chin down in a bashful manner. "You have a gift." He cleared his throat by the hoarseness he felt. She had a way about her that made him want her to see what he saw. Did she understand how remarkable she was? "I'm forever grateful to you for having the courage to do what you did. And for your uncle who inspired you. I see your passion in helping others. By all means, I've never seen you shy away from a challenge. Especially if it meant saving another's life." Bringing his hand to the curve of her cheek, his thumb wiped away a tear that trickled down her smooth, velvety skin. "Take what you learned from your experience and conquer it. There may be a limited number of things you can do in society, but you can still make a difference in whatever you pursue."

Drawing his hand away, he watched her blink from her blatant stare. "Should I ever have my doubts again, I know who I'm turning to."

He smiled. "By all means, I'm here should you ever need my honesty."

A bashful smile crossed her face and she tapped the deck of cards, indicating she was ready to play. "Fruits or vegetables?"

This made him laugh. Immediately he regretted it and sucked in a sharp breath, trying to hide the pain it caused him. Clearing his throat, he answered, "Fruit. Mangos happen to be my new favorite."

The lucky fruit that they bonded over, before the festival. It felt so long ago that they danced together in the streets during Saint Helena's celebration. When the two of them had waltzed for their first time at the town's festival, Jane had made mention of how she tried to learn the waltz with Millie. What intrigued him the most was when she said it was nothing like he had taught her. Ever since she mentioned it, he's been eager to learn her version.

"It's time we switched the game to sixty-six," he offered, as an idea brewed.

A warm smile spread across her face when she met his eye. For a moment, he couldn't remember how to breathe. There was something in the way she looked at him that made him feel he like he could never be apart from her. His hand grazed across the bruise that was marked by the doctor.

"Very well," she replied, her spirits lighter than before.

Clearing his throat, he moved forward with his plan. "May I suggest we add a twist to this game."

She tilted her head to the side. "Oh?"

"I would like to propose a bargain." Shuffling the deck against the food tray, he watched her face fall to one of confusion.

"A bargain? Do you mean a wager?"

Smiling at his idea, he began to deal the cards. "I was attempting to put the term wager aside and go for bargain instead. It sounds more proper, don't you think?"

"The way you're intending to use it has me questioning."

"Alright, we'll call it what it is—*a wager*."

Raising her brow, she replied with a pointed reply, "A lady never wagers."

"Yes, this I know. Then shall we stick with it being called a bargain?"

Tucking her lips together, a laugh emerged in her throat. She looked at her hands and released what sounded like a defeated breath. "Very well. What are we bargaining?"

James couldn't help his triumphant smile and dealt their hands. "Each opponent gets to come up with their own bargain."

Eyeing him suspiciously, she accepted her hand for the game. "Very well, you go first."

"I propose that when I win, you get to teach me the Miss Sawyer Waltz."

Her eyes widened. "I decline your proposal."

Not surprised by her answer, he continued to press. "Why not?"

"May I remind you that you're not necessarily in the best condition to be dancing."

"When I'm better you can show me." He gave her a cheeky smile.

Her eyes widened as though in panic. "I still decline."

"Then you want to propose that you read to me instead?" He couldn't remember the last time someone read to him.

"Yes," she replied with a hint of mischief in her tone.

"Very well. If I win, you'll read to me . . . every day." He was beginning to like this bargain better than his last.

She laughed. "Done. And if I win, you'll get the pleasure of buying me a new dress."

James grinned at her notion. *If she only knew . . .* "Alright, Miss Sawyer, you have yourself a *bargain*. Let the game commence."

❧ ☙

Jane couldn't remember the last time she felt so exhausted. Now that James was on the mend, the past week had been filled with assisting her uncle at the hospital. When she wasn't assisting him, she had been reading to James. She had been close to winning her dress, but he played a card that changed that fate. A card that she suspected he never was dealt, though she could never prove it.

Pausing at the top of the stairs, her nose began to twitch. Jane fumbled for her handkerchief and sneezed into the cloth.

Deep voices rumbled down the blush-colored hall from where she stood. Curiosity took over as she crept towards the half-opened door at the end of the corridor.

"—if only you could have seen it! He pushed me aside and pounded on your chest! You know how Jenny pounds on dough when she's upset?—only he was less forceful." The man laughed. "I never knew he had it in him. That had to have left a bruise . . . Ooh! Those are definitely broken. But that goes to show, there was no way he was going to give up on you."

Clasping her mouth shut, she knocked softly on the door, hoping to interrupt what may be said next. Heavy footsteps padded across the carpet with long strides.

"Good morning, Miss Jane!" Thomas greeted her with his boyish grin. The dark circles under his eyes seemed to lighten with joy. She smiled, relieved to see him back to his usual lighthearted self. She hadn't seen him since he had departed in the middle of the night to carry out his duties. From her uncle's assessment, Thomas had been busy at the fort writing up reports and visiting the wounded men at their homes.

"Lieutenant Thomas! I hope I'm not interrupting anything?" Though she hoped she had. She dreaded the thought of him going into depth on witnessing how she tortured James during the surgery—though James sweetly assured her that she didn't.

"Not at all! Come in!" His smile broadened. Opening the door wider, he stepped aside to allow her through. "I was just leaving to retrieve my bag from my horse. I'll be back in a moment." He winked at Jane before leaving her alone in the room with the door open wide. She stared after him for a moment, wondering how many bags he had.

"Perhaps the lieutenant could use some sleep," she teased with a little concern. "I do believe his bag was on his shoulder." Sitting against the headboard, James gave her a dimpled smile.

"I couldn't agree more," he chuckled. His clean-shaven cheeks showed more color than he had the day before. She smiled, walking towards him. Seeing him every day for the past week had become her favorite part of the day. She loved how they exchanged stories like they were long lost friends. It was intriguing to hear his adventurous tales while sailing the sea. She could never take her eyes off him as he captivated her with the details of his crew and his years of being their captain. There was pride in his eyes when he told his stories, and yet she observed the sadness that hid behind the joy. He had lost a few of his men during the battle, and from what she observed, each of them was more than just a crewmate to James. They were his family.

"How are you faring this morning?" His eyes searched her face, like he was assessing to see for himself.

She smiled. She knew she couldn't hide the exhaustion that lurked there. She could feel the puffiness in her face, and the glaze in her eyes. Not wanting him to fret, she gave him a simple yet truthful answer. "Fine, thank you."

She laughed when his expression doubted her. "I promise. Now, tell me. How are you? Has your pain improved?"

She clasped his hand and stared into his eyes. If there was any pain he suffered, he showed no sign as he looked at her with such softness. "There's improvement each day."

"Good." Her voice quivered, exposing how he affected her more than she cared to admit.

As she went to withdraw her hand from his, he wouldn't release hers. Instead, he gently pulled her into an embrace. Burying his face in her neck, he whispered towards her ear, "I've missed you."

Any feeling of exhaustion disappeared as his words left her speechless. How long has it been since they saw each other? Weeks? Days? Hours? Trying to think logically through the haze that he created, she managed to reply, "It's only been but yesterday." All her muscles became disoriented and she felt herself melt into his arms while he held her tighter. She loved how he made her feel important in his life.

"Are you certain? It feels much longer than that."

She nodded, not daring to trust her voice.

"I don't know how you do it, but this room always becomes brighter when you're here."

"Is that possible?" she wondered aloud, while focusing her gaze on the magenta walls.

James laughed a hearty laugh. "Surprisingly, yes."

Pressure built around her nose, ruining any chance of her lingering close to him. She sneezed a high-pitched sneeze into the handkerchief. "Excuse me," she apologized as her eyes began to water.

"Bless you," she heard both James and Thomas offer.

Jane looked to see Thomas walking into the room, clinging to the same bag that he departed with on his shoulder.

"Thank you," she replied, sounding a bit nasally.

Thomas smirked at James. "I must be daft. The bag was on my shoulder the whole time!"

She rubbed at her eyes and eased herself onto the chair beside James's bed. Thomas must be more exhausted than she felt. When she opened her eyes, she found that both men stared at her with an overly cautious expression.

"Did you have another late-night last night?" Thomas pressed, placing the bag next to her chair. Warmth rushed to her face. She knew he was referring to her nightly reads to James.

Thomas grinned a knowing smile at her. It was as though he could see her feelings for James had blossomed within the past week. There was nothing to hide but she couldn't help the bashfulness it brought.

"Perhaps," she offered and observed a crystal vase full of ebonies. James had introduced her to the beautiful white flower during their excursion to Heart-shaped Falls. She'd fallen in love with him ever since. *Them*! Her eyes widened when she realized she admitted to herself that she was falling in love with him. *No not him, the flowers!*

"Poetry is James's favorite, you know," Thomas encouraged, giving a sly smile. He leaned back as though pleased with himself when James shook his head with a laugh.

It appeared James filled Thomas in on her reads. Not that it was to be a secret. Her uncle knew of her visits and she made certain Millie acted as their chaperone. Poor Millie. After enduring hours of her reading aloud and long conversations with James, she knew she would have to make it up to her.

She glanced at Elaine's leatherbound book of poems sitting on the nightstand. Her friend was so quick to oblige by letting her borrow it.

"So I've heard," she remarked, unable to control the high pitch in her voice. Feeling their questionable stares, she repositioned a flower in the vase. "Captain Norton had given me sound advice on how to keep you preoccupied." She kept her focus on the flowers so she could keep her uninterested facade.

James scrunched his face with disdain. "What exactly did our dear captain say?"

Thomas didn't hide his amusement as he plopped on the corner of the bed and slapped his thigh with a laugh.

Jane contemplated whether or not she should inform James of her knowledge of his latest prank towards Captain Norton. It was a clever trick he played on his friend, but unfortunate for Elaine.

She dropped her hand to the book and stared at James with dawning. Unless he intentionally planned on having Elaine preoccupied with the gentleman, then Elaine's accusation was right! Only with Elaine distracted, James could be free of her flirtatious advances—not keep Jane to himself. She pressed her lips together to keep from smiling. Very clever, James McCannon. She looked at him as he raised an expectant brow.

"I made a promise not to discuss the matter," she finally replied. In the beginning, she never had intentions of reading James poetry. No, she was settled on reading a novel. But after his sly deception during their game, it was the least she could do.

"You…" wincing, he sat up further. "You made a promise with him?" He looked at her as though she had betrayed him.

"Yes, he was concerned about your well-being and your time spent while recovering." Tapping her fingers on the book of poems, she bit her smile back.

He dragged his hand across his jaw, seeming to process the information. "Perhaps, you could read to me from a different book today?" The hope in his voice made her fight a smile. The corner of his mouth raised as though his charming demeanor could win her over.

"Mm." Tilting her head, she pretended to regard his question. "Thank you, but I'm curious to read what William Wordsworth wrote in the Lucy Poems."

Though, she really felt indifferent with the idea of poems. She was more curious by how James was patient each time she read a passage. Never, during any of the readings, did he show any sign of dread or irritation. Instead, he appeared content and at times entertained at parts that were uncomfortable for her to read aloud. She shifted uneasily on her chair while reflecting on the words that she read to James about passion, seduction, and love. That particular book was quickly replaced. Had she known the first book Elaine gave her contained such content, she would have never accepted it.

There had to be a wall he put up that hid him from showing his true feelings and she was determined to shatter it. Eyeing James, she studied his easy-to-please demeanor. Surely, he suffered inner turmoil like Captain Norton had with Elaine. Unless he really did enjoy them? Curious to find out, she drew closer to him and acted as though she was thrilled with what she was about to say. "Some say he wrote the poems about his sister, while others think of Lucy as fictitious."

Thomas smirked and nudged James's leg. "I'm betting it's after his sister," he cheerfully exclaimed.

In a split second, the smile on James's face fell. "I'll be certain to inform you once we find out." His reply was less enthusiastic than what Thomas had shown.

She smiled. *Thank you, Thomas.* With his remark, he helped solidify the matter of James's true feelings. Satisfied that he didn't like the poems after all, she graciously offered, "We can defer to another book when I finish reading this one to you." She swept her fingers across the leather cover to keep her casual composure. James rested his head against the headboard and looked to the ceiling as though helpless. But then his disgruntled expression softened and a smile crept across his face. He looked at her with dawning.

"You still think I cheated." His deep voice sent a thrill throughout her body. She straightened in her chair.

"I know you did."

"I can assure you, I didn't. I was playing by the game's rules."

"What game was that?" Thomas folded his large arms across his broad chest, clearly entertained.

"Sixty-six," James replied. The corner of his mouth lifted while he kept his gaze locked on hers.

She raised her brow. "Normally, I never make such a fuss about those who cheat during a game. But James *made a bargain* before we played and I had expected nothing more than a fair game. Little did I know he'd swindle the cards to get what he wanted." Her eyes narrowed when he gave her a wink.

"A bargain?" Thomas rubbed his chin and looked to James with a perked brow.

"We kept it proper." James feigned an innocent smile. "A wager was out of the question."

Thomas laughed. "What kind of bargain?" he pressed, his eyes twinkling above his smile.

"That I would read to him every day." Had he known she would have picked poetry, she was certain he would have stuck with his original offer. She rubbed her tired eyes as she giggled to herself at her clever ploy.

"If I wasn't so busy helping my uncle gather his supplies for the hospital every day, I'd have more time to read during the afternoon." She leaned against her chair. She was glad her days were busy, for she enjoyed staying up late talking with James about their childhoods, and most recently, poetry. A tickle shot through her nose and she let out another sneeze.

"Are you feeling alright?" James asked, reaching a hand to her. "Perhaps, you should get some rest?"

She glanced up at his worried expression. The muscles in his cheeks tightened. "I just may do that. Then I'll be wide awake to read you another epic poem."

His dimple appeared as he chuckled.

"Lieutenant Thomas," she took to her feet. "It was a pleasure seeing you again."

Thomas stood and offered her a quick bow. "You as well, Miss Jane."

"I did not cheat," James called after her.

She stopped in the doorway and turned to look at him. He gave her a challenging stare, his lips twitching, avoiding a smile.

"Perhaps, we should erase the slate and start again?"

He looked to the ceiling and pretended to stew it over. "And what will we be playing?"

"A game of chess. Then I can catch you in the act, should you choose to cheat—again." Jane raised an accusing brow at him.

"Challenge accepted, but only if I can stick with my original bargain." He grinned, causing her stomach to dip with a betrayed flutter. Having avoided that bargain to begin with, she studied him. James would be difficult. Being a captain, he'd learned to strategize and seize the opponent. But when waiting upon her uncle at the hospital, she defeated many officers with the game. Many of whom were assertive and self-assured that they could never lose against her. And with much pride, she had proved them wrong—every time.

"Fine. Let's say, three past the hour."

"I'll be here." He gave her a wink.

Ignoring how every part of her felt alive, she dipped into a curtsy and left. Sneezing once more, she smiled to herself. She felt confident she had him at chess.

James looked from the doorway to Thomas and quickly relaxed his cheeks as he realized he was grinning foolishly.

Helping himself to Jane's chair, Thomas kicked his feet forward and crossed his ankles. Resting his hands behind his head, he smiled slyly as he observed James. In return, James gave him a challenging stare.

"Don't smile at me like that."

"What, this?" Thomas pointed to his grin that never faltered. "Come now. I enjoy watching you fall head over heels for Miss Jane. And you do it with such style."

He bit back his laugh, "Now that you've ruined the saying, I find it more outrageous than before."

"Nonsense. But I am overjoyed to see you both smiling again. Besides, I never thought I'd see the day that you cheat at a game to get your way."

James groaned into his hand. "I didn't cheat."

He chuckled. "Either way, she knows you don't like poetry."

This broke any defensiveness James was feeling. "I didn't want to tell her, but I feel it's growing on me," he laughed.

Thomas smirked and rubbed his chin. "Is that so?"

"She can read me anything and I'd enjoy it." Sinking further into his pillow, he pictured when she read a poem about philosophy. She made it sound like more of a beautiful story. Her voice was tranquil and soft. Thomas raised a brow and with hesitation pulled a stack of papers from his messenger bag.

"I wish these reports were ones that she could make disappear. Here are the documents of each of the sailors we lost during the battle." With reverence Thomas placed the thick pile on the table.

James stared at the stack of papers where he saw Timothy Haymore's name at the top. The young red-headed lad had finished his night shift. He would have been drifting off to sleep when he was ordered back to his post. James's throat constricted. "What were the casualties?" he hoarsely whispered.

"We lost twenty-eight men on our ship alone. Captain Richard lost twelve."

Closing his eyes, he fought the pain that struck his core, stabbing into his heart. "And how many are injured?" he managed say.

"The Ebony has sixty-seven and the Sphinx—thirty-five."

Opening his eyes, James thumbed through the documents, not daring to peek at any more names. He wanted to save that for a time when he was alone. Unshed tears welled the brim of his lids. All of his crew he knew not only by name, but as a whole. Most of them lived on the island with their families. He couldn't fathom what turmoil their families must be feeling.

"Thank you for bringing these by." His voice grew thicker and raw. "I'll be certain to send my condolences to each of these fine sailors' families."

"They'll appreciate that." Thomas gazed at the pile a moment before whispering, "We were pretty lucky, James."

"We were more than lucky. We were being watched over."

He gave James a curt nod and turned away as his eyes began to glisten.

Laying his head against the headboard, James stared at the ceiling. Both men remained silent for a time as the battle hauntingly echoed through their hearts and minds.

Chapter Six

A stabbing pain shot through James's side while he tried to sit up. He grimaced, letting out a low groan. His right arm throbbed under the sutures where the chunk of wood had been pulled out. His arm muscles flexed, tightening the skin around his wound. A sudden pop sounded from his arm. Quickly, he attempted to put less weight on his right hand. He glanced down at his wounded arm, where a lead ball had grazed his skin. There was no seeing past his sleeve and bandage to know if he had broken a stitch. He'd have to wait until Doctor Brown came to check on him that afternoon, to inform him.

Careful with his movements, he reached for the glass of water on his nightstand and gulped it down. Wiping the beads of sweat off his forehead, he drew a quick breath. Finally! It was pitiful how winded he was after accomplishing a simple act such as sitting up. But he was still proud to have managed that grueling task on his own. He hated tugging on the corded rope of the bell pull whenever he needed any assistance. Staring at the pocket watch on the side table, he rubbed the back of his neck. Two more minutes until three. He had plenty of time to recover from his endeavor. Dabbing his forehead for good measure, he then combed his fingers through his hair.

A soft knock sounded from the door.

"Come in," he called, satisfied by his attempt.

His heart took a tumble as Jane entered the room. Her eyes shone a hazel blue with her sapphire-colored dress. Her pink lips smiled brightly at him. No sunset with its vibrant, warm colors could compare to the feelings she cast upon him.

"Good afternoon, James," she practically sang. "Are you ready to lose?"

He blinked from the trance and noticed the chess board in her arms. Millie followed behind with knitting needles and a large ball of yellow yarn.

Clearing his throat, he smiled. "Ladies, it's a pleasure to see you both."

"Captain McCannon." Millie offered him a small curtsy and hurried to her usual chair in the corner of the room. She sat and continued knitting together tiny loops.

Jane placed the board on his bed then began moving items away from his side table to make room.

"Millie," James called to her. "What project are you working on?" Since seeing her during the week, her yellow yarn was finally taking shape.

"Just a shawl," she meekly offered.

"It's more than just a shawl, Millie. You do exquisite work," Jane proudly boasted while scooting her chair up to the table.

Millie blushed. "Thank you, Miss."

She gave a warm smile towards her lady's maid. "Are you ready, James?" she challenged.

"More than ever," he said confidently. "Ladies first."

She peered up at him and pushed her pawn across the ranks of black and white squares. He followed suit and slid his pawn forward.

"Do you remember the terms?" She moved another pawn.

"Of course," he replied buoyantly. Most of their wooden pieces were set in their positions. "If I win, you'll teach me your fancy waltz." She scrunched her nose with detest. Millie quietly giggled in the corner making James feel even more satisfied with his original *bargain*.

"And if I win, you'll buy me a new dress." Jane slid her pawn across a black square and knocked over his pawn. James grinned, amused that she had regained her composure quickly.

"Yes, to replace the one I removed, to save our lives." He knocked over her wooden pawn with his knight. Jane's cheeks flushed at the bold statement. His attempt to throw off her focus with his brash choice of words was proving to be quite successful.

Clearing her throat, she proceeded to move her knight forward, advancing on his rook. After she placed her piece, she ever so slowly leaned towards him. "Was that part of your naval training, Captain?"

Perplexed by the question and her teasing tone, he stared at her.

She raised her brow then simply stated, "Gown removal?"

Heat rushed up his neck. To hear those words come for her mouth had completely thrown him off his game. He tugged at his constraining cravat. As he retreated his rook, he clumsily knocked over his knight. She gave him a taunting smile. James held his chin high. She slid her bishop across the board and collected his knight. *Don't let her get in your head*, he grumbled.

The game continued, each of them strategically retreating and pursuing each other's pieces. He glanced up from the board and noticed Jane's eyes begin to water.

"Achoo!" she sneezed into her handkerchief.

He paused from the game to study her closely. The rims of her eyes were red and her cheeks were more flushed than normal. Her dark brows were furrowed as she focused intently on the board.

"How are you feeling?" he asked, keeping his concern from his tone.

"Better, thank you," she replied as she positioned her rook down by his bishop. *Bad move.* Advancing his rook behind his bishop, he was ready to capture her rook if she captured his.

"Are you feeling ill at all?"

"No." Her hand hung over her rook. Did she see what he was about to do? Seeming to think better of it, she moved her bishop.

"Millie," James called while moving his queen up one square. "Will you fetch someone to see that Jane gets some tea?" Jane began to scowl from his concern.

"I'm fine, I promise," she protested, while moving another pawn forward. On her feet, Millie clasped her yarn in her hands as she looked between them. James gave her an encouraging nod and watched her briskly head towards the door.

"Millie," Jane called over her shoulder, as he captured her rook with his queen. "Can you see that they add honey?"

Mille nodded and departed.

"You're trying to distract me," she muttered, jumping her knight over his bishop and collecting his pawn. He chuckled.

"It's not a game when it comes to your well-being." He glanced up at her from their board. From her lashes, she peeked at him, then darted her eyes back to their players to move her queen.

After a few exchanges and of capturing each other's pieces, Millie hurried back in with a tray of tea. She placed a cup at each of their sides.

"Thank you, Millie," they said together. Jane glanced up at him and smiled. His heart swelled when she looked at him like that.

The game progressed. She was now down to four players to his six.

"I must say, I'm impressed." He pressed his lips together, giving her an approving nod.

"Why is that?"

"Because no one ever gets this far when they play me at chess. Check." He slid his rook forward a few squares alongside her king. Bewildered, she retreated her king back one space. Right where he wanted her!

She groaned, realizing her mistake. "No, I didn't mean to do that."

James moved his queen and placed her onto the wooden board with a satisfied thud.

"Checkmate," he exclaimed. "I believe you owe me a waltz."

"I never lose!" Her mouth fell. "I can't believe I did that."

A knock sounded at the door.

"Is now a good time to change your bandages?" Doctor Brown appeared at the doorway.

"Perfect timing, Uncle. You've saved me from my humiliating defeat."

"My dear, Jane," he sounded surprised. "You never lose at chess."

"I know," she mumbled.

The gentleman chuckled. "Bravo, Captain. Jane, I believe you've met your match."

"Why, thank you, Doctor Brown. She was a valiant opponent."

Jane scuffed, "Perhaps tomorrow we'll have a rematch?"

Resisting reaching for her hand, he crossed his arms.

"Tomorrow it is."

"Jane, will you be assisting me today with changing the captain's bandages?"

"Forgive me, Uncle, I can't today." Her cheeks turned a darker shade of pink. "I believe Elaine needs help in the garden."

"She just left with Captain Norton to go to the harbor." Her uncle raised his thick gray brows and studied her for a brief moment before continuing to search in his bag. James watched Jane bite the corner of her mouth as though she were at a loss.

"Go ahead and remove your shirt, Captain," the doctor instructed.

Pulling on the corner of his cravat, he undid the bow. Next to him a small wooden castle knocked against the chess board. He watched with surprise as Jane's hands shook while she hurried to slide the pieces into the drawer of the chess board.

"I . . . I believe Millie needs more yarn for her shawl!" Quickly grabbing the game, Jane kept her gaze to the floor and swiftly left the room. Millie followed behind with her arms full of yarn.

James held back a smile as Doctor Brown looked after her with a confused expression. Her sudden departures became the norm whenever the doctor came to change his bandages. Judging by the gentleman's expression, James was suspecting this was out of character for her.

"On a scale of one through ten, where's your pain level today, Captain?"

He held his arms away from his body while Doctor Brown unraveled his bandage around his stomach.

"Between five and six," he grunted.

Doctor Brown peered from his spectacles at him. "That's an improvement since yesterday."

"It is, sir," James breathed, the throbbing in his side increased.

"You can relax your arms now."

Through pressed lips, he puffed out his breath while stiffly lowering his arms. A drop of sweat rolled between his shoulder blades, itching his skin. He reached above him to scratch it, only to be reminded of his tender wound on his arm.

"I believe I broke a stitch on my arm, when I sat myself up earlier."

"I'll look at it in a moment." Doctor Brown reached over to James's side and peeled the final bandage off the sutures and his bruised skin. He grimaced as it felt like dried tar tearing off layers of skin and all its hair. "This is healing very nicely. Your bruises are fading. I'm not seeing any new marks. There doesn't appear to be any infection." He gave an approving nod then cleaned the wound to apply a new bandage.

"I can't thank you enough for all you've done for me," James wholeheartedly stated.

The doctor peered up at him and offered a nod.

"You're very welcome, my boy." Tying off the bandages, he straightened his stance to look at his arm. "You did pop a stitch but it will heal fine without it." While rewrapping his arm he added, "You're healing well. I'll be certain you'll be left in good hands."

James's heart fell from the doctor's words. He'll be left in good hands? As he was about to inquire of his meaning, he was surprised to see Doctor Brown easing into the chair next to his bedside. The doctor's thick gray brows lowered as though heavy thoughts weighed on him. Clasping the blanket, James braced himself for what was to come. The gentleman leaned back and rested his hand on the side table. He paused a moment before meeting James's earnest stare.

"Did you know, after Jane had witnessed the delivery of the two baby goats, she now wants to become a midwife?"

Relieved the doctor wasn't about to deliver daunting news, he relaxed his shoulders. "I didn't know." He and Jane discussed many different topics from how she learned to perform sutures to how she watched her uncle perform surgeries, but becoming a midwife . . . any discussion about the future was usually vague or never talked about. It was as though they knew what lurked around the corner and they didn't want to face the inevitability of her departure for England. Doctor Brown nodded as though James's reply answered whatever may have been running through his mind.

"But I'm not surprised that she does," James added thinking back on Jenny's comment about how Jane should pursue it.

The gentleman stared at him with his brows slightly raised. "You're not?"

"Not at all." He smiled picturing her looking at him with a radiant smile while holding the kid goat. "I could see the passion in her eyes while she assisted me with the delivery."

"Is that so?" Doctor Brown leaned back in his chair. He folded his arms across his chest.

James wasn't certain if he was surprised by his answer or curious. "Sir, after witnessing her suture Lieutenant Wood's hand, I knew medicine was her ambition."

"It is." He smiled and rubbed at his surgical hand. "I assume you already guessed she wanted to be a surgeon?" The doctor peered through his spectacles again at James.

"I had my suspicions, long before she operated on me," James replied.

"And that never deterred you from her," the doctor stated more so to himself than to James. He rubbed at his chin and appeared lost in a thought. "Tell me, Captain, what are your thoughts about her interest in pursuing a gentleman's profession?"

The doctor's gaze pierced him as though he intended to detect any flicker of uncertainty James had towards the question. Was this a test? One that would determine their future together? He swallowed. He only hoped his truthful answer would be enough for the gentleman.

"After she did the surgery on me, I can candidly say she's better than our ship's doctor and probably our island's. I would give her full support if she ever chose such a profession."

Which was the truth, but how to help her get there was another story. There would be many obstacles in her way. But that's not what she decided, right? She wanted to become a midwife.

The doctor stared at James with a blank expression. "If it were only that simple, Captain. She would never be accepted into society as a surgeon. I fear having me as her only family, she's pictured herself following in my footsteps." Doctor Brown stared at his hand. His eyes held a sad gleam as though a distant memory played before him. "I didn't mean for her to go as far as she has with her desire to become a surgeon. You must understand. After she came to me, she was a child needing a lot of love and support. I did everything I could to help her adjust to Bombay and her new life. Along the way, she became fascinated in my profession. Which to my delight, I welcomed, for we drew closer to one another. I only tell you this so you can understand why she has pursued it. Why she may be different from the other young ladies." He flexed his fingers and curled them into his palm. "It was because of my selfish desire to teach her that I put her at risk of being shunned and disgraced by society. I blame myself for not stopping it when I could have long ago."

"Sir, I can see your concern. But I would never consider Jane a disgrace for her knowledge in medicine." Quite the contrary. Despite the rules of society, and how she's supposed to be selective with her skills, he found her even more captivating because of her knowledge.

"I appreciate hearing you say that." The doctor's mood began to shift from solemn to more serious. "I would also appreciate it if you stay discreet about her performing the operation on you. I already spoke with Lieutenant Fletch about the matter and he's agreed not to spread any word about her performance."

"Sir?" James shifted on the bed. He could see how the doctor had great concern about her reputation, but to see him as a threat towards Jane was worse than the wound on his side. Did he not trust him?

Behind the round spectacles, Doctor Brown's eyes tightened. He lifted the glasses and rubbed his eyes. "For the first time in years, Jane has finally discovered a dream that she can pursue. And to be forthright, I'm beyond relieved that she'll be accepted for it. If word spread about her saving your life, it would travel to England. Doctors and midwives that hear the gossip, will see her as a threat. Any trust they have for her will be eliminated.

"You must understand that she's limited on procedures as a midwife. Doctors would view her as a disgrace if they assumed she would be performing a surgery on any mother in trouble, before fetching one of them. It's a cruel and unfair world, Captain. One false move and they'd have her stripped of her license and reputation."

James closed his mouth and nodded. "I would never say a word," he assured. He never thought through the predicament she faced. That night in the harbor, she risked not only her reputation in society, but her occupation to save his life. He rubbed at the tightness in his chest. He could never repay her for what she'd sacrificed, for him.

"That means a lot to me, Captain. She has a great desire to make a difference in her life. Knowing she could never save lives, she's decided to bring life into this world. I'm very proud of her."

James's heart pounded against his chest, threatening to shatter from the question he was about to ask. He didn't want to ask it, nor did he want to think about it. Attempting to straighten, he immediately clenched his jaw. He held in a cry as a sharp ache spread across his stomach from the sudden movement. He squeezed his eyes shut.

"Captain?" The doctor leaned forward in his chair.

"I'm fine," James breathed and held up a hand before releasing a staggered breath. Gradually the pain began to subside. He looked back at the doctor, eager to know the answer. He cleared his throat and asked the question that could end all dreams of keeping her on the island with him. "What is the next step for her in becoming a midwife?"

Doctor Brown eased into his chair.

"In order for Jane to become a midwife, she'll need to apprentice with an experienced midwife. I've heard it can be very competitive for any young woman to enter the field, so I took it upon myself to write to a few friends in England inquiring about a midwife who'd be interested in having Jane follow along."

England. James closed his eyes. The daunting place that lurked in the back of his mind. He used to have pride for his country, now he formed a resentment towards the dreary place and all its glory. It betrayed him, when it offered her everything.

"Your relationship with my niece has taken some surprising turns—for the good, of course. But may I inquire what your intentions are towards her? Considering we will be leaving for England soon?"

James gave a respectable nod and straightened his shoulders. His emotions were being thrashed around like he was swimming against a riptide. The doctor mentioned her reputation, England, and now is questioning his intentions. For weeks he had contemplated his intentions with her. He did his best to avoid her at first, but he couldn't fight the feeling of wanting to be with her.

"Sir, to be honest, at first I had no intentions of having regard to Miss Sawyer."

The gentleman raised his brow.

James nervously fidgeted with the blanket on his lap. "Not that she didn't capture my attention, sir," he rushed. "She certainly captured my attention the first night she set foot on the pier." A smile formed on his face as he pictured the graceful Jane he now knew, wobbling in such a clumsy manner.

His smile fell as the doctor's eyes grew hard with a hint of protectiveness. Not that he blamed him. James swallowed, realizing he sounded like a buffoon, lusting after her and all for the wrong reasons. He ran his hand down his face wishing what he had said could be etched from the doctor's memory. "I did my best to keep my distance, knowing she'd be leaving, but our paths kept crossing, and as they did, each time I had the opportunity to know her better and—" he paused as he looked up and noticed an uneasy expression fall over the doctor's face.

He appeared so vulnerable. Worn, white knuckles tightened as he clung to his medicine bag that rested on his lap. The intimidating stare the doctor had only mere moments before, disappeared. Instead of rosy cheeks, his face paled and his eyes grew heavy with sadness. There was more written in the doctor's expression.

Tiny specs of stubble grazed James's palm as he rubbed against his jaw. Jane mentioned to him how she and her uncle were inseparable. Since the death of her parents, the only time she was apart from her uncle was when he was working in the hospital. They were all the family they had. And from what he had seen, she was the one true joy in the gentleman's life. He glanced at the documents of his deceased crew that were laid neatly on the table. There had been too many families torn apart from this war. What James wanted he knew he could not ask of the doctor. Not at this time. Not for Jane. She deserved more than what he could offer on the island. Not just because she saved his life, but because of her dream, of who she wants to become.

He had no doubt that the selfless, kind, high-spirited woman that captured his heart would be wonderful at it. He sighed, telling his objecting heart there was nothing more for him to say. He would selfishly be taking away all that she held dear if he made her stay. Her education would be far more supreme in England and most importantly, she would be with her only family, her uncle. If he planned everything right, the most he could hope for would be a long-distance courtship. Or . . . James drew in a breath. Within these next few weeks would she agree to a long-distance engagement? He closed his eyes and opened them to look at his hands as they began to tremble. An engagement with Jane. Could he be so fortunate for her to agree to a union? He sighed, attempting to calm the excitement that grew inside him. In a few weeks' time, he'll have correlated a plan to ask for her hand and speak with her uncle in a more formal manner. He wanted to earn the doctor's trust. Earn his approval. Properly court her, to show him and especially Jane, how he'll treat her with the utmost respect that she deserves. Her uncle's opinion mattered greatly to him and he knew it mattered immensely to Jane. James reached deep within himself to gather his courage.

"Sir, I'm in love with your niece," he blurted, closing his mouth before he confessed more. His bandages suddenly felt unbearably tight around his stomach. The doctor looked at him, his brows raised high with surprise, then quickly fell as his eyes softened. He nodded as though to himself.

"There is something else you should know." Doctor Brown's tone was one of hesitation. James's heart jolted. He didn't like the sound of it.

"Our ship's captain came to me yesterday." Doctor Brown stared at his worn hands, "He's informed me that now that the threats have been eliminated, he's wanting to proceed with our journey to London by the end of this week."

James's jaw fell. "This week?" He went to run his hand through his hair but winced as he swiftly lifted his sore arm. "Does Ja—Miss Sawyer know?" he asked as calmly as his voice allowed.

"I'm planning on telling her this evening."

"Do you intend on shipping with them or are you still planning on waiting until our fleet arrives to aid you in your journey?" He clasped his blanket in his hands. The fleet would be arriving within the next three to four weeks. From the urgency in the doctor's voice, James sensed he wanted to leave sooner.

Sadness struck Doctor Brown's eyes. "I've signed a contract with the university for the next two years and am needed right away. The midwife in England wants Jane's presence as soon as possible. I am afraid we must set sail this Saturday."

James stared ahead of him, unable to say a word. His mind reeled while he processed the information.

Doctor Brown stood and spoke softly to James. "I will be certain to check on you before our departure." Clasping his bag, he headed towards the door. "I know this isn't going to be easy for you two. There's a lot to consider. I'll keep her under my wing until you are healed."

James's heart throbbed, lecturing him for ever being wounded. With the click of the door, James felt his dreams slip into the ocean with an anchor labeled "England."

"Saturday?" Jane stood from the bench that sat at the foot of her bed. "But you said we wouldn't have to leave until the next English fleet has arrived."

She paced in front of her uncle, doing her best to keep the panic under control. He released a sigh and slowly sat in a wingback chair next to the fireplace. The bright orange flames crackled beside him, his weary face illuminated from the blaze. Lines deepened between his gray brows and the corners of his eyes. She couldn't help but notice how much older Uncle Duncan appeared than when they had first started their voyage.

"Jane, I must keep to the schedule." He rubbed at the gray stubble on his cheek. With his time spent attending to the wounded at the hospital, he rarely had time to focus on himself.

Slowing her pace, she sat on the bench. She knew her uncle was exhausted with his endless nights.

A twinkle lit his weary eyes and he said, "On the bright side, the sooner we leave for Oxford, then the sooner you'll be off the ship."

As much as she loved her uncle's effort to lift the damper mood, she was in no state of mind to make light of the matter. She looked at him, anxious for him to understand how much she wanted to stay.

"Please, let us stay the extra few weeks."

She clasped her blue dress as she held back the urge to cry out. Her hope twisted and soured while she waited for his response. He looked at her gravely and slowly shook his head.

"I'm sorry, my dear, but I don't want us to be any more of a burden on our friends."

Burden? Jane stared at him baffled. He turned his gaze to the dancing flames. The Keaton's never gave that impression. Quite the contrary, she had overheard the governor teasing her uncle about having them live with them instead of traveling to England for the two years. She went to open her mouth to press further, but he held his hand in the air.

"Jane."

She closed her mouth from his loving, but solemn tone. She watched as he put his hand down and gently patted the armrest. He appeared uncertain with what he wanted to say. Her eyes widened as she studied him. She'd never seen this side of him before.

"Uncle?" she whispered. She swallowed and pressed her bottom lip between her teeth. Her hands tightened the fabric as she leaned towards him. Could he be unwell?

He pulled a letter from his jacket and tapped it against his arm-rest. "I know how hard this journey has been for you. And I know you haven't been looking forward to going to England. When you told me about suturing Lieutenant Wood's hand, I took it upon myself to write to Mrs. Hewitt of Oxfordshire. She's the finest midwife in Oxford's region and she's graciously agreed to have you be her apprentice."

Any feeling of urgency was sucked from her lungs. Jane leaned against her bedpost for support. Wood popped among the flames, breaking the silence in the room. "She wants me to be her apprentice?" she whispered with surprise.

Her uncle twisted his cane against the rug. "I didn't want to tell you like this. I thought I'd have more time after things had died down from the attack to share the news. But I'm afraid the captain of our merchant ship is eager to leave and I need to get back on schedule."

Uncle Duncan handed Jane the letter. She slowly grasped it, baf-fled that her uncle wrote to this woman. She knew he would have had to pull strings to help her gain the position. From what she'd heard from the midwife on Saint Helena's Island, apprenticeships were hard to come by and extremely competitive. Unfortunately, she didn't allow any apprenticeships. Jane had already asked. According to the woman, they were too much of a distraction for her to focus on her patients. Jane carefully studied the letter, feeling small little flutters of excitement build within her.

"I don't know what to say." Any doubt or fear that seeped in her mind from the surgery was replaced with James and his words of support. He made her feel like she could pursue anything her mind was set on.

"You can only imagine my delight after I read her letter. I know you'll be wonderful."

Staring into her uncle's eyes, her heart felt full of gratitude and disbelief. Her dream of becoming a midwife was actually put into motion. She looked back at the open letter in her hands.

"I'll need to tell James," she whispered.

Her uncle was quiet as he stared into the fire. "Forgive me, but I already informed him of the news."

"Why would you feel the need to tell him?"

"I needed to know his intentions towards you."

She threw her face in her hands and released a groan of embarrassment. "You didn't." Slowly she lowered her hands and looked at him. "What did he say?" The speed of her heart pulsed through her veins. Jane's eyes widened. Did he ask her uncle for a courtship while she was gone? She'd heard of couples doing such a thing. Hadn't she? No, that wasn't courtship. They were engaged. The fiancé left for a few years' time during his deployment. But *engaged!* She fanned her hand towards her face, unable to help the exhilaration that swept over her body. Would James make such a notion to her uncle? She could picture nothing sweeter and more perfect than to have him refuse to see her go without claiming her for his own.

Under thick brows, her uncle looked at her with hesitation. Her breath quickened as he began to speak more carefully. Just like he had when he informed her that she could never be a surgeon.

"The captain understands the opportunity that's presented to you and is supportive of your new endeavor."

One by one the butterflies dropped into a dark, empty hole in her stomach. She blinked back the moisture in her eyes. How could she let her mind wander with such preposterous thoughts? Humiliation spread from her chest to her cheeks like a raging fire. "I see," she whispered. Only she couldn't see. Was she blinded by her desires? No, that couldn't be right. He cared for her. She had full confidence that he did.

Taking to his feet, her uncle gathered her into his arms like he usually did when being the bearer of unpleasant news. "With his support, I thought you would be happy." He gently patted her back.

For being such a knowledgeable man, there was one area one would consider him naive—matters of the heart. Never had he been in love before.

Straining a smile at him, she buried her wet cheek into his shoulder. "I will be," she replied.

Chapter Seven

Taking a breath, Jane continued to stare at the door, not wanting to face the heart-wrenching anguish that would pursue. It was the first time in three days since she had the chance to visit with him. The first time since she had left him after their game of chess. Pressing her forehead against the door, she closed her eyes. She didn't want to stay away from him, nor had she attempted to avoid him. Their ridiculous schedules kept conflicting with each other. For preparations of her upcoming departure, she was either packing or running errands with Millie. When she had a chance to visit, he was either resting or with visitors.

A lone tear escaped down her cheek. It wasn't the first to appear since learning about their departure, and deep down, she knew it wouldn't be the last.

She tightened the shawl around her shoulders. At this very moment, her belongings were being loaded into the carriages. All that was left was facing the most dreaded task—saying goodbye. Millie's hand fell on her shoulder. Jane looked to her and saw the sadness in her eyes. Millie nodded at her and stepped to the side, letting her know she was there for her. Her wonderful chaperone. Drawing her head back, Jane wiped her eyes. Her situation wasn't going to disappear the longer she delayed it.

With a trembling hand and little desire, she knocked. Her heart tightened when she heard his deep, rich voice respond, "Come in." She loved how familiar he sounded to her.

Pulling herself together, she opened the door. Still sitting in bed, James flashed her a smile that never reached his eyes.

"There's my favorite doctor's assistant," he called.

A smile formed from his remark and she walked towards him. "There's my favorite troublesome patient."

He chuckled, then winced as he attempted to situate himself better. She hurried to his side to adjust his pillows. Unexpectedly, she felt James's arms wrap around her as he pulled her next to him on the bed.

"James, you're going to hurt yourself!" she warned with a giggle as he drew her closer to his side. She looked over her shoulder, expecting to see Millie behind her but she wasn't. She stood in the open doorway with her back to them.

"I must keep to my reputation of being a troublesome patient." He smiled, this time she saw the joy in his eyes.

"I meant by cheating at games."

"I never cheated. I played most honorably. You seem to have a difficult time dealing with defeat." He brushed her loose curls over her shoulder.

"No, never. I can be quite amiable if the game is played fairly."

"As it was." He leaned his forehead against hers. "I look forward to learning your version of the waltz."

She forced a smile. She wasn't confident it would ever come to pass. Not while she was leaving for England in less than two hours' time.

His eyes darkened as though he had the same thought. Her heart raced, pumping out protests that echoed in her ears. She couldn't leave him, not like this. They'd endured too much together to say goodbye. How could she bear it? She loved him.

"It's not too late," she protested.

"What? Here?" He winced when he pressed his fists into the bed and sat further up.

"No," she hurried, pressing her hand against his shoulder. A soft smile formed on her face as she watched him lean his head back against his pillows, his expression determined as though he was still processing the thought of the waltz. "Not to dance." She drew away from him to get a better understanding of his hesitated smile. "I'll go to the docks to speak with my uncle about delaying our departure, he'll—"

"Jane," James took hold of her hands. "I can't let you do that."

Disappointment stung behind her eyes, blurring her vision. "Why not?"

"Your uncle told me about your training to be a midwife in England. I know you won't be able to get that here."

How did he know that? She raised a questioning brow at him and opened her mouth to speak but stopped when he held his hand up. With a sheepish smile he replied, "I may have had Jenny speak with our local midwife."

Her eyes widened. "You did?"

He intertwined his fingers with hers and stared at their hands. "It's difficult for me to sit back and let you slip out of reach." His thumb caressed her hand. "You have a gift. I'm glad you'll be given an opportunity to use it, especially with the knowledge that you'll gain." His voice was rough like the wretched storm that delayed her on this beautiful island. "I'm happy for your new adventure. And as much as I selfishly want you to stay, I know you need to go."

The sincerity in his eyes spoke of the truth behind what he said. Their future together was unknown. They lived completely different lives and soon in opposite hemispheres. Sorrow burned deep into her soul. How could two things feel so right but the timing be completely off?

His blue eyes began to softly search hers.

"What are you doing?" she whispered.

"I'm trying to lock my memory of your face. You see, every time you disapprove or scowl, you furrow your brows together." He traced his finger above the bridge of her nose. "When you smile, your eyes tighten ever so slightly with a joyous line fanning out." His fingers trailed towards the corner of her eye. "And when you're nervous, or holding back laughter and a smile, like you're doing now, you adorably bite your lip." His voice lowered as he softly traced to her chin.

Jane's heart cried as it was being pulled in many directions. The longing in his eyes made the decision to think of him only as a friend impossible. The unquenchable desire to lean into his soft, firm lips battled at her as she vowed to remain where she was. She closed her eyes, breaking the yearning that her heart desperately wanted to comply to.

"James," she managed to speak in a scarce whisper. "I'm not ready to leave."

"I don't—" He paused and broke free from her gaze. She watched a line form between his brows as he blew out a breath. Clearing his throat, his expression softened. "Soon enough England will be in awe as they discover Miss Jane Sawyer and how remarkable she is."

Unable to speak in fear she'd cry, she offered a small smile. As she went to slip her hand away, his hand held it firmer, refusing to let her go. The lighthearted facade he had displayed crumbled to a pile of despair. His eyes glistened, brightening their blue hue.

"I have full confidence that you'll be a remarkable midwife." She watched him swallow before he made his attempt to speak again, "May I have your permission to write to you?"

A heavy sorrow weighed on her chest and crept up in her throat, forming a lump that would prevent any of her words from sounding coherent. She whispered, not trusting her voice to go louder, "Please do. I'll be certain to write to you as well."

The dimple on his cheek appeared with his smile. "I'd like that." Clearing his throat, he added, "Very much." He gave her hand a final squeeze before slowly releasing it. She hated how cold and empty it felt. "I'm looking forward to hearing about all the wonderful experiences England has to offer. As a former patient of yours, I know your patients will be in good hands."

All the self-strength talks about being able to stay strong and keep her tears from appearing began to dissolve.

"Thank you." She began to fidget with a ribbon on her dress. "Well then, I fear I must be going." She looked up to the ceiling, keeping the tears from pouring out. She didn't want his last memory of her being one where she was sobbing her goodbye.

"Yes." His voice was thick.

She faced him and gave him a smile. "Thank you for many wonderful memories, James."

She noticed the muscles in his cheeks flex.

"I shall always treasure our time together."

Leaning down, she gave him one final kiss on his cheek.

When did they draw the curtains? James glared at the bright, cheerful sun that blazed against the blinding, magenta walls. *And most importantly, why?* For the first time in what felt like weeks, he managed to allow himself to fall asleep. It became a fear when his eyelids hung heavy, threatening to block his vision of the pleasantries around him. For once his eyelids lowered the black curtains, the nightmares came alive.

Splinters of wood exploded through the smoky air. Cannonballs whistled into their target, breaking timber with an effortless snap. The crack of gunfire, followed by the haunting cries of his wounded men. James laid paralyzed on the deck as he witnessed the scene play out before him. Even when he tried to yell orders, no one could hear him. Then there was Thomas running towards him, but faltering when a round of gunfire struck his side. He watched his friend's large green eyes stare empty at him before he toppled to the deck.

It was always that same scene. He never knew if Thomas survived from the shots or not, for at that point he was usually awoken by a loud, helpless scream. By the time he opened his tear-filled eyes, the screams had turned into a sob, echoing in his ears. It used to startle the staff, but he'd found they'd been keeping their distance as of late.

James grunted. The one time his mind was still, the sunshine awoke him. Outside his window, clouds floated lazily in the sky. Normally he would have been drawn to the harbor, but the wind in his sail was gone. Taken by an exceptional woman. Not that it mattered. If she'd ask, he'd give her everything he possessed. His home, his soul, his tattered ship, his heart. He scoffed at the irony. Judging by the emptiness inside, he knew he already had done that. He was alone and numb.

Shifting his weight from under the covers, he propped himself up. Enough was enough. His time spent being bedridden in this pink room had come to an end. He needed air. To feel the wind blowing against him. And he wasn't going to ring the dainty bell for someone to aid him across the room. Gritting his teeth, he lifted his legs, one by one, over the side of the bed. The sharp pain in his side began to stab throughout the wounded area. Instantly, he clutched his side, trying to keep the pain maintained. He was amazed by how much muscle he used in his stomach to perform such a task. *Now to stand and walk*, he encouraged himself. His legs weren't injured during the battle so the task shouldn't be too difficult.

Digging his palm further into his side, he pushed himself off the bed. Through clenched teeth, he paused and puffed out a turbulent breath. His legs trembled. Any thoughts of leaving the room dissolved. "Come off it," he grunted to himself. "Over a month ago you sprinted up Jacob's ladder. You can take twenty steps to the window." Hunched forward, he took a staggered step.

"Blundering fool," he spat, panting more heavily. "Gggaa," he sputtered, forcing his foot to slide forward. He leaned against the bed for support before his body shook his legs out from under him and he fell to his hands and knees. "Mm," he gritted. Clutching his side, he breathed short, quick breaths from his nose to keep from expanding his stomach any further. Drops of sweat lined his forehead, dripping onto the awful, pink carpet. His head spun. Carefully he slid onto his elbow and rolled onto his back. His chest heaved as though he had just finished a race. Why, the sprint up the one hundred stairs of Jacob's ladder was a stroll around the garden compared to those three steps.

A soft knock sounded at the door. He snapped his attention in the direction. *Quit fooling yourself.* He shivered and pulled his blanket down across his shoulders. Footsteps padded as his visitor approached. He looked up at the intruder when silence followed.

Thomas gave him a cheeky smile. "I see you're finally escaping from your bed. It's about time."

The corner of James's lips raised. It became more and more of a relief when he saw his friend, alive and well.

Thomas reached down to him. "Need a hand?"

"No, not yet." Still holding his side, James grimaced, waiting for the pain to subside.

His friend folded his arms over his chest and studied him. "Where were you planning on going?"

James inhaled an uneven breath. "To the window. This room needs a cool breeze to rid the stagnant air."

Thomas chuckled. "I imagine you're already feeling a breeze with what you're wearing."

James laughed and held his side. His nightgown draped securely over his knees. "Don't make me laugh."

"Very well. A few of the crew and I were going over what can be reclaimed from the ship. I happened to find this laying on the deck and thought you may like it back."

Reaching into his pocket, Thomas pulled out the chess piece. James lifted his head off the floor and eagerly accepted the only token he had left of her. He ran his thumb over a chipped section of the queen's head.

"Thank you," he mumbled, his voice too thick to be trusted.

Thomas scooted the wooden chair next to him, and leisurely sat. "Did you commit to anything with her?"

"Just to write," he grumbled, running his thumb back over the broken part. The disappointment in Thomas's face enhanced the storm clouds that dampened James's mood. Deafening silence filled the room and he quietly answered his friend. "If I wasn't confined in this room, I would have already followed her."

"Yes. I would never doubt that. For your career's sake, I suppose it's good you were confined."

James scowled.

"Well, I declare it's time we get you out of this ghastly room."

James grumbled something and rolled his eyes towards the ceiling. The room was only a sliver of what his problems were.

Thomas's lighthearted tone shifted to a reprimand. "I understand you're upset, but being in here is making you worse. It's time to stop sulking and let us focus on your recovery."

There were very few times in his life he could remember Thomas being curt. Rarely was it directed towards him. But what perturbed him more than Thomas's sternness, was what he said about sulking. James turned his head towards Thomas. "I lost a few of my men. Their families are suffering. I've been confined to this blasted bed for days on end, unable to bid my condolences in person. I wrote each of them a letter, telling them of their loved ones' valiant fight. I missed the ceremony of my men's burial at sea—which is still hard to accept that any of them are gone. In my mind, I still anticipate seeing them whenever I get to return to the harbor. And now," he croaked and cleared his throat as it began to constrict. He blinked furiously, wiping the tears. "Now—now she's gone." James stared hopelessly at the queen. Lashing out at Thomas didn't relieve the pain. Instead, regret churned in his heart for his insensitive words. "Forgive me, Thomas," he languished. "I know you were there. And you knew them just as well. That was selfish of me for implying that you wouldn't understand." When Thomas didn't reply, James continued, rubbing his hands over his eyes. "My lack of sleep hasn't helped any of this."

A book slammed shut, causing him to jump. Startled, he looked to Thomas and watched him place the book of poetry Jane had left back on the side table. Having been wallowing in his own despair, he didn't notice his friend had taken to his feet.

"I was there," Thomas's voice shook. "It was horrible." He stared at James with fire burning in his eyes. "I was also there when we almost lost you." His hands shook while he wiped his eyes. "Knowing it was because of me—because you risked your life to save me, tore me up inside. You better believe I understand the turmoil you face. And don't think I don't have the same night terrors that force you to relive the scenes all over in your dreams. I know you have them. The staff were quick to inform me out of concern. But let me tell you James, all of us who survived that battle face the same nightmares."

The pain thumping in James's chest seared his body. He opened his mouth to apologize to his friend. "Thomas—"

Thomas held up his hand. "No." He sniffed and wiped his nose with the back of his hand. "I don't want to hear you protesting or blaming yourself for what happened. There's nothing more we can do. It's done. They're gone. But we're still here. Fortunate to live each day to the fullest or the gloomiest." He threw his hand at James to make his point. "But Jane. She could have stayed. You two could have been together. Why didn't you tell her you love her?" Thomas gripped the book and stared at him with such intensity that remorse overtook James's self-pity.

Grimacing, he sniffed and shamefully muttered, "I couldn't."

"You couldn't," Thomas repeated back, raising his brow. "James McCannon . . . couldn't."

The words struck him with the same intensity as the round that shot his side. He had never given up on a challenge, but this challenge was unique in so many ways. If Thomas only understood the battle . . . he had suffered not to beg for her to stay.

"I'm no coward, Thomas. If you only knew. Every time I saw her . . ." He swallowed to keep the steadiness in his voice. "I didn't want it to be true. I needed more time."

"More time for what?" Thomas asked, staring intently at him. James's fingers curled around a thread on the blanket.

"To prove to her uncle I'd be worthy to ask for her hand," he whispered.

"Why couldn't you have asked her to stay. She would have said yes. You know it and everyone who's seen her look at you knows it. She could still be here had you asked. Then perhaps she could sail to meet with her uncle with the next fleet," Thomas retorted.

"I've thought of that. But I would have changed everything her uncle had planned for her. For them." James's vision blurred. "I couldn't do that to him." He sighed, looking to the ceiling to keep blinking back his tears. "Not after what he's done for me. He saved my life. *She* saved my life. I would be taking away his only family from him. And her dreams." His voice trembled.

"Don't be so daft," Thomas uttered as he stood staring out the window. "The doctor admires you. Don't forget you had also saved her. He'd welcome you with open arms."

"Not if it meant I'd be taking her away from him. She's his everything."

"Yes, and you're hers. He wouldn't risk her happiness to keep her to himself. Besides, rumor has it, he only took the Oxford position so he could see that she'd have a better chance of marrying a worthy gentleman."

James's eyes widened at Thomas. "Not a chance." Adrenaline pulsed through his veins, fortifying his determination. He turned onto his stomach and propped himself on his knees. He tried to remember what day it was and if there would be a ship at the harbor departing for England.

"Keep your gown down, James. I didn't say that to cause you to panic. I only said that so you'd know that the doctor would be more than happy to have you steal her away."

Feeling the muscles in his legs shake, James collapsed to his back breathless. He grimaced as his side ached from his rash decision to rush out towards the pier.

"You would have thought we were under an attack," Thomas taunted.

"You'd be amazed at what love makes a man do. I would have never believed it until now." He rubbed the tight muscles in his chest. James knew he was a pitiful, lovestruck fool in Thomas's eyes, but he didn't care anymore.

"Do you really suppose the doctor would accept my pursuit of his niece?"

"He did while you were here. Why would that change?"

James picked at the carpet feeling extremely foolish for ever doubting himself.

"Thomas, for once I feel you've spoken words of wisdom in regards to my relationship with Jane." Thomas scoffed and shook his head at him. "There's only one thing I can do to make this right. Will you do me a favor and fetch me paper and a quill?"

His lips curled as he peered at him. "Only if you promise to get out of this room by the end of the week."

James smiled at his friend. "I promise."

"Then aye, aye Captain."

"And Thomas," his friend stopped mid stride from the door, "Thank you."

He gave him a half smile and nodded. "Are you ready to get off the floor?"

James stifled a laugh, "Yes."

Chapter Eight

November, 1795

Jane helped her uncle carry their parcels to the front entrance where their butler Neville greeted them.

"Doctor Brown, there's a lady here to see you both." The lean gentleman bowed slightly to them without ever cracking a smile. His eyes were dull, his skin almost ashen. He took the position at their home in Oxford after obeying doctors order to move to the country. She couldn't help but agree more to the decision as she and her uncle welcomed him onto their staff, since their arrival in September. Deep down she hoped the country would soften his countenance. It was as if London's smog affected not only his health, but his spirit. "She declined to give me her name, but I recognize her to be Lady Griftson, the chancellor's wife."

Jane groaned to herself and plucked each of her fingers from her gloves. The lady had sent many notes inquiring to call on them—particularly on her. When the chancellor had offered the position at Oxford to her uncle, he had meant every word about how his wife would love to introduce Jane to the many connections in England. Clearly, the chancellor's wife was eager to get started with her new pet. Jane sighed quietly to herself. She resented the idea of being paraded around like an animal at a fair for the ton to speculate.

She pictured many ideas of ruining the lady's desire to assist her, but she couldn't carry them out. Unfortunately for her, any wrong move would tarnish her own reputation. With her new passion in midwifery, she couldn't risk that. The gossip would ruin any chance of her earning women's trust to be their midwife. Untying her bonnet, she handed it, as well as her gloves and woolen cloak, to Neville. With winter upon them, the days were getting chillier and chillier. She found it hard to stay warm as she missed the warmer climate.

Cushioned steps above the staircase, followed by an excited whisper, drew her attention. "Miss Jane, I'm so glad you're back." Holding the freshly polished banister, Millie leaned as far as she could without toppling over. Her blonde braid dangled over her slender shoulder. "There's a letter for you from Saint Helena." Her green eyes danced with the prospect of it being from James. Jane grinned at her and looked to her uncle.

"May I be excused for a moment?"

In a calm manner, he removed his top hat and handed it to Neville. She fidgeted with the string from her dress while she patiently waited for his permission to be late for Lady Griftson's call.

"Join us in the parlor when you're done," he finally replied while he removed each finger from his gloved hands. Jane laughed as he peered over at her with a gleam in his eyes.

"Thank you!" Relieved his intentional delay was meant to be a tease, she gave him a quick peck on his cheek and rushed up the stairs to where Millie waited. Once to the top, Millie squealed with delight and clapped her hands.

"Is it from him?" Jane asked, breathless from her near sprint.

"There wasn't a name on it, miss, just Saint Helena stamped on top from the postmaster."

Gathering her skirts, Jane hurried to her room with Millie in tow. It had been weeks since she felt this alive. It was a warm welcome compared to the somber environment of Oxford. For the past few weeks, she feared she'd never feel this kind of exhilaration ever again. Not since she left her beloved island.

"Here." Millie hurried past Jane to the vanity where a beautiful cream-colored envelope awaited her. "It's right here."

Jane eagerly snatched the wonderful letter. Her hands shook as she carelessly tore open the casing. Since her arrival three weeks prior, she'd already heard from Elaine, who had written four tear-stained pages expressing her heartache of Captain Richard's departure for Bombay. Then surprisingly, Lieutenant Wood, who had inquired how her journey had been. It was rather brief and straight to the point, but very thoughtful.

"Please let it be his," she whispered to herself. *Please—ah!* Jane bit her lip. Blasted papercut. She sucked in her breath and removed the—pages!

Elegant calligraphy flowed smoothly over the crisp paper. It was such a joyous sight to behold, she could cry. Quickly, she fumbled over the words to get to the signature. *All my love*—she drew the paper back. Slowly, she eased to her stool.

"Whose it from?" Millie bit a nail while she stared with wide eyes.

Jane gave her a halfhearted smile. "Jenny."

"Oh." Millie blew out a breath of disappointment. Jane lifted the corner of her lips, exchanging a knowing smile. Resting her elbows on her vanity, she took the pages and read. Grateful to at least hear from her dear friend.

Every step Jane took down the stairs accentuated the heaviness in her heart. She enjoyed Jenny's letter and the detailed information about the orchard and the island. And according to her brief, regard to James, he was healing well and on the mend. She was glad to hear that, yet selfishly she wanted more.

For instance, could Jenny see regret in his face for letting her go? Or did he mention how he missed her and wished he had asked for their courtship? If only he had. She didn't like feeling like her heart belonged to him when she was expected to court others.

Perhaps she should be grateful Jenny didn't mention any more details of James. She would never ask that of her friend. As tempted as she was to write Jenny and inquire if he had ever spoken of her, she would never do such a thing. Call it pride, but she wanted her friendship to be separate from what had occurred between James and her, and deep down she was afraid Jenny's answer would be no.

Jane drew a short breath. The pain of a dagger twisting in her heart wasn't nearly as bad as it had been during her voyage. Much to her surprise, departing the blissful island was one of the hardest experiences in her life. It was almost as difficult as leaving Bombay, if not more.

"There she is," a rich voice sang out.

Her steps faltered. She had walked heedlessly into the dimly lit parlor. Oxford's sky had a while before it would fill any room in the home with sunshine. An older woman sat plump on the floral sofa, her gray hair pulled elegantly under a heavy hat that was fluffed with cream-colored feathers. She peered at Jane with satisfaction shining in her beady, brown eyes.

"Oh, Doctor Brown, she's breathtaking. My, oh my," the lady muttered through her thin, painted lips. "With her features and figure, she'll be certain to catch herself a gentleman of title." She nodded at her uncle who leisurely sat across from her in a wingback chair. "Not to worry about her being an orphan and all."

Jane's eyes widened at the woman's brashness. She looked to her uncle who gave the woman a curt nod. He held his hand up from the armchair, subtly motioning to Jane to hold her tongue.

"You must be Lady Griftson." Jane forced a warm smile and gave a slight curtsy.

"Oh yes, where are my manners? Forgive me my dear," she replied, picking up her teacup and saucer. Extending her pinky, she took a sip. "You see, I've just been looking forward to taking you in my charge and aid you in finding an eligible bachelor that I've forgotten we've hardly been formally introduced." She stirred her tea vigorously only to place it back on her lap. "And I'm just so thrilled that you will not be a challenge." The lady raised her brow as Jane felt her beady eyes scale her from head to toe. "Rest assured, with coaching on my part, you'll be ready for the season." She placed her hands in her lap and nodded an approval.

Jane's lips twitched when she forced a smile. Uncertain if she dared sit across from this woman, she decided to continue to stand a safe distance in the doorway until she was invited to take a seat. "Though, I believe you'd fare just fine on your own. Goodness. Such a beauty." She raised her tea again, never seeming to catch her breath. "Now my poor friend Lady Scarlet Williams could have only wished for the same fortune." The feathers on her hat floated back and forth, like a hen pecking at the ground, while she continued to babble. "When she first saw her niece, she feared she was never forgiven for a single transgression she may have committed in her past life. Dear me, such a task. But I believe the girl was married after a year. Hmm, yes to the butcher." Her pointed nose crinkled with disdain. "But not you, Miss Sawyer. No, never. Rest assured, you'll be with a gentleman of title."

"Excuse the interruption Lady Griftson."

Both Jane and the lady looked to her uncle. Tea dripped off the woman's spoon as she had stopped stirring the steamy brew for the fourth time. Her uncle interlocked his fingers and leaned forward in his chair. Only such motion occurred when he wanted to settle a discussion. Jane clasped her hands in front of her. One could only hope.

"I appreciate your words of affirmation Lady Griftson, but after our journey from Bombay I've taken into consideration how Jane is a daughter to me." His eyes softly bore on the lady. She smiled politely and lowered her cup. "Thus said, I feel it is my responsibility to introduce her into society."

Jane's mouth dropped. Lady Griftson laughed. "Yes, of course. But please realize that it's only deemed proper for a lady such as myself to take on the role of her chaperone. I shall be able to get her into events and places where many important diplomats attend." She waved her jewel-covered fingers in the air.

"Yes, Lady Griftson, this is true. But with all due respect, I've already received many invitations to the majority of the upcoming balls as well as social calls we've yet to attend due to some gown fittings. One must be up to London's fashions do you not agree, Lady Griftson?"

Beady eyes narrowed at Jane's uncle who kept his features indifferent. "Now that being said, my lady, I know how well informed you are of each potential suitor for my dear Jane. We would greatly appreciate your help in introducing her to many of the gentlemen should we attend the same social gatherings."

With a hint of satisfaction, she gave a soft nod. "Doctor Brown, you must know my disappointment in this arrangement. You, sir, took the fun out of my planning." She raised a thin gray brow and looked at Jane as though she were a prize to be had. "But seeing that you leave me with no choice, I accept. I'll introduce her to only the best of the fold." She placed her saucer on the table next to her. "Well, I see that I'm no longer needed," she huffed. "Be certain that she at least attends Duke Fossey's ball. Everyone who's anyone shall be there.

Rest assured, come the new year, the ballrooms will be filled with fine gentlemen, ready to embrace the new season." Her lips formed into a fine red line.

"I intend to," Jane's uncle replied. "I have the invitation on my desk. I won't delay our answer any longer."

Uncle Duncan stood from his chair.

"Very well." Rising from the sofa, with a less than pleased expression, she said, "I bid you two a good afternoon. Please don't hesitate to call on me should you be in need of any assistance. Doctor Brown."

With a final gaze at Jane, she tsked. "I was so looking forward to our time together. Miss Sawyer, best wishes."

"My lady." Jane curtsied and patiently waited until she heard the soft thud of the front door closing shut.

"Uncle!" Relieved from his decision, she rushed to her uncle to give him a big embrace. Sticking his hand out, he caught himself on the chair before she could knock him off his feet.

"I suppose we will need to get you fitted into some ball gowns."

She chuckled. "I suppose so. We wouldn't want her finding out about your little white lie."

"It was for a great cause." Still holding her in his arms, he lovingly patted her back.

"One that I'm forever grateful for."

Behind his spectacles, his eyes twinkled back at her. "Was the letter from him?"

In her moment of relief to be freed from the lady, she had forgotten all about the letter. Drawing away from his embrace, she shook her head.

"I am sure it will be only a matter of time."

"I suppose." She sighed.

"Come, I have an hour before I leave for my seminar. I want to brush up on your studies with you before you apprentice with Mrs. Hewitt."

Being that she would need to complete courses in anatomy and physiology before she could be midwife certified, her uncle knew the best remedy to keep her mind distracted from the lack of a letter.

James peered through his heavy lids. The unnerving sound of crinkling paper and chuckling awoke him from his restless state.

"I hope you don't mind that I helped myself to some leisure reading." Sitting in a plush, leather chair, Thomas smiled and held up one of many wrinkled papers. Next to him, laid a tray of James's half-eaten breakfast—not by his own doing. Thomas took another bite of a sausage link. "Mmm, James, I never knew you were a poet."

James lifted his head from his cluttered desk. Grumbling in reply, he then peeled a damp piece of paper from off his face.

Thomas tossed the letter over his shoulder and snatched another from the floor, smoothing the creases across his thigh. Clearing his throat, he read, "'My dearest Jane, I shall never forget the day when I first met you. Never mind how I had saved your life and not your favorite dress.'"

Did I write that? James rubbed his puffy eyes.

"'But it was your eyes. Those eyes that sank me into the depths of your enrapturing beauty. You've captured my heart, my mind, my soul, and sadly my sleep. I know I'll continue to suffer until I see your beautiful face again. I shall always regret the day you left this island. I never did tell you to stay like I desperately wanted to. I should have fought for you.'"

James yawned. *I suppose that sounds like me.*

"'I should have told you how much I love you. But alas.'" Thomas stood with his hands clutching the paper, his nose practically pressed against the words that were written. His voice became more robust as he continued to read. "'I shall prove to you and all of Jamestown the sorrow of my mistake. I shall sacrifice the greatest sacrifice that anyone has ever had any satisfaction in. Even my men would not approve of such a thing. Therefore, I do what I must.'"

James raised a thick brow at Thomas's embellishments and stiffly leaned into his wooden chair waiting for his friend's theatrics to end.

"'It grieves many around me to have me do such a thing, but I must, for I love you.'" Pacing back and forth, Thomas shuffled through scattered pieces of crinkled paper. "'Therefore, Jane Sawyer, I shall make a sacrifice of the most considerate act known to man.'" He peered over the scribbled letter and smirked. "'My baths. Yes, my darling, Jane. I shall make all of Saint Helena know how foul I smell because of my agony over losing you. Not even my servants dare enter my quarters for fear of being stricken by my powerful stench.'" Thomas pointed at the food tray to prove his point.

Shrugging his shoulders, James folded his arms across his chest. "I've taken baths."

"'But that's not all, my love. I even grew you a beard.'" Thomas peered closer at the wrinkled paper in his hand. "'Yes, a remarkable beard that shall make any young man cry with envy.'"

Raising a brow of confusion, James ran his hand over the stubble along his jaw, but paused when he threaded his fingers through short facial hair instead. He definitely had a beard. *When did I shave last? What day is it?*

"'My darling Jane, I hope you have suffered as much as I have these past few weeks and accept this horrid scent as a token of my love for you.'" Thomas abruptly looked at James and hurried to his desk, kicking wadded paper along the way. "Quick, rub this letter under your arm. She must always cherish your stench."

"You crazy fool." James snorted. "Back away." He rubbed at his aching side and laughed. "I get it! I look and smell dreadful."

Thomas picked up another half-written letter. "No, having to wash Jenny's manure covered stockings is dreadful. And let me remind you, that was the worst bet I had ever lost to her. You, my friend, look and smell atrocious. I've sailed with better smelling lads than you."

James smirked. "I feel I've been imprisoned in this house for months."

"Well, I'm releasing you." Thomas walked behind James's desk and threw open the heavy blue drapes. Sunshine poured through the window panels, highlighting the wretched mess James had created throughout the night. Half-written paper scattered the wood floor. Puddles of ink dribbled across his paper-filled desk. He rubbed his cheek hoping his face didn't land in one of the ink splotches.

Even the fireplace had scattered specks of ash across the hearth from letters that had successfully entered the inferno of his pitiful words for Jane. One would have thought he was in the middle of writing a novel with all the scratch pieces of papers.

Thomas set the letter on the desk and looked at him with compassion in his eyes. "It's been a few days since we last talked. How are you?"

Waving off the concern, James clenched his side and stiffly stood. "Fine, fine. How was patrolling?" he asked through gritted teeth. The doctor on the island had told him that because of the extent of his wound, it would take months before the pain would subside. Sleeping in the chair all night had him hunched over in pain. Uncertain if he could handle being on his hands and knees, James began to kick the wrinkled paper towards the ash filled fireplace. None of his writings were good enough to send to Jane.

She deserved more than what he had to say. *Forgive me, I was a fool, please wait for me? How would she believe me after I had encouraged her to leave?* The predicament that he put himself in was nothing he'd ever faced before. And he didn't know where to start to make it better. His words on paper always fell flat.

With Thomas's embellishments perhaps he was onto something.

His friend began to help him in his humiliating endeavor and kicked paper across the floor to the mantle.

"Yes, patrolling," Thomas cheerfully replied. "My patrol was quite pleasant. The weather wasn't scorching hot, there haven't been any more reports of French sightings. We're just missing our captain."

"Thomas, you're the captain now." James peered at his friend. "Taking charge and commanding the crew after I was shot proves you've earned the promotion."

Thomas's square jaw shifted back and forth. His boyish face had hardened over the past few months. His green eyes still hinted of his lighthearted manner, but they had grown serious since the battle. James knew each of the remaining crew and townspeople would never be the same after the attack. His men he got to visit with had the same hard look. "Yes, well you know what I mean." He picked up a handful of paper and threw it into the fireplace.

Wanting to make light of the matter, James said, "I'll be back to sailing in a year or so. The admiral sent word that if I were up to the task, he'll be able to assign me a ship and crew."

"That's great news!" Thomas lit a match to start a fire in the hearth. Cream-colored paper ignited, shriveling itself into black ash.

He looked at James with a sheepish smile. "But I hope you don't mind, I already took the liberty of naming my ship Ebony II."

"Only if it's referenced to our island's flower." James looked at Thomas in a serious manner to keep from smiling at his friend's puzzled expression.

"The flower?" Thomas snorted. "Of course not."

"A beautiful, rare flower could be just as intimidating." James broke his serious facade and smiled as he had quoted Jane. That day by the falls was one of many that he would never forget with her. "If not more," he mumbled, remembering how she had made him so unnerved . . . thoughts of her still did.

"Never," Thomas replied with a firm head shake.

"Someday you'll agree with me." James smirked and wiped his sleeve across his forehead as he began to perspire from his movements.

"You keep saying that," Thomas muttered.

Holding his side, James slowly sat in his leather wingback chair next to the mantle and released a heavy sigh.

"If love makes you look and smell the way you do, I shall never desire it." Thomas's nose scrunched with disgust.

James laughed. "I can see how you'd think that."

Thomas added the remaining letters to the fire and poured James a glass of water. Grateful, James took a long sip. After a moment, he stared at his ink-covered fingers holding the glass.

"Thomas." He looked at his friend solemnly. He knew what he was about to say next wouldn't be what his friend would want to hear. "I've put a lot of thought into this and I feel it's best for me to move on. I'm done attempting to write how I feel. She deserves so much more than that."

Thomas's brows furrowed. He rubbed his chin as he appeared to be thinking. "You're certain that's for the best?"

James rubbed at his chest and released a defeated breath. Since Jane's departure, he hadn't been more certain about moving forward than he felt now. He needed to cut strings and create new ties. Holding on to his hope of seeing her in two years had him sleepless and in knots. James looked to Thomas who looked back with disappointment. He nodded confidently at his friend. "I can't continue living life like this. It's time I move forward."

Thomas raised a brow. As he opened his mouth to speak, he was interrupted by a knock at the door.

"Come in," James hollered.

"Forgive the interruption, sir." His housekeeper, Mrs. Peters entered the room. Folding her hands in front of her she continued, "There is a Miss Harrlow here to see you."

James covered his face with irritation. Now with Jane gone, he feared it was only a matter of time before Miss Harrlow swooped in for another attempt to gain his attention.

"Send her in," he replied, ruffling his unkempt hair.

"Yes, sir," Mrs. Peters curtsied and brisked away, closing the door behind her.

The corner of Thomas's mouth raised. "Are you intentionally trying to appear barbaric?"

Straightening his shirt and buttoning his sleeves, James retorted, "Do you think it will help?"

"If by help you mean she will oddly become more infatuated with you? Then yes." Thomas chuckled as he leaned back in amusement. James groaned and ran his hands back through his hair to help tame it. "You know, for the past few months I was beginning to think she'd moved on from you."

James's fingers swiftly buttoned his vest. "What gave you such a fantastic idea?"

"There's been a few occasions where I've seen her sneaking into the mailroom. She didn't seem too interested in seeing her father."

"I'm sure the commissioner's been busy whenever she has stopped by."

"Yes, but the mailroom?" Thomas raised a brow. "You see, my suspicion is that she found herself a sailor, and is trying to prevent his letters from being sent to the house before her dear mother catches wind of their secret love affair."

James laughed. "What an interesting notion. Perhaps, you should address your suspicions to her?"

"Perhaps I should," Thomas retorted. "But I doubt I'll be able to tell if she was truthful in the matter. The woman can be quite deceitful."

"I happen to know a gentleman who has firsthand knowledge of this," James retorted, rubbing the grain of hair on his chin.

"You don't say?" Thomas leaned forward in his chair, playing along with James's sarcasm.

All the playfulness broke when footsteps sounded outside the study's door. He felt the blood in his veins grow cold with dread. "Sailor or no sailor, you are not to leave the room," he ordered his friend from under his breath.

"I wouldn't want to miss it," Thomas smirked and made himself more comfortable in his chair.

The study room's door swung open. James's head snapped up after sliding his arms through his coat's sleeves. Miss Harrlow glided in with a basket on her arm. Her curvy hips swayed back and forth as she floated into the room. Faltering her steps, she held her fingers to her nose with disgust. James subtly raised his arm to sniff. He didn't smell that foul as he had bathed the day prior . . . or was it the day before that? Thomas chuckled behind his hand, raising a brow to say he had told him so. Scrunching her nose, she lowered her hand and continued forward.

"Good morning, gentlemen." She gave a sweet smile to Thomas as he took to his feet, and targeted James. "Forgive me, Captain, for not inquiring about you sooner. I was told you were in such a fragile condition that I wanted to be certain you were better before I made my visit."

James offered her a slight nod. "Thank you for your thoughtfulness."

"Please, gentlemen take a seat." Miss Harrlow waved them down and glided to James's desk. Thomas raised a curious brow at him before gladly sitting. James refrained from rolling his eyes in irritation and carefully took a seat in his leather chair by the fire. He tapped his fingers against his armrest, wanting nothing more than to be done with her visit.

"The tavern gentleman told me that your favorite drink is hot chocolate, so I had him put some aside for me." She pulled out a pouch that had a stamp from one of the countries in South America from her basket. Her blue eyes sparkled as she looked at him. "I also ran into Captain Norton before he shipped out." James noticed Thomas's interest pique as he flashed him a suspicious smile. "He recommended this book for you," Miss Harrlow sweetly smiled at him.

She pulled out a familiar leatherbound book. A book that James was forced to listen to for hours after losing his bet with Jane.

He clutched the chair's arms as a new unfamiliar pain ached in his gut. The pain wasn't from any of his wounds, but from the emptiness that was left when she had departed. Miss Harrlow's voice intruded through his thoughts.

"Perhaps, I could read to you sometime?" Hope filled her face as she gazed at James with anticipation. Thomas covered his mouth as he tried to hide his smile.

"That is very considerate of you, Miss Harrlow, but I will have to decline. Respectfully. Captain Norton, he may have misinformed you." James rubbed the back of his neck as he watched the disappointment cross her face. "Do you remember when we went riding to the falls and we were discussing the schemes Captain Norton and I had played on each other?" James was hoping by mentioning the story it would help her to understand the situation. She slowly nodded, appearing even more distraught. "He hasn't quite forgiven me for not being the one who drank out of the ink filled tea that stained our admiral's teeth black."

"I see." Her smile faltered as she placed the book back into the basket. She quickly withdrew a container. "Well, no matter. I also brought you fish cakes."

"That is very kind," James said with a smile.

"I want you to know," she said, her voice lowering as she took hold of her basket. She briefly glanced at Thomas then back to him. Taking a step towards him, he watched as all her mannerisms softened. "I hold no ill feelings with what has happened between us. I admit I behaved not like myself as I had a bit of jealousy these past few months. Something, I'm not proud of." Her cheeks pinked. She held the basket closer to her and she inhaled deeply. "I'm very grateful for your chivalry, as you rescued the island and . . . all of us from an ill fate."

James stared at her with surprise. He wasn't sure what to expect from her, but that wasn't what he thought she'd say. Thomas cleared his throat, and James realized he had been studying her longer than one should.

"Thank you, Miss Harrlow. I . . ." He went to stand as she inched closer to the door.

"Please, stay seated. You must be exhausted." She gave him a small smile. "I bid you both a good afternoon." Dipping into a curtsy, she closed the door behind her.

James tore his eyes off the door to Thomas, who looked at James with a humorous gleam in his eye. "That was very—"

"Interesting." James finished.

"I have to say, I quite like the more genuine side of Miss Harrlow." Thomas rubbed at his square chin and watched James. James cleared his throat and looked back at the door uncertain what to make of her. *Was she being genuine? Or was it a game to her? She certainly acted sincere and if she was, why, there was hope for Miss Harrlow after all.*

"As do I," James mused. "As do I."

"Well, I must be going." Thomas slapped the arms to his chair and stood. "I'm going to the harbor to see if I can purchase some fish from Mr. Rutkin."

"Before you leave, would you mind taking this letter with you?" James hobbled towards his desk that was now covered with treats from Miss Harrlow. He looked at the empty silver tray where it used to hold a letter for Jane. The one decent letter he approved for that week from the scattered mess of paper. Glancing at the food tray in the corner, he shrugged. "Never mind, it appears Mrs. Peters has already taken it after she delivered breakfast."

Chapter Nine

April, 1796

Jane stood in the corner of Mrs. Dalton's upstairs bedchamber. It was her fourth time visiting the farmer's wife with her midwife, Mrs. Hewitt. The spring afternoon warmed the little room, making it muggy and hard to focus. She gazed around the room noticing how very simple, yet tidy Mrs. Dalton lived. Her furniture was very minimal and the decorations were plain in the loft of the two-story home. Lace curtains draped on either side of a small window, allowing the sun to stream into the dim room. A neatly made bed laid in the center against the wood-paneled wall, with two pillows on top of a floral quilt. To the right of the bed was a small nightstand with a wash bowl and pitcher. On the other side was a rocking chair where the round Mrs. Dalton sat looking extremely uncomfortable and flushed from the room's heat. As directed, Jane watched from a distance as to not hover over the patients, but close enough to take note of the midwife's every move. She had been apprenticing with Mrs. Hewitt for five months now and had enjoyed every moment. Except, for some reason, instead of being invested with every detail their patient told the midwife, Jane found her mind wandering more and more. She watched the stocky, middle-aged woman perform her routine check-up on Mrs. Dalton.

As she continued to observe, she felt her eyes begin to glaze over and her thoughts took her back to a very fond memory. A memory like many others during her stay on Saint Helena that she had pushed aside as she tried to avoid any distraction in her work. She smiled as she could almost feel the warm breeze in the courtyard while she danced with James. She bit her smile as she recalled how flustered he had made her feel when he flashed his dimpled smile. His unkempt, dark hair fashionably tussled, bounced to his every step. His bright blue eyes shone down on her with admiration. A sense of thrill ran up her as she pictured him pulling her closer in his strong arms.

It had been over eleven months since the day of the festival, and she refused to forget any of the details from that celebration.

Was he able to walk now that he'd had this time to recover? She desperately wanted to hear from him but settled with the thought that he probably was too busy to write as he may be focused on his duties and recovery. Jenny had written to her a week ago, telling her not to give up hope on ever hearing from him. Elaine, too, gave her the same support. Surprisingly, it was her uncle who was extremely disappointed that she hadn't seen a letter and told her to move on if he hadn't written soon. She briefly closed her eyes, pushing aside the hurt that had resurfaced in her heart. According to her uncle's timeline, she had a week left to hear from him before she needed to move forward with her life. But how could she do that when all she ever thought about between midwifery and the dull dances in England, was him?

"Oh," Mrs. Dalton murmured, pulling Jane back from her thoughts. The woman's red apple cheeks reddened more with discomfort as Mrs. Hewitt pressed firmer. "Is he doing alright? He was sure to kick me earlier today in my ribs. I had to give him a scolding for doing such a thing to his mum."

"Your baby seems to be doing just fine, Mrs. Dalton," Mrs. Hewitt replied with a crisp tone. "I'm only feeling where he's positioned."

"Miss Sawyer," Mrs. Hewitt called over her shoulder. "I would like you to come over and tell me the baby's position."

Jane nodded and gave Mrs. Dalton a warm smile. The woman released an exasperated breath and leaned her head against the rocking chair.

"Mrs. Dalton, you may feel a bit of discomfort while I feel around for your baby." Jane always appreciated how her uncle had always given his patients a fair warning before his procedures and she felt it best that she'd do the same.

"Get on with it," Mrs. Dalton impatiently breathed. "I had five youngens already. I'm used to all this poking and prodding. But I must say, you ladies are by far gentler than that doctor in town, Mr. Pitts. He was the one who delivered my first before I found Mrs. Hewitt. Thank the heavens," she breathed. "He was rough on me and my child."

Jane listened to Mrs. Dalton while she placed her hands around her lower stomach. She had heard of how doctors arrogantly believed that they knew more about the female anatomy than women. With that belief, the doctors also felt they knew how to deliver the babies better than midwives. Why, they even unnecessarily aided deliveries with their metal instruments which the midwives were unlawfully allowed to use—it was despicable. Jane gritted her teeth as Mrs. Dalton continued to tell her horror story of a delivery.

"—Why, he used these clamp looking gadgets to hold onto my dear little Jacob's head to pull him out of me. Mm hmm, that's definitely his foot, right there." Mrs. Marlow remarked as Jane felt around the baby's foot after it kicked against the side of the woman's stomach. "Anyway, that was the worst pain I had felt in my whole life when he yanked my baby out. I nearly passed out." Mrs. Dalton started fervently fanning herself with her handkerchief. Her voice began to quicken as she continued. "He stretched my legumes . . . no, my lent, my lapels, my—"

"Ligaments?" Jane asked through pursed lips. Mrs. Dalton reminded her of Millie at the moment. 'Saint Hell-ina,' Millie had said as she remarked how much she was going to miss the southern island. She sucked in a breath as she had a sudden sense of homesickness. At the time they had sailed away from Jamestown's harbor, she had hidden her tears from Millie and her uncle.

Feeling the baby's elbow, she continued down towards its head. She had refused to show them how much she was going to miss not only the island but everyone on it. Particularly one gentleman who seemed to have a hold of her heart.

"Yes, my ligaments down there. I've never been the same. I even told Laudy, my husband," she addressed Jane, "that I was done having children. But the good Lord had other plans. Why, Jacob, my poor child, had bruises on his head for weeks." She released an exasperated breath. "He still ain't right in the head," she mumbled. "The boy still can't tell the difference between a rooster and a chicken."

"Jacob is a fine boy, Mrs. Dalton," Mrs. Hewitt said assuredly. "And don't you worry a bit about your delivery. Between Miss Sawyer and myself this next delivery will be as easy as baking a pie."

"Oh, pie does sound delicious. I've been having so many cravings with this pregnancy." Mrs. Dalton licked her lips. "Apple pie. I look forward to 'em apples when they're in season."

"The baby's head is positioned here," Jane informed Mrs. Hewitt, as she held in her laughter from the woman's sudden craving. Her left hand pressed against Mrs. Dalton's lower stomach. "And his bottom is here." She pressed her hand against the firm round rump on top of Mrs. Dalton's belly. "It is in the occipito anterior position. Which is a very good position to be in for your baby," Jane addressed the hungry woman. Mrs. Dalton gave a curt nod and continued to fan herself.

"Would you care to feel for yourself Mrs. Dalton?" she asked, lifting her hands off the woman's belly.

The woman began feeling across her stomach. "His shoulder is right here." Jane watched in awe as the baby rolled like a wave across her stomach. "This is definitely a knee. And his foot," she pressed against the top of her belly down, away from her ribs. "His foot is now kicking me ribs," she said breathlessly.

"I'm impressed you're able to distinguish the difference," Jane said with a smile.

"This is me fifth child, Miss Sawyer. I've had loads of experience to tell what body part is what."

"So, I see."

"Very good," Mrs. Hewitt praised. "Miss Sawyer, can you measure how far along Mrs. Dalton is?"

Jane bit her lip. In the beginning, she was very skeptical with Mrs. Hewitt's odd technique of measuring. Had she not witnessed the accuracy, she would have been concerned of the woman being a fraud. But much to her surprise, every time they measured it matched with the mother's estimation as well as the delivery date. Proceeding with her mentor's invitation, she felt below Mrs. Dalton's belly button. Just as she was taught, she began to measure with her fingers from the top down to her pelvic bone.

After having measured many women's stomachs, she began to feel more confident with the technique. "I believe Mrs. Dalton is thirty-two weeks."

Mrs. Dalton tsked. "I'll be. For as peculiar as it is to be measured like that, I'm surprised by how right you are. Give or take."

Mrs. Hewitt's brown eyes twinkled with pride. "Very good, my dear. Not every young apprentice calculates that so easily."

Jane felt her cheeks warm as the two women looked at her, "Thank you."

"Well, Mrs. Dalton, is there anything else that we can do for you before we see you again next week?" Mrs. Hewitt asked as she gathered her medical bag.

"Yes." The woman's voice was breathy as she leaned forward on her wooden rocking chair. "How do I help my aching feet? They get so swollen by the end of the day."

Jane glanced down at the women's white stocking covered feet. Her poor ankles were definitely swollen as they appeared to be rolling over the top of her shoes.

"Have one of your children pour you a large bowl of cold water and then I want you to soak your feet in it every night. Little Sarah and Ann can help make dinner and get the littles ready for bed. Then for the finale, have Mr. Dalton rub your feet," Mrs. Hewitt said encouragingly. Mrs. Hewitt's manner was always one of being friendly, but as a respectable midwife in the county, she carried herself with so much dignity and seriousness that Jane rarely saw the woman's radiant smile.

"I'll see if I can convince Laudy of that." Doubt filled Mrs. Dalton's face. She grunted as she pushed herself off the rocking chair and grabbed her apron from the arm of the rocker.

"If he doesn't, then tell him I'll visit with his mum,," Mrs. Hewitt replied with a stern look in her brown eyes. "She'll be certain to give him a talking to,"

"He'll be sure to listen to me for certain." Mrs. Dalton laughed. "His mum had the worst labor in the county with him. How long did it last Mrs. Hewitt? Three days?"

"Four days."

Jane's mouth dropped, "Four?" She followed the two women out of the muggy bedchamber and down a narrow creaky stairway that led to the front door of the small cottage.

"I remember it as if it were yesterday. Laudy's mum did every-thing she could to hurry the labor along, but nothing worked. Not even walking two miles to her neighbors to drop off a basket of eggs. That woman persevered," Mrs. Hewitt said as she walked ahead of her. Jane noticed how nothing fell out of place with Mrs. Hewitt. She was very particular about how things ran with her appointments and with herself. Her appointments all had an order of how she examined her patients, her medical bag was set with her tonics in alphabetical order. Even her silver hair stayed in perfect place with their pins as she stepped down each stair. Jane felt very fortunate to be following along a woman who took pride in everything that she did.

"Lucky for me, his mum reminds him of how treacherous preg-nancy was for her every time she sees me and my belly. She always sees that Laudy takes extra care of me during my pregnancies. Even though they were nothing like hers."

"As he should," Mrs. Hewitt said assuredly. She grabbed her hat off a hook on the whitewashed wall.

"About my payments," Mrs. Dalton wrung her hands together. "We've been in a bit of a bind with some of our crop and I fear we won't be able to—" She furrowed her pale brows as Mrs. Hewitt held her hand up to keep her from proceeding.

"Never mind payments. Right now, I want you to focus on grow-ing that baby and then we can discuss the matter. We'll see you next week."

"Oh, thank you!" Mrs. Dalton's face lit with relief. "I promise, I'll make those payments as soon as I can."

Just then the front door burst open and a little girl bolted through the door giggling with a younger boy chasing her. Jane did her best to scoot out of the way of the chase but found herself a roadblock to the little girl.

"Dear me!" she exclaimed, gazing down at the freckled little girl who had grabbed hold of her dress to keep balanced. Holding the sweet little child's shoulders steady, Jane looked down into the girl's wide, frightened eyes. "Are you alright?" Jane quickly asked as the girl's red-stained chin began to quiver.

"Josephine Ann Dalton!" Mrs. Dalton exclaimed with horror. "You get in the kitchen right now and fetch me water, vinegar, and a rag!"

The little girl didn't have to be told twice. She sprinted to the kitchen with her brother in tow. Jane was a bit confused as to why the girl needed to fetch vinegar, but a fermented smell began to tinge her nose. She glanced down at her pale-yellow gown and saw two small red handprints stains on the skirt of the cotton material.

"Oh, Miss Sawyer, I'm terribly sorry. Oh, and your fine dress too!" Mrs. Dalton's face paled, her green eyes wide with disbelief. "We'll get the stains out, miss. Don't you worry your pretty little head."

"Please, there's no harm done. I'll be able to get it out when I get home." She offered a reassuring smile. The last thing Jane wanted was to have Mrs. Dalton's stress about her dress as well.

"No, Miss Sawyer. Not beet stains. Your dress will be ruined by the time you get home. If not already," she mumbled.

The little girl, Josephine, came running into the room and placed a rag and a little wooden bowl into her mother's hands.

"How many times did I tell you to stay away from the pickled beets?" she scolded. Rushing to Jane's side, she fervently poured what looked to be muddy water on the rag. Jane looked up at Mrs. Hewitt with surprise as the farmer's wife began to quickly dab the skirt of her gown. Mrs. Hewitt pressed her lips together to hide her smile.

"Just a few dabs, miss, and this will help treat the stains. I apologize. I keep tellin' her to wait till supper, but that girl is always hungry." Jane watched as Mrs. Dalton shook her head. Her auburn strands bounced with the movement. "If I had a gown your size, I'd let you borrow one of mine. But my only good dress is my church dress and I know I was never your size before I was even wed. Such a slender figure you have. But a mighty fine figure—might I add. Just the right curvature," Mrs. Dalton rambled, keeping her focus on the stain. She continued to dab fervently on the material.

Warmth rushed to Jane's cheeks. She didn't know what to say to such remarks. With wide eyes she looked at Mrs. Hewitt in hopes she'd intervene. The woman's eyes tightened and her cheeks rose higher as her lips pursed tighter together. Goodness, was she about to laugh? Jane had never seen the woman laugh.

"Please, Mrs. Dalton, I'd be happy to take care of the rest when I get home," she finally managed to say.

"Very well, at least I managed to get some of the coloring out," Mrs. Dalton said with heavy breaths. "Usually, I can get more out but for some reason it's not working." The woman blew an auburn strand of hair out of her face and straightened upright while holding her back. Jane glanced down and saw purple smudges surrounded by saturated pink and yellow circles. She bit her lip, not sure how she could hide the large wet markings during her walk home.

"I thank you for your thoughtfulness, Mrs. Dalton," Jane said with a smile.

Mrs. Marlow shook her head with disapproval and rested her hands on her waist. "I'm uncertain about having another child."

"You'll do splendid." Mrs. Hewitt softly patted the woman's back. "Send word if you are in need of anything."

"Good day." Mrs. Hewitt bowed her head in farewell.

"Good day, Mrs. Dalton," Jane offered and followed Mrs. Hewitt towards the front yard.

"Good day, ladies! And thank ya." Mrs. Dalton brought her arm up to her forehead and wiped at the glistening sweat that had formed.

"Come, Miss Sawyer," Mrs. Hewitt called over her shoulder. She pulled out a gold, chained pocketwatch from her skirt pocket. "Let's go over today's visit."

Jane was always impressed how fast the woman walked with her short little legs. Hurrying to the woman's side, they hastened their way past the untrimmed yard, toward Mrs. Hewitt's horse on the other side of the picket fence.

"Miss Sawyer, did you notice how anxious Mrs. Dalton became when she mentioned payments?"

Jane leaned her head down towards Mrs. Hewitt as she began her lecture. The woman always gave council as they left each of their patient's homes.

"I did."

"I want you to remember this, a good midwife will never put their patients in a position of stress. Money is something that you have to accept you may never see from some of these ladies. They may be struggling to get by and as payment may offer you some of their eggs, bread, or some of their harvest. Going into this field of work, you will run across situations like this and you'll have to make the choice on whether or not you will continue to be their midwife. But Miss Sawyer." Mrs. Hewitt grabbed her horse's reins and looked at Jane with severity. "That being said, an opportunity to help another in need is more rewarding than money. Trust me."

Jane nodded. "I couldn't agree more, Mrs. Hewitt."

The corner of the woman's mouth began to twitch upward. Before Jane could catch the smile, the woman turned her back on her to step on the mounting stool and jumped onto her horse. Jane grabbed her medical bag from the grass and handed it to the midwife.

"Thank you, my dear," Mrs. Hewitt said, tucking the bag in front of her. "Now, tomorrow we are double booked so I thought it would be best that you see Lady Bingham on your own."

Jane couldn't contain her excitement. "I would love to!" she exclaimed. Mrs. Hewitt looked down at her with a twinkle in her eye. She gave her an approving nod.

"After hearing that Doctor Brown's niece wanted to become a midwife, I knew I couldn't refuse the opportunity to have her apprentice with me. I was curious to see what your skills were and if he had taught you any of his medical procedures. To my delight you've surpassed my expectations on performing checkups and did exceptionally well with the delivery I coached you through last week."

"Coming from you, Mrs. Hewitt, it is an honor to hear such words." Jane pressed her hand to her warm cheek.

"I'll see you Thursday, at noon, at Mrs. Ludwick's. You'll do her checkup and afterwards we'll discuss Lady Bingham's progress." Mrs. Hewitt tightened her hold on the reins.

"Yes, ma'am," Jane said with excitement.

"Good day, Miss Sawyer." The woman tapped her horse with her heel and trotted down the dirt road.

Jane stared after her, stunned by the praise. The way the midwife kept her lips pursed, she had had a feeling the woman hardly gave such approval.

Walking off in the opposite direction from Mrs. Hewitt, Jane headed down the narrow dirt road towards her house. Usually she rode her horse, but on rare days when the weather permitted, she preferred to walk. The road was surrounded by thick forest on one side and beautiful farm fields on the other. The three miles to her home would go by fast with the beauty that surrounded her. She strolled along, enjoying the birds soaring and singing above her. Their joyous songs reminded her of the birds on Saint Helena, their tunes were always bright and cheerful. A gentle, cool breeze blew by and she caught a strong scent of the fermented beets. She glanced down at her dress. It was the plainest dress she owned and wore it specifically on days when she did her patient checkups. A lot of her other gowns were a bit more fashionable and she didn't want any of the patients feeling uncomfortable when her dresses cost her the same as some of their monthly wages. She brushed a loose strand of hair off her shoulder and stopped as the earthy fragment grew stronger. Looking in both directions of the road to be certain she was the only one on it, she lifted her gown closer to her nose. There was a tiny hint of vinegar on her dress as beets and dirt filled her nose. Jane chuckled with disbelief and picked wildflowers to cover the large stain. All of that dabbing and talk of her figure for nothing but a ruined dress. That is unless Millie could help her treat it.

"Oh, Millie won't be thrilled about this stain," she muttered to herself. Eager to treat the stain, she quickened her pace and rounded a corner.

A gentleman with broad shoulders sat finely on a sleek black horse. Her heart took a sudden gallop and her steps faltered. Squinting her eyes from the sun's glare, she peered at the gentleman while trying to discern if he had the same coloring of hair as James. *Could it be him? He certainly had the same broad shoulders yet this gentleman was slenderer in size.* Gathering her pace, she discussed the matter in her head. *Then again, muscle loss was to be expected during recovery.* Hope filled her. There was no harm in discovering if this mystery gentleman was indeed him. Biting her lip to keep from calling out, she grabbed her skirts and quickened her steps towards the rider. With the sun shining in her eyes, she couldn't make out the gentleman's complexion nor hair color, especially since his top hat covered most of his head.

Curiously she watched the horse pull the reins and walk towards the tall grass on the side of the road.

"Come on, Daisy," the gentleman said with irritation. The horse refused to listen as it kept fighting the reins. With an exasperated huff, and a flick of its tail, Daisy began to graze.

Her heart slowed to disappointment. That wasn't James's voice. James's voice was deeper. Releasing her skirts, she maneuvered to the side to pass. She just needed to stop thinking of him. Feeling irked to have allowed her thoughts to get the best of her, she swung the flowers against her dress.

The gentleman pulled harder on the reins and the horse grunted in protest but finally obliged and proceeded to walk.

"That's it. Good girl. No, no, come on, Daisy," the gentleman objected with a grumble. Daisy lowered her head to stop and take another bite. "I have carrots in the stables. You can eat then."

He pulled firmly on the reins, leading the horse towards the middle of the road. Avoiding being stomped on, Jane cautiously stepped off the road to pass. Humorously she watched as the horse had stopped again, refusing to move.

"Excuse me," she said to make the irritated rider aware she was passing, with hopes she wasn't trampled on.

"Miss," the rider greeted and tipped his hat.

Sulking in her disappointment, she didn't glance in his direction. Her eyes trailed down to her skirt where her stains greeted her with a bright welcome. Swiftly she covered her dress as much as she could with her flowers, grateful the gentleman couldn't see them from where he sat. The sound of horse's hooves began to clamp against the dirt next to her. From the corner of her eye the black horse was drawing nearer. For a moment she was a bit confused as to why the gentleman began to ride so close to her, but it dawned on her as she watched the horse stretch its neck towards her flowers and began nibbling on the petals.

She smiled with relief. "Oh, why by all means, help yourself."

"I'm terribly sorry, miss," said the flustered rider as he yanked on the reins. "I don't know what has gotten into her today."

Jane briefly glanced up at the gentleman only to notice that he appeared younger than most gentlemen in the area. His green eyes reflected his repentant tone. She offered him a small smile. "It's quite alright. I'll pick more flowers along the way."

Not wanting to linger with the gentleman, she released her flowers to the horse and carried on. But what happened next was not what she expected would happen. With one long stride, Daisy stretched her lips to Jane's skirt, and began nibbling on her dress!

"Gracious!" she exclaimed, pulling her skirt from the horse's lips.

"Whoa!" the man yelled. Daisy's ears twisted back, but she refused to listen as she eagerly pursued Jane and clasped the beet stain portion of the dress between her teeth. Managing to free the material out of the horse's mouth, Jane pushed Daisy's muzzle away to give herself distance.

"Eh," she grimaced as Daisy snorted on her arm as though in protest. The gentleman jumped down and ran in front of the horse to separate her from Jane.

"I'm so sorry, miss! Daisy! Stop!" he ordered as Daisy proceeded to stomp her hooves with determination.

Holding the dry patches of the skirt in her hand, Jane looked down at the beet stain that now had horse saliva mixed with pieces of chewed up flowers and grass. *Millie is really going to be disappointed.*

"I suppose that's what I deserve after having beets on my dress," she mumbled to herself, wiping the thick mucus Daisy shared with her off her arm.

"I'm terribly sorry, miss! I don't know what has gotten into her," the man continued with a quiver in his voice. "Did she hurt you?"

Feeling his gaze on her, Jane quickly folded the material of her skirt on top of each other to hide parts of the stain. Warmth spread to her cheeks, and she tried her best to avoid meeting the eager gentleman's eye.

"Not at all." She kept her response short, feeling desperate to disappear from the situation. Above, a crow cawed, and Jane couldn't help but feel it was laughing at her.

"I'm truly sorry."

"It's quite alright," she called over her shoulder, eager to hide the horrid display from the stranger.

"Just a moment," the man called to her. Hurrying to her side, he yanked Daisy's reins to keep up.

"As much as I enjoyed getting well acquainted with your horse, I don't hold ill feelings," Jane said, hardly glancing his way. The tall man chuckled and she felt her eyes flick back on him as she now caught a glimpse at how handsome he appeared. He quickly removed his hat and offered her a charming smile while his green eyes sparkled in the sunlight. His nose was perfectly straight, his cheekbones high with long sideburns that were neatly trimmed on the side of his cheeks.

"Pray, tell me your name, miss?"

She looked his way, nervously picking up her pace. "Miss Jane Sawyer, sir," she replied, never daring to inquire of his name. His long strides matched her steps with ease. She could feel his eyes staring at her as she looked ahead.

"Are you from here, Miss Sawyer?" he asked casually, placing his hat back on his head. She could hear his smile as he spoke. Not wanting to explain to the gentleman how long she'd lived in the area, she said, "My uncle and I live in a cottage, down the way." The large oak tree on the corner waved its large branches towards her. It was her mile marker from her house.

The man continued to cheerfully address her, "I moved to Oxford a few months ago, so I still find myself meeting neighbors as I'm in London often for either Parliament or other official business."

"I see," she responded politely.

Leaves rustled above them on tree branches that hovered over the road. They walked in silence as Jane didn't know what more to say. She hadn't been alone in a gentleman's presence since her time in Saint Helena. Not that she hadn't had a few gentlemen who had asked to call on her—which she conveniently denied due to her busy schedule with Mrs. Hewitt. But truth be known, it was how she preferred it. It was cruel to give false hope to the gentlemen callers when her heart was set on another. Her uncle on the other hand was becoming more anxious about her passing up opportunities, while he was worried James didn't hold the same esteem towards her as she did him. It was silly for him to even worry. Of course, James felt the same as she . . . didn't he? Being in the presence of this gentleman, her doubts surfaced. Usually, she was able to brush aside any uncertainties in stride, but this was different. It began to seep into her thoughts like a fog spreading across the fields at the governor's plantation. She knew he wanted to keep in touch. When they had said their goodbyes, she knew his feelings were deeper than friendship and her hope was as they wrote to each other, perhaps something more could blossom. But without any letters, there was nothing to hope for. She clasped her hands in front of her to keep from playing with the ribbon hanging from her bonnet—and to conceal the mess on her dress.

"I normally don't make assumptions, but are you by chance the niece of Doctor Duncan Brown?" He gazed at her with curiosity.

"I am." She briefly smiled, grateful for the distracting question. She always enjoyed hearing people speak of their knowledge of her uncle. The gentleman's face lit up when she looked at him.

"I've been eager to meet his acquaintance," he said with a smile. "I've heard many marvelous things."

Jane offered a polite nod and kept her gaze on the trees ahead of them. She didn't like how he was becoming more enamored in conversing with her.

"Then you're the apprentice of Mrs. Hewitt who's been tending to Lady Veronica Bingham. I have heard you two visit the manor, but I must admit I was detained to make my introductions."

The tightness in Jane's chest released as she registered who the gentleman was. "Why, you must be Lord Bingham! Lady Bingham has told me so much about you." She relaxed her stance and released her breath as she realized she was speaking to Lady Bingham's husband. All the minuscule feelings of flattery immediately disappeared. It was such a relief knowing the gentleman had no regards to her other than as his wife's midwife. She had recalled Lady Bingham mentioning how her husband was out of town frequently and for long periods of time. "How is Lady Bingham feeling?"

Feeling more at ease, she relaxed her guard, and offered a smile. For a moment he didn't reply. His eyes fixated on her. It was as though he was at odds with himself. Daisy stretched her lips towards Jane's skirt, breaking him from whatever she saw cross his face. "She is well," he finally replied, shoving Daisy's muzzle away from her.

Jane bit the corner of her lip as she tried to discern if he was being truthful, his hesitation made her doubtful of his reply. She decided she'd have to be extra assertive at her visit with Lady Bingham in case there was something the lord wasn't telling her.

"Tell me, Miss Sawyer, how are you and your uncle liking Oxford? If I do recall, Lady Bingham mentioned you had traveled here from Bombay."

"We did. We've been enjoying our time here, quite well." At least she'd been enjoying meeting many women during her visits with Mrs. Hewitt. The dances that she'd been forced to attend were usually all the same. The gentlemen took extreme measures to outshine each other and flaunt their money and status in society. Little did they know, she never was interested in any of those things, nor any of them as a person.

Lord Bingham stared at her a moment before blinking and quickly nodded with satisfaction. "I'm glad to hear it." He adjusted his hands on his reins as Daisy drew closer to them and nudged Jane's side with her nose.

"Daisy," he scolded. "I do apologize, but she is my sister's horse. I had left mine to rest in the stables."

He pushed Daisy's muzzle away again as she attempted to get closer to Jane.

"I'm afraid the beets on my dress have caught her attention." She smiled at the beautiful horse and then to Lord Bingham.

"Is that what it is?" he exclaimed, as though relieved.

"Why, yes." She looked at him confused, unsure what else he'd think it was. "One of Mrs. Dalton's children had helped herself to the jar of pickled beets and upon running into the house, collided into me." She laughed, shaking her head at how the little girl looked at her with such surprise.

Lord Bingham chuckled and scratched behind his head. "I must confess after discovering you were Mrs. Hewitt's apprentice, I thought that perhaps . . ." He paused then chuckled again only to hide his amusement with a straight face. "Forgive me, Miss Sawyer, but I just assumed you were coming home after a delivery."

Jane's eyes widened at the gentleman and gazed down at her yellow dress that was stained with purple and pink splotches. Warmth spread to her cheeks at the thought of how disgraceful she must have appeared. Did he suppose she caught the baby with her gown?

"Please, I didn't mean to embarrass you," he rushed. He fidgeted more with the reins in his hands. "It's not that terrible. I only . . . I . . . I'm not doing well with this. Do you mind?"

Jane raised her brow when he offered her the reins. Hesitantly she accepted them, uncertain as to why he was giving them to her. The lord hurried to the side of the road, gathering long stems of flowers in his hand, he began to tug and pull at them until he managed to yank a handful of wildflowers. Taking long strides back to her, he collected the reins from her hands.

"For you," he said, handing her the bouquet. She couldn't help but smile as half of them were still attached to their roots. She held the flowers away from her already soiled dress as chunks of dirt fell to the road. Lord Bingham took a breath and quickly shook the roots in Jane's hand.

"My apologies, I uh . . ." He patted a root for good measure then looked up at Jane. "I realized Daisy had sabotaged your, uh, concealment so it's the least I can do." His green eyes were bright as he appeared desperate for her acceptance.

"Thank you," she smiled. "And I suppose I can see how one would think that, my lord."

He let out a hearty laugh and nervously wiped his forehead. "No, Miss Sawyer. But thank you for being polite for my foolish assumption."

She looked away as she had caught his gaze. There was an odd way he had looked at her. She became quiet as she wasn't certain what to make of the situation. He wasn't flirtatious. He wasn't overly friendly, except maybe perhaps the flowers, but then again it was to make up for Daisy eating hers. She quickened her pace. Peering at him from time to time, she noticed that he too appeared as disgruntled as she felt. His strong jaw was tight and his eyes squinted as though he were deep in thought. Perhaps, she was the one being too friendly?

Jane had thought she was being reserved but perhaps not enough? She gazed past the tall oak trees that were scattered on her uncle's property. A carriage that she didn't recognize pulled into the drive and stopped in front of their two-story cottage. She quickened her stride, curious as to who had arrived. She watched as a woman stepped out of the black carriage with a large feather bonnet. Another woman, who appeared younger with a smaller bluebonnet followed suit. Jane's heart leapt into her throat when she recognized the young lady's golden locks as they shimmered in the sun. A grin spread across her face.

"Miss Sawyer, there's something I need to tell you." She heard Lord Bingham begin to say to her. "About my relations to Lady Bingham."

"Forgive me, my lord," she interrupted, "but there's someone I must see." She dipped into a quick curtsy. "It was a pleasure making your acquaintance."

Lifting a section of her dress to prevent herself from tripping, she quickened her walk to a half run down the road towards her drive. "And please give Lady Bingham my regards!" she called over her shoulder. She caught a glimpse of Lord Bingham with his top hat pressed against his cravat and Daisy nibbling at his boots. He smiled with a humorous gleam in his eyes and watched her hurry away. Jane ignored the oddness of his behavior and began sprinting down the pebbled drive towards the two ladies.

"Jane!" The young woman yelled, waving her white parasol through the air. She laughed as Sophie Kensington, her best friend from Bombay, started running towards her.

"Sophie!" Jane yelled back. She ran faster, ignoring her bonnet as it bounced off her head onto the tiny rocks behind her. The last time the two of them ever ran freely like they were was when they were children running through the coffee fields in Bombay. Sophie's feathered bonnet slid off her head exposing more of her beautiful blonde locks. Her traveler's cloak whipped behind her legs. Lady Kensington stood next to the carriage with graceful poise and smiled at the two before carrying out her instructions to the coachman.

"Jane, my dear friend!" Sophie exclaimed breathlessly with open arms. Her friend abruptly lowered her arms and brought her hands to her mouth.

"Jane, oh my, oh! Is that blood?" She came to a stammering stop. Her round emerald eyes widened as she studied Jane's dress. Her thick dark brows raised with uncertainty.

"Not you too!" Jane laughed, gasping for her breath. "It's beet juice!"

Sophie's round face relaxed and she laughed with relief with open arms to her. The two friends embraced each other, giggling with joy.

"Sophie, how I missed you!" Jane exclaimed, drawing in a breath. Sophie drew back as Jane wiped at her tears of joy. "Why wasn't I informed that you were coming?!"

"I'm so glad you weren't!" Sophie clapped her gloved hands with satisfaction. "I had told father to be sure to write to your uncle and say that this was going to be a surprise."

"It certainly was," Jane said, still gathering her breath. "How long do I get to have the pleasure of your company?"

Her friend's smile faltered. "Unfortunately, two nights and then we are to continue our journey to mama's sister's home in Birmingham."

"That is too bad," Jane let out with a heavy sigh. "But I'm excited to have you for any time at all."

Sophie squeezed Jane's hand and looked down at the replacement flowers Lord Bingham had given her. She raised Jane's hand to get a better glimpse of the stems. Running her fingers over the roots, she laughed.

"I see nothing's changed with the gentlemen," she teased with a smirk.

"Please." Jane playfully swung her bouquet towards her. "They're to replace what his horse happily ate."

"Either you're playing naive or you're hopelessly a lost cause," Sophie declared, rolling her eyes.

"A lost cause?" Jane looked at her with offense, though a smile crept on her face as she couldn't help but find the humor.

"What was the phrase Elaine used to tease you with?" Sophie asked as she tapped her chin.

Jane shook her head with a smile. "I'm not sure what you're talking about."

"Oh yes!" Her face brightened and she playfully waved her hand in the air with confidence as Elaine used to when they were younger. "When you have it, you have it." She practically sang the words, mimicking Elaine.

"No." Jane laughed and hid her face in her hand from embarrassment.

"Oh yes," Sophie teased with a nudge.

"I can't believe I had forgotten about that." She shook her head and laughed again from the memory.

At the time, Elaine had full confidence that every young man in Bombay had his eye on Jane. When Jane passed a few gentlemen on her way towards Sophie and Elaine in the market, the men tipped their hats at her—as gentlemen usually do.

But Elaine had to prove a point and with a smug smile, she had looked at Sophie and Jane and waved her hand in the air with a grand gesture saying, "When you have it, you have it," before she unintentionally tripped over a rope holding a merchant's tent. Jane bit her lip as she could picture the scene as though it happened last week. Even though the remark was directed at her, Elaine certainly had the charisma and charm that had gentlemen rushing to her side to give her aid.

"Well Jane, you still have it. The men are like little flies hovering and fighting over a prized possession." Sophie's fingers danced up Jane's arm. Jane playfully swatted her hand away.

"Not in the least." She gave her a look of warning. Her friend laughed at the expression.

"Come," Jane said with a chuckle. "I need to retrieve my bonnet. Then we'll see that you're settled in your room."

"My room? You mean your room? I believe we're sharing." Sophie looped her arm through Jane's and gave an excited squeeze. With her home being smaller than the home in Bombay, they had only one bedchamber available for guests, which under the circumstances was reserved for Sophie's mother.

"We shall never get any sleep, shall we?" Jane smiled, knowing their late-night chats would go into the early morning hours.

"It's been over a year, my friend. I don't see how that's possible." Sophie grinned at Jane who couldn't help but smile in agreement. She didn't realize how much she needed her friend until they ran into each other's arms. Jane felt lighter as the looming doubt that fogged her mind brightened.

The two ladies stepped onto the stone walkway that led to the quaint home. Her uncle decided that with their short duration at Oxford they'd settle in the countryside where it was a little bit quieter. She loved the peace and serenity it brought as it helped balance the reverberating evenings and weekends when she attended many social gatherings with him.

"Forgive me for not asking sooner, but how was your voyage?" Jane asked.

"It was quite uneventful. No seasickness, no storms and uh . . ." Sophie paused to give Jane a sly look. "No handsome captain rescuing me from Jamestown's harbor."

Heat rushed to Jane's cheeks from the memory of her arrival at Jamestown, Saint Helena. She had written Sophie, telling her about the horrendous storms they had sailed through to get to the island. The treacherous waves left her a bit off balance causing her to gracefully misstep into the harbor. Thankfully, Captain James was there to rescue her before she drowned. That was such a miserable yet exhilarating day.

Her heart sank. The warmth in her cheeks began to fade as the blood drained from her face. She slowed her steps and glanced at Sophie, uncertain what to say. Every barrier she had placed to protect herself from her reality had fallen. She crossed her arms and pressed them close to her body, feeling exposed. All the ache her heart had carried since her departure from Jamestown emerged. Her friend stared at her with concern.

She forced a smile and with a tease she managed to say, "That is too bad."

Opening the door to her home, she walked through the threshold. It was frustrating how James kept slipping into her thoughts, more so today than the past few weeks. Sophie continued to peer at her as though she was trying to decipher her reaction—not that she blamed her friend. Jane needed to regain her composure before Sophie began to interrogate her on the topic.

"Let's see that you're settled into our room, shall we?" she asked, hoping to rid her intrusive thoughts.

Sophie gave her a soft smile, though uncertainty spilled from her expression.

"Goodness, my sweet Jane!" Lady Kensington approached the two young women from a small parlor to the foyer where they stood. Her blue muslin dress swayed effortlessly around her as she walked to them. Her tall, graceful frame gave Jane the impression of a Greek goddess from childhood stories. Her blonde curls were pinned perfectly on her head and her brown eyes sparkled along with her beautiful smile. The resemblance of Sophie to her mother was so striking to Jane. They could have been twins had it not been for the maturity in Lady Kensington's appearance and the green of Sophie's eyes. The woman took long strides towards Jane with extended arms and lovingly embraced her. She felt herself melting from the woman's comforting touch. Her familiar floral perfume brought a sense of home with her hug. She took a deep breath, inhaling the sweet familiarity.

"Lady Kensington, it is so nice to see you again." Jane smiled as the woman drew back.

"It's wonderful seeing you," Lady Kensington's rich voice sang as she peered into Jane's eyes. "If it were berry season, I would have guessed you had a run-in with a bush," she stated humorously, her gaze trailed down to Jane's dress.

Jane chuckled at Lady Kensington. "You're the first to have guessed the closest, my lady." She perked an accusing brow at Sophie. Her eyes narrowed in protest.

"Jane, you mustn't blame me for assuming otherwise," Sophie defended, removing her traveler's cloak. Their butler, Neville, appeared and grabbed the cloak and bonnet from Sophie. "With your passion in life, one would only assume the worst. Besides," she turned her attention to Lady Kensington, "if you were to have seen her running towards you. I believe you would have thought the same."

"I can only imagine." Lady Kensington's smile broadened. "Pray tell, what is it?"

"Pickled beets," Jane sighed.

"Ah, I fear this may be the last you see of your dress."

"I was afraid of that," she replied, defeatedly.

Lady Kensington gave her a sympathetic smile and stepped towards Sophie to fix an out-of-place curl. "Jane, I was informed by your butler that your uncle shall be returning home within the hour. I do believe we plan on attending a musical medley tonight at the chancellor's home, is that still, correct?"

"It is, your ladyship."

"Splendid." Lady Kensington gave an approving smile. "Hurry along ladies and get yourselves ready. We do not have much time."

Jane dipped into a small curtsy and led Sophie up the stairs to her room.

Chapter Ten

Applause rippled throughout the room and Jane found herself joining the audience as they all began to take to their feet. Cheers were offered when the pianist took his bow.

As the performance commenced, Sophie and Jane linked arms trailing behind Lady Kensington and her uncle towards the grand hall. They squeezed together through a narrow doorway to where a small orchestra played while many people mingled.

"Doctor Brown!" Lady Griftson exclaimed, fluttering her fan across her face. The chancellor's wife excused herself from an older couple and hurried towards Jane's uncle.

Squeezing Sophie's arm, Jane subtly leaned towards her friend.

"Brace yourself," she warned under her breath. "The lady is determined to play matchmaker."

Guests strolled around them as they stood at the edge of their party. Jane was about to explain further what was to come when she was suddenly taken aback by what she saw. Her friend, who despised being a prospect to any lady's agenda, began to run her hand over her styled curls and adjust the pink sleeves on her shoulders. The unusual reaction of primping left Jane speechless. Could Sophie really be thrilled about the prospect?

Meeting her eye, Sophie began to whisper with a smirk, "Come, Jane, it's not that I'm desperate to be married. I'm just excited to be conversing with one of these noble gentlemen about anything other than the war."

Jane bit her lip to keep from groaning. Clearing her throat, she leaned towards Sophie while keeping a watchful eye on Lady Griftson who was conversing with Sophie's mother. She knew it was only a matter of time before the lady would want to examine the new prospect in her matchmaking game.

"Then you best not tell the gentlemen where you're from," Jane said, lowering her voice. Sophie's brows raised above her emerald gaze with confusion. "These gentlemen are no different than the men back home," Jane assured. "Though, in my opinion, they're far worse, for they have no experience in fighting a war, but speak as though they were in the frontlines."

Sophie's mouth dropped. "Surely, it is not that bad."

Jane knew how Sophie dreaded any topic of war, as she had experienced firsthand the horrors of bloodshed. It was assumed that the admiral's daughter would somehow share her father's passion for fighting for England and all Her glory, but that couldn't be further from the truth. Sophie wanted nothing more than for the war to end, and that included all conversations regarding it. After experiencing years of bright explosions lighting up the night sky from battles that were too close to home, and sporadic attacks in the market from the Mysore, that killed innocent lives, Jane understoof her friend's apprehensions

"It is, and then some. To avoid talk of war, it's best if you avoid questions on where you're visiting from," Jane whispered when she noticed Lady Griftson glancing their way.

Jane knew firsthand how mentioning Bombay or Saint Helena Island were trigger words that led to full discussions of how people knew a fellow who had served in the area or had lost his life from an attack.

"I'd rather speak of this gloomy weather than talk of the French or the Mysore." Sophie groaned. "It's like a plague."

Patting Sophie's hand in support, she leaned closer to her as people squeezed past them. "Then direct the questions towards the gentlemen and you'll do splendidly. I've found most gentlemen thrive on talking about themselves," she teased truthfully, giving her friend a gentle nudge.

A sudden smile spread across Sophie's face. "I have an inkling this challenge may end up being very entertaining." Her green eyes sparkled, lighting her face. "Jane, our task for the evening is to do everything possible to dodge any question regarding our home in Bombay. The first one to surrender that bit of information whether it's about you or I will owe the other person—"

"The fluffiest pillow?" Jane cut in with a laugh.

Sophie smiled, "And the softest side of the bed."

Knowing the bed was equally soft, Jane quickly agreed. "Done. Though, most of the attendees know where I'm from."

"Then we will have to mingle with those that you do not know," Sophie said while adjusting her gloves.

"Fine," Jane agreed, fully aware that if Lady Griftson had her way, she'd introduce Jane and Sophie to a group of single gentlemen that she had never been acquainted with. As if on cue, Lady Griftson turned her attention from Uncle Duncan and Sophie's mother to them.

"Oh," she purred, slowly waving her fan across her rouge face. "Lady Kensington, why this must be your daughter. Such a stunning beauty. I can see the resemblance between you two." The lady closed her lace fan and held it firmly in her hand as she looked Sophie up and down. Sophie's mother subtly smiled with pride.

"Lady Griftson, may I introduce my lovely daughter, Miss Sophie Kensington." Lady Kensington elegantly gestured her gloved hand towards her daughter. "Sophie, this is Lady Griftson, the wife to Chancellor Griftson of Oxford University."

"How do you do?" Sophie dipped into a curtsy.

Lady Griftson's smile broadened. Jane fidgeted with a button on her glove as she could see a plan brewing behind the lady's twinkling eyes. Usually, she never liked the lady's mischief, but with Sophie by her side and having the new challenge in a small game, she found herself eager to begin.

"And Miss Sawyer, it's such a delight to see you again." Lady Griftson nodded to Jane. Her tone was less ecstatic than the one she used with Sophie. She could only assume it was due to the lady's failed attempts at finding Jane an eligible companion. Not that it was the lady's fault. She had made many valiant efforts in finding agreeable gentlemen, but they were left with disappointment at Jane's lack of interest. It was hard for her to discern if it was due to a bad batch of potential suitors or if it was because she kept comparing them to James. Either way, he made it difficult for the gentlemen to compete for her attention.

"My lady." Jane dipped into a curtsy of acknowledgment.

"Most excellent," Lady Griftson murmured as though she had settled on a plan. She threw her fan against her palm and smiled brightly at Uncle Duncan and Lady Kensington. "Would you two mind if I borrowed these young ladies for a moment? There are a few attendees I would be delighted to introduce them to."

Jane caught Uncle Duncan's humorous expression as he brought his hand to his mouth to cover a chuckle. After months of many social events and conversing with the lady, he knew how Jane dreaded being trapped in one of Lady Kensington's snares of introductions.

"Of course," he replied, seeing that Jane didn't give him a look of distress.

Sophie's face lit when he mother also agreed, but she smoothly kept her smile small. Yet she squeezed Jane's arm, as though she were ready to start a race. *Why she's practically bouncing in her slippers.*

"Well come along, the night has yet to begin." Lady Griftson motioned to them to follow her with a wave of her hand. Following along, as though they were led by a rope, Jane watched as long feathers bounced in the lady's silver curls. It was remarkable how the lady parted the sea of people as she neared. The guests smiled politely with a bow and curtsy but never pressed to start conversing with the lady as she bid them a quick wave of greeting with her fan. *They obviously sensed she was on a mission—a dreadful mission.* Jane started to regret her acceptance of Sophie's challenge. Many of the older guests smiled or whispered behind their fans while they watched their procession. They clearly knew of their hostess's pursuit. Jane forced herself to hold her chin high and kept her eyes on the woman's feathers. It was as though the *ton* were speculating which of the two ladies were going to find their companion by the end of the night.

"Is there something out of place on my gown?" Sophie whispered to her. Jane bit back a smile. The room buzzed around them with fervent chatter, Sophie could have spoken at a normal volume and nobody would have heard her. Fortunately, those who looked at them were very few in comparison to the number in attendance at that evening's musical concert.

"No. I've found they like to keep tabs on who we are and who we'll be paired with in the coming weeks," Jane said through a smile as she recognized one of the women in the crowd as Mrs. Hewitt's patient. The woman nodded warmly towards Jane in acknowledgment.

"Aren't they intrusive," Sophie stated, appalled.

"Are you surprised?" Jane asked, laughing. "They are no different than those from home."

"I suppose," Sophie said, still speculating. They approached the back of the room. A large, green plant on a column fanned out in front of a gold-trimmed wall, camouflaging the view of a gentleman that had his back to them.

Sophie quickly hid her disapproval as they came around the plant, exposing not one but three men in black evening attire.

"Good evening gentlemen," Lady Griftson sang with delight.

The three gentlemen abruptly stopped their conversation, smiles from their former conversation slipping as they turned their attention towards them.

"Lady Griftson," answered the tallest man in the group. Jane recognized none of them—it would seem Sophie's game was about to commence. He quickly nodded his head respectfully to her. The ruffled brown hair and thick sideburns made him appear to be the more adventurous one of the lot. Jane carefully studied each of the men as she was trying to decide if they were the type who were open to Lady Griftson's matchmaking or if they were annoyed at the prospect.

The two other gentlemen were attractive in their own manner, both the same height, but one held a larger midriff than the other. The rounder fellow scrunched his crooked nose as he studied both Jane and Sophie. He must only want the enjoyment of his friends and not the attention of young ladies.

"May I introduce you to Miss Jane Sawyer and Miss Sophie Kensington?"

Each of the gentlemen bowed to them as though on cue.

"Ladies," Lady Griftson purred. "May I introduce to you Mr. Andrew Cady." The ruffled brown-haired gent lifted his hand to his heart and bowed while keeping a steady eye on Sophie.

"Lord Peter Reeves." The rounder fellow who was closest to the plant, offered a curt nod. He looked to the ground, avoiding any eye contact with any of the ladies.

"And Mr. Taylor Burgess," Lady Griftson finished with glee. The thin-haired gentleman flashed Jane a charming smile and quickly winked at her when Lady Griftson turned her attention from him. Captain James's face flashed before her eyes as she noticed the gentleman's dimple. Any confidence that she had towards the challenge dispersed as her heart staggered. She looked down at her gloves, deciding they were worth more of her attention than the bachelors in front of them.

She wanted nothing more than to support Sophie in her endeavor of having an enjoyable conversation with a gentleman, but with James's dimpled smile in mind it would be very difficult.

"Oh, dear me," Lady Griftson rang next to her. "Looks to me that my husband needs my assistance." Jane snapped her head up and stared wide-eyed at their hostess. *Surely, she wasn't going to leave them?* Usually, the lady waited until the conversations started before she left Jane hanging dry with a gentleman.

"You must forgive me." Lady Griftson waved her jewel-covered hand in the air as though this were a minor hiccup. "I can only be stretched so thin tonight." She chuckled as everyone smiled politely at her. Everyone that was, except for Jane. Jane clasped Sophie's elbow ready to lead them away and into the crowd.

"We best be going too," she replied with a smile. She was beginning to feel extremely uncomfortable by the thin-haired man's flirtatious stare. Sophie glanced at Jane with a questionable brow.

"No, not at all. Stay." Lady Griftson patted Jane's arm as though she settled the matter. "You all enjoy yourselves." The lady's eyes sparkled as she walked away from them and disappeared into the large gathering of finely dressed guests.

"Miss Kensington," the ruffle-haired Mr. Cady said. "Are you from around here?"

Sophie gave a quick excited glance at Jane and smiled towards the gentleman. "No, I'm passing through on my way to see my aunt. Are you fine gentlemen from Oxford?"

"I'm from London," Mr. Cady replied, running his white-gloved hand over his sideburns, "but these two hail from Oxford." He addressed both gentlemen to his left—the crooked-nosed Lord Reeves who crossed his arms over his round midriff and Mr. Burgess who continued to study Jane.

"Miss Sawyer, are you from here then?" Mr. Burgess asked with a smile that brought out his dimples. Her heart sank. Jane ignored the resemblance of his dimples to James's and looked at how he strategically combed over his hair to hide the thin areas.

"Yes, my uncle and I live a few miles from here." She glanced coolly at Sophie whose corner of her mouth quivered as though she tried to not smile.

"I don't believe I've ever seen you in Oxford before. Have you lived here long?" Mr. Burgess pressed with another dimpled smile. A server holding a silver tray and flute glasses approached them. Each took a glass and turned their attention back to Jane. Sophie raised her brow waiting for her to miss her chance of winning the challenge.

"Not at all. But I find myself enjoying the country immensely." Quickly raising her glass to her lips, Jane took a sip to keep from saying anything else.

"You're from the city?" the serious Lord Reeves asked. He peered down his crooked nose at Jane with beady, dark eyes.

"No," she smiled politely, lowering her glass. "I've been to London on a few occasions though. Have any of you been to the operas?"

The gentlemen exchanged a curious look between each other. Ignoring their exchange, Jane glanced around them at the unfamiliar mingling people. She and her uncle had attended many social gatherings in Oxford but the chancellor and his wife drew a more extravagant crowd. A more refined bunch than she was accustomed to. The women wore exquisite gowns with their hair done to perfection. The jewels were by far the most extravagant pieces and their spouses appeared very dignified in their tailored suits. In Bombay, many of the men's suits were either too loose due to the diet change from England or too tight as they discovered a new specialty treat, like pedas. Many of the English officers swiftly took to the sweet, doughy desserts.

"I've attended the operas many times, Miss Sawyer," Mr. Cady mused, drawing Jane's attention back to him. "Miss Kensington, do they have operas where you're from?"

Sophie took a sip from her glass then smiled. "Nothing in comparison to London's."

"And where exactly did you say you're from?" Lord Reeves asked as though annoyed.

"A place that's too boring to discuss," Sophie replied and flashed them a sweet smile. "Tell me, Lord Reeves, what is it that you enjoy doing in Oxford?"

The gentleman stared at her with more annoyance as he tightened his beady eyes. Smugly, he raised a brow and replied. "Things that are too boring to discuss."

Sophie laughed, ignoring his snide remark. "My dear lord, how dreadful. Hopefully, Mr. Cady and Mr. Burgess can help change that."

Jane took another sip of her drink as their challenge was becoming nothing more than a disaster. Thankfully, Mr. Cady and Mr. Burgess chuckled at Sophie's remark.

"You set yourself up for that one, Reeves." Mr. Burgess slapped Lord Reeves across his shoulder. His dimples deepened as Lord Reeves appeared to have growled at the man. Jane's heart stammered and she quickly studied the gold trim design on the wall.

"You'll have to forgive our friend. He doesn't like decoding things," Mr. Cady replied, taking a sip of his wine.

"But Cady and I love a challenge," Mr. Burgess continued, catching Jane's eye to give her another wink. "From what I gathered, with where you're from, there's not much countryside, the operas are nothing compared to London'd, and it's quite boring."

Jane glanced at Sophie knowing quite well their game flopped as the gentlemen were determined to guess their origins. Sophie's jaw tightened when she gave her a sideways glance.

"It would have to be a factory town," Mr. Cady mused.

"Yes, but which one?" Mr. Burgess smirked.

"My guess is it wouldn't be a coastal town," Mr. Cady continued, rubbing the side of his fluffy sideburns as he pondered.

A familiar gentleman's voice rang out to the side of Jane, causing her to jump. "Good evening gentlemen. Ladies."

Jane peered from the corner of her eye at Lady Bingham's husband. The gentleman gave a charming smile to each of them and paused on her. She darted her eyes away from him to look over his shoulder for his wife, but she was nowhere to be seen.

"Ah, I thought I spotted you earlier—" Mr. Burgess began to greet the gentleman at the same time Sophie whispered into Jane's ear. "I think it's time for us to make our escape."

Jane nodded in agreement but before they could offer an excuse, Mr. Burgess extended his hand to them. Jane blew out her breath wishing more than anything to leave. "May I introduce to you Miss Kensington and Miss Sawyer from where-we've-yet-to-discover?"

Lord Bingham offered a bow and smiled at Jane. "How do you do Miss Kensington? Miss Sawyer." She offered a small smile of acknowledgment.

"Mr. Burgess, I'm afraid I have the advantage in your quest," Lady Bingham's husband said with a small smile. The three gentlemen looked to him with intrigue. "You see I already know where Miss Sawyer is from and after seeing the greeting she exchanged with Miss Kensington earlier this afternoon, I have a hunch she's from the same city." He smiled at Sophie who looked at him as though impressed. Jane subtly nudged Sophie's elbow to draw her attention. Glancing her way, Sophie caught Jane tapping her finger against her glass twice with a slight head shake as she exchanged their secret code that indicated the gentleman was not available. Sophie acknowledged with a sip from her glass.

"Pray tell," Mr. Cady pressed. "I'm most curious about their whereabouts." Giving a broad smile, he looked at Sophie. Lord Reeves scoffed with annoyance.

Lord Bingham's thick brows raised with curiosity. Jane took a sip from her glass to avoid catching his gaze.

"I can't let you fellows have it that easy," Lord Bingham said with a taunting smile. "If the ladies are making you guess, then I'm afraid you're on your own."

Lowering her glass, she looked up at Lord Bingham with surprise. A feeling of respect filled her. He gazed down at her, giving her a small smile.

On the other side of her, Sophie laughed. "It's really not much of a secret."

"Then you must enlighten us. For surely, I've never seen such beauty like I have tonight," Mr. Cady boldly stated. Hiding a chuckle behind her glass, Jane couldn't help but see how Mr. Cady resembled that of a love-struck puppy with his tousled hair and thick sideburns. He even had the chocolate brown, puppy eyes that looked to her as though he'd obey her every command.

She smiled at Sophie as her friend's mouth fell for a brief second before she collected herself. From what Jane knew of her friend, Sophie never had a gentleman speak with such boldness. They usually refrained from such talk as they knew better than to flirt with the admiral's daughter, which in these men's case, they didn't know. Lady Griftson had graciously failed to inform the gentlemen of whom their relations were. Sophie's cheeks flushed further as she appeared to not know what to say.

"We're from Bombay," Jane surrendered. She had lost the pillow but it was worth the sacrifice as she quickly drew the attention off of Sophie's flustered state.

"Ah Bombay!" Mr. Burgess said with excitement. He carefully brushed a few loose strands of hair over a thinned area with his hand. "Such a hostile city, but one that I never would have guessed was boring."

"Yes, not with all the attacks it receives from the Mysore," Mr. Cady added. Jane exchanged a knowing glance with Sophie whose eyes filled with dread. *And so it begins.*

"Have any of you tried the pastries tonight?" Sophie asked, as though determined to change the topic.

As though uninterested in what she said, the gentlemen continued.

"You know, I've heard plenty of stories from a few soldiers who've been to Bombay. Such a dreary place," Mr. Burgess announced with a small shudder of his narrow shoulders.

"Mm, I find it quite charming," Jane said, trying not to sound too defensive of her beloved home. "And there haven't been any attacks in the past year from the Mysore."

"Yes, but there certainly have been plenty of attacks from the French in that area," Lord Reeves said with certainty.

"Have you gentlemen heard of the battle off Saint Helena Island?" Mr. Cady asked. "From what I've heard, it was one of the fiercest battles that's taken place at sea in the past year or so."

A sudden tightness formed in Jane's stomach. She gripped her glass tighter and curled it toward her chest, readying herself for what usually followed. She had heard many people refer to that battle and the praise that they gave Captain McCannon and Captain Norton. Her stomach turned from memories of that night where the town was in devastation and later, she found James, laying feverish on the Sphinx. Like at other social gatherings, she tried to stay focused on keeping an impassive expression to hide her emotions that were tied to it. But tonight, was more difficult. She drew in a breath, bracing herself for all the praise and acknowledgment that James rightfully deserved.

"Had we lost that battle, the French would've had leverage over our English trading company," Mr. Burgess said.

"Yes, being one of the company's main ports, that could have ruined us." Mr. Cady added. "The captain of that ship was brilliant, sailing between the two ships like he had." Mr. Cady glided his gloved hand straight in front of him as though it were the ship.

"It was suicidal," Lord Reeves muttered, swirling his glass in a bored manner.

"Come now," Lord Bingham objected. "Having come across two French frigates miles from the harbor left the captain no choice but to fight with what he had. The captain's not only brave but a hero."

"The man's a lunatic," Lord Reeves scowled above his crooked nose. "He killed most of his crew by entering that battle. Things could have turned out for the better had he waited for reinforcements instead of trying to be the hero."

Jane went to open her mouth to defend James, but she was so baffled by the man's ridiculous notion that she couldn't gather her thoughts.

"I believe the gentleman had no other choice but to face the tyrants," Sophie declared. Lord Reeves began chuckling and rolled his eyes in a mocking way at her.

Jane gritted her teeth together feeling rather irritated with his belittling gestures. She ignored Mr. Cady's take on the matter as she still felt herself fuming. On rare instances, she'd crossed gentlemen who felt women should never talk freely about politics or war and unfortunately for them, Lord Reeves was one of them.

"The captain was of stable mind, Lord Reeves," Jane added to Sophie's remark. "Instead of fleeing adversity with his tail between his legs, he faced them with his *prepared* crew. As an officer in the navy, I'm sure he wasn't going to let the opportunity pass when the two ships they needed to catch were right under his nose. That's not only courageous but noble, sir."

"Well said," Mr. Burgess cheered, raising his glass to Jane.

"I agree, Miss Sawyer," Lord Bingham added to her side.

"I hate to disappoint but the man's a fraud," Lord Reeves countered with a sneer. "Had the other English ship not intervened, then that captain and his crew would have died in vain. He doesn't deserve any advancement in his rank." Jane exchanged a disbelieving look with Sophie. She curled her fingers into a fist, the man's words igniting fury inside her. "He's arrogant and from what I've been told," Lord Reeves continued as he lowered his voice to address the group, "a disgrace as he's quite a philanderer with the ladies that sail through Saint Helena's port."

Sophie gasped. Jane's cheeks warmed immensely by the notion. Sophie subtly grabbed Jane's arm showing her support.

"By the bitterness in your tone, you sound as though you personally know this gentleman," Lord Bingham noted, rubbing his chin as he observed Lord Reeves.

"Not personally. But an old acquaintance who served in the navy was suspended from his duties due to this captain's falsehood."

Jane's mind raced as she tried to figure out what fabrication James could have said of another. Knowing his character, James would never do such a thing. Unable to restrain her anger any longer, she addressed the wretched man.

"Sir, one should hold one's tongue before spreading such false notions of a person—" she started, but was interrupted.

"Forgive me if I offended you, Miss Sawyer, but who's to say that they're false?" Lord Reeves challenged while staring intently at her. Jane's lips pressed as she glared at the infuriating man.

"I noticed that the gardens are open," Lord Bingham quickly intervened. "Would you two ladies like to join me for a stroll?"

"That's a delightful idea," Mr. Cady replied. He placed his empty glass on the table next to him, appearing eager to leave the tense conversation.

Jane ignored the two gentlemen as she fumed. She opened her mouth ready to unleash everything she knew about James and his honorable character.

"Pray tell who your source is, sir," Sophie demanded, cutting Jane off before she could retort. The gentlemen in the group began to shift uncomfortably as she held a surprisingly commanding tone. One that she learned from years of listening to her father.

Lord Reeves laughed. "Why would you like to know, Miss Kensington?" he asked, narrowing his beady eyes. Even with all the loud voices of the guests around them, Jane felt as though the group could hear a pin drop from the sudden stillness.

"Peter," Mr. Cady whispered sharply in warning. Lord Reeves held up his hand to his friend waiting for Sophie's response. Mr. Burgess was quiet as he kept his glass to his mouth, hiding his humored smile.

"Because a person who spreads such tales about an officer such as Captain McCannon, who, might I add, has served with extreme loyalty to the crown and country, deserves to be flogged." Sophie held her chin high and kept her challenging stare on Lord Reeves.

"I highly doubt that would be possible," Lord Reeves smirked.

"Why is that?" Jane asked. Her voice sounded weak as she felt tiny little prickles work their way up her spine. She began to remember the one man who crossed James. She suspected who the informant would be, but she needed to hear the lord say the barbaric man's name. Was he truly associated with him?

"The lieutenant that was falsely accused is none other than Sir William Howard, Duke of Brandon's nephew, Lieutenant Stephen Howard."

Blood drained from Jane's cheeks. Lieutenant Howard's sneer crossed her mind as she remembered vividly the nightmare of the man who cornered her in an alleyway in Jamestown. She wrapped her arm around her waist, holding in a shudder.

Sophie laughed callously, "I would never believe a word that man has said. And if you were wise, neither would you."

"So, you know him?" Mr. Cady asked. His ruffled hair made him appear more distraught with his serious expression.

"Not directly," Sophie started.

"Then perhaps one should hold their tongue before falsely accusing the gentleman," Lord Reeves smugly replied.

Sophie's eyes narrowed as her glare threw daggers at Lord Reeves. Mr. Cady groaned, running his hand over his face. The evening had taken a horrible turn for the worse and needed to end. Jane took a deep breath and pushed aside the haunting memory the lieutenant had left with her. She stepped towards Lord Reeves whose smug smile broadened.

"Lord Reeves," she said calmly though every vein in her body pulsed fiercely out of fear and fury. "I can assure you that Captain McCannon is one of the most honorable of gentlemen, who fought valiantly to protect Saint Helena Island and its people. My uncle and I can attest to that as we took care of the wounded when they returned from the battle. Yes, he lost some of his crew—which he did grieve over, but mind you, each of those men who were lost had joined the navy to protect their country—our country. They didn't die in vain because of their captain's decision to fight, but for the protection of their families and friends. You speak of war as though you lived it, sir, but how naive are you to speak from a source who lacks any credibility to his name except for that of his uncle's?"

For once, during the duration of knowing Lord Reeves, he didn't throw a snide remark. Instead, he stared at Jane with wide eyes. Lord Bingham cleared his throat next to her and took a satisfied sip of his wine.

"Fascinating," Mr. Burgess muttered. "Peter, my friend, I'd say this was the first time a lady has finally put you in your place." He slapped his friend across his shoulder. Wanting nothing more than to leave the group, Jane took the first opportunity that was offered.

"My lord." She looked to the gentleman at her side. Lord Bingham's brown eyes sparkled with admiration as he looked at her. "I believe you mentioned the gardens?"

The corners of his mouth raised. "Yes of course."

"Uh, Miss Kensington." Mr. Burgess lowered his glass and appeared to be in deep thought. "You wouldn't happen to be in relations to Admiral Kensington, would you?"

Sophie held her chin high with pride. "Yes, he's my father." Raising her brow at Lord Reeves, she accepted Mr. Cady's arm. Seeing the wind knocked out of Lord Reeves's sails had Jane's heart pumping with triumph. Satisfied he would no longer speak of the matter to anyone in attendance, at least for the evening, she offered a slight nod of farewell.

"Ladies." Mr. Burgess smiled broadly with his dimples. She quickly looked away. She had had enough reminders of James for the evening. "This evening has been most entertaining. Truly a pleasure to have met you." He offered a bow and looked with satisfaction to his friend, Lord Reeves.

"Indeed," the man muttered with irritation.

Jane turned without another word for the gentlemen. Her pulse pounded throughout her body as though she had faced her own battle. She drew in short breaths as she tried to calm herself from all the memories. In all the weeks of being in England, she had endured many discussions of the battle that took place off of Saint Helena's Island, yet never once did she join the conversations to tell her account. But when one had the audacity to speak about James and tarnish his admirable character . . . She clasped her shaking hands together. Chatter flooded around her as she withdrew from her thoughts and noticed all the conversing people. Her eyes widened when she remembered it was Lord Bingham who had led her away.

"Miss Sawyer, there's something I must tell you," he whispered, his gaze tenderly bore on her.

Jane released her breath that she had been holding and stopped walking. Standing in the middle of the grand hall with strangers all around her, she wanted nothing more than to escape tot he comfort of the cottage.

"The gardens you mentioned are closed?" she asked, wanting to distance herself from the married gentleman. His brows raised.

"What? Well, no. I'm not sure," he started appearing a bit confused. Sophie and Mr. Cady quietly approached their side.

"I appreciate the excuse of the gardens to leave the conversation, Lord Bingham. That was very thoughtful of you." Jane smiled up at him though she wasn't quite sure what to make of his expression. His thick brows furrowed tighter as though he was losing his grip on something. But what? He opened his mouth and quickly closed it as he appeared uncertain what to say.

"Miss Kensington and I best be leaving." Jane smiled softly at him. Sophie nodded in agreement and slipped her hand from Mr. Cady's arm. He had appeared too smitten as he gazed at Sophie to understand that they were leaving.

"Mr. Cady," Sophie said with a smile as he took her hand and kissed it.

"Will you ladies be attending the ball here tomorrow night?" Mr. Cady eagerly asked. Jane smiled, thinking how he seemed to beg for a treat.

"We will be in attendance," Sophie replied with a hint of pink to her cheeks.

"Most excellent," Mr. Cady beamed. "I would be honored if you saved me a dance. Perhaps the dinner set?"

Sophie smiled. "Certainly."

"Until tomorrow night."

He bowed to her and then to Jane before retracing his steps to where they had left the despicable Lord Reeves.

"Lord Bingham, give Lady Bingham my regards. I shall see her in the morning." Jane curtsied a goodbye to the gentleman. He ran his hand through his hair as though conflicted.

"I shall," he hesitatingly replied, then bowed. "Good evening, Miss Kensington. Miss Sawyer."

After seeing the lord depart, Jane looked to Sophie and shared an exhausted nod with her. It was clear neither of them wished to stay in the home a moment longer.

❧ Chapter Eleven ❧

lowing out the candle, Jane fluffed her lumpy pillow for what she hoped would be the last time. Swiftly she sank under the chilled covers next to Sophie.

"Jane, are you certain you don't want this pillow?" Sophie whispered into the dark bedchamber. "I feel the challenge should be eliminated. Our evening was nothing but a disaster."

"I'm quite certain." Jane scooted herself deeper under the covers, the smell of melted wax tickled her nose. "Besides, you're my guest, so there's no need to discuss it further."

Closing her eyes, Jane attempted to push aside the evening's tormenting conversation. Never mind Lieutenant Howard and how Lord Reeves knew him, though the thought of him and his possible whereabouts greatly disturbed her. What affected her most was that she had to remind herself multiple times that James was not a philanderer. Nor that he would ever prey on her. Even though there was a time when her insecurities took over and she thought that perhaps James may have been in love with another—Miss Catherine Harrlow. Thank goodness he cleared that up during the evening they had gazed at the southern lights.

Jane's heart leaped as a memory she had buried under all her midwifery work surfaced. Her lips began to tingle as though she could still feel his lips pressed firmly against hers. She threw her pillow over her head when she felt the same surge of excitement she had experienced while in his arms. Ugh! She wanted to yell into her pillow. Why must these feelings intensify? They'd been apart over nine months!

"I can't believe that pompous man would say such things about the captain," Sophie grumbled while adjusting her covers.

Jane squeezed her eyes closed as her heart pounded harder against her chest at the mention of James.

"Are you alright?" Sophie whispered, lifting the corner of the pillow off Jane's face.

"No." She threw the pillow off and blew out an exasperated breath.

"Is it your pillow?" Sophie asked. Her voice hitched as though she were holding in a giggle.

Jane laughed. "If only it were."

Shifting next to her, Sophie propped herself on her elbow. Through the darkness, Jane could feel her intense stare. "By all means, tell me what it is. For surely it's serious if it's bothering you more than your feather-clumped pillow."

She laughed some more and threw her pillow back over her warm face. "It's foolish, really," she muffled into the silk fabric.

"Foolish? This I must hear." Sophie lifted the pillow off Jane's cheek. Jane glanced over at the outline of her dark figure.

With the curtains drawn in her small bedchamber, she couldn't make out her friend's expression but the curiosity in her tone told her she wanted to know everything. She bit her lip as she was about to confess something that she had kept to herself since she departed Saint Helena Island.

Releasing a muffled groan, Jane surrendered her buried secret that no one of Oxford knew. Except of course for her uncle and Millie. "I lost my heart to someone."

An exasperated sigh came from her friend. "Love isn't foolish," she stated as though she were an expert in the matter.

Lowering the pillow to her chest, Jane folded her arms and hugged it tight against her body. "It is if it keeps you awake at night, leaving you to wonder what the future holds."

"I'm certain he's written many sappy letters about your future together. That would keep me up at all hours. Where do you keep his heart-stopping letters, anyway? Are they under the mattress?" Sophie giggled and began reaching over her side of the bed to feel for them.

Jane laughed. "If I had any, I would have already shared with you the best parts. But I have yet to receive them."

"What?" Sophie shrieked and sat straight up. With panic in her voice she continued, "Do you mean to tell me after one year, you haven't received a letter from him?"

"Nine months," Jane corrected, brushing aside Sophie's startled tone. "And it's alright. This isn't surprising to me. Jenny mentioned how busy he's been preparing for a new assignment. I'm certain I'll receive a letter any day now." At least, that's what she'd been telling herself every day since her arrival to Oxford.

"Oh no. No, no, no." Sophie scooted closer to her. Jane could hear the hesitation in her voice when she said, "I never thought I'd see you fall and become a victim to this."

Scoffing, Jane threw her arm over her eyes. "Sophie, I haven't fallen prey to anything. This is different." She knew what her friend was referring to. Their fears of being misled by any military man was something they'd vowed they'd protect each other from. They'd witnessed many young ladies fall for a gentleman in the military. Many of them were promised love, a family, and security, only to be left heartbroken by their lies and deceits, all in the name of a good time.

Sophie rested her hand on Jane's arm. "Remember when we were younger, we promised each other that no matter what, we would never commit to a relationship that's not reciprocated. Especially if it were a long-distance relationship," she said, her voice softening to one of sympathy.

Jane offered a smile, though she doubted Sophie could see her through the darkness. "I appreciate your concern. I do. But I promise, there's nothing to fret about. I know he cares for me just as much as I him."

"Alright," Sophie said with hesitation. She played with the end of her braid for a moment before pausing and looked to Jane. "Have you written to him?"

How was she to answer? Having promised her uncle to only write when she received word from James, she didn't dare send any of her letters. But she couldn't help herself from writing about her day to him and she kept those notes in a hat box all the while pretending they were shipped to him.

"I have but they were never sent. Do you suggest I send him one in order to receive a reply?" Her tease got the reaction she was looking for.

Sophie's head snapped in her direction. Her gasp was one that filled the quiet room. "Don't jest about such an indecent thing. He needs to be the one that takes the lead on this."

Refraining from laughing at her friend's response, she continued with her tease. "Should he, though? Perhaps, if I wrote to him, it would give him enough encouragement to write me back."

Jane nudged Sophie as she groaned into her hand. "I don't think I can take you seriously anymore. If you want to ruin your reputation, by all means write to him. Just don't tell me."

"Sophie," Jane laughed and intertwined her arm through Sophie's while resting her head on her shoulder. "I won't. I promise. I didn't expect that you would get so upset by it."

"I can't help myself. I don't understand how I'm more upset about this whole thing than you. It's as though you have a pile of letters already stashed under this mattress. I do not understand."

"I have nothing to fret." Settling into her covers, Jane released a contented sigh. "And now I know where you would stash your lovers' letters."

Sophie laughed. "I have no such letters."

They laid in silence and stared at the canopy above them.

"Jane, do you plan to wait for him until your uncle is done? I can't imagine him being able to visit you here. Not within the next year and with his duties on the island."

Jane didn't reply. She knew Sophie wouldn't be thrilled by the idea. But it didn't matter. She had full confidence that if she persevered for two seasons in London, that upon her return to Bombay, they could delay their trip in Saint Helena. With no doubt, James would be waiting for her, and their relationship would pick back up where they left off. She just needed to be patient as their letters would lead to it.

"Then that's it. You'll pass up on every opportunity for a chance to be with him, even when he hasn't written you." The edge in Sophie's tone was one of panic. Clearly, she had never experienced love before.

"If you knew him the way that I do, you would know that it will all work out. He's an honest man." Jane picked at a piece of lose thread on her blanket.

"I'm certain he has the very best intentions. But that's exactly what Gretchin said before her heart was broken into tiny little fragments."

Breaking the thread off the blanket, Jane groaned. Of course, Sophie had to mention poor Gretchin. The young lady spent the summer by a lieutenant's side. He vowed he would write to her before he sailed off into the horizon to never be heard from again. That was until Gretchin's brother received word that the lieutenant had a fiancée waiting for him in England. Sophie threw the blankets off herself and began pacing the room. "We need to come up with a plan so you're vulnerable. If word gets back to him that you're waiting, it could give you the opposite effect than what you hoped. Mama has told me that gentlemen appreciate ladies who are hard to catch. It's like an odd game to them."

Considering how Lady Kensington invaded the stone fortress to the Admiral's heart, she had no doubt the lady knew all the tricks on how to win a gentleman's affection.

"That may be true but James isn't one to play games. Unless, it's one of chess." She smiled to herself but she stopped by the sudden pause in Sophie's padded steps. Her friend impatiently crossed her arms over her chest, and give Jane a hard stare that ended all arguments. She shivered and surrendered any thought of putting up a fight. "What would you have me do?"

"Has he promised you anything?"

"Just to write." She blew out a breath and sat up. Taking Sophie's fluffy pillow, she threw it over her lap and hugged it to her chest.

"So, no engagements, no promises that he will visit?"

"No." She didn't like where this was going. If she hadn't put all her faith in him, she could easily see why one would doubt her waiting for him at all.

"Did he speak about seeing you again?"

"Yes!" Jane eagerly offered. Finally, she had something hopeful to give her. "He said he looked forward to our next meeting." The words slowed from her lips as the statement held little promise for the future.

"May I be bold with you?"

Jane gave a half-hearted laugh. "I believe you already have."

As though that were permission enough, Sophie carried on. "With bad weather, it takes less than two months for a ship to voyage from Saint Helena Island to England. Add roughly ten minutes to write a sweet yet simple letter, that's plenty of time for you to have received a letter by now. Especially if he was lying in bed while he recovered from his injuries, unless of course both his hands were broken?"

Jane bit her lip.

"One could have only hoped," Sophie said with a sigh, and threw her hands up.

It made perfect sense for Sophie to be in disbelief. Jane would have too had she not experienced what she did on the island with him. Which was why she refused to let doubt seep into her mind.

"He promised he would write, so I believe he will write."

"Jane," Sophie's voice softened. "Unless he's been captured and being held captive with his hands in chains, he has every opportunity to write to you. And let me assure you that he is not in a cell somewhere," she added with confidence. "I know my father met with him when we passed through." Jane plopped her body back against her pillow. She hated how Sophie brought forth valid points that went against everything she hung on to. "I'm not trying to be difficult," Sophie whispered. "Jane, I love you as a sister. I hope you understand that I intend to fulfill the promise we made to each other so many years ago. I know you care deeply for him. I just don't want you waiting for something that may not happen. And I especially don't want you to get hurt. I could never forgive myself if I allowed that to happen while you pine away."

"Which I won't." Jane closed her eyes, wishing she could end the conversation. All the talk of eliminating his excuse as to why he didn't write was beginning to wear away her resolve.

Sophie released a heavy breath, "Which you won't," she surrendered. "You are as stubborn as my father when he refuses to back down on any of my requests. But I need you to make a promise with me. The one with the unbreakable seal we made when we were children."

Holding the pillow tighter to her chest, Jane grew uncertain with what she was about to ask. "The butterfly promise?" Stifling a laugh of disbelief. They hadn't made the sealed promise since Sophie lost one of her mother's bracelets while they played dress up. Thankfully, it reappeared in her jewelry box the following day. They assumed one of the maids had found it lying on the floor.

"Yes," Sophie held out her hand. "Are you ready?"

Curling her hand into the blanket, Jane leaned away. "But what am I promising you?"

"That you will allow other gentlemen to call on you."

"Sophie," she protested.

"Just until you receive a letter," she rushed, kneeling next to her on the bed. "If it weren't for hearing so much about this captain's aimable character, I would have told to you to move forward with or without a letter."

"Fine. And when I do receive his letter—which will be soon—I shall continue in my contented ways of avoiding any gentlemen callers."

Sophie sighed. "Thank goodness my father speaks highly of him."

Jane smiled. Coming from Sophie's father who was hardened by the effects of war, that spoke volumes.

With their hands clasped together they each placed a kiss on the back of each other's hands to seal the promise. Jane couldn't help but laugh at how the motion brought out their younger selves.

"Thank you." Jane could hear the smile in her friend's voice. "You know who's been trying to catch your eye tonight?"

"No." Jane groaned as the joyous memory dispersed into a feeling of regret. She could picture Sophie smiling next to her as she ignored her objection.

"Lord Bingham. And may I add he's rather handsome."

"And may I add he's rather married? First, you protest me waiting for James and now you encourage me to seek out one who's very married. Honestly Sophie, what is the matter with you?" Jane swatted the pillow she had clung to at her friend's arm.

"Married? The gentleman could have fooled me. And don't swing my pillow." Sophie clasped the feathered pillow and smoothed it out. "I don't want it to get clumpy."

Jane lifted her lumpy pillow and softly swung it at Sophie's face. Sophie gasped in surprise then immediately swung her pillow back in retaliation.

"Now Jane, behave yourself." She threw her pillow next to Jane and crawled to get to her side of the bed. "I'm going to sleep."

Jane chuckled as she heard the smile in Sophie's somewhat serious tone. Finding herself now hanging over the edge of her bed, she took another swing at Sophie. Immediately, Sophie responded, hitting Jane hard in the head with her plush feathered pillow.

"Jane," she hissed through laughter. "You're going to make my pillow lumpy."

"Then don't hit me," she whispered with gasps of laughter. She swung again but was blocked by Sophie's lump-free pillow. The two continued to swing their pillows at each other, but stopped as feathers began to float around them. Jane's sides ached from the joyous, somewhat quiet laughter.

Settling back under the covers, with her pillow half-filled with feathers, for the first time since arriving in England, she was able to drift off to a deep slumber.

The next morning, Jane rode one of their horses to Lady Bingham's manor. Easing in her saddle, she peacefully studied the beautiful scenery around her. Green rolling hills with rows of thick, luscious trees outlined the farmers' properties. The country offered a wonderful escape from the busy city of Oxford.

Jane smiled as the sun peeked through thick, white, cotton clouds in front of a blue backdrop. She loved Oxford in the spring. After freeing her thoughts with Sophie, she felt a sense of calmness with the muddled matter of Captain McCannon. Even the usually gray-pearl colored, cloudy skies were nowhere in sight. Loosening her reins, Jane drew in a deep, satisfied breath. It was going to be a rare, beautiful afternoon.

Lady Bingham's parlor was a delightful, spacious room. Light pastels for the furnishing and wallpaper proved to be quite charming for the country estate. Jane's eyes scaled the quaint room while she waited for Lady Bingham to make her appearance. She clenched her medical bag in her lap as she sat on the edge of a blush-colored sofa. Gold-flecked framed paintings of gardens and the surrounding farmlands neatly scattered the walls with an organized purpose. Jane peered to see the fine print in the corner of one of the paintings and noted it was one of Lady Bingham's works. She had heard the lady was extremely talented in the arts. If only Sophie was here to be able to appreciate her work.

"Miss Sawyer. It's wonderful to see you again," Lady Bingham greeted with a sweet, rich voice as she approached the parlor. The young woman who was a year shy of Jane, appeared flushed as though she had sprinted to the room. Jane lowered her bag to the carpeted floor and quickly stood to take her curtsy. Pausing her steps, Lady Bingham winced as she calmly clasped the side of her stomach. The wispy, blue material of her dress that draped over her stomach hid any indication that she was with child, but Jane knew she was more than halfway through her first pregnancy. Had the lady not been so sick during her first trimester, Jane figured she would be showing more of a bump.

"Lady Bingham, it's a pleasure. How are you feeling this morning?" She couldn't help but feel concerned as Lady Bingham's dark, arched brows furrowed further together while she gently rubbed the side of her hidden stomach. Her bright green eyes winced and she rubbed harder.

"I've been better," she breathed. Her high, apple cheeks raised, squeezing her eyes as she released a slow, heavy breath.

Nodding with understanding, Jane calmly approached the lady's side.

"Come, take a seat."

Lady Bingham laughed. Her thin upper lip disappeared as she smiled at Jane. "Please, don't think I'm being a softie, Miss Sawyer. It's not painful. Really. It's just more of an annoyance."

"I would never think such a thing, Lady Bingham," Jane assured her. "On the contrary, I think you're very strong having endured the first trimester like you did." She bit her lip as she remembered the severity of the woman's morning sickness.

Lady Bingham frowned and followed Jane to a wingback chair. "Thank heavens, that part is over with. I told my Bingham if all my pregnancies are like this, then we may be settling for just one," the young woman breathed as she slowly eased herself on the seat cushion.

"I'll pray that it doesn't." Jane smiled, grabbing a pillow from the sofa, and tucking it behind the lady's lower back.

"Please do," she exasperated. "For I fear my husband won't be satisfied until he has at least seven children."

"Seven?!" she smiled as Lady Bingham nodded and rolled her eyes.

"He wants to outdo his older brother, who currently has six little ones."

Jane held in a smile as she pictured Lord Bingham being clambered by seven little children. If he struggled controlling his horse, then he would certainly be in for a surprise. Grabbing a footstool, Jane lifted the lady's stocking covered feet and rested them on it.

"Out of all the things he wants to outdo his brother with, I don't understand why he chose children," Lady Bingham muttered, gazing with a perturbed look in her emerald eyes. "But then again, I suppose they're competitive in everything together. Hunting, money, boxing, sports . . ."

Jane pressed her hands on her waist as she was trying to picture Lord Bingham being the competitive type. He didn't seem to be aggressive with anything, yet Captain James and Lieutenant Thomas were certainly competitive and neither of them were aggressive . . . *argh!* Jane brushed a loose hair off her face. *Must he always enter her thoughts?* Lady Bingham was still naming different things her husband and his brother were competitive at but Jane was too determined to dive into her work. She needed the distraction.

". . . best tailor, finest horse."

Jane smiled to herself. He certainly lost in that category.

The lady's tone was becoming more irritated as she continued to list off their pettiness. "Who shot the largest turkey . . ."

"My goodness, please tell me his brother doesn't live nearby?"

"Gracious, no. He currently lives in London," Lady Bingham smiled with satisfaction.

"Thank goodness," Jane laughed. "Now, why don't you tell me what sort of pain you're experiencing right now."

The lady took a few short breaths as she continued to rub her stomach. Anticipation built as Jane's mind raced with all the supplies she was going to need if indeed the lady was going through early labor. Really early! She counted in her head how many weeks the lady would be . . . Why, she was still only at week thirty!

"It's more annoying than anything," she started. A dark curl fell over her flushed cheek. "It's as though she is tapping the same spot in my stomach over and over again."

"May I?" Jane asked calmly, though her mind raced with a list of supplies.

"Please, by all means." She lifted her small hand away from her stomach as Jane leaned down and felt through all the thin layers of fabrics. A rhythmic twitching motion came from under Jane's fingers.

"Are you feeling it only in this section?"

"Yes," the lady answered, her tone pitched higher than normal. Her eyes grew with concern as she looked to Jane for answers.

Jane looked up and smiled at Lady Bingham with relief.

"I do believe the baby is hiccupping, my lady."

"Hiccupping?" Lady Bingham sat further up as she began to feel her stomach again. "I didn't realize they could do that in the womb."

"Just for a short time. Some believe it's the baby testing their lungs."

"Fascinating," Lady Bingham marveled while staring at her tiny bump.

"Any other pain? Cramps? Swelling?"

"No cramps, but a little swelling in my ankles." The young lady lifted her skirts to show Jane her stocking-covered ankles. "I did take a morning stroll so I do believe that's the reason for my swelling."

Jane nodded and pressed her fingers into the lady's ankles and felt how slowly the woman's skin raised back against her fingertips. "Yes, be sure to drink plenty of liquids. That will help reduce some of the swelling." Jane then pressed her fingers against the lady's wrist to check her pulse. "I'll also leave you with a few herbs in case the swelling worsens."

"I appreciate that. Perhaps, I should stop walking for a time to keep my swelling down."

"On the contrary, walking does wonders for one's health and the health of the baby. That is as long as you're feeling up to it." Jane retrieved her bag from off the floor and placed it on the small table next to Lady Bingham. Swiftly, she dug through the organized tinctures of herbs. "And socializing with friends and loved ones will also do wonders for your spirits." Jane casually added, pulling out the bottles she wanted to help aid the lady's swelling. After hearing all that her husband and his brother were competitive with, she knew the lady was in dire need of social interactions.

"Socializing is one of the few things I avoid these days," Lady Bingham breathed as she shifted uncomfortably in her chair. Her oval face pinched in discomfort until she found herself better situated.

"Why is that" Jane turned her attention from her tinctures towards the lady.

"With my husband out of town, I haven't felt comfortable parading around with my belly showing." The lady subconsciously rubbed her stomach as she spoke. "Nobody in Oxford knows of my pregnancy and I would prefer him to be by my side when our friends hear of it."

Lost in thought, Jane placed the tinctures on the table. In case of the loss of a pregnancy, she knew many women kept the secret that they're carrying to themselves until the birth of the baby.

"Forgive me for asking, but were you not attending the musical performance at Lord and Lady Griftson's home last night?"

"No." The lady absentmindedly played with the chiffon fabric of her dress.

"Then your husband was in attendance without you?" Something felt off with Lord Bingham and she couldn't quite put her finger on it.

"Bingham?" she smiled wistfully. "He's been out of town for the past month. Why do you ask?"

Jane's cheeks flushed. "Forgive me my lady, I thought I had heard he was in attendance."

Lady Bingham laughed. "I'm most certain he'd rather be there than in London where his brother couldn't pester him."

London? Jane's eyes widened and she drew back. *Then who was the gentleman she kept referring to as Lord Bingham?* A prickle ran up her back, warming her face.

"Bingham would have loved to have felt these hiccups," Lady Bingham absentmindedly sighed to herself.

Jane closed her mouth and pushed aside the thought of this Lord Bingham—no this, imposter! Quickly, she proceeded with measuring the baby with her hands.

"It feels as though the baby is right on track." Finding any excuse to hide the bewilderment on her face, Jane pulled out a scrap piece of paper from her bag. Uncorking her ink bottle, she dipped her quill feather in and began scribbling her notes on the paper. Her back was strategically turned towards Lady Bingham as she knew the warmth in her cheeks would reveal her perturbed thought of the mysterious gentleman.

"The baby's measuring at thirty weeks," she said over her shoulder. Corking her ink bottle, she returned it in its rightful place in her bag with the quill. Slowly she waved the sheet of paper to help the ink dry faster. *Didn't the gentleman say he was living here? But then why didn't he correct her?* Shame filled her as she realized the gentleman had tried to explain himself to her but she kept interrupting him to leave.

"Why, Lottie May," Lady Bingham coed towards her stomach. "You're growing before my eyes."

Shaking her head to push the matter aside, Jane closed her bag and held out her hand for the lady.

"I see you've already decided on a name," she mused as she assisted her to her feet.

"Yes. Lottie May," she smiled brightly.

"That is a beautiful name."

"Thank you." Getting to her feet, Lady Bingham pinched her face as she stood and released a heavy sigh. Knowing the woman's muscles and ligaments were stretching and pulling from the baby's growth, Jane sympathized with her discomfort.

"Here are two tinctures that you can add to your tea whenever you're feeling swollen. You'll only need two drops."

Lady Bingham graciously accepted the tinctures and smiled. "Thank you, Miss Sawyer. Hopefully, I won't be needing them too often."

Jane nodded and hoped for the lady's sake she was right.

"And what should you name the baby if it is a boy?" She casually grabbed her medicine bag that sat next to the plush chair.

"There's no need to decide that. I'm most confident she's a girl."

"How are you so certain?" she asked as this was the lady's first time experiencing pregnancy and she didn't have as much knowledge carrying babies as others like Mrs. Meers.

"This sounds a bit silly." She laughed as she walked with Jane out of the parlor room. "But I've heard that if you hold a pendulum over your stomach, it will tell the baby's gender." Looking over her shoulder as they stopped in the front foyer, the lady lowered her voice and looked intently at Jane. "So, every morning this past week, I've attempted it and sure enough the pendulum swung back and forth." The lady's eyes gleamed with excitement.

"Then that's to mean it's a girl," Jane guessed as she had never heard of this technique before. She's heard of how women carrying a girl would lose their beauty and give them uneven skin tone and possibly pimples. On the contrary to baby boys, they added more of a glow to the mother's skin.

Jane never knew the lady before her pregnancy, so she would never know if her skin had changed. The lady's skin was a little pink, but she held a beautiful, even glow. If Jane were to have to make an assumption based on her skin alone, she would have guessed she was carrying a boy.

"Yes!" she practically sang, trying to keep her excitement from bursting from her lips. "I've never had it swing in a circle over my stomach, otherwise I wouldn't be so certain."

"Does Lord Bingham know of this assessment?" Jane humorously asked. She loved how the lady couldn't stop smiling with the idea. Lady Bingham's smile swiftly fell and she shook her head.

"Heaven's no. He would be terribly upset as he wants our first child to be a son." She rubbed her stomach and sighed. "Heaven forbid that his brother's first child was a son. They're like silly little schoolboys always trying to outdo one another." Lady Bingham clasped Jane's free hand and held it tight. "That is why we must keep this between us. The longer he thinks we're having a boy, the less talk there will be of his brother."

"Yes, of course," Jane replied, trying not to look too worried about the brothers' unhealthy competitiveness.

A door slammed towards the west wing of the estate, drawing their attention. The steps were heavy and quick as though whomever it was, was very irritated.

"Good gracious," Lady Bingham released Jane's hand and bit down a smile. "I believe Daisy may have finally gotten the best of him."

Jane tucked her bag closer to her side as she drew nearer to the woman. "The best of whom, my lady?" She held her breath as she suspected to be the gentleman riding Daisy the day prior. Her heart began to quicken as the steps grew louder and the gentleman had yet to make his appearance from around the corner that led somewhere deep into the home.

Giving Jane a side glance, Lady Bingham's arched brow raised higher on one side. "Lord Evans," she smirked.

A deep, familiar voice came from the hall. "Veronica," he frustratingly called.

"I'm in the foyer," she calmly replied.

"I better be going," Jane whispered to the lady. She didn't like the idea of being between the two when he clearly sounded disgruntled but more than anything she wanted to disappear from the soon-to-be uncomfortable encounter.

"No, please stay, Miss Sawyer." Lady Bingham softly placed her hand on Jane's arm. "I would love for you to meet my brother." The lady smiled sweetly at her. An unsettling knot formed in the pit of her stomach as she caught a spark of interest in the lady's eyes. A gleam that Jane was well too familiar with from Lady Griftson. Lord Evans stormed around the corner, with his riding crop clenched in his gloved hand. His riding attire was unkempt, full of dust and tiny twigs. He quickly ran his hand through his ruffled golden hair as his nostrils flared.

"Veronica, your horse lacks any common sense from any normal—" He stopped and took a double take towards Jane. She peeled her eyes away from his gawking stare while warmth spread to the top of her head. *It was as though I didn't inform him of my visit,* she thought by his surprised stare. His mouth clamped shut and he swiftly brushed off his jacket doing little to help his cause as one of the sleeves had a tear below the shoulder.

"I beg your pardon, Miss Sawyer." He bowed, his cheeks darkening in hue as he turned his gaze towards the floor. *Lord Evans?* Jane pressed her lips together as she began to count in her head the numerous times she had called the gentleman "Lord Bingham."

"My lord," Jane quickly curtsied, wishing she were anywhere but there while she felt Lady Bingham's observing stare.

"Why, you two know each other?" Lady Bingham's voice rose and looked between the two with great interest.

"We met the day prior," Lord Evans stated. His voice sounded more serious than Jane had ever heard before—which didn't mean much given how she knew him for only a day. She tightened her hold on her bag as she was uncertain if he was irritated at her or because he had clearly fallen off of Daisy.

Lady Bingham looked at Jane with an expectant stare as though she wanted her to expound on the matter. Jane offered a small smile but remained quiet. She didn't want to elaborate her part of how her beet-covered dress was eaten by Daisy, nor how she had humiliatingly assumed Lord Evans was none other than Lady Bingham's husband. Lady Bingham looked between them and finally broke the silence.

"Well, since introductions are not in order, I suppose poor Daisy needs a visit after what you put her through." Holding the side of her stomach, Lady Bingham gave her brother a taunting smirk as he irritatingly stared back at her. "Charles, would you be a dear and see Miss Sawyer out?" Her tone was sweet but the order behind it was obvious. Lord Evans released a breath and looked away from his sister's encouraging smile.

"Of course." He straightened his riding jacket, giving no indication whether or not he was pleased with the idea.

"Miss Sawyer, it was a pleasure seeing you again." Lady Bingham smiled at Jane with a satisfied twinkle in her eye.

"And you as well, my lady." Jane had lost her smile as she wished nothing more than to continue to be as professional as the lady's midwife, not an opportunity for the lady's brother. She watched as Lady Bingham departed the foyer in the same direction from where Lord Evans had entered.

"Miss Sawyer," Lord Evans said, while stepping forward and holding his hand out towards her medical bag. "May I?"

Since his entrance, Jane couldn't help but notice Lord Evans was now smiling at her. All the irritation that he had shown with his sister had disappeared.

"Thank you." Jane loosened her hold on her bag and handed it to him. Smoothing out the front of her cream-colored gown, she began towards the opened entry door. Keeping her gaze from his, she looked forward as she walked beside him.

"Miss Sawyer," he started when they began down the outdoor steps. Jane clasped her dress and carefully took a step on the stairs. Her breath caught in her throat as he had spoken her name. "I do beg your pardon as I'm in an extremely undignified state of dress."

She couldn't help but smile. "I believe our roles may have switched since yesterday." Poor Millie was determined to rid the stain and had spent hours scrubbing the dress with hardly anything to show for it as it still held the beet smudges.

He chuckled. "I suppose you're right."

She briefly smiled at Lord Evans while she led them towards her horse. Being that it was a quick visit, she hadn't bothered sending her horse to the stables and had left her mare by a large, wispy tree a few yards from the circular brick drive to graze.

"I understand Daisy is your sister's horse?" Jane bit her lip as she let the word sister pass. She peeked from the corner of her lashes at Lord Evans who broadly grinned at her from the clarification. She darted her eyes forward, uncertain if she should show any encouragement towards the gentleman. Her heart began to tug, conflicted on whether or not it was appropriate to be engaging with the gentleman any longer. She clasped her hands as she wanted nothing more than to fidget with the ribbon on her dress.

"Yes, that dreadful thing you call a horse is my sister's." Lord Evans chuckled.

"Then may I ask, why do you ride her?"

"So my sister wouldn't be tempted to, given her condition," he muttered. "She adores that horse and insists that she gets her daily exercise." Lord Evans winced and began to rub his lower back. "Though, after today's ride, I'm going to have to convince the stable master to take over."

"Was she going after flowers?" Jane couldn't help but tease while approaching her mare. She gripped her horse's reins and gently pulled her horse away from nibbling at the manicured grass. Feeling a bit uncertain what to make of her comfortable mannerism towards the gentleman, she focused on stroking her mare's auburn muzzle.

He laughed, patting her horse's shoulder. "No, Daisy decided to commandeer my ride and gallop through the trees. I had to bail before a branch got the best of me."

Jane's eyes snapped over at Lord Evans, who was smiling at her. Her horse shook her head from Jane's hands and began to nibble at the grass again.

"How dreadful. Lord Evans, are you alright?" She immediately turned her attention towards his dusty clothes to be certain nothing was bleeding. Her attention was quickly grasped by his tall, lean muscular figure. Realizing what she was doing, she snapped her eyes back to his long face.

"It's good to hear you finally call me by my given name," he teased. His green eyes sparkled as he continued to watch her. Warmth spread up Jane's spine to her cheeks.

"I do apologize for the accusation," she started, feeling extremely ashamed for calling him Lord Bingham on a few occasions.

"Yes, I was hoping you could make it up to me," he stated, combing his fingers through his wavy golden hair as it had fallen over his eyes.

"Make it up to you?" Jane tugged on the reins and began walking away from the gentleman as a thought had broken through her barrier of embarrassment. "I have nothing to make up," she replied and led them around a manicure bush, back to the brick driveway. "You, sir, never corrected me."

"I tried, but you always found an excuse to leave."

Jane peered at him as he held a guiltless smile.

"You could have corrected me after I had first made the assumption."

He rubbed at his strong jaw. "Forgive me, I didn't know how to tell you at first. Will you let me make it up to you?"

She laughed, but quickly withdrew her smile and looked at him intently. Sophie's request ran through her mind as she thought of the idea of giving the gentleman a chance. She gripped the reins tighter and cleared her throat.

"What did you have in mind?"

Lord Evans's eyes brightened. He switched her bag and crop to his other hand so he could straighten his jacket more.

"Will you save me a set for tonight?"

Jane bit her lip as a smile formed. "I'm afraid my dance card is full, sir."

She was intending to tease of course, but deep down she wished her statement was true as a trickle of excitement quickened in her veins from the thought of dancing with him. Lord Evans chuckled and took long strides along the grass to catch up to her short, eager steps.

"Ah, you must be mistaken for a different dance because according to my sister, there are no dance cards tonight."

Jane's cheeks warmed being called out in her fib. She blinked to release herself from his green eyes and swiftly looked away.

"I see." Warmth spread through her body. Clasping her horse's reins, she looked away from him towards the iron gates of the estate's entrance. She felt she was facing a crossroad as Captain James's blurred face appeared across her mind's eye. His crisp image had become less prominent than it had before and more a mere clouded image from her memory.

Lord Evans took a step closer to her. She caught her breath as he was intimately close—at least for her. She took a step back, giving themselves more than enough room for her comfort.

"Then I shall accept your offer of a dance. Now I must be going." Her cheeks continued to warm as he smiled with victory. Brushing a lock of hair off his forehead, he took a step towards her. "Then may I assist you onto your horse?"

He lowered her medical bag and crop to the brick driveway, freeing his hands. Sucking in a sharp breath, Jane took another step back. She nervously played with the reins in her hands.

"No, thank you. I feel like walking." She smiled though she felt he could see through her weak facade.

He glanced up at the sky. "It is a beautiful day for a stroll." Picking up her bag, he walked around her to tie it to the back of her horse's saddle.

"Then, I shall look forward to seeing you tonight." He grinned, taking a small step away.

Jane nodded. "Good day, Lord Evans."

He bowed with a full grin, "Good day. And Miss Sawyer?"

She glanced over her shoulder at him. He raised his hand towards the back of his neck.

"You have a little feather in your hair."

Jane quickly reached up and patted her hair until she felt the escapee. Slowly she pulled it out. How Millie hadn't noticed it was beyond her.

"Thank you," she softly said.

With a smile, Lord Evans bowed and departed for the home.

Slowly walking back to her cottage, Jane studied the little feather, wondering why she had allowed herself to make such a terrible promise.

Chapter Twelve

Jane ran her fingers down the silk coral gown as she stared at herself in the mirror. Her curls were perfectly pinned in place, threaded with stringed pearls. Her high cheekbones of her heart-shaped face—slightly pink. Having slept more than usual, her blue-green eyes were well rested and bright.

"Here they are, miss." Millie held up two dainty silk slippers. "They were hiding with the other slippers you purchased yesterday."

Jane gave a half-guilty smile. She never liked to shop frivolously. Yet her uncle had stayed true to his word to Lady Griftson and had her fitted for ball gowns. They had shopped for many weeks, doubling her wardrobe with extravagant gowns. There had been many times when she began to protest, but he would hold up his hand and tell her he'd hear none of it. He wanted the best London had to offer her. At times she was fearful of what society was doing to his pocketbook, but he reminded her that her parents left him with a large inheritance for her. With only a small memory of her mother being all about status, she would probably be very pleased that he invested in her dresses. She ran her fingers down the elegant dress that was fit for a duchess.

"It's too much." She bit her lip as Millie helped her slip into her shoes. "He did too much," she whispered.

Millie brought her hands to her narrow hips. "Miss Jane, this is London. You know he's wanting you to feel comfortable amongst the *ton.* Though, his idea of blending in with them only makes you stand out." She grinned proudly at her. "You're beautiful, miss. I'm sure you'll dance with many fine gentlemen tonight."

Jane's cheeks flushed as there was one gentleman in particular she was going to dance with. Fervently, she reached for the back of her dress as her heart raced with apprehension. "Millie, will you help me with these buttons please. We need something with a little less . . . appeal."

Millie's green eyes widened, "I'm sorry, miss. I didn't mean to offend."

Jane fanned herself as she felt the gown was constricting her. "No offense taken. Please hurry," she breathed.

Millie hurried to her back and swiftly unbuttoned the bodice. Jane turned and leaned against her bedpost. She took slow, steady breaths as the loosened gown didn't help the tightness in her chest. A familiar ache began to gnaw at her as she thought about the captain.

"I'm not ready." She closed her eyes, her heart pounding loudly in her ears.

"Aw, Miss Jane," Millie patted her shoulder, "There, there."

"I didn't mean to fall in love, Millie," she whispered. "How am I supposed to move forward with Sophie's promise when I can't picture myself being without him? I just need his letter to end all doubts." She wrapped her arms around the ache and carefully sat on her bed. "Why is it taking so long?"

Millie grabbed Jane's fan and slowly waved it across her face. Having done Sophie's hair earlier, Millie had caught wind of the demand for Jane to move forward. "Perhaps the letter was on a ship that got lost at sea? Or it fell out of the mail carrier's bag . . . every single time . . ." Jane raised a doubtful eyebrow. "Oh, miss, there are many places it could be. May I make a suggestion?"

Releasing an exasperated breath, Jane nodded, eager to hear whatever advice Millie had for her. Even though she never said anything, Jane knew Millie adored James and assumed she didn't like the idea of her moving on from him—yet she was being supportive with the plan as best she could.

"Supposedly, fraternizing with other gentlemen helps distract the pain, miss."

Fraternizing? Her ears perked up more. *They're not enemies.* "Do you mean conversing?" she asked.

"Of course, mangling the gentlemen will provide you great comfort."

Jane pressed her lips together to keep from laughing. *Now I'm going to maul the gentlemen?* She looked away and suppressed a laugh. Clearing her throat, she glanced at Millie, "You're right. Mingling will bring much comfort."

Millie smiled up at her. "And may I point out one other thing, miss?"

"Of course." Jane grabbed her gloves that lay next to her and pulled them on, bringing them above her elbows. *Millie certainly is a wonderful distraction,* she thought with a smile.

"I'd hate to put more of a burden on you but changing your gown won't help you blend in." Millie brought her hand to her waist and looked at Jane from head to toe. "You will be noticed no matter what."

Having forgotten that her dress was draped open in the back, Jane looked up from her white gloves. "Thank you. Forgive me for making such a fuss." She swallowed down her hesitation. "Will you button me back up, please?"

A light tap came at the door and Sophie entered the room in a dazzling satin green gown.

"Oh, Jane! Was that gown made in London? It's beautiful! I need to convince my father to buy me a new ball gown." Her bright smile faltered as she noticed the somber mood.

"Whatever is the matter?" She glided across the room with her dress swishing around her. Clasping Jane's hands, she stood in front of her with a look of concern.

"I fear my nerves are getting the best of me," Jane said through a halfhearted laugh.

"Of course, they are," Sophie said, voice soft. "You're allowing yourself to tear down walls to allow others in. That couldn't be easy."

Jane blew out a breath as the discussion of James and her feelings was getting tiresome.

"I suppose it's time for me to take courage as I fraternize with the gentlemen tonight." She stood and smiled at Sophie who looked at her in confusion.

"Fraternize?" she asked, playing with her pearl necklace.

Millie hurried behind Jane and started buttoning up her gown. "She's going to converse with the gentlemen," she replied excitedly, poking her head around Jane's bodice.

Sophie glanced at Millie then at Jane and smiled, her face brightening with understanding. Through the years of knowing Jane, Sophie had had countless conversations with Millie and knew of her way of switching words. But there was something more to the glint in Sophie's eyes that made Jane hold her breath. She was up to something.

"Fraternizing. Why Millie, that's a wonderful idea!" she exclaimed.

Keeping herself still while Millie finished the last of her buttons, Jane carefully studied her.

Sophie laughed to herself and began to pace in front of them. Her dress shimmered and elegantly floated around her like a small wave at Saint Helena's shore.

"Jane." She finally stopped with a grin. "Tonight shall be unforgettable."

"Will it?" she asked, suspicious of what she could mean.

"Yes! Oh, this will be fun," Sophie laughed. She clapped her gloved hands with glee and began to pace, a habit she formed from her father when he would strategize. Jane peered down at Millie who looked back at her just as puzzled as she felt.

A string orchestra resounded through the swarming ballroom. Jane peered breathlessly towards the high ceiling trimmed with exquisite Palladian designs. She continued to observe her surroundings to keep from making eye contact with any of the gentlemen gathered in the ballroom. Three magnificent crystal chandeliers lined the center of the ceiling with brightly lit candles. The room was twice the size of any ballroom she had been in Bombay. She waved her fan across her warm face, something she had to repeat every few minutes. So far this evening she'd danced with seven different partners—some capable of dancing, and others . . . she flexed her sore foot against her thin slipper . . . not so much. Her last partner was a bit too earnest in his fancy footwork and he stomped on her foot one too many times.

"Now remember," Sophie said breathlessly next to her. "We are to continue to dance with every gentleman who comes our way." She squeezed her side and released a heavy breath. Jane could tell by her vigorous breathing that her corset was just as constricting as hers. "Once the clock strikes one, we may rest our feet."

Sophie straightened her bodice and waved her fan across her slightly flushed face. She had endured just as much twirling, weaving, and hopping as Jane, yet she still appeared flawless. It was remarkable how none of her golden curls were out of place.

"I fear my feet may give out before then," Jane groaned as she had unavoidably locked eyes with a potential disaster of a partner. The short gentleman raised his brows in acknowledgement and began making his way through the sea of ladies in ball gowns and gentlemen in their prestigious black attires. *Fraternizing.* A term Sophie was taking out of context, as she was determined that the two of them not avoid any of the unlikely fellows who came their way. Jane drew in a staggering breath. Instead, they were to make themselves vulnerable by staying put and allowing any awkward gentlemen to freely converse with them.

"Jane, dear," her uncle said while returning to her side. "You look like you could use a refreshment." He smiled, holding out a glass of punch.

"Yes, please." She eagerly closed her fan and accepted the glass. Taking a long sip, she welcomed the thirst-quenching punch.

Gaping at the glass, Sophie began to lick her lips. Jane lowered her cup and laughed. As tempting as it was to finish her drink, she handed Sophie the rest of her punch.

"Why don't you ladies come enjoy the gardens?" her uncle suggested. His thick brows hung low over his spectacles like he was trying to understand Jane with her unusually cordial behavior toward the gentlemen of Oxford.

"I'm afraid I won't be able to leave this spot for another hour," Jane replied with a hint of exasperation in her tone. Wringing her fan, she watched with dread as the shorter gentleman drew nearer. Her uncle followed her gaze and narrowed when they landed on the gentleman. Just then, both Jane's and her uncle's eyes widened as the man bumped into a fellow guest causing him to spill his drink down his front. She bit her lip, knowing nothing good would come from dancing with him.

"Are you certain?" he asked, giving Jane every opportunity to disappear before the clumsy gentleman approached. She wanted more than anything to join her uncle and leave the stuffy room, but she was adamant she would keep her promise to Sophie.

"Mm-hmm," she murmured, watching in horror when the gentleman laughed at his accident and backed away, only to bump into a woman behind him.

Her uncle chuckled. "Very well, then I suppose I will stand by in case you need me to come to the rescue." Her uncle's brows raised above his spectacles. The blundering gent was beginning to wipe the red-faced gentleman's saturated vest with his handkerchief.

"Doctor Brown, you spoil her," Sophie chimed in, as she humorously watched what had transpired. She took the remaining sip of the punch and said, "But I am afraid you are not allowed to interfere."

"I am not?" Uncle Duncan asked, removing the empty glass of punch from Sophie's hand.

"No," Jane replied. "We are to make ourselves available to every gentleman who appears interested in dancing with us." She fidgeted with the fan that dangled on her wrist and she searched the crowd for any other gentleman to meet her eye before the other man approached them.

"Even if that gentleman were to have two left feet?" Uncle Duncan asked with a twinkle in his eye.

Assuming he had just witnessed her dancing with her last partner, Jane replied, "Especially if he has two left feet." She flexed her sore foot again.

"We are to take this very seriously," Sophie added, raising her chin.

Jane wanted to laugh as her friend was the one who came up with the *"thrilling"* idea.

"I see. Is there a wager to be won with this?" Her uncle rubbed his chin and continued to watch the scene unravel. Jane assumed his question was to help answer the purpose of being trodden on by these incompetent dancers.

"There should be," she muttered, glancing at her friend.

Sophie raised her brows as though she didn't hear nor care about Jane's discontented tone.

"Just the thrill of dancing," Sophie replied, with a bright smile.

Jane laughed and looked at her uncle who still seemed confounded by the idea.

The short gentleman had finally approached Jane as he finished muttering to himself. She was too focused on the man to notice an older gentleman had accompanied him. The gentleman bowed elegantly to her uncle.

"Lord Rowley," her uncle greeted the man with half the enthusiasm that he usually merits.

The man stiffly raised his chin. "Doctor Brown, may I introduce you to my nephew? Mister Percy Acker."

Mister Acker ran his hand through his slicked black hair and straightened his cravat.

"Mister Acker," he offered a head nod. With hesitation, her uncle held his hand out to Jane. "This is my niece, Miss Jane Sawyer, and her friend, Miss Sophie Kensington." Freely he waved his hand in her direction. "Miss Kensington is visiting us from Bombay and has been delighted by the enchanting music. Haven't you, Miss Kensington?"

Jane's eyes widened at how her uncle eagerly drew Mister Acker's attention from her towards her friend. Sophie shot her uncle a look of warning which caused him to smile into his hand.

With a delighted smile, she spoke through her teeth. "I have, indeed, Doctor. Do you dance, Mister Acker?"

Mister Acker squinted his eyes as though to smile.

"Miss Sawyer has been telling me how she hopes to dance every song tonight as she shares my delight of music."

Had Jane been standing closer to Sophie, she would have elbowed her.

The gentleman eagerly nodded. "I do. In fact, it is the reason why I have asked my uncle to bring me here. Miss Sawyer—" He bowed a very low bow to her, as if he were going to kiss his knees.

She pressed her lips together, not daring to look at Sophie nor her uncle, knowing their surprised expressions would cause her to break from her calm composure into bursts of laughter.

"Miss Sawyer, might I request your hand in this next set?" Appearing to force a smile, the corner of the gentleman's mouth twitched. In the background of chatter, the violin slowly lulled, ending the song that had played.

"You may." Her voice sounded higher than she intended. To avoid looking at Sophie and her uncle, she kept her chin high and awkwardly accepted the gentleman's upper arm while he led them past his uncle, the stiff Lord Rowley, to the dance floor. She couldn't help but notice how his nose lined perfectly with her shoulder.

"I'll have you know, I'm an expert in the minuet," he whispered up to her.

She glanced from his proud face towards the other dancers and noticed their positions were not one of the minuet but of the gavotte, one of the more difficult dances of the evening. *Did he mean the gavotte?* It was quickly answered when he left her side. He crossed the floor to face the opposite of her and placed himself in the position for the minuet.

"Sir—" Jane started but stopped as the gentleman wouldn't have heard her through the chatter of the guests. She covered her mouth and watched him proudly nod at people that stared in his direction. Desperately wanting to hide behind her fan, she observed him pivot on his feet. Bouncing on his toes, he took his position. A couple next to Jane began whispering to each other and laughed while her partner remained oblivious. Jane clasped the fabric of her dress in her hands, uncertain how to continue the dance with him standing on the opposite side of her. She glanced around trying to decide whether or not she should leave the dance floor as she and her partner were clearly ruining the lineup for the dance. Thankfully a gentleman next to the mistaken man subtly whispered something to him. Her partner's eyes widened in alarm and the blood in his face drained. Feeling self-conscious for him, Jane looked around and met Sophie's eye. Across the way, she stood next to her partner and hid half her face behind her fan. Her round cheeks pushed against her eyes while her shoulders shook in laughter. Biting her smile, Jane avoided any temptation to join her, and quickly snapped her eyes forward while her partner scurried across the dance floor to her side.

The music commenced with the strings fervently striking their first chord. Jane held back a smile as the gentleman released a heavy breath and took out his punch-stained handkerchief. Abruptly he wiped his forehead and tucked it back into his sleeve.

This is certainly going to be thrilling, Jane smiled to herself.

The dance began with hopping and Jane met the lady across from her as they skipped towards each other and switched sides. Her partner soon followed suit, breathing heavily while skipping to her side.

"Are you alright?" she asked with a breath.

"Yes, yes," he blundered, and wiped away a drop of sweat off his temple. He avoided her gaze and Jane couldn't help but feel unconvinced by his response. Not while he kept gasping for air. The group swiftly began to hop forward and hop backward. On cue to the beat, Jane turned to skip in the circle, but bumped into her partner as he had gone in the wrong direction.

"Oh, I'm terribly sorry," he muttered, taking out his handkerchief and dabbing his forehead again.

"Are you certain you are alright?" Jane pressed, worried he was overexerting himself.

"Miss, I am perfectly fine," he replied with annoyance. His eyes hardened when he looked at her. Jane offered a polite nod, settling that his pride was more affected than anything else. Clasping her skirt, she held her chin high and pressed on with the dance.

Five! Five times the gentleman bumped into her before the set was mercifully over. Unfortunately for either of them, the second dance was not a minuet, and no better than the first. The poor, red-face gentleman bowed to Jane then walked off into the sea of people before she could ever utter a word. Had she not been embarrassed for the both of them, she would have been more offended by his rudeness at abandoning her on the dance floor. She drew her fan and briskly cooled her warm face, looking through the parting people for Sophie.

"Tell me you aren't feeling black and blue after that?!" Sophie exclaimed, rushing to Jane's side.

"You saw?" she asked with dread. She waved her fan closer to her face when she received sympathetic looks from a few of the ladies in passing.

"N-no," Sophie hesitated with large eyes. "Not at all," she forced through her teeth. "But he could at least have the decency of escorting you back to your uncle, considering all that you endured."

"Yes, or perhaps thanking me for putting up with him slamming into me. One would have thought we were playing a sport." Jane swatted Sophie with her fan. "Have I already mentioned to you that this is beyond thrilling?" she teased, and rubbed her tender arm from where her partner had elbowed her. "I honestly believe my arm is bruised after he skipped into me."

"Was it after the first skip or the second skip?" Sophie taunted over her shoulder, leading them around a couple to their self-assigned spots, where her uncle was supposed to be.

"Both," Jane groaned. "It's very fortunate he left when he did. I was almost tempted to encourage him to ask you to dance."

"You wouldn't!" Sophie exclaimed.

"Considering how this is your brilliant idea and how you both love the minuet, I thought it would be very appropriate." Jane grinned a teasing smile at Sophie when she had stopped walking to face her.

"Well, then I'll be certain to send my partners your way after they've stomped on my feet." Holding out her stubborn chin, her green eyes twinkled with laughter.

"Fine," Jane retorted, the corners of her mouth twitching while she feigned an uncaring expression. A part of her suspected she may have already done such a thing as a few of them came her way after dancing with her.

"Fine," Sophie retorted.

"Fine." Jane bit back a smile and she stepped next to Sophie to turn and face the dance floor. Both ladies crossed their arms, not glancing in each other's directions. Jane was hoping to see her uncle with another glass of punch, but she noticed he was otherwise engaged with a few young gentlemen who were probably a few of his pupils.

"Miss Sawyer, Miss Kensington!" Lady Griftson announced, huffing in their direction. Sophie and Jane broke their facade and gave each other a side glance.

"What a delight to see you two tonight," she practically sang. Her shimmering eyes gazed upon them with determination.

"Lady Griftson." They both curtsied and smiled at the extravagant lady. She positively sparkled, covered in jewels from the crown on her head to the rings on her fingers.

"Yes, yes. Now, Miss Sawyer, I cannot tell you how relieved I am to see you dancing tonight." The woman's tone rang with sincerity, though she held her hand over her full bosom while she looked at her with sympathy. "But may I offer some assistance with finding a more appropriate partner for you? I could not help but witness your last partner and his horrifying display. Bless dear Lady Rowley as her nephew is not very—well let's just say, he's not suitable for you."

The corner of Jane's mouth raised and she glanced at Sophie. Sophie held her hand to her mouth to hide her smile. Their task that night may have to come to an end if Lady Griftson was indeed intending on commandeering their dance partners.

"No," Lady Griftson continued. "What you need is a more handsome gentleman. One who can dance as elegantly as his partner. Let me see . . ." Lady Griftson narrowed her eyes as she began scouring the room.

"Excuse me, Lady Griftson," a lean gentleman, with round spectacles, approached and bowed. His friend, who could mistakenly be taken as his twin, stood behind him. "Would the—"

"No, no, no," Lady Griftson interrupted. She scrunched her face at both men with disappointment. "Forgive me, but these ladies are otherwise engaged." She waved her hand to dismiss the poor gentlemen away. Bowing respectfully, they departed.

"Take note, Miss Sawyer. You mustn't allow yourself to dance with just anyone." Lady Griftson peered down her nose at her and carried on. "Otherwise, every gentleman who is the lowest of the low will assume they have a chance. Now, I do realize you cannot refuse them outright, but for the sake of your reputation, ensure that you're otherwise engaged when the runts come to call." The lady's beady eyes scanned the room back and forth, like she were reading a captivating book, just to prove to Jane that she could find her better. "This is why your uncle shouldn't have declined my offer. This would never have happened."

Baffled at what took place from the lady's brazenness, Jane and Sophie exchanged surprised glances.

A loud gasp came from the woman's lips and she clasped both Sophie's and Jane's arms.

"I don't believe it," she gawked, staring towards the entrance of the ballroom. "He came!" The lady clapped her hands with excitement. "His sister would be so proud, as he usually avoids any dance of the sort. Ladies, now this sort of gentleman is a catch."

Jane's heart raced at Lady Griftson's words. She began to speculate that the gentleman the lady referred to was none other than Lord Evans.

"Yes, he would make a fine match with either of you," Lady Griftson beamed, staring in the gentleman's direction.

"And who is that, my lady?" Sophie's brow arched slightly as she appeared perfectly collected by the news.

"Lord Evans!" Lady Griftson looked at her with a satisfied smile. "His residence is in London, but he's been coming to Oxford to visit with his sister Lady Bingham while her husband's been away." She brought her hand to her heart as though she were trying to control her excitement. "She and I have been trying to get him to come to the dances for months, but he always had an excuse not to come."

Jane looked away from the lady, determined to hide the warmth in her cheeks. Deep down she hoped she wasn't the reason for Lord Evans's sudden appearance. Though, a small little voice in the back of her head was telling her she was. Jane nervously pulled her white glove higher up her arm.

"Oh look, he's coming this way." Lady Griftson examined them. "Miss Kensington, straighten your necklace and Miss Sawyer . . ." She eyed Jane up and down as a tailor would with a project that needed major adjustments. "Smooth your hair. You have a curl that has gone astray."

Jane immediately turned her back toward his direction. Her heart began pounding in her chest. Part of her wanted to hide from him, to hide and bury the nervousness that built by the idea he wanted to dance with her. But a small part cried out for her to take a chance. She was feeling so torn. Biting her lip, she tucked the loose curl behind her ear. Next to her, Sophie raised a brow while she watched Jane fidget with the ribbon on her bodice.

"Are you alright?" she whispered.

Jane offered her a half smile but remained quiet. She hadn't told Sophie about Lord Bingham actually being Lord Evans.

"Lord Evans," Lady Griftson sang on the other side of Sophie.

Sophie's eyes widened with recognition. She tucked her lips together as she realized Jane's mistake. Jane released a subtle breath to turn and face him. Trying to keep herself somewhat concealed, she peered at him through her lashes. She couldn't help noticing how he appeared quite dashing in his black, tailored evening attire. His blond hair combed up and back, his thick brows neatly trimmed and his angular cheeks were freshly shaved down to the narrow of his chin. Jane released a breath, grateful Lord Evans kept his eyes solely on Lady Griftson.

"May I introduce you to two of the loveliest ladies in attendance tonight? Miss Sophie Kensington and Miss Jane Sawyer?"

Releasing her ribbon, Jane clasped her hands behind her back.

"Yes," Lord Evans said with a hint of a smile. "I had the honor of meeting the ladies last night. Miss Kensington. Miss Sawyer, it's nice to see you again."

He bowed, not indicating that they had any effect on him. On the contrary, though polite, he appeared rather bored. Sophie raised a questioning brow to Jane and dipped into a small curtsy. Jane followed suit, not saying a word. She suspected the gentleman had been sought after by many mothers seeking a suitable husband for their daughters, or by bored ladies who enjoyed seeing to the task themselves. Lady Griftson's watchful eye studied the exchange with disappointment. She let out a low sigh and rushed to save whatever she had in mind.

"Lord Evans, we were just discussing the dancing tonight. Both these ladies have yet to find a suitable partner." She lifted an expectant brow at him.

"So, I've seen." The corner of Lord Evans mouth raised and his eyes twinkled as he briefly looked at Jane. Jane's eyes tightened when she met his gaze.

"Yes." Lady Griftson's confidence began to waver. She glanced around and fervently waved her fan across her front. "Well . . ."

"Miss Sawyer," Lord Evans's low voice broke through any doubt Lady Griftson might have had. The waving stopped and her face illuminated when she gaped at Jane. "Would you do me the honors of accompanying me in the next dance?"

Feeling everyone's eyes on her, Jane clasped her hands tighter.

Giving him the same bored look he gave her, she replied, "As long as you promise not to step on my feet, my lord."

His eyes held a humorous gleam while the corner of his lip twitched. Lady Griftson nervously twisted her fan like she intended to strangle it. Quickly she uttered, "Of course she would be honored to dance with you, Lord Evans."

Not showing any acknowledgment towards the appalled woman in front of him, Lord Evans kept his gaze on Jane. "Very well, as long as you keep your feet out from under mine, then you have my word."

Next to her, Sophie looked at Jane with a slow smile forming across her face.

"Then I suppose I shall accept your offer," Jane replied, holding in her laughter. She didn't dare give Lady Griftson any satisfaction in the knowledge that, truth be known, she was surprised to find that she was looking forward to their dance. If the lady had caught a speck of interest, word would spread through the ballroom about the two of them and speculation of them courting would soon arise. Jane wasn't ready for such talk.

Lord Evans clasped her hand and wrapped it through his arm. As soon as they were a safe distance, away from prying ears, he leaned his head towards her. "You look very lovely this evening."

Jane felt as though the room became a blaze. Anyone who watched them would notice the color the gentleman sent to her cheeks.

"Thank you," she nearly squeaked. Wishing she could fan herself, she kept her eyes away from his and focused on the dancers that formed two long lines. He gently squeezed her hand as he left her side to stand across from her. She drew in a breath, trying to calm her nerves. *A promise is a promise*, she reminded herself, yet she couldn't help but feel like she was betraying James.

The minuet began with the loud orchestra, though she hardly heard the music. Her mind raced along with her beating heart, filled with doubt and excitement. She smiled on cue as they stepped towards each other. He smiled back—*good gracious, he has a handsome smile.*

Her cheeks warmed further when they clasped hands. They danced in silence until the second minuet began.

"Miss Sawyer, have you ever seen Wytham Woods?" he whispered before they turned out and around the couple behind them.

"No," she quickly replied. She'd passed the road that led through the woods, but never ventured in the direction.

"May I ask if I can take you on a picnic?"

Clasping hands again, Jane was overwhelmed with the idea. "A picnic?" she softly asked, in hopes the couples on either side of them didn't hear her over the music. The two stepped down the line and turned out around the couple behind. Meeting again, he held her hand even more gently.

"Yes. A few of my friends are gathering there for a picnic and I wondered if you'd join us."

Feeling more comfortable with the idea that others were involved, she released the breath that she had been holding. "That sounds delightful." She walked around a lady and faced Lord Evans who was now facing her in the opposite direction. His green eyes shimmered under the candlelight as he briefly looked her way. Stepping away from each other, they circled and clasped each other's hands again. Lord Evans smiled at her while they drew closer to one another—*perhaps too close,* she thought when her breathing quickened. Continuing down the line, the music began to lull.

"Will next week be too soon?" He took a bow as the music came to an end.

"No." Jane curtsied along with the other ladies in the line. "But I'll have to speak with Mrs. Hewitt to see what our schedule entails."

Lord Evans smiled. "Yes, of course."

Taking her arm through his, he escorted her off the dance floor towards Lady Griftson who now stood next to her uncle. Jane pressed her hand against the pearl necklace on her neck as it suddenly felt tighter than before. She glanced up and caught Lord Evans's eye.

"Thank you for the dance, my lord." She smiled, lowering her hand. "You've proved yourself quite a capable dancer."

"And you, Miss Sawyer." The corner of his mouth raised into a small smile. His gaze locked with hers without any show of hesitation.

Her chest tightened while the room grew unbearably warm. "I rather enjoyed our dance."

To say she didn't enjoy the dance with him would be a lie, but she wasn't ready to admit it. "Thank you again," she breathed, looking away. She swallowed a dry swallow that didn't relieve her parchedness as her surroundings began to close in on her.

Lord Evans furrowed his brows. "Are you alright?" He took a step closer which made her withdraw further.

"Yes." Her voice sounded high and unfamiliar to her. "I fear the room has gotten a bit stuffy for me." She laughed, drawing her fan and waving it across her face. "Please excuse me, I'm in need of some fresh air."

Lord Evans nodded and held out his hand to give her support. "Let me accompany you."

"No, no." Jane smiled to hide the panic that flared from his remark. The thought of him joining her only worsened her feelings. Ignoring his offered hand, she quickly collected herself and folded her fan. "Thank you, my lord, but I'll be just a moment."

"Of course." Lord Evans offered her a bow.

Jane squeezed her way through clusters of people towards the glass-paneled wall. Multiple French doors opened to a large balcony where she rushed through and hurried down the steps to the gardens. Her ears rang slightly after giving herself enough distance from the vivacious ballroom. She drew in the fresh spring air, relieved it helped lighten the weight on her chest.

"I can't," she muttered in frustration.

The cold air glazed her skin, but she didn't care. She made her way around darkened flowers to a moonlit bench and plopped down, burying her face in her hands. Her heart slowly pulsed back to normal as she drew in more deep breaths.

"Why, James?" she whispered into the darkness.

Music lulled through the air to where she sat. It was a beautiful, slow tempo for a waltz. She wiped away a tear that rolled down her cheek and looked up into the vast, night sky. Stars scattered across the black canvas. With its distinct 'W' shape, the constellation Cassiopeia shimmered above her. Being the queen and mother of Andromeda, Jane couldn't help but chuckle to herself as she wiped another tear.

One of her favorite memories on the island was when they had gazed at the southern lights. Jenny had told her rendition of the beautiful goddess—Andromeda being placed as a sacrifice on a rock to be eaten by a sea monster—only for Jenny it was a shark that was determined to eat her. Then there was James. Jane's heart pounded fiercely, a flurry coming alive in the pit of her stomach. The cool night air hardly soothed the heat that caressed her skin. She pressed her hand to her flushed cheek and began to think of every detail of that night. How his eyes were filled with such passion when he gazed at her. A jolt of excitement rushed through her for a brief moment. She sighed slowly, closing her eyes. When she opened them again, she stared up at Cassiopeia.

"James McCannon," she whispered towards the constellation, as if somehow the goddess would send her message to him. "Please hurry."

She wrapped her arms around her body and continued to gaze . . . wishing there would be an answer—soon.

❧ Chapter Thirteen ❧

May, 1796

"James!"

From the dirt road, James watched Thomas walk through the tall grass. His necktie hung loose around his neck. Slipping his arms through his coat sleeves, he continued to call out to him. "Are you all set?"

James adjusted his hold on his sack and grinned at his friend. "As set as I'll ever be."

Chuckling, Thomas began tying his necktie. His knee-high boots crushed the grass in his way. "Well, that sounds promising. I'm certain the ship's captain will be ready to greet you with open arms. How are you feeling?" Making it onto the road, he ran his hand through his unkept hair. A small twig fell from the motion.

"Like I'm about to take the largest leap of faith off of a cliff's edge. How was working in the orchard?"

"Fine, fine." A cheeky smile spread across Thomas's face. "You have nothing to worry about. It's been over ten months, I'm certain she's never forgotten about you. Why, Jenny mentioned how in her last letter she inquired how you're doing."

If only that was the least of his fears. Having never heard back from her, at times James couldn't help but wonder if she had indeed found herself a gentleman in England. Thank goodness, he had Jenny to reassure him that wasn't possible, otherwise he would have found himself going mad with doubts. "Did she happen to mention if Jane received my last letter?"

Thomas shook his head. "She didn't. The last I heard was that she's still waiting to hear from you."

"That's reason enough to hope." The sack over his shoulder was growing heavier by the second. He adjusted it. Releasing an exerted breath, James didn't pause to slow his pace down the dirt road. Dust drifted around his boots, tickling his nose. With the remaining of his belongings stuffed in a sack over his shoulder, he was eager to board the ship that was set to sail within the hour.

"I'm such a bloke, hand that to me." Thomas took the sack from James's shoulders. As willing as he was to pass it up, James looked at him confused. Thomas threw the sack over his shoulder and sighed. "Mrs. Haymore mentioned how you were digging boulders from her fields the other day. I know the doctor wouldn't approve of that, not while you're still on the mend."

James rolled his shoulders and rubbed at the throb on his side. "I couldn't let her carry on that work alone. Timothy would be rolling in his grave if he knew his ma was taking on those physical demands."

Peering at him from the corner of his eye Thomas offered a nod of understanding. The widow, Mrs. Haymore, had six little mouths to feed. With her oldest son's passing from the battle, her days around the farm were quite burdensome. "I'll be sure that they're taken care of."

"I appreciate that."

They walked in silence towards the harbor. Tall grass waved on either side of them from a slow-moving breeze. The bright blue sky carried thick cotton clouds. It was the perfect omen for the first day of his voyage.

"Now, what is the first thing you're going to do when you get off that ship?"

James released a heavy breath. This plan he had been brewing since the first week Jane left for England. "I'm going straight to Oxford."

"And what do you plan on saying to her?"

Having played out their conversations many times in his head, James laughed to himself. "Things," he replied, not willing to share the ridiculous nonsense that he had come up with.

A slow smile spread across Thomas's face. "I have an idea."

In the low-hanging branches to the side of the road, birds began singing a cheerful tune. It was as though they were oblivious to how his friend's ideas were never pleasant or simple. "I don't know if I want to hear it."

Thomas's smile broadened. "Come now. This is to benefit you."

James laughed and kicked at a stone on the road. He watched it skip over other rocks until it rolled into a shallow ditch. "I'm glad you accepted," Thomas said before he carried on. "In order for you to come off confident and dashing to the young lady, I only feel it right if we role-played this."

James's eyes snapped to Thomas who raised a slight brow as though to dare him to offer him a challenge. "You must be joking."

"When it comes to Miss Jane, I never joke. She's earned all my respect, which is why I'm so willing to help you in this. In fact, I'll even be willing to sacrifice my dignity to act as her. Are you ready?" He held his chin high and offered a serious expression.

James tilted his head and peered over at his friend. "I'll pass on this one."

"Come now, just imagine how impressed she'll be by your responses."

Thomas snatched a wildflower and pulled at its petals. Batting his lashes he said in a high-pitched voice, "Why James, how I missed you. When did you arrive?"

James began to laugh. Taking the flower from Thomas's hand he threw it towards the grass. "And that's enough of that."

"But we're just getting started." Thomas raised his pitch again. "Why didn't you write me?"

"I thought you said you'd give her all your respect." James couldn't help but feel defensive when he addressed Thomas. "And I did." He'd seen the letters to know that he'd written to her.

"Then why didn't I get them?" Thomas lowered his voice but kept battling his lashes, which only provoked James to shove him away.

"You look ridiculous when you do that."

"What this?" Thomas laughed, fluttering his lashes again. "I do believe this is what the ladies do to catch a man's attention."

"Stop," James groaned. "It's as though you have dirt in your eyes."

Thomas perked up. "I shall use that line the next time I see any young lady fluttering their lashes at me. 'My dear lady, do you have dirt in your eyes?'"

"If they ever bat their eyes your way." James laughed.

"Please, now's not the time to discuss the ladies in my life." Thomas gave him a cheeky smile. They both knew Thomas never loved any woman in his life other than his mother and perhaps Jenny—but that was more of a sisterly kind of love. "This is about you and Miss Jane. Let's try this again." Speaking in his normal, deep voice he continued. "Why didn't she get the letters?"

"I don't know," he sighed. "And in all seriousness, Thomas I have no idea where they could have gone. I wrote her every week. There was no way all of them would have gotten lost at sea."

Thomas rubbed at his square jaw. "You don't suppose her uncle kept them, do you?"

Running his sleeve across his forehead, James then shook his head. "No. Before their departure I had asked him if I could write her, and he said that he expected nothing less from me. I had even written to him, inquiring if he had seen any of my letters addressed to her but I've heard nothing back from him either. I'm at a loss for words as I have no explanation."

Dirt crunched under their boots as they walked in silence. Thomas looked at James and gave him a shrug. "I'm terrible at writing so I never reached out to her to know if she received my letters. At least we know that she's heard from Jenny, Miss Elaine and . . ." He paused. "Speaking of Miss Elaine, there she is."

James squinted as the sun shone bright in her direction. Miss Keaton strolled towards them with her parasol shading her from the sun's glare.

"Good day, Miss Keaton," James hollered, tipping his hat. Miss Keaton's eyes coolly narrowed at him when she glanced up from a letter in her hands.

"Perhaps it's not a good day," Thomas muttered under his breath.

"Do you think the letter is from Richard?" James whispered back as she drew closer to them. A shiver ran up his back when her eyes hardened and she kept her cold gaze solely on him.

"You don't suppose he stopped courting her?" Thomas added quietly.

"I wouldn't be surprised, Richard never stays put with one lady," he muttered back. "But then again, I was surprised they were ever together in the first place." Miss Keaton lifted her chin higher and pursed her lips with disdain. "Isn't it a beautiful day?" James added, uncertain what to make of her flaring nostrils. He removed his hat and quickly exchanged a look of confusion with Thomas before she stopped in front of him.

"Captain James McCannon," she growled, tucking her letter into her little purse.

"Yes?" he asked, unsettled that she was directing her aggravation at him. As fast as he could blink, she lifted her empty hand and gave his cheek a hard slap. James stared wide-eyed at the angry woman. She glared back at him as though he had done something outrageous to her.

"Uh," Thomas started and removed his hat. "A curtsy would do just fine for me."

"Tell me it's not true!" she demanded, her eyes never straying from James.

"I wish I could, but I don't know what you're accusing me of." James clenched his jaw, bracing himself when her hand balled into a fist.

"Miss Harrlow!" She waved her parasol in the air adding to her dramatics. "I just ran into her when I went to send a letter. I just can't believe you would stoop so low."

James exchanged a confused expression with Thomas. "Stoop so low, how do you mean?"

Miss Elaine's mouth fell. "I can't believe you would think otherwise. Going from Jane to her would be like drinking out of the Thames River."

James grimaced at the thought. "Are you accusing me of courting Miss Harrlow?"

With her hands on her waist, she starred at him with wide eyes. "Are you not?"

Out of all the rumors, how could she believe this one? He drew in a deep breath to keep his voice calm. "No."

Miss Elaine raised her parasol, shielding her from the sun's rays. Her nostrils flared as she looked between him and Thomas. "Does that woman not have a decent bone in her body? She led me to believe that she was talking about you . . . sorry, James . . ." She ran a lace gloved hand across her cheekbone. "For your cheek." Right when James was going to forgive her, she hurried and added, "But you can only imagine how furious I was when I heard that you've been courting that wretched woman."

"Is that what she's claiming?" Thomas smirked as though he could read the dread on James's face.

Why, did I ever accept Miss Harrlow's peace offering of fish cakes? He dragged his hand down his face. "What exactly did she say?"

With a huff, Miss Elaine shook her head with disbelief. Her curls bounced by the movement. "The audacity of that woman. While I was at the harbor, I thought I'd go to the mailroom to drop off a letter for my dear Richard. She happened to be there as well, oddly organizing the letters to only be tossed in the mailbag. Honestly, the woman must be dafter than a fish. As I was ignoring her odd ways, I overheard her gushing to one of her friend's about how her captain was soon fully recovered so he could take her riding around the island. I just assumed she was talking about you."

"Never." The blood boiled in his veins when he stepped towards Miss Elaine. "Never would I consider courting that woman."

A dainty hand fell to Miss Elaine's chest. "Thank the stars. I was ready to recruit Jenny in knocking sense into your thick head."

Uncertain how to take the remark, James met Thomas's eye. Expecting him to laugh at this predicament, he instead found his friend's eyes widening. "Miss Elaine, this wasn't your first time finding Miss Harrlow in the mailroom, was it?"

She peered up at him with a hint of confusion. "It's not."

"How frequently would you say you've seen her in there?" Thomas adjusted the sack on his shoulder. His thick brows pinched together as if he were on the brink of solving something.

James studied him, putting the pieces together. *Miss Harrlow. Organizing the mail. Miss Elaine in the mailroom. Misleading her.*

"I see her more than I would ever care for as I write to Richard every other day."

James leaned away from them, feeling his stomach drop. "Miss Elaine, did she ever mention a secret lover to you?"

"That woman?" Miss Elaine laughed. "We all would have heard about it by now as she's not one to keep much of a secret. Even if it were her own."

Thomas raised a brow. "I caught her searching through the mail. My suspicions were she'd found herself a lover that she kept quiet about. Especially, if she were hiding the letters from prying eyes."

The lady's curls bounced when she shook her head. "I would have heard such rumor from a few of her friends. The only soldier that she's spoke of and has had her eye on is this captain right here."

She closed her parasol and smacked James on his shoulder with it. James grimaced. His mind raced to all the times Miss Harrlow paid him a visit. The visits were always brief and she was always delightful but he could never forget how she treated Jane, nor the lies she had spread. He had hoped she had changed her ways but now that he thought about it, he never really knew her to know for sure. "Jane's letters," he ran his hand down his face.

"Do you suppose Miss Harrlow has stolen them?" Thomas's tone was one of skepticism.

Miss Elaine gasped. "Oh, I do." She drew a letter from her purse and began reading the unfamiliar handwriting. "How often would you say that you wrote to Jane?"

"Every week," James pulled out his pocket watch. He had less than an hour to make it to the docks and at the pace they were going, it would take him the rest of the afternoon. "I haven't much time before my ship leaves. Come, Thomas, let's hurry." Nodding a farewell to Miss Elaine, he quickened his strides.

"Yes, sir," Thomas secured that sack over his shoulder and matched James's pace.

"Wait," Miss Elaine grabbed his arm and hurried by his side. Her parasol towered over her head and his shoulder. "Here, I'll talk while we walk."

James peered at Thomas who shrugged. It was more than a year ago that he wanted nothing to do with Miss Elaine. Now that she wasn't so clingy, he found her somewhat decent to be around.

"Are you sailing to your new assignment?"

He raised a brow, surprised she knew about his plans. Jenny and Thomas were the only ones he had mentioned them to.

Staring at the letter, she added. "I overheard my father saying you were being reassigned off the island."

Ah, he mumbled to himself. And he had mentioned it to the governor.

"I am—" he started but couldn't continue as she shrieked in his ear. "Sophie! I have many words for you." She looked up from her letter to James with large eyes. "Please, tell me you're going to see Jane before you're stationed to wherever it is."

"That is my plan—"

"For goodness sake, you better," Miss Elaine rushed, holding her letter towards him. "Jane's obligated to accept any gentleman caller until you write to her."

"But I have!" James blurted, he raised his hat and raked his hand through his hair. "How am I going to prove that to her and her uncle that I've kept my word? I have nothing to show for it. Just suspicions."

"If you mention how Miss Harrlow may be behind it, Jane will never doubt you." Miss Elaine began to pant as she seemed to struggle to keep up with the two men.

Thomas nodded in agreement. "Jane's not naive to that woman's tactics. She wouldn't put it past her."

"Yes, but there's no proof. I can't go off of my suspicions." James slowed his pace to keep Miss Elaine from gasping. Rubbing the ache in his side, he groaned with frustration.

"Oh, I'll get your proof." Miss Elaine tucked her letter back in her purse. With her hand on her waist, she drew in a breath. "Leave it to me." The corner of the woman's mouth twisted into a smile. "I'll keep you informed as soon as I hear what she's done with the letters. Your job, James, is to show Jane that you never forgot her. After this letter I'm certain she'll need that reassurance."

James's mouth fell. What did that letter say? Who did she say that it was from? "Thomas, I'll see you soon. James, safe travels. I'm going to find Jenny." Taking a deep breath in, Miss Elaine turned in the opposite direction from them and headed towards Jenny's family orchard. Her parasol bobbed in the air with her fervent steps. "And this does not mean your forgiven for having me read poetry to Richard," she called over her shoulder. "I'm doing this for Jane not for you."

The corner of James's mouth raised as he remembered how he tried to keep Captain Richard from pursuing Jane. He never thought his plan of convincing Elaine that Richard had feelings for her would result in them forever being together. Nor that Richard would put up with the poems for so long.

"God speed to you both," James called with a chuckle. He ran his hand through his hair and plopped his hat back on his head. Panic began to prick at his heart from what Miss Elaine had said of Jane being encouraged to be courted. He had no doubt that she would be pursued but what worried him more was if any of the gentlemen would win her heart.

Thomas cleared his throat. "I'm certain you have nothing to fret. Jane would never move on from you."

James could hear a pinch of doubt in his friend's tone. Rubbing the back of his neck, a feeling of regret began to churn in his stomach. He should have promised her more than just to write.

"I could only hope. But if all this time she's never received one of my letters asking for me to court her, I'm certain she has many reasons why she shouldn't hold on."

Sucking in a deep breath, he knew the next month at sea was going to feel like an eternity.

Sitting in her garden, Jane peered at her textbook. It had become her favorite place to escape there in Oxford as she enjoyed the fresh air. On rare occasions she'd catch a glimpse of home when the sun peeked through the muted gray sky. A cool breeze blew past her, shaking the narrow leaves of a horse chestnut tree, across her way. She tightened her shawl across her shoulders.

Mrs. Hewitt proved to be a marvelous instructor and she had allowed Jane to assist with two births the past week. Both mothers and babies were doing splendidly. She smiled as she reflected on each miracle. She was extremely grateful Jenny had aided in her decision to become a midwife. It was very gratifying.

"Miss Jane," Millie's steps crushed the pebble rocks on the narrow path. Tightening her grip on her shawl, Jane's heart leapt into her throat at the woman's approach.

Seeing the anticipation on her face, Millie shook her head, and her slender shoulders hunched forward. "It's from Lord Evans."

Jane gave a halfhearted smile and glanced down at a pale yellow flower. She hated how she kept anticipating a letter from a certain someone. She placed her book on the bench and plucked the yellow primrose. Twisting the spring flower in her fingers, she released a heavy sigh. If only she could bloom like the flowers behind their cottage did with all the gray sky. Not that Lord Evans wasn't sunshine in her life. He certainly had been a perfect gentleman when they'd seen each other on a few occasions. The last visit was a week ago when they had gone horseback riding together. He took her to a hilltop so he could show her why Oxford was nicknamed the "City of Spires." The scenery was breathtaking and his company—she smiled to herself—it was quite enjoyable.

Millie pulled out the letter from her pocket, "Do you think he's coming to town again?" Her round, green eyes were wide with curiosity.

"Perhaps," Jane accepted the letter. Since the actual Lord Bingham had returned to the estate to tend to Lady Bingham and their new daughter, Lord Evans returned to his home in London to attend parliament. With Sophie at her aunt's and Lord Evans in London, Jane longed for their surprise visits.

"I'll see you in an hour, miss." Millie bobbed in a curtsy. Her thick, blonde braid fell over her shoulder.

"Have my morning hours already passed?" Jane peered up at the clouded sky. It became hard to discern the time of day with the sun constantly hidden.

"Yes, miss. And may I say I'm excited to see you in this ball gown? There're so many beautiful beads, you'll be dazzling."

Jane smiled. "I appreciate your kind words, Millie. I'll be in shortly."

"Very well, miss," Millie said assuredly.

Jane was too focused on opening the letter to notice Millie's departure. She slid a piece of paper from its encasing and read.

My dear Miss Sawyer,

*How London is even more dreary without your beautiful smile.
I'm afraid my spending time at Oxford isn't an option for a while.
It is my impression that you and your uncle will be in London for
a fortnight. I have inquired of your uncle if the two of you would
join me at the Royal Opera House. He's given me his approval yet
I seek your answer.*

*Would you do me the honor Miss Sawyer, and join me at the
opera? I eagerly look forward to your response.*

Sincerely, your friend,
Lord Evans

Folding the letter, Jane smiled as she tucked it in her pocket. An
opera. She had mentioned to Lord Evans that she had yet to attend
one. He made true to his word as he was determined to be the first to
take her to the musical theatre.

Gathering her book against her side, she hurried her way inside to
write her reply—yes.

June, 1796

The morning hour fog blanketed the congested Port of London. James
wrinkled his nose from the foul stench of rotting fish and sewage lurk-
ing in the Thames River they traveled on. A bell rang in the distance,
alerting sailors at the harbor of a ship's departure. He leaned forward,
grasping a line and peered from the ships deck towards the brick buildings lining the street along the docks. His knees buckled back and
forth as he tried to keep himself from diving into the vile water to
speed up the daunting process of docking. He had spent most of his
time at sea planning for this day. He watched as the ship eased her way
through the crowded water of other merchant ships of various sizes.

Twisting his hand around the course rope, he ran through the
plan in his mind. From the dock he'd catch a carriage to his parents'
townhome. Usually, this time of year, they were in the city attending
a few events with friends. And if they had received his letter, they
wouldn't be at all surprised by his visit. After the briefest of hellos,

he'd take one of their carriages to Oxford as he didn't trust his side to handle the ride on saddle—not yet. Then he'd knock on Jane's front door and pray that she'd be home for him to sweep her in his arms and—

"May I speak freely with you, Captain?" Lieutenant Tuft's approach startled James from his thoughts.

The older gentleman stood by his side. The man's eyes squinted, when he looked to the pier, deepening the weathered lines on his face. Never had James had the pleasure of being approached by the quiet gentleman. At sea he always kept to himself. Then on a few occasions the lieutenant would offer him a brief nod whenever James attempted to start a conversation, but that was as far as it went.

"You may." James's knees stilled.

"I've never seen a wounded soldier have such perseverance that he went from barely walking to climbing up and down ratlines in a matter of weeks. I marvel at your recovery, Captain."

James felt his jaw slack when the lieutenant looked at him with the deepest respect. "I appreciate that, Lieutenant." He'd never forget the pain and sweat that he had to endure during those trying weeks at sea. It was brutal climbing the ratlines, but very rewarding as his desperate need to gain his strength back was successful.

A bell rang out from the ship's deck and an officer called out to the sailors to prepare the lines to dock. James removed his hat and ran a trembling hand through his hair. Tugging on his coat sleeves, he drew in a foul breath of London's air and slowly released it.

"Good luck with your endeavors, Captain," the lieutenant offered, before giving him a brief nod and limping towards the steps to the quarterdeck. James couldn't help but stare after him in disbelief. It was humbling to have received a moment of the gentleman's time.

The ship slowed as men on the pier pulled rigging lines in the opposite direction.

Careful not to twist in a way that could hurt his side, James reached down and lifted his sack.

Hurrying onto the damp deck, his pace was confident and determined. His gaze searched the street in front of him for any sign of a hackney coach. A dark carriage stationed next to a darkened streetlamp caught his eye. James watched as a tall figure emerged from its coach. The person's hood draped over their head concealing their appearance. With long strides, the person headed in James's direction. Walking around a barrel, James kept his eye on the figure. With only a few steps to go before they crossed paths, the gentleman lifted his head and looked James in the eyes with a broad smile across his face.

"Captain McCannon," the familiar deep voice called. "What a pleasure to see you again. Do you have a moment?"

James's pulse throbbed in his throat. He took a deep breath to keep calm, as he knew his plans to see Jane were about to crumble.

"Yes, sir."

Chapter Fourteen

My Darling Jane,

Do you remember that night you ruined my pillow and made it lumpy? What about the time you tricked me into dancing with the gentleman who smelt atrocious? Well, I forgive you for it and hope you forgive me for ever telling you to move on with love. I met someone. We only danced once but that's all it took for my heart to be taken with him. So please, reconsider my words. I desperately wish I could tell you more about the gentleman but my time is short. By the way, Father will be arriving in a few days from London. While he was out on a special assignment by yours truly, I found a way to get the frugal man to buy me a new ball gown. Between you and me, I may have accidentally left my aunt's puppy in my room where my least favorite gown happened to be left airing out. 'Tis a shame, really. I may have even smiled after I saw the shredded fabric and pictured a London dress in its place. I'll see you in London soon.

Enjoy your first opera with Lord Evans. I expect you to give me every detail. And I mean every detail!

Much love,
Sophie

Jane stared out into the dark evening sky from their carriage window. The early June heat began to thicken the air. Not a star could be seen from London's smogginess. Their horses' hooves trotted with a continuous rhythm along the cobblestone street. The iron clad wheels of the carriage echoed loudly between tall brick buildings.

"You'll love the opera, my dear," Jane's uncle said, eyeing her while she wrung the fan in her hands. "The music is marvelous and the singers are extremely talented."

She nodded. The corner of her mouth rose and fell quickly as she continued her gaze out into the darkness. The opera was far from her mind at the moment. What had grasped her attention was Sophie's letter. As much as she enjoyed hearing from her friend, her words about meeting someone had her thinking too much of her first meeting with . . . she released an exasperated sigh—Captain McCannon.

"It was very considerate of Lord Evans to invite us to join him in his box seats," he added, cleaning his spectacles with his handkerchief.

"It was," she replied quietly, glancing at her fan. She twisted it between the clutch of her hands. Captain James never gave her any indication to hold on, for he still had yet to write. Though, somewhere around the broken pieces of her heart, she refused to think he had given up on her.

"Jane." She looked up, to see her uncle was at the edge of his seat. "We're here."

She tightened her stance while she swayed forward with the carriage and the horses came to a halt. The coachman opened their door. The flickering light of the lamppost on the sidewalk dimly illuminated the cab. Shifting himself towards the doorway, her uncle departed. Jane released a breath and followed suit. Crisp cool air struck her face. It was a cooler evening than what it had been the previous night. She tightened her hold on her cloak.

Her uncle held out his hand for her, aiding her onto a large, stone sidewalk. Her red silk gown swooshed around her feet as she stepped forward. Torches flickered off tall, thick stone columns, illuminating the grand steps towards the crowded entrance. Couples, dressed in their formal attire, strolled up the stairs in front of them. Her eyes followed them until they landed on Lord Evans. The tall, dashing lord smiled at her and hurried down the steps to where they stood. She observed how elegantly he held his head high. His blond, wavy hair stayed in its place with every bounce in his step.

"Doctor Brown," he bowed towards him. "Miss Sawyer." His green eyes shone bright when he turned his gaze to her. He took hold of her gloved hand and brought it to his lips.

She held her breath, waiting, perhaps even hoping his kiss would be an escape from any doubts she was beginning to form towards him. He kissed her hand and lowered it back to her side. She released a staggered breath. Nothing, she felt nothing. Not even one flutter. Was she numb from feeling? She gave him a smile, trying to hide her disappointment.

"Lord Evans," her uncle said beside her. "We're very grateful to have an opportunity such as this."

"Doctor Brown." Lord Evans smiled at him with great esteem. "It's my honor to have you and Miss Sawyer accompany me tonight." He glanced at Jane and offered his arm. "Shall we?"

Smiling, she wrapped her arm easily through his. She lifted her skirt and ascended the stone stairs, being careful to avoid tripping on the beautiful material of her new satin gown.

Her uncle had yet again insisted on buying her a gown for the opera. Why she had to wear a new gown for the occasion was beyond her. If she had a choice, which she felt she didn't, she would have worn one of her gowns from Bombay. She was beginning to fear London's society was having an effect on him. Or perhaps it was Lady Griftson and her not-so-subtle jabs at finding Jane a suitor. Either way, she was going to have to speak with him about the unnecessary expenses.

The dazzling foyer of the opera house was beyond words. The room was magnificent with high vaulted, patterned ceilings. A grand staircase greeted them with a deep crimson red carpet. The landing at the top of the stairs divided into two separate staircases that led toward the opera boxes. Jane smiled, thinking of the exhilaration of racing Sophie up such stairs. After passing her cloak to a steward and collecting her number, they eased their way through the masses across the marble floor and climbed the carpeted steps. Excited chatter echoed off the gold-trimmed walls around them. With every step

Jane took she felt the anticipation grow within her. They walked down a long corridor and paused at the heavy, red drapes covering one of many entrances. An usher swiftly pulled a drape back and beckoned them in.

Lord Evans assisted Jane to her soft, velvety chair then sat on her right while her uncle sat slightly farther away to her left. She peered over the banister, gaping at the exquisite scene before her. Two-stories below them were rows of half-filled chairs. To her amazement, the stage was close enough that she could see the large orchestra in the pit below the stage.

"It's beautiful, isn't it?" Lord Evans softly said to her side. Jane drew her eyes away from the spectacular view to look at him. His freshly shaved face was so close to hers that she could see a fresh cut on his cheek where he was nicked. She leaned back ever so slightly.

"It is." She smiled and looked back towards the audience while she felt him study her.

"I'm glad you think so," he added, his eyes softly gazing into hers when she looked his way. "Do you have any plans while you're here in London?"

She began to fidget with the fan around her wrist as she knew where the question would lead. Was she ready for it?

"There are a few dances that we'll be attending. Other than that, my uncle will be busy meeting with colleagues until our return to Oxford."

Lord Evans leaned further on his arm rest, and lowered his voice to her. "Miss Sawyer."

She could feel the temperature in the room rise. Her uncle was on her other side completely engrossed with the orchestra as they went from discord to a beautiful harmony that swelled the room as the musicians tuned their instruments. His fingers tapped his armrest as he was eager for the music to commence.

"If it's alright with you, I hope to see more of you within that time."

She caught Lord Evans's earnest gaze as he searched her eyes for her answer. Her breathing quickened and her thoughts barreled over each other. Weeks ago, Sophie had encouraged her to move forward with her life, but mere hours ago her letter apologized that she ever suggested it. What should she say?

Her uncle's voice seeped through her mind, *You can't set your heart aside for something that may never happen. Give others a chance.* Of course, he had said that after he saw how torn she was when she began to receive flowers and notes expressing Lord Evans's admiration for her. She bit her lip and sucked in a sharp breath. Perhaps he was right? Her feelings for James ran extremely deep, yes, but what was she to do when she never heard from him? should she continue to move forward with the promise? After all, Lord Evans had been nothing but kind to her. Lord Evans slowly began to back away from her, his face filling with doubt. Quickly, she made a rash decision that she hoped would void any hesitation towards him.

"That would be nice," she said softly, resting her hand on the arm of her chair. He grinned and clasped her hand. Bringing it to his thin lips, he gently kissed it. She smiled but she didn't feel it reach her heart. Instead of the joy she had hoped to feel, it was quite the opposite. Her heart ached and she was extremely confused. Tears stung her eyes. Promptly she looked away and began to fan her face in an attempt to help dry them.

Thankfully, the flames from the crystal chandelier started to dim, hiding her glossy eyes. The rest of the audience had trickled in and were all situated in their box seats and the seats below. The strings and woodwinds in the orchestra began the vibrant intro to the opera.

"There's a pocket on the side of your chair. In it you'll find your binoculars," Lord Evans whispered, and pointed towards the fabric next to where she was sitting.

"Thank you."

She slipped her hand into the pocket and lifted the dainty binoculars to her eyes. She smiled as the small stage now appeared larger and closer to her. She could even make out the musicians' faces. Woodwinds, strings, and brass rang out with song. The curtains parted and a man bellowed out in spinto. Tiny bumps ran up Jane's arms in an exciting chill. She leaned forward, taking in his glorious voice. The music was all in Italian, but she understood some of the words as her uncle had insisted that she study a little of the language while she was young. The melodies altered from fierce, to soft, to fleet and calm. By the third act, tears escaped her as the melody and words from the song were filled with immense passion. Lord Evans politely handed Jane his handkerchief. Grateful for the offer, she dabbed her eyes and continued to enjoy the soul-stirring music.

The curtain closed and intermission began. The flames on the walls flickered brighter once again. Jane's uncle turned towards them, his eyes twinkling with glee. "Wasn't that wonderful?" But before Jane and Lord Evans could respond, his gaze had turned across their way. "Ah, if you two would excuse me for a moment, I see a colleague of mine that I'd like to converse with." He squeezed Jane's hand and left their box seats.

"How are you enjoying the opera, Miss Sawyer?"

She hesitatingly looked up at the lord. Ever since she said she'd like to see him again she had been feeling regret.

"I loved it. The music was so moving," Feeling it impossible to look at him, she stared at his handkerchief in her hand. "Forgive me, I never expected to cry like I had." She held the fabric out to him but he put up his hand to decline.

"Keep it. You may want it for the second half of the act." He smiled.

Jane laughed. "You're probably right. If you'll excuse me, I better freshen up."

"Of course." He stood, and held out his hand to assist her.

"I'll be gone for a moment." He gave her a nod and stood in his place while she left. On the other side of the curtain, she released a heavy breath and drew in another. She needed to regain her composure. She made her way through the crowded hall towards the ladies' room, mentally giving herself encouragement while trying to clear her mind of any thoughts regarding Captain McCannon. *You can do this, Jane. He's a wonderful gentleman. He's kind, handsome, a good brother, a decent dancer*—she maneuvered herself around a couple—*and he's excellent with communication. He writes to you. Weekly.* She sighed once in the sanctuary of the ladies' parlor. If he's so wonderful, then why didn't she feel anything spectacular?

She approached a water basin and a pile of clean cloths. Running the water over the cloth, she blotted her face and eyes. Perhaps her heart was hardened? Did these past few months turn her cold from feeling love again? She glanced up at the mirror and stared at herself. Her blue-green eyes were bright with a touch of pink along the rims from her tears. She lifted her chin and ran the cloth down her slender neck. If she opened her heart to the idea, then perhaps she would feel something more than an occasional racing heart. The strong flutters she once had with Captain James were dormant. She just needed to be open to the idea of being able to love again and then those feelings would come alive again. Feeling more confident that being closed-minded was the issue, Jane stood in front of the mirror and gave herself a quick look over. Patting a curl back into place, she smoothed down her red gown and made her way back into the chatter of the mass of people in the hall.

She peered around ladies with feathers in their hair and gentlemen smoking their cigars to the identical curtain-covered doors. Along the columns she noted numbers indicating the booths but regretfully couldn't remember the number of their booth.

A group dispersed from the front of a doorway, allowing her to glance at the number. The red curtains began to part, and she glanced its way. Within that moment, time slowed. Her steps staggered and blood drained from her face and limbs. She tried to blink to assure herself he wasn't there, that it was all a nightmare of her imagination, but she couldn't peel her horror-stuck stare from him. Her pulse pounded against her neck, her heart having decided to sprint fast away from the situation. But her mind couldn't keep up. No, she couldn't move!

Lowering his cigar, a sinister smile crept over his face as his eyes fell on her. She caught her breath and forced her legs to do what felt to be an impossible task—run!

She moved swiftly, briefly rubbing her arms that began to throb from the memory of his grasp. Peering over her shoulder, she saw him watching her, like a vulture to his prey. She squeezed her way between a couple and turned down the staircase to hurry from his sight to the floor below.

"Excuse me, excuse me," she frantically said as she rushed down the hall. Peering back over her shoulder, to her horror she saw his stringy, auburn hair bob up and down while he weaseled around people towards her. She wanted to scream, to cry out for help but her panicked beating heart felt as though it was caught in her throat. Determined to lose him, she darted for the nearest exit. She was vulnerable being in the open of the hallway, even though she was surrounded by many attendees. Her crimson red gown didn't help—making her stand out from the other young ladies who were wearing dark hues of blues and purples. She slid herself between the curtain of a box seat, attempting to avoid any movement of the drapes.

Cautiously, she faced the exit and grabbed the fabric with shaking hands to peek through. Slightly hunched, she blinked multiple times as she became lightheaded from her escape. She unsteadily released a breath as she watched people pass in front of the drapes. The lieutenant stopped in front of where she hid. Her chest burned as she forced her gasping into a more short, shallow, and quiet breath. Carefully, she released her shaking hands from the velvety curtain, leaving a small gap to still peer through to see him.

Lieutenant Howard ran his hand over his slicked hair and threw it against his thigh. His lips curved over his teeth with a snarl. He looked around, fervently scanning the crowd. After what felt to be a lifetime, he pivoted on his feet and stormed down the hall towards the stairs.

Slowly releasing a quivering breath, she straightened her stance. Freeing her skirt from her fearsome grip, she brought her trembling hands to her chest, attempting to hold herself together. It was close. Too close. A shiver ran up her spine and she shook.

"Excuse me," A deep, rich voice said from behind.

Her panic-stricken heart stammered. The hair on her neck stood as she recognized the voice. She slowly turned, uncertain if it was all in her head or if she had indeed heard him. With whatever air remained in her burning lungs, she gasped.

He lifted the corner of his mouth, exposing a dimple. The dreadful dimple that she had wistfully dreamt of so often.

The darkened corridor began to spin. Her vision darkened and her body became light. She felt herself floating down into darkness—away from a horrid man and away from the one she longed to see.

"Jane," his velvety voice called. She flinched as she felt something gently patting her cheek. "Jane . . . Jane," he pleaded.

Am I dreaming? This must be, if I'm hearing him. She nestled into her pillow, refusing to wake.

"Jane," he softly called again. Gradually, her senses were waking as she became aware that she wasn't wrapped in a blanket but rather in a strong arm curved around her back. *No, this can't be a dream. Not again.* A large hand softly stroked her cheek.

"Jane, please wake up," he whispered.

Her eyes fluttered open as she instantly remembered what had happened. He was staring down at her with his worried, striking blue eyes, and her stomach began to twist and pull in all different directions. She gripped his arm, trying to straighten herself to stand. He began to assist but once her feet were steady, she pushed him away. Not the best idea. Her hand flew to her head as she felt the room spin around her.

"Jane, are you alright?" he asked anxiously. His hand rested on her back to steady her. She avoided his eyes, afraid he'd see the pain he had caused her the past few months.

"Please, I'm fine," her voice quivered. Angry tears began to form at the brim of her lids as her voice gave away her emotions.

"Jane," James pleaded, taking a step towards her.

She threw her hand up, to stop him from getting any closer. She blinked hard, holding back the tears. Then, with all the strength she could muster, she looked into his handsome, desperate face. The very tan face she yearned to see every day since they had been apart was in front of her. *At the opera? Why? And with whom?*

"I need to return to my seat. Good evening, Captain or Major or just whatever you are," she stammered with frustration. She hated that she revealed that she heard about the advancement that he may or may not yet receive. It only made her appear as though she hung to his every movement.

His face fell. Before he could say another word, she slipped out through the curtains

She barely made it into the hall when she collided with her uncle.

"Jane!" he exclaimed, shocked by her state. "Are you well?"

"I am not." She blinked harder, determined to keep it together. "I'm so sorry, uncle, but I must go. I'll meet you at the house. Please inform Lord Evans I'm unwell."

Her uncle was about to say something but Captain James hurried through the curtains. Her uncle's surprised expression turned into a look of understanding. "Take the carriage home, dear. I'll find other means." He gave her a kiss on her cheek.

She nodded and scurried down the hall, distancing herself from all the whirlwind of emotions she was feeling.

From behind, she heard her uncle exclaim. "Captain McCannon! It's so great to see you on your feet again!"

The walls of the opera house were closing in on her as she eased her way through the crowded hall towards the grand stairway. Her chest tightened. *Steady, Jane!* She drew in a sharp breath and blew it out as her head was spinning. Her shoes clacked against the marble floor of the foyer. Fortunately, the steward heard her approach.

"Doctor Brown's carriage if you please." She did her best to keep the quiver out of her voice. Extending her number to the steward, her hand noticeably shook. The steward bowed then snapped his fingers. A servant hurried to his side, listening to the steward's instructions and left to carry out the orders.

Eager to escape, Jane pushed the heavy doors open, leaving behind her cloak. Releasing a shiver, she welcomed the cool night's breeze that blew through the night's fog.

Why was he here? Most importantly, why didn't he tell me he was coming?

She wrung her fan on her wrist and aimlessly took heavy steps down the stone stairs. She clasped her side, pushing against her constricting corset as her breaths came short and fast. Disappointment flooded her mind as a memory swamped her. A memory from Jamestown's festival that she thought she had buried. She was everything Miss Catherine Harrlow hinted she was. *A simpleminded lady who fell into his distorted trap.*

Argh! She stopped at a darkened column and crossed her arms over her chest. *What has this night come to?*

"I'm dreaming," she concluded. She squeezed her eyes shut, picturing how the nightmare will pass when she awakes. Slowly, she squinted through her lashes and caught the fluttering of a flame in a lantern above. Disappointment crashed over her.

Footsteps began to softly approach her direction. Her heart tightened, not ready to face the raw feelings he caused to surface. The footsteps stopped behind her. She wiped her tear-stained face as his hands clasped her arms.

"Please," Jane began, turning to look up at James.

Cold pricks ran through her body. Her eyes widened. She opened her mouth to scream but his hand roughly covered it, muffling the sound. Viciously, he wrapped an arm around her body, and pulled her into the dark shadow of the column. Shoving her against the cold stone pillar, he pushed her head back with his boney hand still covering her mouth. He lifted her chin with his thumb, forcing her to look into his ghastly face.

"Miss Sawyer," he spat, pressing himself against her.

Jane thrashed against the weight of his body. She screamed with all her might into his hand and pushed her head off the column but was thrust back by his force.

A loud thump echoed in her ears, followed by a sharp pain behind her head. Darkness filled her vision as she felt her body grow frail from her head slamming against the column. She lifted her heavy lids as she felt Lieutenant Howard's grip tighten to hold her up.

"No, you don't. You get to listen to me," he breathed, sending the aroma of liquor into her face. Instinctively, she gagged into his hand. Her groan muffled against his sour palm. "Do you know what you put me through?" He clicked his tongue as if to scold her. "They suspended me as an officer in the navy for six months. I was outraged . . . My uncle—he almost disowned me," the man growled. "I've had to redeem myself by sweet talking with his friends and charming my way with their hideous daughters." His lip curled with disgust. "I'm a puppet on a string and it's all because of the false accusations you claimed."

Tears began to pour down Jane's cheeks onto his hand. Her body, weak from all the emotional turmoil of the evening, had quit trembling.

"I'm glad you find my story despairing," he sneered, pressing closer into her to hold her up. "I feel the only thing that will correct this is if you—"

"Howard!" a voice roared through the darkness.

From the corner of her eye she saw a large figure come thundering towards them through the fog. Lieutenant Howard loosened his grip on her and turned, catching a fist to his jaw. Stumbling back, he released her.

She collapsed to her hands and knees, shaking. The steps began to spin under her. She clasped her throbbing head to steady herself.

"Are you hurt?" James asked with urgency. He crouched down next to her, hovering his hand over her shoulders. Through the quivering, she managed a slight nod.

In the shadows, Lieutenant Howard let out an angry yell and charged James. He stood, swiftly blocking the lieutenant's blow. James grabbed his arm, twisted it around his back and pinned him against his body. He wrapped his other arm around Lieutenant Howard's neck to keep him from escaping.

"You just couldn't stay away, could you?" James fumed.

Lieutenant Howard grunted, struggling to get out of his hold. "I have my reasons, thanks to you and that good for nothing, little—"

James's arm tightened against Lieutenant Howard's neck, causing him to gasp.

"Enough," he snarled.

"But I'm just getting started," Lieutenant Howard choked out in a hoarse voice. Forcefully, he pounded his heel into James's foot, loosening his hold.

Jane's eyes widened and she screamed out in horror as Lieutenant Howard brought his head forward and fiercely thrusted it back into James's face. She gasped, helplessly watching James stagger back, covering his forehead.

Lieutenant Howard turned to face James with a menacing laugh. "Look at yourself, the pathetic captain who killed over half his crew for his own victory," he sneered.

Her heart quickened. James's wounded side from the French attack was now exposed to the man. Scrambling to her feet, she charged.

"Stop!" she yelled, clasping his raised arm.

Lieutenant Howard looked over his shoulder and laughed at her. With one swift shake, he threw her back to the stairs.

Catching herself on her hands and knees, she winced, grateful that all the layers she wore under her skirt cushioned her from the fall. Desperately hoping she had bought him enough time to defend himself, she looked up at James.

He staggered back and shook his head. In the distance a constable's whistle blew. Lieutenant Howard went for another punch but was immediately blocked. James thrusted his fist into the lieutenant's stomach, causing him to hunch over in agony. Grabbing his shoulders, he shoved the lieutenant down on the hard step.

"Stay there," he grumbled, wiping at his brow again.

"I don't take orders from you," Lieutenant Howard shot back. "I won't make the same mistake as your crew did." The flickering lamp above casted shadows across his wrathful expression. He went to stand but James threw his fist to his face.

"Never, ever talk about my crew again," he breathlessly said, his voice husky. He grabbed the half-conscious man's lapel and pulled his bloody face towards his. "And don't you ever go near her again," he growled, casting him back on the step. "Your career in Her Majesty's Navy is officially finished."

Lieutenant Howard let out a painful moan and he curled up on the stair.

A constable ran up to Jane's side and assisted her up. She briefly explained what had happened and pointed her shaking finger towards the abhorrent man.

Relief washed over Jane as she watched Lieutenant Howard being dragged away by the constable and his partner. She collapsed on the steps and continued to shake uncontrollably. She caught her breath when large hands rested briefly on her shoulders. She quickly assured her panicked heart that it was James. Glancing up, she saw through the shadows how he was in his shirt and waistcoat and her eyes trailed down to his hands where his coat was draped around her shoulders. She grabbed the lapels and pulled his coat tighter around her.

"Thank you," she whispered.

A grunt sounded next to her as he sat by her side. A wonderful citrusy aroma filled her nose, bringing her back to her time with James on Saint Helena. She closed her eyes, clinging to those memories and the joy it brought as she tried to escape what had happened.

"Are you alright?" His voice was hoarse.

Peeking through her lashes, she watched him rub his hands together. The sharp pain in the back of her head turned dull. It was still pounding but not nearly as bad. Resisting the temptation to touch it she kept her hands tucked into his coat.

"I knew he was in England," she said, voice shaking. "I just didn't think we'd cross paths—at least that's what I was hoping." She wiped a stray tear.

James clenched his jaw. He released his hands and lifted his arm, drawing it around her shoulders. "You're safe now," he whispered. He offered her a reassuring squeeze, then surprisingly kissed the top of her head.

Jane's heart filled with hope but it quickly shattered as she convinced herself to stop. *Any friend would offer such a kiss. It's been months without a word from him, don't be like the other ladies, "distorting" his actions.* She looked at her gloved hands that were folded into each other. *Why did he make this so hard?* She released a sigh. *Oh, Jane. You really are mindless.*

"Thank you for rescuing me—again," she whispered.

James held her tighter against his side.

"Now I do need to go," her voice quivered.

Swaying to her feet, the warmth of his body was quickly replaced with the chill of the night. She went to release a hold of his coat on her shoulders, but his hand secured hers. It was warm, and felt so right as it protected it from the night air. She closed her eyes as her heart yearned to be with him. He let out a heavy breath and stood.

"Please, let me escort you home." His voice was one of pleading.

Hesitantly, she looked up at him to object, but then noticed something shimmering in the lamplight just above his eye. She had been selfishly lost about herself that she had forgotten all about the hit he took from Lieutenant Howard.

"James, you're bleeding!"

All the conflicting feelings rushed out as she grabbed the handkerchief from the corner of her bodice. She reached up to place it on the cut of his brow. He winced when she applied the pressure. Jane's eyes scanned down from his face to his disarrayed dress attire. Blood had dripped onto his white cravat and his satin waistcoat. She began to scold herself for being so self-centered.

"Come," she said softly, keeping her eyes away from his face and safely on his cravat. "Let us get you cleaned up."

She glanced through her lashes at him and noticed how his eyes had brightened. Without further reply, he wrapped her arm through his and led them to the carriage that had arrived on the street.

Chapter Fifteen

As directed, James held his hand to his brow with the handkerchief. Sitting across from each other, they rode in silence through the foggy streets of London. He ran his hand through his tousled hair. After months of rehearsing what he would say to Jane, he found himself at a loss for words.

Never had he expected to see her at the opera, let alone at his seating area. He had thought it quite odd that a lady would duck behind his curtains. When he decided to approach her to see if she was alright, he had to blink multiple times to be certain he was truly seeing who he saw. The recognition of her brown curls and the silhouette of her beautiful face was unmistakable, and it had taken all his restraint not to pull her into his arms.

He rubbed the back of his neck and glanced her way. Loose, dark curls draped across her shoulders, a few perfectly framed her face. She stared intensely out the window, wringing her fan in her hand. He looked away, watching darkened windows of buildings pass by. The rhythm of the horse's hooves was slow and steady, unlike his rapid pulse. Reflecting on how she fainted in his arms like she had before, he knew someone had frightened her.

He drew a deep breath as his anger began to fume. The familiar stabbing, dull pain in his side intensified. The weeks at sea had given him time to strengthen his muscles. Unfortunately, tonight only reminded him that he wasn't all the way healed. Thankfully, nothing bad came from their fight—for him at least. Attempting to ignore the discomfort in his side, he shifted again on the hard bench.

For the first time in the duration of their ride, Jane glanced up at him. Her beautiful eyes were unreadable as they bore on him.

"We will be there soon," she softly assured, looking back towards the window.

Continuing to hold the handkerchief, James studied her stiff posture. How he wished he knew what was going through her selfless mind. She must be terrified by what she had gone through. A subtle tremor in her chin caught his attention.

"Are you cold?" he asked. His voice was rough, breaking the unsettling silence in their coach. Even with his coat around her shoulders, he wondered if the shock of the night had taken an effect on her. He inched himself to the edge of the bench, ready to move by her side.

She shook her head.

"I'm fine, thank you." She spoke softly, yet her voice sliced through the stillness of the carriage. James caught a despairing expression flash across her face as she gazed back out the window.

His stomach dropped. Lieutenant Howard wasn't the only one who had inflicted pain on her tonight. His heart grew heavy, understanding a lot of the grief was caused unintentionally by him.

The clapping of the horses' hooves slowed to a stop. The driver opened their door. He stepped out with the soiled handkerchief in one hand and turned to assist Jane with his clean hand. The few strands of curls that broke free from her loosened hair bounced on her shoulders. He offered his arm, which to his relief she accepted again.

"I'll be out shortly," James informed the driver.

With her arm through his, they walked up the steps to her townhome. She opened the front door, letting them in. Only the foyer lamps in the home were turned on, casting shadows on the walls. To their left was a long entryway table with two brass chamber candlestick holders on top.

Jane walked over and pulled out matches from the drawer. Striking the box, she created a flame and lit the candle. Holding the candlestick in one hand, she reached up with her other to dim a lamp on the foyer's wall.

"It's to let my uncle know, I made it back," she whispered over her shoulder.

"You have a very nice home," James noted, attempting to fill the silence.

"Thank you. It's not ours." She took a breath as she stood on her toes to reach the lever on a lamp better. "A colleague of my uncle's is letting us reside here while my uncle attends to meetings. The gentleman doesn't live here, he just graciously offers the home to any of the professors while they're in town on business."

Noticing that she was struggling to turn the knob, James came up from behind. Without a thought, he reached over her shoulder and effortlessly turned the tight lever. He paused when the familiar scent of her perfume engulfed his senses. Swallowing, he lowered his arm, brushing her soft curls with his fingers in the process. She glanced over her shoulder at him. Her eyes wide and glistening in the lamplight. Drawing in a staggering breath, he took a few steps back.

Giving him her full attention, she faced him.

Great heavens, she was even more beautiful than he remembered. He stood immovable, not wanting to break from her stare as she searched his eyes.

"Come," she said softly, walking down a dark hall. Her crimson gown swished around her swift, moving feet. "I'm afraid we're on our own," she said over her shoulder. "Anticipating a late night," she pushed a door that led into the kitchen open, "we told our staff not to wait up for us."

He loosened his cravat as it tightened around his neck and followed her through the door.

"Please, take a seat," she directed, pointing towards a stool by a long table. "I'll be just a moment." Draping his jacket at the corner of the table, she disappeared with the only candle into the pantry. The kitchen darkened except for the moonlight seeping through the windows.

Stiffly, James sat on the hard surface and anxiously looked for something to do. Spotting a tea kettle on the counter, he went over and lit a fire in the hearth. Pouring a pitcher of water into the kettle, he placed it on a hook and anchored it over the small flames. With the fire crackling, he scoured the kitchen for teacups. He opened and closed cabinets until he reached the last cupboard, full of glasses and teacups. Bringing the porcelain cups out, he placed them on the table in front of two stools.

Light began to illuminate as Jane came in carrying a bag and other objects in her hand. She placed them on the table next to the candle.

"Take a seat, please," she commanded while opening the bag.

Slowly, he eased himself onto a stool. He watched as she appeared to be flustered. His mind raced with things to ask for a distraction.

"Have you completed the midwifery course?" he blurted.

"Mm, I finished my fellowship last week." Her response was one of politeness but her tone was short.

James rubbed his hands together. "Then you're officially a midwife?" He smiled, seeing that her features softened.

"Yes," the corner of her lips lifted.

He was beginning to find it hard to breathe as he stared a moment too long at the curvature of her soft lips. Pouring tonic on a strip of fabric, she briskly applied it to his wound. James tightened his fist, and kicked his foot out from under him, grimacing from the intense burn the tonic caused to his cut.

"Oh!" She bit her lip. "I'm so sorry," her voice rang unsteadily. "I should have warned you about the stinging effect."

"That is not a sting," James grunted, forcing himself to breathe. "I feel like I'm being branded by an iron poker."

He would have thought she did it intentionally had she not lifted the candle to the bottle's label. Her eyes widened and she pressed her lips together.

"Jane?"

Quickly she hurried to the pitcher and poured water over a rag. Hurrying back, she dabbed his cut.

"I may have gotten my bottles mixed." She bit her lip as she appeared to be holding in a laugh. "I, uh, used a tonic that is specifically for sore throats."

"Salt water?" James asked jokingly.

She tucked her lips under. "Perhaps. And maybe a little bit of cayenne."

His mouth fell.

"Fortunately, it's just as effective as the other tonic." She paused then added, "Just a bit more of a burning sensation." She began to laugh a nervous chuckle, but covered her mouth with her hand. "I am sorry," she stated in a collective manner.

Glancing at her supplies, she grabbed a needle and hurried to thread it. She leaned closer, while appearing to attempt to find the best angle to suture. Her gown pressed against his legs. In the moonlight, he watched her cheeks darkening. Her chest rising and lowering at a fast rate. With the slightest touch, she placed a hand under his chin and angled his head back. Tightening her eyes, she brought the trembling needle towards his brow.

"Jane," he whispered, hating how the evening had turned for her. "It can wait."

Reaching up, he pinched the needle and lowered it back to the table. She looked at him confused, but glanced elsewhere when he clasped her trembling hands in his. She closed her eyes and a tear dropped to her cheek.

"Why are you in London?"

He nodded and guided her to the stool across from him.

"While Admiral Kensington was passing through Saint Helena, I spoke with him." He cleared his throat to rid the hoarseness. "Due to the extent of my injuries, he requested that I take a year off of active duty. So, I made a petition to him. I asked that I work in London's war department for a year after that." He swallowed and clasped her chin, bringing her gaze to his. Her beautiful eyes shimmered in the moonlight. He softened his voice to a near whisper as he continued his confession. "You see there's someone in England that I long to be with. The idea of not seeing her for another year had me in complete turmoil." His thumb brushed a tear off her cheek. "I realized it was foolish of me to attempt any form of communication from afar. Especially when I desire only to speak with you in person."

She looked at him, only this time her eyes narrowed. She pressed her lips into a firm line. Whatever he had said, had ignited a torch within her. He leaned back, feeling the heat of her stare.

"Is that why you never wrote me?" she exclaimed, drawing her hands from his. "Because you found it foolish to attempt any form of communication overseas?"

"What? No. Of course not—"

"For months, I haven't heard from you. And here you are in London?" She brushed a strand of hair off her cheek and huffed with frustration. "Tell me, Captain James McCannon, at what point were you going to inform me of your stay?"

He ran his hand down his cheek before curling his fingers into a fist. "Jane, I did write to you. I have many who can attest to it. I just can't prove to you where the letters have all gone. Not yet." Her mouth parted as she appearted to grasp what he said. "And I only said that it was foolish to form communication while apart because of the grueling agony I dealt with while waiting to hear back from you. Forgive me, I can only assume that you have felt the same." James raked his hand through his hair. "And believe me when I say I was planning on seeing you—immediately." She raised a brow at him, clearly confused. James continued carefully, though with a rush, eager for her to understand. "I only arrived this morning. As I was leaving the harbor to take a carriage to Oxford, Admiral Kensington met me at the docks. He asked that I attend the opera in his stead. When I explained to him that I had pressing matters, he informed me that it was a direct order. Never in my career would I have thought attending an opera was an order. It was such an odd request, that I began to rebuke it. But once again he ordered it, and the sternness in his voice had me feeling I had no choice in the matter. I suppose it worked in my favor as my order led me right to you."

The anger she had shown dispersed into a small smile.

"Sophie," she whispered.

"Sophie?" James furrowed his brows. If Sophie was the reason, he was possibly forgiven then this person he was forever indebted to.

The smile disappeared when she looked at him.

"I do not understand. I have not received any of you letters."

With no surprise by her declaration, he nodded. "That is what I've been hearing." He winced as his wound above his brow began to burn again.

"Forgive me but I still do not understand. You said that you did write?" She bit the corner of her mouth as she studied him.

"Yes. After many letters and not hearing back from you, I had a feeling something was amiss."

"That doesn't make any sense," she retorted. "I was receiving letters from others on the island just fine."

"I know," he drew in a breath to keep his voice from rising. "You can only imagine my frustration when I heard about that. So for months, I thought perhaps I sent them to the wrong address. After hearing how Jenny had heard back from you, I had her watch me write out your address to be certain I had it correct." James stared at his palms when he mumbled, "I felt like a schoolboy again as she told me how my r's needed improvement." He felt helpless as he left her with no answers as to where the letters may have gone and he didn't want to throw out Miss Harrlow's name, not without any evidence. All he had were suspicions and any false accusation would only make him feel worse.

The burning ignited above his brow. He formed his hand into a fist to keep from rubbing it. "Gah," he uttered. "Is it supposed to burn again?" he asked through gritted teeth. He ran his hand over his forehead to wipe off the sweat that had built.

Jane tucked her lips under as though she fought a smile. "There may be some residue of salt on your skin. Here—" Her satin skirt ruffled around his legs when she stood. Softly, she placed her fingers under his chin and lifted it towards her. He scarcely breathed when she brushed a lock of his hair away from the area. Avoiding his eyes, she kept her focus on dabbing his wound. He didn't dare admit the burning had disappeared as soon as she made the first dab.

"It is good to see you again." His voice was hoarse and low. Her cheeks darkened. He briefly caught her eye before she looked back to his brow. She bit her lip and lifted her needle to stitch.

"Here comes the first poke," she gently warned.

James was too distracted by her nearness to notice any pricks. The urge to pull her into his arms began to increase as he watched her focus on suturing. Her brows drew close together in such an adorable manner while she concentrated. He crossed his arms, pressing them against his pounding chest. Fervently, he tapped his heel against the kitchen floor to keep himself distracted from her.

"You only need two stitches," she said quietly, snipping the thread.

"Mm, hmm," he mindlessly grunted.

She arched a questioning brow and looked to his bouncing knee. He immediately stopped and tucked his feet under his stool.

Unfolding his stiff arms, he surrendered and reached for her. She took a step back, away from his touch and closed her eyes. When she opened them, they were conflicted. *Why?* She shook her head. Her breathing staggered as her chest rose and fell unevenly. Staring down at her hand, she looked back at him.

"I need your cravat and waistcoat," she ordered.

James's eyes widened with surprise. "You need my—" He stopped his stammering and glanced down at his blood-soiled vest. Understanding washed over him. "Why Miss Jane Sawyer," he began to taunt. Slowly, untying his cravat, he stood and took a couple steps towards her. "I didn't know you could be so direct with unclothing a gentleman," he jested, placing his cravat on the table by her hand.

How he wished the room were brighter to see her cheeks turn a lovely shade of pink. He waited for her retort but instead, she bit the corner of her mouth and turned away. Taking the soap in her hand and his cravat in the other, she hurried to the kitchen's tin tub. James unbuttoned his vest and followed close behind. Removing the vest, he stood next to her and grabbed the bar of soap from the bottom of the tin pan and began scrubbing the stain. She glanced through her thick lashes at him but quickly focused on his cravat when he stared back. A smile began to spread over his face.

Remembering the handkerchief that she loaned to him, he went back to the table to grab it. As he picked it up, he noticed embroidered letters in the corner. He held the cloth closer to the candle. C.L.E. His heart began to sink. *Was there another? Is that why she was reserved?* The tea kettle began to whistle causing Jane to jump at the tin container. James dropped the handkerchief in the dish pan before removing the pot off the heat.

His mind swarmed as he tried to discern who was C.L.E. Grabbing the candle, he walked into the pantry to see if he could find her a tea that she would enjoy. Picking a bin that said fresh leaf tea, he brought it to the table. Never having made tea in his life, he began spooning out the tea leaves into their cups.

Could it belong to a lady friend? he began to hope to himself. But there wasn't any lace to be found on the fabric as the ladies usually preferred. After the fifth spoonful, he brought the kettle over and poured the steaming water. His stomach knotted. *Confound it! Of course she would be pursued by other gentlemen.*

He was such a fool for not sending any of his letters through with Jenny. That would have been worth the humiliation she may have added.

Breathing deeply through his nose, the letters C.L.E. ran through his mind. Stirring their tea with a spoon, he sat, disheartened, on the stool. He glanced her way and watched how she peered at his saturated vest. *Had she already moved on?*

"These will have to sit overnight," Jane mumbled. Defeated, she rinsed her hands.

Consumed with heat and dread, he began rolling up his sleeves to brace for what he was about to ask.

"Jane," James said softly. "Was it just you and your uncle at the opera tonight?"

He held his breath when she took her time answering. Slowly, she wiped her hands on a rag.

"No," she answered with slight hesitation in her voice while making her way towards him. "We attended with Lord Evans." She spread her gown out as she sat next to him.

James clenched his spoon and stirred, accidentally sloshing his tea as he repeated the unfamiliar name in his head. The potent aroma of herbs tinged his nose.

"Were you with anyone at the opera?" she stared down at her teacup in her hands. The steam curled up towards her face.

"Yes," he answered truthfully. Jane's eyes widened and she looked at him. "My parents." He gave her a crooked smile when she scoffed. He would never admit it out loud for fear of sounding condescending, but he found her quite adorable when she made that face.

Together they lifted their cups and took a sip. Instantly, he regretted it. He held his breath and swallowed the sour leaf particles. Jane rushed to the tin tub and covered the side of her mouth to hide her spitting out the repulsive liquid.

"Mm," he muffled, and smacked his lips. "Not bad." His voice cracked from the powerful aroma that was still stuck in his throat.

She cleared her throat and walked back to her seat. "Well, that was interesting." Holding up her tea, she peered into it. "Was this your first time making tea?" Her lips tucked together, holding back laughter.

"Perhaps," he offered. "Why don't you enjoy another sip while I explain how I made this wonderful concoction."

"Oh," she giggled. "I think I'll let it brew a little longer before I do such a thing."

"That may be a good idea."

"You do realize the strainer, by the kettle, is meant to strain the tea leaves?"

"Mm?" James took another sip, refusing to let her see how horrible he thought it was. Her eyes grew large as he swallowed. She held in a smile while his eyes began to water.

"It's a tad strong," he choked out. "Perhaps, we'll need more water." She giggled at his raspy voice.

"Just a little," she said, wiping her eyes. "But thank you, that was really sweet of you to make us your special tea." She grinned up at him. He went to adjust his cravat but swiftly rubbed his neck when he realized it was sitting in the kitchen's tub. He glanced at the particles floating in his tea.

"I missed you," he whispered, daring to look at her. Her eyes glistened under the flickering candle light. Without thinking, he clasped his hand around her irresistibly soft cheek. Realizing what he did, he was about to withdraw, but stopped when he caught her eye. Her captivating eyes stared back at him with longing. He leaned closer but not by much. The thought of a Lord Evans sitting next to Jane at the opera's balcony lingered in his mind. He immediately lowered his hand and clasped it around his warm cup for restraint. Clearing his throat, he slowly stirred his tea.

"Believe it or not, I even missed you reading me poetry," he said truthfully, with a half-smile.

Jane stifled a laugh. "You missed me reading you poetry?"

"Yes," he said softly. "I love hearing the gentleness of your voice. And I especially loved watching your eyebrows scrunched together in discomfort when you came across a poem written specifically about lovers. I've never seen you squirm so much."

"I did not," she protested, biting her lower lip to keep from smiling.

"I also noticed you stopped reading anything regarding romance after the first two days." James chuckled, pausing inches from her face. His eyes dropped to the fullness of her lips. The corners of her smile fell as her eyes lowered down at his. His hands gripped the hot teacup more firmly.

"Please," his voice was low and rough. "Please tell me I'm forgiven."

The quickening of his heart was the only sound he could hear while he watched her stare at her tea. After what felt to be a lifetime, she turned from her cup and met his eyes.

"Yes, I believe you," her voice broke.

"Thank you," James nodded, feeling relieved. Yet there was still something that weighed on him that he needed to know.

"Tell me I'm not too late." He could barely make the words out. With a saddened expression, she lifted her hand to his cheek. His pulse raced from her gentle touch.

"James," she whispered, leaning closer to him.

A crashing wave of panic surged through him as she held her solemn expression. Leaning back towards the shadows, he hid the dread that surfaced. *Please, no. Please don't let it be so.*

"Oh James," she whispered again, this time a smile hinted from the corners of her mouth. "I shall tell you tomorrow." Patting his hand that rested on the table, she drew away and flashed him a mischievous smile.

For a long moment, he sat there baffled. The wave of panic stilled, resulting in him taking a moment to register what she had said. *She'll tell me tomorrow?* Biting down the corner of her mouth, she turned to stir her tea. *Was she teasing him?* Clenching his fist, James blew out an exasperated breath. He grabbed her stool and slid her into him, caging her in with his leg stretched out behind her. She gasped with surprise.

"For the past year, I've thought of nothing but you and now you're telling me, I have to wait until tomorrow?" he demanded.

"I waited nearly twelve months to hear from you," she retorted. "What's one more night?"

They stared into each other's eyes with fierce determination, neither turning away. Their breathing staggered as he held her close.

In one brief moment Jane lowered her facade. Immediately, James knew what her answer was as her eyes betrayed her. What he needed now was for her to understand that he was still in love with her.

"I can't wait until then," he muttered, leaning closer to her. With his body facing her, he scooted to the edge of his stool. "Jane." He tenderly took her hand and pressed it against his fiercely beating heart. The love that he felt for her reflected back from her glistening eyes as she stared into his, never blinking away.

"This," he breathed. "This is how I feel every time I think of you, let alone when I am around you." His voice was barely a whisper. "My heart, mind, and soul haven't been the same since I've met you, and, frankly, I dare say that I like it."

She was motionless, feeling his heart pound beneath her light touch. "I—I will not yield," she stammered, a tear dropping down her cheek, "to your persuasion, sir." She breathed a staggered breath.

James chuckled, releasing her hand back to her lap. "No, I dare say you won't. Regardless, I desire nothing more than to be with you. My heart cannot deny how I feel whenever you come into my mind or whenever we're together."

The corner of her mouth raised. Slowly, she returned her hands to his chest, her touch warm, soothing and yet invigorating. He swallowed, his heart echoing through his head, drowning out any voice that kept him from reaching out to her.

"For the past few months my doubts took over, as they convinced me that I was the only one who felt this way," she whispered.

He clasped hold of her waist. His fingers gently dug into the fabric of her gown as he fought the urge to pull her towards him. He dropped his head, pressing his forehead against hers. "For twelve long, miserable months, I could only think of you." His voice was low and rough. He leaned forward, his lips barely brushing hers. "May I?" he whispered.

She released a shaky breath, "Yes."

The word filled James like he had been famished for years. Eagerly, he pressed his lips against hers. Her hand combed through his hair, drawing him impossibly closer. His heart pounded fiercely in his chest as she kissed him back with the same desire. His hand flew from her waist to the nape of her neck. Together they drew back, breathing with short deep breaths, both staring at each other with wide eyes. He grazed his fingers across her jaw, stirring the hunger for more. He stared deep into her eyes and saw the same intensity that burned through his veins reflected there. Instinctively, he leaned in and kissed her again.

Her lips tasted better than he remembered. It was as though every kiss and every touch filled the emptiness in their hearts from all their months apart. Releasing a reluctant groan, he loosened his hold, softly kissing her cheek, her neck, until he managed enough willpower to draw away from her but still close enough to be in her arms. Her eyes fluttered open and she exhaled a shaky breath.

"To think I was going to tell you that you were too late," she breathed through a whisper.

James smiled at her lighthearted manner and held her closer. Somewhere in the kitchen a clock chimed, ringing out a reminder that his time there was long past. Withdrawing, he clasped her hand, and brought it to his lips. "When can I see you next?"

"Come by the house tomorrow, around noon."

James nodded, catching his breath. "I'll be here."

With her hand in his, he kissed it tenderly. Reluctantly he stood, unrolled his sleeves and threw on his jacket. If he had his way, he'd stay longer and talk through the night with her. Tucking her arm through his, he grabbed the candle and walked with her down the dark hall to the foyer.

"Goodnight, Jane." He gave her hand another kiss before he quickly pulled her into his arms for another embrace.

"Goodnight," she whispered, bringing her arms up around his neck.

Squeezing his eyes shut, he inhaled deeply into her curls before releasing her. She smiled, a soft loving smile. Holding her hand until their fingers slipped apart, he departed from her home.

Stepping out into the cool night, with his heart warming his soul, James headed to the carriage. Giving the address to his parents' townhome, he leaned back against the bench. For the first time in a year, all the unsettling agony of not knowing what the future held dissolved. The fog was finally lifted.

A breeze rustled the leaves above where Jane sat. She had been pacing the gardens when she stopped to sit on a bench under a shaded tree. She closed her eyes, and tilted her head back, soaking in the gentle rush of the wind. Cradled in her arms she held a clean cravat and vest—thanks to Millie's assistance.

Her conversation with Lord Evans that morning had gone smoother than she thought it would. After handing back his handkerchief and giving him a brief explanation of her history with James, he smiled at her and told her he wished her the best. Evidently, he had been suspicious of an attachment the night she had so vehemently defended James at the musical concert.

"Good afternoon."

She jumped, startled by the deep voice. She fluttered her eyes open against the bright light. A tall, dashing gentleman stood before her. His dimpled smile beamed down at her. Since she awoke that morning, she had had to tell herself many times that the night before wasn't a dream. A smile swept over her face.

"James." She removed his articles of clothing from her lap and stood to face him. He clasped her hand in his and kissed it.

"Please excuse my tardiness. I got here over an hour ago, but I've been conversing with your uncle in his study."

She stiffened as the blood drained from her face. "What did he say?" Horrible scenarios played out in her mind as she feared he had chastised James for the lack of communication. She had already spoken with her uncle earlier that morning about how James had written to her many times, but for some odd reason the letters never arrived. As silly as it had sounded repeating the words, she had hoped he would believe him, like she did.

She began to nervously clench the fabric in her hand. Even though her uncle assured her that if she trusted James, then so did he, she didn't feel convinced. She couldn't picture her life without James again, nor live her life with her uncle's disapproval of him. But then again, he did say he held great esteem for James after she explained how he rescued her—again—from Lieutenant Howard. *Surely, there's nothing to fret about,* she assured herself. Glancing at James he began to chuckle at her worried expression.

"Everything is fine." James smiled and kissed her forehead. "Your uncle holds no ill feelings towards me. In fact, he said he would love to attend." Still holding her hand, he led her to sit with him on the bench.

"I know. I suppose my thoughts got the best of me . . . Attend what?" she asked, suspiciously. Her eyes quickly gazed over his stitches and the purple bruise that stained around his puffy brow.

"Attend the ball my parents are throwing in a fortnight."

"A ball?" Jane asked with surprise. *His parents?* She began to fidget with the cravat on her lap. She had forgotten they resided nearby.

James nodded. "My mother throws a ball once a year at their country estate."

She swallowed, looking at the now wrinkled cravat. "Where is your parents' estate?" she asked, quickly smoothing out his necktie that laid on her lap.

"It's outside of High Wycombe. I've discussed it with both my parents and your uncle." The corner of James's mouth lifted. "You and your uncle will be staying at the manor for two days."

He pulled out an envelope from his coat and handed it to her. Jane Sawyer was written with exquisite penmanship on the front. *Two days?* She glanced up at him, still startled by the news.

"I wish I knew what you're thinking right now." He studied her intently with his bright blue eyes.

Jane smiled, hiding the nervousness she felt. "Only that I see nothing wrong with your r's and that I would be honored to attend."

He grinned. A lock of her hair escaped a pin as a cool breeze blew across them. The hair tickled her cheek. He clasped it, gently tucking it behind her ear. His fingers lightly brushed along the side of her neck, stopping at her collarbone. Her skin tingled where he touched. Flustered that he still had that effect on her, she subtly rubbed her arms, and glanced away towards a rose bush. A memory filled her mind of the night that they watched the southern lights.

"You know," Jane said and peered at his tanned face with a smile. "I do believe you never told me about the challenge Thomas gave you the morning of the race."

James laughed and rubbed the back of his neck. "It must have slipped my mind." Clasping her hands in his, he appeared as if he were observing the drastic difference between her creamy, soft hands to his dark, calloused ones. "In my defense, I was too distracted that night."

Her cheeks grew uncomfortably warm. He wasn't the only one distracted that night. He had told her he'd surrender anything for a kiss. His thumb tenderly ran over her hand.

"The challenge was if I won the race up Jacob's Ladder, then I got to bid on your basket. If Thomas won, he would bid on your basket. Except, his intentions were one of a test to see how deep my feelings were for you. Evidently, they ran deep, as I set a new record." He smiled as their eyes met.

"You raced to bid on my basket?" Jane said aloud, feeling flattered that he'd even agree to such a notion.

His eyes softened. "As disappointing as it was that I didn't win your basket that day," he smirked when Jane bit her lip, "I'd hoped I'd at least win your affection."

Feeling too abashed, she looked down at their hands and marveled how his large hands cradled hers with such tenderness and love. Her heart quickened as though to confirm what she thought.

"James," she said softly. "You won more than just my affection—" She looked deeply into his blue eyes. He stared back at her with such earnestness. She went to open her mouth to tell him how much he meant to her, but the words wouldn't come. He brushed a curl over her shoulder as their gaze carried the unspoken words between them. Sweetly, he lifted her hand to his lips. She closed her eyes, allowing the touch of his warm lips to fill her heart.

"That is more than I could ever have hoped for," he whispered. "I wish I didn't have to leave you now, but I'm afraid I have to report at the war department within the hour." He cleared his throat and straightened his back. "This week will be busy as I transition, but I promise, I'll pay a call as often as I can."

"Alright," she breathed.

The corner of his mouth lifted, deepening his dimple. He went to stand and held his hand out to assist her up.

"Just a moment." Jane grabbed the clean cravat and waistcoat and handed them to him.

"I'm impressed you were able to remove the stains." His hands grazed the freshly cleaned clothing as he accepted them.

"Millie was a great help."

She bit her lip, reflecting on Millie's appalled expression as she caught Jane nearly annihilating the fabric.

"You two did me a great favor." He grabbed his clothing and tenderly kissed her on her cheek. "Thank you," he said softly. Gratitude filled his eyes as he looked between her and his clothes.

"You're welcome."

Overwhelmed with a mixture of disbelief and excitement, she gave him a final wave goodbye while watching him depart through the garden gate to the street.

Pebbles on the path crushed against each other. Jane's head snapped towards the direction and saw her uncle walking down the path.

"Uncle." Jane ran her hands over her dress, feeling exposed from the intimate scene he may have witnessed. "I didn't see you there."

"Well, I simply couldn't leave you two unchaperoned in the garden now, could I?"

He stopped in front of her and leaned on his cane. Jane's eyes widened and she looked down at the bench only to be relieved the rose bush had hidden them from her uncle's line of sight.

"You look flushed my dear, are you alright?"

Her hand flew to her cheek, and her words began to stumble together. "Yes, of course. I—" She stopped, when she caught the gleam that danced in his eyes. "Uncle, did you come over to tease me?"

"Not at all," he chuckled, sitting on the bench. Patting the open seat next to him, Jane obliged and stared at the garden gate James had departed from.

"I was very skeptical," he started, interrupting the clamping sound of a carriage rolling by.

Jane turned her full attention towards him.

"About the letters and his intentions." He nodded towards the gate. Her chest tightened with nervous anticipation. Behind his spectacles, he tightened his eyes. He stared with disbelief as though whatever he was thinking was unraveling before him.

"Yes?" her voice cracked. She straightened her back.

He scratched his forehead with the top of his cane. "I had to ponder what you said. And then after speaking with him, I came to a conclusion."

"What was that?" she swallowed. Her breathing quickened while she held herself impossibly still on the edge of the bench.

"That no gentleman, in his rightful mind, would move to take a new position in order to be near the one he loves, even though he has no idea if she feels the same way. That was a huge risk for him to take."

She released a staggered breath. Judging by her uncle's serious expression, she was uncertain if he approved of James's bold move.

"Yet, I suppose being an officer in the navy, the captain is used to making such daring decisions." He rubbed his chin and stared ahead. "Fortunately, as long as I've known him, he seems to make the right move each time." He smirked, and crossed his arms as though amused.

"So you believe he wrote?" She leaned towards him.

"I do. It would be out of character for him not to."

Jane's brows raised as she didn't expect his reply to be so matter-of-fact.

He smiled again. "You see, as an officer, he's used to strategizing. In order to survive, it's expected of him. I believe his first mission was to write to you to try to see how things went. And since that clearly failed, as he never heard back, he had a backup plan. Which I must say, should have been his first plan."

"What do you mean?"

"He should have set sail a long time ago." He lifted his cane in the air and pointed at the gate.

"But he was still recovering!"

"True, but a year of watching you mope was far too long for me."

Jane couldn't hide the surprise from her face. She closed her mouth and pressed, "So you approve of him?"

His eyes tightened and he subtly nodded. "Very much. He makes a fine suitor."

"Oh, thank goodness!" Jane stood and threw her hands to her temples. "For a moment I was worried you didn't approve!"

"I'm glad to see what I have to say on this particular topic matters to you," he teased and smiled his genuine smile.

Jane knew he was being lighthearted but sensed a hint of sadness in his tone. "Of course it matters, and it always will."

She sat next to him and leaned against him as he wrapped his arm around her shoulders. He held her close into his side, never letting go as they listened to another carriage roll by. There was a sense of change that filled the air. It felt new and exciting yet almost serene.

When the street was quiet again, he tilted his head towards her. "You'll always be a daughter to me," he whispered, with a slight break in his voice.

"You'll always be a father to me."

She looked up and watched the corner of his mouth raise. He patted her shoulder and continued to hold her like he used to when she was a child.

"Before I forget . . ." Her uncle pulled out a letter from inside his coat pocket. On the front was Jane's name and her address to the cottage in Oxford. The penmanship of Elaine Keaton looked rushed with each letter at a slant. Jane's uncle lifted a brow at her and flipped the post over. On the back of the post was written, "Urgent! Matter of importance!"

"Do you think it's urgent?" Jane laughed when her uncle began to smile.

"I can only assume it is a matter of importance," he teased. "The postal carrier did have it delivered here instead of Oxford. I'm amazed how word gets out regarding people's whereabouts."

"Only in London." Jane accepted the letter and placed it on her lap. As though to answer her uncle's curious expression, she said, "I'll read this at a different time. I assume it's nothing more than her letting me know that James is on his way to set things straight."

Chapter Sixteen

Jane, my dear sweet friend,

The things I must say but where to start with such little time. The next ship departs for England in less than an hour. Alright, straight to the point. I saw James yesterday before his departure for England. He's been writing letters to you but for some reason they're not getting to you. And for your sake only, I've recruited Jenny and we decided to look into this. With three words I present to you James's letter thief. Miss Catherine Harrlow.

To even write her name makes me want to burn this letter. Well, I cornered her in the dress shop today and made a few threats regarding my father telling her father about the fibs she's been spreading. Especially it being about our island's hero. Basically, I played the political card being that my father is the governor and hers is just a councilman and we wouldn't want any ties to such deceit. It all worked in my favor. She practically spit her confession at me. Like a hissing cat. Now that I think of it, I'm going to need a bath, to rid myself of her.

What I heard through all her appalling spit was that she was the one who had been stealing the letters. Her plan was to have James move on to "manured-filled" pastures since he never heard *back from you, and for you to be left heartbroken as he never wrote. That foul woman.*

I was honored to have the pleasure to inform her how her plan backfired. She may have shed a few tears when I told her that he was on his way to confess his love for you. I couldn't help but smile at that.

Jane, I hope this letter will validate what he says about writing to you, because he truly did. And I know he loves you. I hope I'm not too late with this as Sophie mentioned something about a butterfly and a promise. I sure hope that butterfly passes so you're not sealed to that promise anymore. And with earnest prayer, I hope James's ship gets caught in a few storms while my ship presses forward to get this letter to you.

Much love,

Elaine

Jane tucked the letter in her reticule. Having reread the letter a few times since she'd opened it, she wanted nothing more than for James to see it as well. Minus the prayers Elaine offered for his storms. She would never wish that on anyone.

"Miss Jane," Millie beamed. "There's a captain downstairs, waiting to strut with you in the park."

Jane bit her cheeks, "Do you mean stroll?"

"Yes, miss."

"I'm on my way." Jane smiled and draped the reticule around her wrist. After a year of confusion and misunderstanding, James would too have his answer.

⁂

"Millie! Have you seen my slippers?" Jane called over her shoulder. She dropped to her knees and lifted her bed skirt. "The blue ones that match my gown? They're not in my boudoir where I last had them."

Frazzled, she crawled on the carpeted floor, looking under her bed in nothing but her chemise and corset. Her corset dug into her stomach, making it difficult to breathe. "And what of my dress? Is it downstairs being aired out?"

She had had the satin blue gown specifically made for tonight's ball but now when she needed it, it was nowhere in sight. She could have sworn she saw Millie unpack it here at the McCannon's estate that morning.

Millie giggled from behind. Jane blew a chunk of hair out of her face and staggered to her stocking covered feet.

"Millie, this is no laughing matter. I have less than an hour to dress and for you to do my hair."

"Forgive me, miss. Not to worry, your gown will be up shortly. Shall we get started on your hair?" Millie took her hand and led her to her vanity.

"I'm sorry. I'm a mess." Jane let out a heavy sigh and looked at her reflection in the mirror. Her cheeks were pink, her hair in disarray. She looked far from being presentable. "Tonight is a big night." She grabbed the pearls and began to twist them in her hands. Having met James's wonderful parents, she wanted nothing more than to make a good impression for them and especially their son. "I get to meet the McCannon's friends and their acquaintances. I need to appear some-what pulled together."

Millie smoothed a few of Jane's loose curls with a balm.

"Miss Jane, by the time I get through with you, your Major won't notice anything but you."

"With people congratulating him on his advancement, I have my doubts." She bit her lip, wishing a sliver of what Millie had said would be true.

Millie giggled, pulling out a gold ribbon. *Gold? But the blue ribbon was the one I had picked for my dress.* "Miss Jane, I've never heard of a gentleman sailing across the ocean to reprimand the lady he loves."

Jane felt heat rushing to her face. *Goodness, nor have I.* "Reprimand?"

"Yes, miss. To win your heart like he did from one of those love stories."

She grinned up at Millie as the last of the ribbon was weaved into her hair. "Yes, Millie. He certainly *redeemed* my love."

A soft knock sounded at the door. Jane swiftly reached for her silk robe, and slid it on while Millie went to meet the caller.

"Millie!" Sophie said with delight. Giving her a quick embrace, she hurried past to Jane.

"Sophie! How did you—how—"

Her friend threw her arms around her neck for a loving embrace. "Surprised?"

"Well, yes!" Jane drew away. "And your gown!" Holding her friend's hands high, she admired the beautiful shimmery, cream-colored material that wisped around her hourglass figure. "Is this the one you had made in London?"

"It is! Don't you love it?" She spun, letting the dress billow elegantly around her. "I was so grateful it was finished before tonight's ball."

"It's absolutely stunning." Baffled, Jane continued to stare. "Sophie, what? I mean when?—" She stumbled over her words as the questions flooded her.

Sophie laughed with glee. "Your major sent us an invitation a week ago."

"He did?"

"Uh huh." Her round green eyes twinkled with mischief. "I must confess, I met him downstairs, and Jane, I cannot express how happy I am for you! Please tell me if he has a brother or a friend that's just as handsome?"

Jane laughed. "Whatever happened to you and that gentleman you met at your aunt's?"

"He wasn't the one for me. After hearing what happened with you and your major, I decided there weren't enough sparks between us."

"Sophie," Jane shook her head with disbelief, "You shouldn't be holding out due to how I feel with James. Your love may be different."

"That may be true, but after telling my mother about your relationship, she agreed with me. It's better to wait for love than to rush into it."

"Clearly, it wasn't meant to be if you're feeling fine with it." Jane watched her carefully to see if she could catch a hint of sadness. Her cheerful green eyes, with her broad, white smile, hinted at no such thing.

A firm knock sounded at the door and the ladies turned to look. Millie scurried excitedly across the carpeted floor and opened the door.

"Millie, it's good to see you!" Jenny's voice cheerfully rang. Jane's mouth fell with surprise. Jenny paraded into the room with a rather large smile. Her chocolate-brown eyes beamed with excitement when she saw Jane.

"Jenny!" Jane ran to her friend and gave her a long embrace. "My goodness I cannot believe you are here! You look beautiful!" She blinked, feeling her eyes dry from her blatant stare. Jenny's pale blue satin ball gown complimented her auburn brown hair and her less tan complexion beautifully.

"Thank you, my friend." She grinned, holding the skirt of her dress and waving it around with admiration.

"What are you doing here?" Jane asked with a delighted laugh.

"Thomas is doing some training in London for a few weeks." She paused, giving a sly smile. "He escorted me here. Evidently, I'm becoming an old maid so Mrs. McCannon convinced my mother that I should spend the summer here with them. I have a feeling that James is behind all this. A while ago I told him I was desperate for a break from the orchard."

Jane wrapped her robe tighter around her body.

"Is he here too?" she asked, peeking around her friend towards the doorway.

She shook her head. "Not yet. He'll be arriving soon."

From the corner of her eye, she noticed Sophie approaching with a warm smile.

"Oh, forgive me, Sophie!" Jane stepped back, allowing her friend to join.

"No need for introductions," Sophie said with a gleam in her eye. "Miss Jenny and I met while I was passing through Jamestown."

"Elaine, introduced us," Jenny stated. "And we've already said our greetings downstairs."

"I should have known." Jane looked between the two friends, thrilled that they connected.

Jenny gently clasped her hands and examined Jane up and down. "I see you still need to get dressed for the ball." She exchanged a knowing smile with Sophie.

"Are you here to assist me?" she teased, referring to the last dance Jenny had assisted her with for Saint Helena's festival.

"Actually, yes!"

Jane raised a brow, not certain if she was being serious behind the excitement in her eyes.

"Bring it in," Jenny called towards the open doorway.

Sophie exchanged a curious glance with Jane and smiled with excitement. Entering the room, a maid came holding a long white sheet high above the carpet. Grinning, Millie joined the other side of the sheet to help support it. Jane studied it, confused about what it could be.

"Well, go on," Jenny encouraged, nudging her softly against her arm. "Take off the cover."

Taken aback by the surprise, Jane slowly approached the sheet and curled her fingers around the white fabric. Giving a gentle tug, the sheet fluttered to the floor. She blinked, inhaling a soft gasp as she marveled at the gown before her. Why, it was the most gorgeous, deep green gown she had ever seen.

"Jane Sawyer," Sophie breathed from behind. "I heard it was exquisite, but I never pictured this." Jane's fingers grazed the satin fabric. Softly pinching the skirt, she fanned the front revealing tiny, gold-embroidered designs scattered underneath and at the hem of the gown. Astonished, she traced up the fabric towards the bottom of a tight bodice trimmed in gold thread. "I've never seen any gown like it," Sophie continued.

"It's so beautiful," Jane barely whispered. "Did he—"

"Mm hmm," Jenny beamed.

"When?" Jane continued to trace the hours of embroidery work.

"Before the attack. He came to my window, shortly after we saw the southern lights. Thank goodness I was still awake otherwise he would have received an earful. He drew out the layout of the gown and was persistent that the color was emerald. I've never seen him so enthusiastic about anything other than sailing."

Jane laughed a joyous laugh.

"My goodness, he's thought of everything," Sophie marveled.

Jenny's smile broadened. "Millie helped me with the sizing. And of course, the shopkeeper was beyond thrilled to help Jamestown's finest captain."

Jane continued to stare at the gown as Millie and the other maid carefully draped it on her bed. "You brought this gown all the way from Saint Helena?"

"I did."

"I'm at a loss for words." Sniffing, Jane turned to Jenny and gave her a long embrace. "Thank you," she whispered over her friend's shoulder.

Drawing away, Jenny clasped Jane's hands within hers. "I cannot wait to see you in this magnificent gown tonight. But I must be off." She gave her a quick peck on her cheek. "I promised James I would tell him your reaction after you saw the gown. Miss Sophie, I'll see you down there." She smiled and hurried out of the room.

Jane blinked over at Sophie who squeezed her hand. "Tell me, how long did you know about this?"

Sophie regained her smile. "Not long at all. Jenny pulled me aside to tell me about it before I sought you out." She gave Jane a tight embrace. "I must apologize for my doubts with him. I'm extremely happy you found each other."

"Your doubts are understandable. And I'm so grateful you had your father make that odd order for James to attend the opera. I don't know what you said to him to get him to play along but I'm very glad you did."

Sophie began to giggle. "As soon as I overheard my father speak about Captain McCannon making a request to work at headquarters, I knew exactly why he did that. It took me some time to convince my father to meet him at the docks but once I told him about the two of you, he eagerly complied."

Jane stared at her with disbelief. "I'm forever grateful that you did. Thank you."

Sophie wrapped her arms around Jane. "What are friends for?"

"I beg your pardon, Miss Jane." Millie had reentered the room and smiled timidly at her. "We don't have much time to get you dressed. Come."

"I'll meet you downstairs," Sophie said with a laugh. "You're in good hands." She winked at Millie and departed the room. Jane brought her hands to her forehead and released a breath.

"Are you feeling alright, miss?" Millie asked, the smile fading from her face. She lowered the petticoat in her hands and looked at her with concern.

Jane wiped the moisture from her eyes. "I don't remember the last time I felt this overwhelmed with joy. It's better than any dream."

"Would you like me to pinch you to prove you're not asleep?"

"I'd rather not," she laughed. "This is something I would never want to wake from."

"You certainly deserve the most happiness, miss. Now come, the major's waiting for you."

"Yes, I must not keep him waiting." Taking another breath to calm the flutters, Jane stepped into the petticoat that Millie held for her.

After being draped, pulled, and pinned, Millie popped her head from behind her. "Finished!" she announced, wiping her forehead with her hand. Jane grinned and hurried to step in front of her full-length mirror.

"Millie," she gasped.

Gazing into the mirror, her eyes trailed each of the golden flowers down to the bottom of her skirt, then back up over her bodice. She almost didn't recognize herself.

"Miss Jane, you look so beautiful!" Millie exclaimed.

"Thank you," she breathed with astonishment. "And not to worry, Millie, I will keep you informed about my evening after I have returned."

"Please do, miss. I love the stories you tell me about the two of you." Millie grinned, her round eyes twinkling with excitement.

After squeezing her hand, Jane hurried and grabbed her fan, loving the sound of her gown swishing and how her soft green slippers comfortably cushioned each of her steps.

Right as she went to open the door, a knock sounded on the other side. She opened it, excited to see James standing in front of her, his smile beginning to falter as his eyes took her in.

"James, I love it!" She fanned out the skirt for him to see. "It's the most beautiful gown I've ever seen!" She awed, at the well-crafted, gold trim shimmering in the lamp light.

Noticing that she was met with silence, she looked up from her gown to him. Dressed in his fine, blue, naval officer uniform, James blatantly stared at her. His cheeks flushed and his eyes soft, yet wide with surprise. He blinked, and cleared his throat before opening his mouth to mumble, "It is."

She stood on her toes and gave him a gentle kiss on his cheek. "Thank you."

His hand reached for her waist like he was about to draw her close to him, but stopped when he looked over her shoulder and noticed Millie standing in the room behind them. Clasping her gloved hand instead, he leaned down towards her ear. "I've never had anyone take my breath away like you do. You're stunning," he whispered, gazing down at her. She stood in the doorway, lost in his bright eyes. Music floated through the hall from the downstairs ballroom.

"Shall we?" he whispered.

"Yes," she replied, wrapping her arm in his.

A slow smile swept across his face as he led her down the hall towards the stairs where Jenny waited. Once she eyed them, she moved ahead, to give them space but staying close enough as though she were—"Our chaperone?" Jane asked, smiling by how Jenny stayed so far ahead of them.

"Yes," he chuckled. "It was her idea. She convinced your uncle that she'll escort us to the dancehall."

Jane laughed. The way Jenny escorted them wouldn't have been up to anyone's standards of the definition.

Next to her, James began to smile.

"A penny for your thoughts?"

Meeting her gaze, his smile faded into one of reverence. "I'll never regret the day your dress got caught in those branches," he began, releasing a staggered breath. He sounded hoarse, his voice lower than usual. It caused a thrilling shiver up her spine. She stared at him a moment trying to understand his meaning.

"Are you referring to the infuriating branches?" she asked slowly, catching a smile forming on his face. His dimple deepened.

"Yes, the very ones that protect the delicate fauna from falling in the river and drowning," he replied, bringing Jane back to their first conversation at the governor's plantation.

"You have definitely helped me find beautiful green vegetation." She stopped on a stair and fanned out the skirt with laughter. James smiled and pulled her into him with one arm.

"That was the day I knew you would change my life."

"And you changed mine."

His eyes traced over her face before he released her and took a step back to kiss her hand.

Together they entered the crowded ballroom. An applause broke out when James's father, Admiral McCannon, announced his arrival. Many people wanted to give their praise to James for his valiant effort and victory in the battle he fought the year prior. Jane followed his motion as he held her proudly by his side to speak with them. After numerous conversations, she eased her hand on James's arm when she saw a familiar face approach.

"My dear Jane," her uncle proudly chimed. "You are breathtaking." He gave her a kiss on her cheek.

"Thank you, Uncle."

Her uncle's eyes twinkled at the two of them and nodded as though in approval. "Be certain you take time to dance with her," he advised. He patted James's arm before heading towards Admiral McCannon.

"I definitely plan to, sir," James said with a chuckle.

"I'm not so certain we'll make it to the dance floor," Jane teased, seeing a couple nod at him. He smiled and, out of courtesy, nodded back.

"I didn't invite you to a ball just to socialize," he whispered into her ear.

"You didn't?" Jane hummed, peering at him from the corner of her eye. "You do realize, you came home as a war hero?"

"If they only knew you were the one that saved that war hero," James stated. Jane shook her head.

"My uncle was the one that saved you, James." She lowered her voice when a different couple nodded at him. He smirked and met her gaze.

"If you only knew." A soft melody echoed in the room. "But that will have to be discussed another time. Come." The muscles in his cheeks flexed as he kept his stare on the dance floor. "I've been wanting to do nothing more than to dance with you."

Jane laughed when his steps quickened, and he led her towards the dancing couples.

"James! Jane!"

Thomas stepped in front of them, his broad shoulders blocking any view of the dancers. He smiled a crooked smile, his cheeks barely widening over his broad neck. Under his square jaw, he straightened his cravat and tugged on his waistcoat.

"Thomas," James muttered, shaking his head. "Every time."

Jane smiled, knowing what he meant.

"Well, it's great to see you too," Thomas smirked.

She watched humorously as he laughed and hugged him with a quick pat on his back.

"Where's your officer's uniform?" James asked, eyeing the black dress attire.

"Yes, my uniform. It snagged on a nail this morning, so it's being mended," Thomas shrugged, "and I don't at all miss it. I finally get to attend a dance without someone inquiring about all the war I've seen. But that's beside the point . . . Miss Jane," he kissed her hand. "I hear congratulations are in order."

For a split second she watched James's jaw clench. Thomas raised his thick brows and quickly said, "About becoming a midwife, of course."

"Thank you," she replied, noticing how James's face began to relax. He gave her a small smile when he met her gaze. Nervously, Jane fidgeted with a button on James's sleeve. The expression she caught didn't seem too happy and she couldn't fathom why.

"That's right!" Jenny pipped in, drawing to Thomas's side. "Both of you have made wonderful achievements."

Thomas clapped his hands and rubbed them together. "This calls for a toast!"

Frantically looking around the heads of the ladies and the gentlemen in attendance, Thomas paused and raised his arm.

Over his shoulder Jane caught Sophie's eye as she admired her emerald gown. A wide grin spread across her face, brightening the room. She gathered her skirts and hurried to her through the sea of people.

"Now with the four of us being together again," Thomas began when a servant approached him and offered the tray of drinks. Grabbing two crystal glasses, he began to hand them over to Jane and James. "And with your advancement to major, my fine man."

"And you a captain," James reminded, accepting his glass.

"Yes!" Thomas continued, "and Jane becoming England's favorite midwife."

She smiled, accepting her glass.

Grabbing the remaining two glasses from the tray, Thomas added with a smirk, "And to Jenny for finally venturing off the island."

"Very funny," she retorted, extending her hand out in front of her for her glass.

"Jane!" Sophie exclaimed, with a bright, beautiful smile. "Your gown is so—oh!" She halted as a glass full of punch sloshed right into her stomach.

"Blast!" Thomas exclaimed, quickly drawing back his arm.

Jane covered her gasp as she watched her friend's face go from joy to utter surprise. Punch dripped off Thomas's gloved fingers onto the marble floor. For the first time since she'd known him, he grew quiet as he stared in alarm at her friend with his mouth ajar.

"Oh no, Miss Sophie!" Jenny exclaimed next to her.

"Yes, I couldn't be more sorry," Thomas stammered. With both his hands preoccupied with drinks, he began attempting to wipe the reminiscence of the drink from off her skirt with his elbow, only succeeding in sloshing more drops of punch onto the floor and Sophie's dress. As amusing as it was to watch him, it just kept getting worse.

"Sophie," Jane gasped, lowering her hand from her mouth. She watched her friend slowly close her eyes and opened them to evaluate the damage. The beautiful cream-colored gown had crimson punch dripping down the bodice and skirt. She took a deep breath and clenched her fingers into fists.

"Come." Passing her glass to James, Jane stepped towards her friend. "Let us get you cleaned up. I'll have Millie give you the gown I was going to wear tonight."

"No, no Jane, you stay," Sophie protested with a high pitch to her voice.

"Yes, I'll help Miss Sophie wash up," Jenny piped in. She held Sophie's arm and began directing her towards the hall.

"Are you certain?" Jane stepped closer to her, but stopped when Jenny held a commanding hand up.

"Jane, please stay. We'll find Millie and we won't be long."

"Yes," Thomas declared. "Jane, you stay with James, Jenny and I will help her." Holding the drinks high, he motioned on where to go. Jane bit her lip to keep from smiling. His tan face was paler than she had ever seen before.

"To help her wash up?" James muttered under his breath. He quickly held his cup to his smile when he caught Thomas's flustered expression.

Sophie glanced at Thomas for the first time since the accident. She peered at him with a quiver in her chin while she pressed her full lips into a fine line. Her emerald eyes blazed with fierce loathing. Without a word she turned and walked with Jenny out of the ballroom.

Thomas stood with his back to Jane, watching in silence while Sophie disappeared in the sea of ballgowns. Turning around to face them, he closed his mouth. "Miss Sophie. Such a beautiful name." He mumbled as though to himself. Jane eyed James and tucked her lips under when he kept rambling. "That was quite mortifying." He took a sip of his drink and studied it for a moment. "Miss Jane, you don't suppose she's one to hold a grudge?" He raised a hopeful brow then took a sip from the other glass in his hand.

"You did ruin her dress," James stated, trying to hide his smile.

Slowly, Thomas lowered his glass from his lips and blatantly stared at his friend. "I have many words I want to say to you right now," he retorted. "You're very fortunate Miss Jane is standing here."

"I couldn't agree more." James grinned at her before kissing her hand.

"I'm going to change my gloves and rid myself of this disaster." He held the two glasses up towards them. "Cheers to you both. Miss Jane, I do hope James dances with you before the end of the night."

"Thank you, Thomas," James retorted. Thomas smirked at him before he left.

James leaned towards her ear, drowning out the chatter and music around them. "Would you care to venture out with me?"

She laughed and nodded. With how things were going, she was ready to escape with him before it took another interesting turn for the evening.

"What do you have in mind?" She lifted a brow when the corner of his mouth raised and he clasped her hand in his. Without delay, she kept pace with James as he weaved them out of the crowded room towards the pavilion. They paused on a few occasions when he accepted handshakes and pats on the back. Jane watched with amusement while he excused himself from any conversation, never releasing her hand. She laughed when the cool night air finally greeted them with a soft breeze.

"The pavilion?" she breathed.

"Not exactly," James muttered, pulling her close into him while eyeing the couples around them. "There's a better place I have in mind," he said, lowering his voice so others around them couldn't hear.

Feeling a sense of thrill, Jane allowed James to discreetly lead her away from the fairly popular pavilion to the grounds near the manor. Hand-in-hand they walked in the shadows of the trimmed shrubbery, listening to the orchestra as the music drifted faintly around them.

"Now that I have you alone, I was hoping you would help me with something?" James twirled her around to face him.

"And what are you needing help with?" she asked suspiciously. Shadows from branches above them played across his face. He grinned at her and held out his hand.

"Would you do me the honor and teach me the Jane Sawyer waltz?"

She laughed and quickly covered her mouth. Clearing her throat, she kept the smile off her face. "Well," she sighed. "If I must."

"A bargain is a bargain." He winked at her, referring to her loss at their chess match.

Jane smirked. "First, I'll take your hand." She grabbed his hand, stepping towards him.

"You'll place your other hand around my waist—not too close," she breathed, pushing him back a step. He smiled audaciously at her.

"A couple must have some distance apart in order to move," she reprimanded, her nose practically touching his chin. He chuckled.

"Since my last instructor took the lead, I feel it only appropriate that I do the same," she taunted, alluding to their first waltz together. "And one, two, three." She pulled his hand and began leading him in a circle. His feet shuffled along to the rhythm of the faint music. "You're doing splendidly Major James," she teased as she led them around shrubbery.

"This was the waltz you were so embarrassed to show me?" he asked, with a doubtful tone. "I'm not sure how different it is from what we did at the festival," he challenged. Jane smiled sheepishly, knowing he had suspected much more to her waltz.

"Very well, as my pupil requested." She straightened her shoulders back. "Now remember, to understand the dance, you too must take part in every detail of it." She extended her hand up in the air, stopping their dance. "Now, go ahead James. Twirl around my finger." She bit her cheeks to keep from giggling. James stared at her, refusing to move. "Well go on," she encouraged.

James shook his head and with one swift motion he grabbed her hand, spun her around and dipped her low to the ground. Jane stared at him in surprise as he held her steadily close to his body. His face was so near to hers all she needed to do was lift her head and their lips would touch.

"Tell me," he smiled impishly. "Was this part of your waltz?"

Trying to catch her breath, she felt her head spin. "It is now," she breathed, her pulse speeding up in her chest.

James grinned down at her. His eyes roamed her face, lingering longer on her lips. Ever so smoothly, he lifted her up. His face filled with desire as he tightened his grip around her waist, pulling her closer.

"Jane." He said her name with reverence, as he traced his fingers up her arm to the base of her neck. Bumps scattered across her skin.

"Yes?" she managed

His hand cupped her jaw. Tenderly he brushed his thumb against her warm cheeks. "I'm in love with you," he whispered, staring into her eyes. His thumb smoothly made its way across her lips, making her tremble. Lifting her chin ever so gently, he whispered, "There are many things I want to say." His eyes darted from her lips. His breath staggered. She watched his throat bob as he swallowed. "Jane," James breathed, gazing at her with such tenderness. "When you gracefully came into my life that day on the pier—" He smiled as she scrunched her nose. "I knew, I wanted to get to know you better. What caught me off guard from the beginning was not only are you beautiful, but I found you to be witty, kind, and extremely humble."

She blinked fervently as her eyes stung with tears. He tenderly held her hand and then tugged on each finger of her glove until it slid off, exposing her skin to his gentle touch. Reaching into his pocket, he pulled out a chipped, black wooden chess piece. He held the queen up to her, the same queen she had given to him the night he confessed that she was his queen. His lucky charm. She blinked, surprised he still carried the piece with him. His eyes glistened in the moonlight and he stared deep into hers, warming her cheeks, her heart, her soul.

"I have never met such an extraordinary woman as you." Her hand trembled when he placed the queen into her palm. "Will you do me the honor of becoming my wife?"

She covered her sob and drew in a breath. "Yes," she managed to whisper.

Her heart stopped as he looked at her with deep admiration. Wrapping her in his arms, peace traveled through her body until it enveloped her heart. With the queen clasped in her hand, she laid her head against his chest.

"You made me the happiest man," he whispered.

She sank further into his loving embrace. "I never knew I could feel such peace. It's as though I've finally found home in England."

He grinned his crooked smile and tenderly kissed her lips. Jane slowly opened her eyes, entranced by the pleasure she felt whenever his lips met hers.

"And where would you like home to be?" he whispered. His breath was warm on her lips, bringing a tingling sensation.

"Anywhere you are. But if I had a preference, then it would be Saint Helena."

"After your uncle completes his contract at the university and I at headquarters, I'll take you there."

With a contented sigh, she whispered, "James McCannon, I love you."

The corner of his mouth raised and she felt herself melt into his arms. Laying her head against his shoulder, they swayed contentedly to the soft music coming from the manor.

After but a moment, she felt his lips soft against her hair as he whispered, "And I love you."

Epilogue

One year later, one wedding later, and one voyage later.

"Jane, my love," James called from the dining room of their cottage in Jamestown. "Have you tried this tea your uncle has sent us? It has a peculiar taste to it. I'm assuming it's from India?" She heard him smack his lips in the other room. "I can't quite discern the spice they used."

Jane stood in the kitchen with the door propped open, restocking her medical bag with gauze. Being the island's new midwife, she had performed an early morning delivery that had gone wonderfully.

"I haven't," she paused, collecting her thoughts. "What is it called?" Her uncle knew she loved tea, especially darjeeling tea. But since he decided to stay in London for another year, she couldn't fathom how the Indian tea would have been sent to them. Unless he had written to an old colleague in Bombay, because she could never find the tea anywhere in England.

"Oolong," James said.

Oolong? Why would he send us black tea? He knew she didn't like the taste. Jane walked over to the dining room where James was sitting. He took another long sip then set the cup down. Noticing a film on his lips, she covered her mouth in surprise.

"James," she pressed her lips together to avoid the laughter that was about to erupt, "did it specifically say from my uncle?"

Holding up a note, he took another sip. Jane peered at the unfamiliar handwriting.

"Hmm," she fought back a giggle, "I'm very certain that's supposed to read 'Much love and best wishes, Captain Richard Norton', not Uncle Duncan."

James sat for a moment staring at her with a perplexed expression. His eyes widened and he shot up from his chair. He ran into the hall to look in the mirror. Jane stood in the dining room giggling to herself.

"Why, that scoundrel! I'm to report to the fort tomorrow! Are you laughing? Jane!" he called out to her. A moment of Jane's giggling passed before James strolled into the dining room doorway. "Jane, my love." He gave a mischievous smile that bared all his black-stained teeth. Pushing his shoulder off the doorframe, he took long strides towards her.

"Oh no, you don't!" She hurried to the opposite side of the table from him.

"Just one kiss," he begged.

A giggle escaped before she quickly covered her mouth.

"Not a chance." She tried to sound convincing but her abrupt laughter encouraged him more. She darted in the opposite direction as James took a few steps closer.

"My darling Jane, I feel I haven't kissed you in such a long time." He held a solemn expression with a gleam in his eyes. They both stopped moving as they were on opposite sides of the wooden barrier.

"I believe you kissed me after you came home from the fort, an hour ago."

Imitating her movements, Jane's heart raced as she still found him drawing closer.

"That's an eternity ago!" His long strides started closing the gap.

Trying to escape through the door, she was cut off as James quickly turned around, ran, and caged her to the wall with his arms. She burst into fits of laughter as she moved her head around avoiding his wet kisses.

After many failed attempts, he stopped and stared intently at her.

"Jane McCannon, may I please kiss you?" He attempted to give her a disheartened look but his vibrant eyes betrayed him. "It doesn't even have to be a short one." He flashed her a cheeky smile, displaying the disturbing film on his teeth.

"Not even a peck," she muffled, pressing her lips together while still giggling.

"Fine," he surrendered, releasing a defeated sigh. Drawing away from her, he held his hand against the wall above her shoulder. His head dropped, emphasizing his distress. Gently patting his cheek, she slid away from him to the doorway.

"James," she taunted. "You have a little something right there." Acting innocent, she pointed at her teeth.

James gave a sly smile, deepening his dimple.

"Jane—come here!"

He chased her around their home until her bursts of laughter caused her to be caught. Wrapped in his arms, she surrendered to a kiss, a very long one.

Acknowledgments

There have been many people who've helped me in this journey, and because of their encouragement, time, and wonderful feedback, I have gotten this far.

To my husband, Sam, thank you for giving me your honest opinion and helping me bounce ideas off of you. And my sweet Miles, you are the sunshine in my world. Love you, kiddo.

Xela Culleto, there was no mistake we were supposed to sit at the same table for bunco. After discovering your love for writing, I knew you came into my life when I needed guidance the most. It was because of you and your shared experiences as an author that I was able to get this far. Thank you for your encouragement, your wonderful feedback and friendship.

A special thanks to Kyenna Weston, you gave me the direction I needed to be able to add more depth to the story. You taught me how to dig deep in becoming a better writer. Thank you for your inspiring words and council that helped me stretch and grow.

Jenna and Beth, I love having you two in my corner. Thank you all for your kind words. I appreciate how you've supported me since the beginning of my journey.

Karen Thornell, you have been such a wonderful friend and support to me as I needed guidance with this story. Thank you for always being willing to read through scenes to help me organize my thoughts!

Whitney Hurst, I can't thank you enough for reading through this whole manuscript. You helped inspire me as your feedback gave this story the plot that it needed. I'm forever grateful for your honest opinions.

And much appreciation to my sister-in-law, Ariel Fisher. Thank you for sacrificing a second of your busy schedule to help me navigate through the tech world. Girl, you have an amazing talent and may I add, wonderful taste.

Many thanks to my friends and family for your love and encouragement. Mom, Colin, Sarah, Jenn, Kristen, Josh, Erica, and Travis, thank you all for listening to my excitement as I tell you the "cliff notes" of my stories.

To the Cedar Fort Team. Thank you for always being flexible and willing to work with me. I appreciate all your hard work to help my novels be marketed and published. Your skills and kindness have made it such a delight to publish through you.

And last but most importantly, I want to thank my God, for helping me navigate through my own uncharted waters.

About the Author

Heather Fisher grew up living in some of the most beautiful parts of the country. While living in the Northwest, her family would go on many road trips to camp. On those long road trips, daydreaming and reading became her favorite pastime as their destinations were always, "just around the corner." She currently lives in Utah with her husband, their fun-loving son, and their cat, Leo. After becoming a mother, she was reminded of her childhood dream to become a writer. When these thoughts and dreams persisted, she began putting them into words. She is grateful for the opportunity to become a writer, and for those long road trips that first inspired her.

You've dreamed of accomplishing your publishing goal for ages—holding *that* book in your hands. We want to partner with you in bringing this dream to light.

Whether you're an aspiring author looking to publish your first book or a seasoned author who's been published before, we want to hear from you. Please submit your manuscript to

CEDARFORT.SUBMITTABLE.COM/SUBMIT

CEDAR FORT HAS PUBLISHED BOOKS IN THE FOLLOWING GENRES

- LDS Nonfiction
- General Nonfiction
- Fiction
- Cookbooks
- Juvenile & YA
- Children's Books
- Biographies
- Self-Help
- Regency Romances
- Comic & Activity books
- Cozy Mysteries
- Children's books with customizable character illustrations